Amber Hollow

Amber Hollow

Edgar Swamp

Edited and Typeset by Amnet Systems
Cover design by Amnet Systems

ISBN-13: 9780578496443

CONTENTS

PROLOGUE

NBC Channel Seven News, Milwaukee, Wisconsin, 7:00 a.m., July 15, 1991:

"Good morning, I'm Tricia Mapplethorpe, bringing you an exclusive story that is rapidly developing in the early hours of Monday, July 15.

"Craig Rawson, a dairy farmer from the town of Crandon, in Forest County, was the first to alert authorities that at approximately three o'clock this morning he saw large plumes of black smoke in the sky northeast of his small township, over the village of Amber Hollow, roughly sixty miles away. Firefighters were deployed from both Crandon and Rhinelander, and reports from the scene describe a large fire tearing through the unincorporated burg, igniting everything in its path. Bulldozers have been brought in to create containment lines in the outlying forests, and crop-dusting planes are being used to drop foam retardant in an attempt to stabilize the situation. Per this report the fire is only ten percent contained as firefighters battle tirelessly to keep it within the confines of Amber Hollow in an effort to save the large expanse of forests that surround it on all sides. So far, rescue crews have located two survivors, both suffering from smoke inhalation and second-degree burns. Unfortunately, neither of them were physically able to answer queries made by investigators.

"I'm Tricia Mapplethorpe, and we'll stick with this story as it unfolds, bringing you updates on the hour…"

ABC Channel Five News, Green Bay, Wisconsin, 12:00 p.m., July 15, 1991:

"Good afternoon, I'm Jeffery Winters, bringing you an update on the blaze that firefighters are calling an unparalleled catastrophe: at the time of this report, firefighting crews have been working non-stop to contain a fire that broke out in the wee hours of the morning in the remote village of Amber Hollow, an unincorporated township in Northeast Wisconsin. The Rhinelander fire chief stated that the fire is about twenty-five percent contained, but is still ravaging the community as firefighters from Wausau and Green Bay have been recruited to aid the workers who have been battling it since roughly four o'clock this morning. Their efforts to keep the blaze from getting bigger have been hindered by strong winds from the northwest, as well as the extremely hot summer temperatures and unusually low humidity. The Governor has declared a state of emergency, calling upon the federal government for backup should that become necessary. At this time, the fire marshal of Green Bay, Calvin Lemory, doesn't expect that will be needed, but if conditions worsen, he reassured us that any measure would be taken to ensure the safety of the preserved woodlands. Although there are no other townships in the path of the fire, the Elfin National Forest is due north, home of many endangered species including but not limited to gray wolves, badgers, and bald eagles.

"Only three survivors have been located of the approximately six hundred people who reside in the isolated community, and have been taken to hospitals in Green Bay for treatment of second-degree burns and smoke inhalation. There is still no explanation for the cause of the fire, as those who survived have been unable to respond to the investigators. I'm Jeffry Winters, and we'll keep bringing you updates throughout the day..."

CBS Channel Ten News, Madison, Wisconsin, 5:00 p.m., July 16, 1991:

"Good evening, I'm Carol Traynor, bringing you an exclusive story that has shocked and horrified people around the nation over the last two days.

"Amber Hollow, a small, secluded village in Torrance County, Northern Wisconsin, is the scene of an unprecedented tragedy, leaving firefighting investigators baffled as to exactly what happened. Authorities surmise that the blaze started around midnight on Sunday, July 14, and aided by strong winds the flames ravaged all of the scenic business district and then spread to outlying homes, businesses, and farms in the surrounding area. Firefighters were able to effectively contain it to the limits of the village, saving the area from what could have become an out-of-control wildfire, but the entire township is gone. There is no known cause for the fire just yet. It has been speculated that it may have been initiated by mismanaged fireworks, although there has been no substantial evidence to confirm this. As of four o'clock this afternoon firefighters report that they have the fire one hundred percent contained, and expect it to be completely extinguished by tomorrow morning. However, they have informed us that of the village's population of approximately six hundred people it has so far been determined there are only five known survivors, all of whom have been transported to hospitals in Green Bay to be treated for burns, smoke inhalation and various injuries. For now, their names have not been made public, nor has the Torrance County Sheriff's Department offered an official statement regarding this disaster. All that is known at this time is that one of the survivors is in a coma, three are suffering from first and second-degree burns, and one of them, an eleven-year-old girl, has a sprained wrist, a concussion, and other superficial wounds. With the exception of the patient in a coma, they are all expected to make a full recovery.

"Arson and homicide investigators from the Brown County Sheriff's Department in Green Bay are handling the case, and promise to release a statement later this week as more facts are collected. In the meantime, we can only pray for those who survived, and mourn for the extraordinary number of lives that were mysteriously lost in what surely has to be one of the biggest calamities in Wisconsin history. I'm Carol Traynor, and we will continue to follow this story as more details emerge…"

Excerpt of testimony given by one survivor of the Amber Hollow tragedy, July 18, 1991:

"...every summer we celebrate bath-steel days, and I was with my mommy and daddy and my brother Timmy. Everyone in town gets together and there's a band and fireworks and games. We were eating hamburgers and corn on the cob and potato salad, and mommy let me and Timmy have a soda. I had a Coke, and Timmy had a Mountain Dew. My daddy always has a beer, and mommy has wine, but they say that we can't drink it 'til we're grownups, which is OK with me because I think it smells funny. Anyway, we were listening to the band, and they played all kinds of songs I like, you know, from the radio, and then they lit the fireworks. I don't know what happened then, I was really sleepy, but I remember hearing somebody shout something, and then a woman ran by me and she was bleeding. Then my mommy and my daddy grabbed me and Timmy and we were running away from the village square, you know, where they had the stage for the band, and then everybody was screaming and I smelled smoke. It was hot, really hot, and it was hard to breathe. And then my daddy fell down, and he dropped Timmy, and they just laid there, bleeding, and mommy started screaming, and...and...and..."

At this point in the interview the little girl broke down in tears and had to be consoled by one of the detectives. When asked her name she said she didn't know, however, in most cases of mild brain trauma amnesia is seldom permanent, which is indicative of a favorable prognosis. After receiving a sedative to calm her anxiety, she slept soundly.

Passage from the Amber Hollow Chamber of Commerce Information Center, courtesy of the Wisconsin Bureau of Tourism:

Founded in 1735 by an ordained Jesuit priest named Solomon Marquette, Amber Hollow is a scenic retreat far from the hustle and bustle of larger cities like Wausau, Rhinelander, Green Bay and, farther to the south, Milwaukee. Known for its beautiful apple orchards and pumpkin patches, it is a place of extraordinary beauty.

The earliest settlers were mostly fur trappers and missionaries, hunting fox, badgers, and deer while sharing the word of God with the native Americans who then inhabited the area. The village is a picturesque wonder of natural bodies of water and is in fact split down the middle by the Iron River, making it the perfect location for logging operations and paper mills, although citizens of the Hollow never embraced such enterprises to make their fortune. The small township avoided these industries because they feared the pollutants would take a heavy toll on the river, and villagers relied on the abundant supply of fish, such as smelt, perch, pike, and trout, to supplement their diet. To this day there are no manufacturing operations in business on the stretch of river running through the village, leaving the water practically pristine thanks to the hundreds of acres of preserved forests to the north.

Bloodlines run deep in Amber Hollow, as many generations have chosen to stay and raise their families as opposed to making a life elsewhere. Agriculture was the mainstay well into the twentieth century, but large-scale farming operations were never needed to support the villagers because ample reserves of gold were discovered in the late seventeen hundreds, guaranteeing wealth and abundance for many centuries to come. To this day, vast troves of gold-enriched wealth still sustain the community; however, the Hollow gives the impression of being "preserved in time" as the residents eschewed many modern conveniences, instead following the traditions of their ancestors. This is evident in the architecture and design of the business district, as well as the homes, although they are equipped with electricity thanks to solar and gasoline-powered generators. Automated farm machinery is also employed, as well as the convenience of modern automobiles.

Tourism in Amber Hollow isn't a booming trade; nevertheless, folks are encouraged to enjoy day-visits to the orchards, fish on the river, and stay at one of the many bed-and-breakfast hotels nearby in Crandon that offer all the best amenities. For more information call (715) 555-5721.

PART ONE
THE TRAGEDY

CHAPTER 1

FRIDAY, JULY 19, 1991

Detective Jeremy LeFevre stared at the report that sat on his desk, his brain slightly muddled from the early morning humidity coupled with lack of sleep. It was only ten o'clock but it was already at eighty-five percent, and would probably drop by only ten percent as the sun streaked mercilessly across the midwestern sky, and that didn't bode well for his slumber. Nor did being assigned the task of lead homicide investigator in a case that was receiving more headlines than all of his other cases combined. This dubious honor was bequeathed to him and his partner by Captain Martin, and it wasn't without a small amount of pity that his superior gave him the job. Amber Hollow wasn't in their usual jurisdiction but since Green Bay was the nearest "big city," his department was tapped for their resources. The request had been made by the Crandon police department, the closest neighboring town, and why they hadn't called in the Rhinelander PD was beyond his pay grade, although it certainly wasn't the first time he'd assisted with out-of-town cases. The Brown County Sheriff's Department was often tasked with assisting in statewide homicides committed in smaller towns, effectively giving him something else to do other than investigate vehicular manslaughter cases and hunting accidents, of which there were many.

Most recently, in April 1991, a teenager named Bruce Brenzier shot five members of his family with a deer rifle before placing them in the family's station wagon and setting it on fire in a park near Balsam Lake. The crime was committed in Polk County, in Northwest Wisconsin, along the Minnesota border. Despite the considerable distance from Green Bay, Jeremy and his partner had been called in to assist with the interrogation. Thanks to a spring lull, they were the most readily available. Now that was one kid who really gave Jeremy the creeps. He had large, brown, dead looking eyes, like a shark's, and his face was slack and emotionless. He gave his confession in a muted voice, betraying no remorse. That was what had really bothered Jeremy. The kid hadn't reveled in the act, but he didn't appear to regret it either. His trial was currently pending, but last Jeremy had heard, his defense lawyer was working on an insanity plea.

Considering the current case, he wondered when the Feds would get involved, send some of their best and brightest to shadow him and his partner, most likely mire the whole investigation in red tape. Since the entire population (with the exception of five people) were dead, a tragedy of this magnitude would surely warrant the unsolicited expertise of the FBI. It was just a matter of when.

He set down the report, ran a hand through his hair and then wiped his hand on his shirt. The AC was blowing cold air through the vents, helping to dry the sweat on his brow, but he had the window of his office open to let out the stale air that had accumulated over the course of what had already been a very long morning. He and his partner, Detective Sadie Conrad, had conducted their first interview with the as of yet unnamed little girl yesterday, but they hadn't obtained much information from the poor, addled child, nothing to shed any light on what had transpired on Sunday, July 14. Reports from the scene of the tragedy from firefighters, arson specialists, and forensic investigators described a vague picture; so far there was no concrete information, just a lot of dead bodies. With the exception, perhaps, of the report he was looking at. It offered no obvious clues, only made what they were up against a bigger challenge, but for now it was all they had.

"Hey," Sadie said from behind him, two cups of coffee in her hands. He turned, offered her a smile.

"Hey yourself." He took the proffered cup and sipped it slowly even though he need not bother because it was lukewarm. He tipped the cup too far and spilled some on his shirt and cussed under his breath. Of course he was wearing white, and he'd wear the stain all day like a badge of dishonor. He dabbed at it with a napkin, but all he did was smear it around. Sadie smiled at this, and his scowl deepened.

"Great. I'll never get this stain out. Might as well throw the shirt away."

"Have your laundry professionally done. I know you bachelors are helpless when it comes to domesticity."

"You got that right." Jeremy hadn't always been a bachelor, he was divorced, had been for over five years. The split had been amicable, though, and there were no children to worry about. And even though it had been a while, he wasn't in a hurry to hook up again anytime soon. He'd been on that merry-go-round, and at the robust age of thirty-five he felt a good turn at being single might be what the doctor ordered. This way he could focus on his work. He'd taken the position with the Brown County Sheriff's Department after the separation, eager to rid himself of the persistent memories by getting a fresh start. So far, it had been working beautifully.

Sadie eyed him with the tolerant gaze of a long-time co-worker, amused at his discomfort. He wasn't what you would call a good-looking man, in fact he had a nose that looked like a dog had taken a chomp out of it, accompanied by blunt features that ostensibly affirmed his French heritage. His hair was short and black, and it looked as if he'd either gotten a bad haircut from an amateur barber or he cut it himself with a dull knife. All that said, he still wasn't a bad catch for some lucky lady, she thought. His patience and cordiality made up for his physical features.

She pulled a chair over from the corner of their office and sat down next to him, looking at the photocopied report, although from her vantage point, she could only make out the large type of the masthead, not the rest of the text. She furrowed her brow and sipped her coffee, absentmindedly running a hand over her tight black curls. She used to straighten her hair with harsh emollients and a curling iron until one of her sisters accused her of being an "Aunty Tom." Since then, she let her Afro grow however it wanted while keeping it reasonably trim. She didn't often let other people make decisions for her, but being African-American (and a woman, no less) working as a homicide detective in a small Midwest city, she wanted to assert herself as a strong-willed, independent thinker. Besides, she was proud of her heritage and saw no need to mask who she was.

"I suppose you think this is funny," Jeremy said, after trying spit on the stain and making it worse. It now looked like a Rorschach drawing. If one squinted hard enough, they could possibly discern the scowling face of a drunken leprechaun.

"Of course, I do," she replied, and he guffawed, admiring her honesty. He looked at her appreciatively.

"I'm glad I can entertain you."

"And how."

Sadie possessed a demeanor that made her increasingly attractive the longer you knew her. She was smart as a whip but she enjoyed being silly, could laugh at high-brow humor as well as slapstick. When she laughed, the rust-colored spattering of freckles that spread across the tops of her cheeks and over the bridge of her broad, flat nose twinkled like a galaxy of stars, which in turn were complimented by a smile that was as disarming as it was inquisitive. She was a bit on the heavy side, the unfortunate result of long hours sitting at her desk typing reports and eating fattening foods, but she was in good health. Like most Wisconsinites she loved cheese, and often had a bag of cheese curds readily available for snacking on when she needed to do research. She, too, was unmarried, and as her twenty-ninth birthday drew near, she knew she probably (according to her sister) should be, but she had a boyfriend she saw a few times a week and that was good enough for her. It was nothing serious, she often stressed when asked, so it was widely thought she just kept him around for the occasional company on a lonely night.

"What are you looking at?" Sadie took another sip of her coffee and grimaced. There wasn't enough sugar in the world to make the Brown County Sheriff's Department coffee taste any better, and they could thank Sandra Kendrick for that, as she was the one responsible for the pot in the break room nearest their department. That woman probably couldn't boil water to cook an egg.

"The latest report. You're just in time, take a look at this."

She leaned in closer to read the text, each of them mulling over it as they drank their tepid, rancid coffee. Sadie could smell the pleasant scent of Jeremy's cologne, but beneath it there was a sour hint of BO. She could forgive him for that, though, as it was so damn humid. She'd used enough antiperspirant this morning to give herself Alzheimer's twenty times over, most likely, so she certainly wasn't one to judge. Besides, it was a *manly* smell. Nothing wrong with that.

"What do you think?" Jeremy asked her after she'd read it all, and she shrugged.

"I'd say that this case is definitely going to be a barnburner."

"Pun intended?" he said, smiling, and realizing her choice of words, she shook her head.

"No."

"If it helps, that's exactly what I thought too, minus the 'barnburner.'"

"What's next?"

"Let's talk to the next survivor on the list, the woman with the least severe burns. We'll see what she knows. Hopefully she can give us something more than the kid did."

"Give her a break, she's only eleven years old, and she has a concussion. I can't believe you insisted on talking to her so soon." She frowned at him in a stern, motherly fashion, and as he was wont to do, he took the bait.

"I know, my bad," he said, obediently hanging his head. "But if they are awake and coherent, we need to get their statements."

"The little girl was barely coherent."

"She made sense to me."

"You just said it yourself: she didn't give us anything."

"I guess so, but we have a job to do." He tipped her a wink, wanted her to know that he agreed with her but was ready to defend his actions as a bona fide necessity. She begrudgingly accepted with a snort and he knew he was forgiven. "You ready?"

"Let's go." She set her cup down on his desk. "And on our way, let's stop and get some real coffee, huh? This crap is giving me a stomach ache."

"Motioned seconded," he agreed, and this made them both laugh. As the day progressed, humor would be hit or miss, but for the time being the laughter felt good, a way to dispel the gloom created by the case. "I call shotgun," he said, and she nodded.

"Of course you do, you lazy bastard."

And they exited the office in the direction of the cruiser.

• • •

The antiseptic smell of the hospital gave Sadie the willies. She associated it with the horrific battle with cancer that had consumed her mother. The last month of her life had been excruciating, not only for her but for the rest of the family. How many nights had she taken turns with her brother and sister sleeping in the hospital chair, just waiting for their mother to die? Too many, and even though the pain was now a dull ache, it still hadn't gone away, even after two years. Being in a hospital brought it all back, the smell of urine and sweat, the sounds of the nurse's soft-soled shoes whisking across the tile floor, the soft burble of voices over the intercom. Over the years she'd gained a good working knowledge of the "coded" messages the staff sent the doctors, indicating a patient suffering from myocardial infarction, or an epileptic having a seizure. If she ever had to spend so much as one night in a hospital in one of those depressing beds, she'd probably beg for humane euthanasia.

"Can I help you?" the woman at the desk asked disinterestedly.

"Homicide detectives Conrad and LeFevre to see a patient, please."

That got her attention. "Yes?"

Sadie glanced at her pocket-sized notebook, turning pages until she found the correct one. "Sylvia Albright, please. She's in the psychiatric ward."

The nurse looked visibly disturbed, nodding her head quickly and averting her gaze.

"Certainly, yes. One of the candy stripers was just in with her. She's awake and having something to eat." She regarded them briefly before looking away. "She's in room three sixteen; that's on the west side of the building."

"Thank you."

Heading to the bank of elevators, Jeremy checked to make sure his walkie-talkie was silenced. He didn't want the hiss of static to awaken anyone from their much-needed slumber. Twisting the dial, he made a mental note to turn it back on as soon as they were finished. He didn't want to miss a single transmission, not at a time like this. He also turned off his pager; if anyone needed him, it could wait until they were finished with the interview. The elevator came, they stepped inside.

"The latest bit of news," Jeremy said, referring to the report they'd just read, "let's keep that to ourselves until we see what she has to say, OK?"

"Why?"

"Just humor me."

"Sure."

They got out at the third floor, made their way down a long corridor that to Sadie's olfactory senses smelled worse than the lobby. She especially didn't like this floor; it always made her feel even more uneasy. The overhead fluorescent lights seemed too bright, the natural light through the patient's room windows offering a muted quality that made the day somewhat surreal. Outwardly, the psychiatric ward appeared no different from the rest of the hospital, unless one studied the patients carefully. Eyes as empty as moon craters stared from hooded lids, drool oozing miserably over scabbed lips. Some brooded; others laughed uncharacteristically in regard to their surroundings, while others muttered nonsensically to themselves. Not exactly a place where anyone would want to spend a lot of time, in Sadie's humble opinion.

No more than two hundred yards down the corridor brought them to the woman's room. Sylvia was sitting upright in the bed, spooning Jell-O into her mouth from a paper cup, staring out the window. Her face was red and blistered, looking raw and gruesome under the harsh lights, and her hands and arms were covered in gauze. Despite her injuries, she was only hooked up to a blood pressure machine, which droned a steady beep-beep-beep as it monitored her vital signs. Her eyes were fixed on the landscape outside in a desultory manner that was somewhat disquieting, and Sadie was given to think the woman was most likely medicated. She appeared to be in her late twenties, maybe early thirties, but it was hard to tell exactly because of the nature of her burns.

"Ms. Albright?" Sadie asked from the threshold, and the woman jumped as if jolted with a stun gun. When she looked from Sadie to Jeremy her eyes grew wide and her nostrils flared.

"Yes?" she asked in a meek voice, the spoon frozen halfway to her mouth, the Jell-O precariously perched there, looking in danger of spilling on her hospital gown.

Sadie took a step forward. "I'm Detective Conrad, and this is my partner Detective LeFevre. We'd like to ask you some questions about what happened on Sunday night."

The woman sat very still, her eyes a startling shade of green. They darted back and forth from Sadie to Jeremy, the spoon forgotten in her hand. Gravity finally won out and the Jell-O dropped onto her hospital gown, but she didn't appear to notice.

"May we come in?" Sadie asked, pitching her voice low, trying not to startle the poor woman any further, but she surprised them by uttering a deep, guttural laugh.

"You guys are detectives and you have to ask? Does that mean I can say no?"

"Afraid not," Jeremy said, walking into the room and taking a small recording device from his pocket. He'd had the presence of mind to preload a fresh cassette beforehand. "We're both very sorry for what happened. Please accept our most sincere condolences. Nevertheless, we need to ask you some questions. We're hoping that you can help us."

"How come they won't let me watch TV? Is the set broke?" She pointed to the TV on the wall, and Jeremy glanced at it a second before shaking his head.

"It's not broken. The doctors don't want you to get upset, not after everything you've been through."

"After what I've been through?"

"Yes, Ma'am."

"How do you know what *I've* been through?"

"We don't," Jeremy said, "so you'll have to tell us."

Sylvia Albright of Amber Hollow, Wisconsin, eyed the two of them intently before noticing she was still holding the spoon. She set it down on the nightstand next to her and then the cup of Jell-O. She still didn't notice (or didn't care) about the gelatin on her gown.

"What do you want to know?"

Sadie and Jeremy exchanged a quick glance. What did they want to know? The entire village was gone, burned to the ground, her family and friend's dead, and she asked them what they wanted to know? It was becoming apparent why she was in the psychiatric ward and not the burn center. Sadie wondered if the woman's answers could be considered pertinent, given the nature of the circumstances.

"What we want," Sadie said softly, "is to figure out what happened that night. Are you aware that you survived a massive tragedy?"

The brief smile that had played across the woman's face was gone, exchanged by an expression of fear that was seemingly boundless. She again looked from one face to the other, licking her lips nervously. She began to mutter, but it was too low for either of them to hear.

"What was that, Sylvia?" Sadie prompted. "What are you saying?"

She quit muttering and stared at Sadie for so long the detective began to feel uncomfortable. It was something in the woman's eyes, some secret she wasn't sure she should share. She took a deep breath, exhaled.

"You have no idea what happened." A statement, not a question. "Am I the only survivor?"

Sadie opened her mouth to say no, but a quick glance from her partner stopped her from even forming the word with her lips.

"Tell us what happened," Jeremy said instead of answering her question, and their silence seemed to calm her even more. She closed her eyes, leaned back into her pillow, and exhaled more sharply, this time with an air of resignation.

"I'll tell you, but you have to promise to keep me safe." Her eyes were still closed, her voice carrying a dreamy quality to it.

"We promise," Sadie said. "That's our job."

"OK. But remember, you promised."

"We did, and we mean it," Jeremy said. "Now please, tell us to the best of your recollection what happened."

He turned on the tape recorder, holding it close to catch every word. She opened her eyes and fixed them with a long stare before drawing another breath, shaking her head, and beginning to speak...

CHAPTER 2

SYLVIA ALBRIGHT'S TESTIMONY

"We've long been a very private community. We didn't need the help of outsiders because we were independently wealthy. We were open to tourists, but we never encouraged anyone to stay for very long. Did you know that we discovered gold in the early seventeenth century and had no need for out-of-town developers? Well, if you didn't, now you do. The village sustained itself quite comfortably for a long time without having to expand beyond the borders established over two hundred years ago, and probably would have for a long time to come if this hadn't happened. People came to us over the years, land developers, real estate moguls, business franchises, and we turned them all away. We liked things as they were, you see, very simple. We did change with the times, of course. We had TV and modern conveniences, but we were never driven by greed, not enough to allow a Wal-Mart, not even a Bed, Bath, and Beyond, and I wouldn't have minded not having to drive a hundred miles to buy some of their lotions and hand towels, but that's the way it's always been.

"And it worked fine for a long time, but then Anthony Guntram had to go and ruin it for all of us. He is…was…our mayor. We elected him a long time ago, and we thought he always had everyone's best interests in mind. He was the valedictorian of his class in '69, a natural leader with an abundance of good sense, but sometimes a little bit of a dreamer. Maria Clancy used to say that if his head wasn't attached to his shoulders by his thick, bull neck it would float away like a helium-filled balloon. Isn't that

funny? Can you just picture that? Anyway, he and his assistants were in charge of the city treasury; they held in their hands the entire destiny of our township. And none of us had any worries, because the gold mine showed no sign of running out. Isn't that crazy? Wisconsin isn't exactly known for gold mining, but there it is.

"None of us knew that Anthony was spending the money—our money—on extravagant things for himself, and not only that, gambling, whoring, and drugs too. Turned out that bastard had a taste for high-priced call girls and blackjack, but that wasn't the worst of it. He apparently made friends with some mobsters down in Milwaukee, and they got him hooked on cocaine. Those mobsters, well, they can get you anything you need, and they got it for him all right. The son of a bitch was buying it by the kilo, definitely high as a kite from sunup to sunset. I'm sure he was giving it away to his cronies too, some bottom feeders like those McAuley boys, and you better believe he went through all of the town's reserves in no time. Well, it probably took a few years, but none of us were aware of it, we thought everything was just peaches and cream, until late last spring, when he finally called a town meeting, told us all it was urgent.

"He hemmed and hawed for a while, muttering things about latent accountability, and the stress of being the one in charge, until he eventually got to the part about the mob and his gambling, whoring, and drug problem, and then he dropped the bombshell: the village was not only flat broke but in debt up to its eyeballs and the mobsters wanted the money back they'd loaned him plus interest. He told us he was sorry, that he hadn't meant it to come to that, but we all knew he wasn't, not really. That cocaine can make a monster out of you. His wife was probably the most upset, and she left him faster than you can say 'pass the Peruvian flake,' but Anthony said he would make it right, he'd take care of the problem. Thing was, what could he do? According to the village treasurer, Daniel Chimeres, there was nothing left. And we didn't have much else in the way of revenue. Our tourist industry didn't bring in enough to run the snow plows in winter, nor did we have any industrial manufacturing that could make up the

difference. It wasn't like we were useless, there were a lot of folks with good educations who could have applied themselves to any number of trades, but that wasn't going to get us out of the hot water he'd put us in. And the kicker was that the mobsters wanted the gold mine…what Anthony owed them, well, they figured that would pay it off. This sent everyone into an uproar, that Anthony would bankrupt us and give up the rights to the only thing that was supporting our community, and I'm sure most of us left that meeting thinking very bad things about good old Guntram. I know I was. I'm just a homemaker. I never went to college, and my husband has been dead and in Heaven for many years now. I never remarried, didn't see any need to.

"So, the rest of us, we had a meeting, in secret without Anthony. We figured maybe if we could talk to the mobsters, you know, work out a deal with them, they might see it in their hearts to take the debt out on him. You know what I'm saying? Now, I'm a good Christian woman, and I fear the righteousness of our Lord and Savior Jesus Christ, but this was Anthony's mess, and he dragged us all into it. Maybe, we thought, they could just take it out on him and leave us alone, let us try and pick up the pieces of our lives in whatever way we could. Maybe pay them off with some of what the mine put out, and then, you know, we'd open the town to fast food joints and super stores, maybe sell off some of the land that realtors wanted to develop, some of the apple orchard and pumpkin patch land. Build some hotels, maybe allow a paper mill or logging operation to set up on the banks of the Iron River…we were just trying to be practical, trying to protect ourselves from needing government assistance, which we may or may not have been eligible for, being independent for so long.

"Problem we had was, we didn't know who these mob guys were, and it wasn't like we could just go and ask Anthony, not without making him suspicious. So, Al Bougie said he'd try and wring it out of him, you know, have a few drinks, get Anthony to loosen up, hopefully cough up a name that would lead us somewhere, but before he could have that talk, why, Anthony disappeared in the middle of the night. Just took off for God knows where. I've never been the type to hate, I think hate is a terrible thing, you know?

But I hated Anthony Guntram, oh Lord, yes, I did, and so did everyone else. What he'd done, you see, was leave us to whatever fate it was these mobsters saw fit to mete out on us. Left us to die.

A month went by, May turned into June, and everybody was pitching in to do whatever they could to keep us afloat. We continued our discussions about bringing in a McDonald's and a Burger King, maybe allow Marriot's to build a hotel. Because that was what we had to do; start selling Amber Hollow off in chunks just to keep the lights on. We had to sell something, and we had to let out-of-towners in. Did this make us mad? You bet it did. Our beautiful, private little parish with hundreds of years of history was about to be raped by capitalistic America. Just made me sick. But we went on as best as we could, tried to keep positive in light of a bad situation.

"Now, every year, we celebrated Bastille Days, because of our French heritage. It was a local tradition. On July 14 every year we all gathered in the village square and brought food from our gardens and set up carnival games for the children and Justin Freeport and his band The Merry Tricksters set up on the gazebo and played all the hits from the radio. They were good, those boys, and we looked forward to hearing them every year. The big event though, was the fireworks display. That was how we ended the night every year, after everyone got their fill of corn on the cob and potato salad and burgers and hotdogs and homemade apple pie. We had some of the best orchards in the greater area, and were those apples sweet? Why, you bet they were. Hardly needed sugar to make 'em taste so good. And everything was going fine, everyone having such a nice time watching the fireworks. And that's when we heard the cars approaching, a lot of them too. Sounded like a whole presidential motorcade.

"They drove all the way up to the village square, over a dozen cars, filled with men who made their living hurting people. Right there in the middle of our Bastille Days celebration they came, acting like they owned the place. Al Bougie was the one who met them, flanked by Joel Adderley and Raymond LaCroix. He told them to come back the next day, that *they'd sit down and talk about things, but the mobsters, well, they were fixing to take matters into their hands right then and there. The talk went on for a little while until it got kind of heated, and after that, why, that's when it happened.*

"The guy in the lead, I'll bet he was the mob boss, he waved his hand and his men spread out on both sides of him. They all had guns, and they looked like automatics to me. I'm no gun aficionado, but I've seen enough war movies to know what a machine gun looks like, and that's what they had. They pointed them at us, and everyone got real scared, started to run, and that's when they open fired.

"People were running every which way, and the sound of the guns was so loud it overtook everything else, except for the screaming. I saw Mary Beth Witherspoon's head explode right in front of my eyes. One minute she was standing there, trying to corral her children and the next thing she had no head and she was lying on the sidewalk, her legs kicking as her blood ran into the gutter. I've never been so afraid in my whole life, and I'll tell you it's a miracle I'm not laying there dead with the rest of them. I don't know how I escaped, just that I ran and hid in the hardware store behind a shelf of half-penny nails and calk guns. Then I smelled smoke, and when I felt brave enough, I stood up and had a look. They'd set the town on fire, and everything was burning. I saw my friends and neighbors running for their lives, the lot of them on fire. More gun shots rang out, and I watched as they fell twitching and screaming, rolling around in the flames. It was like Hell opened up beneath our village and just swallowed it right up. I can't describe it any better than that. Well, I hunkered down for a while until I realized the hardware store was on fire, and then I ran out the back door and made my way toward the Hollister's farm. The air was so smoky I could barely breathe, and I could smell the stink of burning flesh...it was awful, you never forget that smell. And in the stables at the farm I could hear the horses whinnying and trying to get free. I opened the gate, slapped one on the ass and yelled at it to git, but those horses were too dumb or too slow and they cooked too.

"I don't remember much after that. All I know is that I must have blacked out, and then I woke up here. Now I'm talking to you."

At this point in the interview, Sylvia Albright yawned expansively, told the investigators she was tired, and that she needed to get some sleep. The interview was then concluded but plans to cross-examine her were made for the following afternoon.

CHAPTER 3

A VISIT TO THE MORGUE

"**H**er story wasn't very convincing to me," Jeremy said as he climbed into the standard issue Crown Vic, taking a seat on the passenger side. Sadie did all the driving because she was more sensible behind the wheel. He had a tendency to tailgate other cars when he thought they were going too slow, and this led to confusion because the offending vehicle often thought they were getting pulled over. "Because she's on psych meds, we'll have to consider the fact that her testimony is tainted."

"She didn't seem that crazy, and her story corroborated the latest evidence," Sadie pointed out. "You think she made all that up? That was a pretty detailed account."

"I don't think she made it *all* up," Jeremy said, turning his pager back on before buckling his seatbelt. "But she basically recited the city's Chamber of Commerce blurb and went running with it from there."

"There isn't a lot of gold mining in Wisconsin, is there?"

"I have Corey looking into it, but no, I don't think so." Jeremy considered it a moment. "I should also have him see if the Marriot Hotel corporation made plans to purchase land in Amber Hollow."

"Might be a good idea." She looked at him quizzically. "You think they didn't have a gold mine?"

"I don't know, but for there to be a gold mine that sustains a town for hundreds of years…sounds kind of fishy to me."

"Then maybe they *were* connected with the mob."

"There is definitely more than meets the eye going on here."

"So where to, chief?"

Jeremy fixed her with a look that made her smile. He hated it when she called him "chief."

"I think it's time to see exactly what the new evidence turned up."

"So…"

"Time to pay our good buddy Allister a call."

Sadie shuddered, firing up the engine and putting the car in drive. Allister MacArthur wasn't necessarily someone she liked to see at any time of day, but just around the lunch hour was the worst. If she'd just eaten, she felt like puking. If she hadn't, she wasn't hungry until dinner, and that said a lot for her. She wasn't one to miss many meals.

"Whatever you say, chief."

"Just drive."

• • •

The temperature in the morgue was more agreeable than it was upstairs, but that was only a small consolation for what they were about to see. Jeremy had an iron stomach; he could look at a corpse while eating a sandwich and think nothing of it. Sadie, on the other hand, could take or leave it. Mostly leave it. And it wasn't her aversion to the dead, she was a homicide investigator after all, it was all the other smells that accompanied it. Like the hospital, the antiseptic odor brought to mind too many memories, ones she'd like to bury in her subconscious if she could. Women half-melted in the driver seat of their car, arms melded with the steering wheel, the children's car seats a slimy wash of blood and tattered clothing; gunshot victims with loops of intestines hanging out of their abdomen; cyclists practically flattened after a run in with an eighteen-wheeler…she'd seen a lot of things during her time on the force, images that could haunt you in the wee hours of the night, when sleep was elusive.

At the double swinging doors Jeremy paused.

"After you," he said, and she frowned.

"After *you*."

He grinned. "Glad to see chivalry isn't dead."

"In your dreams, princess."

He rapped once and then entered, the cold from the outer chamber becoming much cooler, as it needed to be. It had to be pretty frigid to sustain the flesh of the recently deceased so they could be properly examined. Now, to be fair, Green Bay's morgue didn't see a whole lot of action. The city boasted a very low yearly homicide rate, so most autopsies conducted were in regard to crib deaths, drug overdoses or vehicular homicides. This week, however, the morgue was working overtime because of the large case load, which meant long hours for MacArthur, who only had one assistant, and he was barely competent enough to get the body temps correct and tag and bag the various body parts. Presently, that doofus was on donut and coffee duty, the one thing he was extremely adept at.

"Hey Allie, how's it hanging?"

The coroner looked up from the body he was elbows deep in, was about to make a snide remark, when he saw Sadie.

"You're lucky you have female company, Jerr. I was about to tell you what was hanging, and how low."

"Hey," Sadie said amiably, "I'm just one of the guys, remember?"

"The day you walk in here sporting a handlebar mustache is the day I'll believe that," he said, removing and setting down a blood-spattered bone spreader on a stainless-steel table, and Sadie blushed slightly. Allister may have been an old crank, but he was still sort of handsome, in a creepy, horror movie mad scientist way. Besides, she ate up compliments no matter where they came from.

"I received a report from the forensic investigators," Jeremy said, sidling up, but not too close. He didn't mind the bodies, but if he could keep a good arm's length away, that was fine by him. And this one, well, it didn't look pretty. Not that it should, of course, but unlike the majority of the corpses that had been discovered this one wasn't completely crispy fried, in fact, there was enough left to easily see it was the remains of a young woman. "What's the word?"

"Always one to get right down to business, I see," Allister said dryly. "You sure you don't want to talk about the Packers first? You think they need to draft a better back-up QB if Majkowski gets injured?"

"You know I'd love to sit here and talk about the Packers but humor me and tell me what we're looking at."

"So, the report...what did it say?"

Jeremy looked at the body, what was left of it anyway and then glanced sidelong at Sadie and saw that she'd removed a handkerchief from one of the many pockets of her uniform and was covering her nose.

"There's masks over there if you want to wear one," Allister offered, and she shook her head.

"I'm fine."

"The latest report we saw before interviewing one of the adult survivors stated that there was evidence of physical trauma. Apparently, some of the corpses retrieved weren't just burned alive, they suffered serious bodily harm first."

"Correct," Allister concurred. "As you can see by the ligature marks on the remains of this woman's arm something was wrapped around her shoulder that literally tore her arm off."

"Hmm," Jeremy pondered, examining the body more closely. "What type of ballistics have you found?"

"Ballistics?"

"Yeah, are we talking large caliber automatics or handguns?"

Allister paused from what he was doing. Behind him, on the other eight slabs in the room, were bodies covered with plastic sheets. Personally, Allister didn't care if they were covered or not, but it was standard policy. No one else in the department (except maybe Christopher Dolce) liked looking at them, and he'd been sent to the department shrink more than once for that peculiar habit.

"Must be some misunderstanding," Allister said, peeling off one glove to wipe sweat from his forehead. How he could be sweating in this meat locker was anybody's best guess, but so it was. "Why do you ask?"

Jeremy hesitated, a look of confusion on his face. "Forensic investigators on the scene said that several bodies they found showed signs of physical trauma, suggesting violence by some other means than being burned to death."

"Yes, that corroborates evidence I have found. So, what's with the ballistics report question?"

Jeremy glanced at Sadie, she shrugged. "The survivor we just talked to said that they'd been ambushed by mobsters. She said they were all gunned down in the village square while they were celebrating Bastille Days."

Allister arched his eyebrows, two of the thickest, hairiest eyebrows one ever laid eyes on. For all practical purposes, they looked like two caterpillars either making love or fighting to the death.

"As you can see there are signs of trauma, but I haven't found any bullets, nor shrapnel of any kind."

"What?"

"Am I speaking English?"

Jeremy glanced at Sadie again. "Is he speaking English?"

"Appears to be."

"So," Jeremy said, "what *have* you found?"

"Nothing but trace amounts of various accelerants, but those are standard in cases of a fire," he said and then laughed at the puzzled looks on their faces. "Man, this is priceless, and me without my Polaroid."

"Accelerants?"

"You know, butane, propane, gasoline, natural gas, but those are to be expected because they are commonly found everywhere."

"So, by 'nothing,' you mean…?"

"This body shows definite signs of trauma, but no apparent reasons as such."

"No bullets, no blast residue from a bomb?"

"Did I not just say the word 'nothing'?"

"That's what he said," Sadie supplied, and Jeremy frowned at her. "Sorry, but you seemed like you weren't getting it."

"Then how did they die?" he asked. "How did this person die?" He pointed at the cadaver on the table.

"No idea. It's apparent that something literally pulled her apart, but I haven't found anything, no identifiable marks signifying a tangible object that did the physical trauma."

Sadie and Jeremy were silent for a moment, digesting this fact.

"Well, that negates the testimony from Sylvia Albright," Sadie said, and Jeremy nodded.

"I knew there was something about her story that didn't add up."

"It does explain why she's in the psychiatric ward at Bellin."

"Well, do tell. Your star witness sounds like she's off the rails." Allister was now putting on another glove, preparing to continue with his examination.

"So, if they weren't rubbed out by mobsters," Sadie said, "then what the hell *did* happen?"

Allister paused, glove half on, a perplexed expression on his face. He shook his head, and in this gesture, there was a look of resignation.

"I don't know, but that little tidbit is going to make my job a lot harder."

"What do you mean?" Sadie asked, adjusting the handkerchief as some new, odoriferous scent wafted her way.

"Well, I've done pre-exams on all the bodies you see here." He waved one hand, indicating the tables and their less-than-savory cargo.

"Yeah?"

"None of them have any bullet wounds."

"Are you sure?" Jeremy said, and Allister rolled his eyes.

"I think I'd know a bullet wound when I saw one."

"Have you performed a full examination on all of these bodies?"

"Are you aware of how long it takes to examine one, much less eight corpses? I'll be at this through the weekend, and I had plans to play golf at Mystery Hills with some of my buddies."

"I'd like to feel sorry for you," Jeremy said, "but it also makes our job a lot harder too. Apparently, our first witness lied to us, and Christ knows why she'd do that."

"Well, when you put it that way, I guess my job is easier than yours."

"I don't think so," Sadie disagreed, and they all laughed.

"OK, thanks Allister. Keep us posted on what else you find."

"Will do," the other said and, as they turned to go, he added: "So who do you think the Packers are going to play in the Super Bowl this year?"

Jeremy was about to say "in your dreams" when Sadie said: "The Buffalo Bills."

The two men exchanged a look that said, "Dames? What do they know about football?" and she scowled. "Come February, you two are going to look pretty stupid when I'm right."

"Of course, we will, Sadie," Jeremy said. "Of course, we will."

CHAPTER 4

EXAMINING THE EVIDENCE

Jeremy wolfed down his Suburpia sub sandwich while Sadie picked at hers without much enthusiasm. Thanks to their visit to the morgue, her Gold Coast sub with extra onions wasn't too appealing.

"You want your chips?" her partner asked through a mouthful of meatball and the look of distaste she gave him made him laugh, spraying marinara and mozzarella on his Apple computer screen. "I'll take that as a no," he said, reaching into the bag of Old Dutch sour cream and onion chips with one hand while using the sleeve of his already coffee stained shirt to wipe the screen.

An updated report from the forensic team was cued up before them and, like the first one, didn't offer any answers. It corroborated what Allister had told them, that various flammable accelerants were discovered at the scene, but again, these were all common incendiary materials found everywhere. Since the entire village was engulfed in flames, it was only logical that propane, gasoline, butane, and natural gas would all be present. What was conspicuously missing so far, however, was blast residue from fireworks, such as sulfur, strontium, lithium, and phosphorous. Based on what Sylvia Albright and the little girl told them, there was a fireworks display; surely arson investigators would have found these compounds at the heart of the burn zone.

"You'll be a great catch for one lucky woman someday," Sadie commented dryly, and this time when he laughed, he covered his mouth.

"I already failed in that department," he replied. "Roxie is all I need from here on out."

"And all she sees are your good qualities, no doubt."

"Damn tootin'."

Roxie was Jeremy's Rottweiler, an ex-drug-sniffing dog that he'd taken in when she'd been officially retired at age eight and needed a new home. He loved her dearly, more so than he had ever loved his wife, Sadie suspected but didn't say. She could see it in his eyes whenever he talked about her, which was often. A source of hilarity incurred by said mutt was her inability to "officially" retire. Whenever he walked her (or his faithful dog walker, Karen, a woman whom he'd been correct in entrusting the love of his life to due to her unflagging optimism and availability) she was forever in work-mode, alerting him (or Karen) to the possibility of drugs at any one of his neighbor's homes.

Now, Green Bay wasn't exactly the epicenter for illegal drugs in the state of Wisconsin, but if you needed anything from pot to cocaine to LSD, they could be found without too much trouble thanks to their neighbors to the south, Milwaukee and Chicago respectively. In both Sadie's and Jeremy's experience drugs weren't a big problem in their city. That said, the upstanding denizens of their semi-rural metropolitan did enjoy sparking up the occasional (OK, maybe daily) doobie, and this was an endless source of attentiveness on the part of his erstwhile best friend. Every few houses on her walk she'd stop and go into her stance, letting Jeremy or his dog walker know that there was the presence of drugs in their neighborhood, at which point some good-hearted citizen would come strolling out, on their way to some respectable job or another, and wonder what it was they'd done to invite her attention. Jeremy was always effusive about his apologies; he had no problem personally with marijuana. Anyone he'd ever arrested who was violent, they certainly hadn't been toking up on the old ganja. No, those folks were too busy munching their way through a bag of corn chips and laughing themselves stupid watching *In Living Color*, *Married...with Children*, or that cartoon family *The Simpsons*.

"This doesn't make sense."

"I think we've been saying that all day." Sadie belched, politely covering her mouth with her fist. "Has Corey gotten back to you yet?"

"No."

Corey Lindsley was their gopher/researcher. When something needed to be looked up, he was their guy, no matter what it was. Rainfall average for Brown County in 1989, football scores, road closures due to heavy snowfall, possible suspects in a homicide investigation and, in this case, one mysterious gold mine in the unincorporated burg of Amber Hollow, and any successfully operating gold mines in the greater Wisconsin area, plus anything else he could scrounge up. He was also in charge of coffee and donut duty.

"How does a whole village of people die violently with no apparent reason for their deaths?"

"I don't know," Sadie said, setting her sandwich down. "I think we have a mystery gang!"

Jeremy ignored her Scooby-Doo reference, scrolling through the report to the end, unsatisfied.

"And why would Sylvia Albright lie to us? What does she stand to gain?"

"Maybe she's in cahoots with the mobsters?" Sadie joked, and Jeremy smiled. He knew there was a reason he enjoyed working with her, besides her intelligence and tactical skills. Her sense of humor was contagious.

"Something odd is definitely going on, something that she feels the need to cover up."

"Maybe she *is* nuts," Sadie said. "It's possible our witness is in the Bellin psychiatric ward for a reason."

"Did she seem crazy to you?"

Sadie gave this some thought. Over the years she'd dealt with crazy people, plenty of them. In fact, she had a cousin who was schizophrenic. She was well versed when it came to people suffering from mental disorders.

"No," she said at last. "She didn't."

"Then why would she tell us that story?"

"She's probably lying because whoever did this, they'd come after her. You remember what she asked us right before she told her story, and what you led her to believe?"

Jeremy frowned, thought about it a second. Then it came to him. "Yeah, I do."

"Why would she say that?"

"Good question."

Yes, a good question indeed. Right before she'd given them her bogus testimony regarding what occurred on the night of July 14 she'd asked: "Am I the only survivor?" at which point Sadie had been about to tell her no, when Jeremy intervened, leaving her query unanswered and allowing her the belief that she alone walked away from a tragedy that killed everyone she'd known and loved. With this belief, she'd still given them a false account.

"Whoever did this, she's afraid of them."

"Yep, apparently enough to cover for them."

"Does this mean we're dismissing the mobster theory?"

"Consider that formally flushed down the proverbial toilet."

"If you think so—" Just then Sadie's desk phone rang with a shrill clamor that made both of them jump. She picked up the receiver and punched the button for line one." Detective Conrad," she said and then listened for a moment before putting her hand over the mouthpiece and whispering the word "Corey." "Where are you?"

"Tell him to bring us some coffee," Jeremy said, and after waiting for his reply she relayed the information.

"You were, really?" She laughed and then seconds later said "bye" and hung up. "He's on his way in," Sadie said, "and he called to ask if he should pick up coffee. How thoughtful!"

"It's his job," Jeremy groused, but he shot her a wink.

Ten minutes later a young man entered the room carrying a cardboard tray from Molly's Roasted Beans, three jumbo-sized cups nestled within.

"It's about freakin' time," Jeremy said, and Corey grinned.

"I got here as fast as I could," he said, setting the tray down and taking one for himself. "Dig in."

"No donuts?" Sadie asked, and Corey made as if to go when Jeremy waved him back.

"Cop humor, son. You'll have to get used to it."

"Of course," he said, his smile only partially faltering.

"Have a seat," Jeremy invited, and the other complied. He'd only been working for them over the last six months, from right out of the police academy, and he wasn't yet quite certain how to interpret everything they said.

Corey sat in one of the office chairs, sipped his coffee.

"So, what do you have for us?"

"Not much of anything, I'm afraid. The citizens of that village were really private, unbelievably so, even. It's like they didn't want there to be anything left behind in the event of a catastrophe."

"There's this wonderful new invention, maybe you've heard of it, called a computer?" Jeremy said. "Did you check to see if there were any town records listed on a state of Wisconsin data page?"

"First place I checked," Corey said, "and the only thing I found was the Chamber of Commerce piece. The community records for Amber Hollow apparently were either in ledgers or typed legal documents, and if that's the case then we can assume they've all been destroyed."

"Um, you know what the word 'assume' means, right?" Jeremy said, and Sadie had to contain a chortle that was threatening to burst from her lips.

"Wow, you guys must think I just fell off the hay wagon, huh?" Corey joked, and when neither one was quick to deny it, he continued. "I know it isn't right to simply make assumptions, but it's as if the place doesn't exist."

"Well," Jeremy said, "they don't exist, at least not anymore."

"Touché," Corey said. "I suppose the most likely place the records would be is in a safe or vault in the town hall, maybe the bank." He looked from Sadie to Jeremy. "I suppose we could check there...are either of you skilled at safe-cracking?"

"Speaking of banks, tell us about gold mining in Wisconsin," Sadie said, ignoring his attempt at humor and sipping her coffee appreciatively. The boy was a little green around the gills when it came to police work, but his memory was impeccable. He remembered that she liked two sugars and a touch of French cream.

"Not a whole lot to tell. Gold was discovered in the eighteen hundreds, but mostly gold flakes, not nuggets. According to the latest data regarding gems, minerals, stones, and chemical elements in the state of Wisconsin, gold mining has never been a viable financial option."

"So...?"

"So, there's never been enough for anybody to make a living on. There are some tourist towns where you can pan for gold, and you might actually find some, but like I said, nothing but gold powder or flakes, no nuggets. No one in the history of Wisconsin has ever made a living off of mining gold."

"And yet, Sylvia Albright and the Amber Hollow chamber of commerce information details that they were a self-sustaining community because of a prosperous gold mine, which they also claim they discovered in the seventeen hundreds. Why would they make something like that public?"

"Beats me. According to people I contacted in surrounding towns and villages—"

"You actually did some phone work?" Jeremy gaped, and the boy flushed slightly.

"Well, I figured I might as well do a little more digging. If I didn't, you would have asked me to, anyway."

"Damn straight," Sadie said. "So, what did they tell you?"

"The people in Amber Hollow kept to themselves. They held no close ties with any surrounding communities, in fact, where they are—were—located, they were isolated by roughly a hundred miles on all sides."

"You're saying there were no neighboring communities they did business with?" Jeremy said, furrowing his brow.

"No, I'm not saying that," Corey said. "They received deliveries from neighboring towns: soda, beer, various sundries—"

"Did he just say 'sundries'?" Sadie cackled, and Jeremy snorted laughter.

"I think he did."

"They didn't have any close ties with neighboring communities, but they did have stuff delivered," Corey continued, unfazed. "I spoke with a manager at the Wal-Mart in Rhinelander who told me they delivered all kinds of things, but that was it. I guess none of the truck drivers wanted to stay the night."

"Define the 'surrounding communities'."

"Crandon is the closest town but calling it a town is being *very* generous. Blink your eyes driving through, and you'd miss it. And Rhinelander is the closest city, and they are about a hundred and twelve miles away. Amber Hollow was nestled into a small pocket of land along the Iron River in the farthest reaches of Torrance County. Very secluded."

"How far away is Crandon?"

"About sixty miles."

"So, they weren't isolated by a hundred miles on all sides," Jeremy countered, and Corey nodded sheepishly.

"Sorry, but because it's so small I wasn't counting it."

"The Devil's in the details, son."

"They never needed assistance of any other kind?" Sadie marveled. "Medical, financial, infrastructure? That's impossible!"

"They wouldn't need financial aid, what with owning a prosperous a gold mine," Jeremy said, and Sadie could practically see the wheels turning in his head. "To convert the gold into spending money, though, they'd need some assistance. I'm sure they weren't paying the truck drivers with gold nuggets."

"Probably not," Corey agreed. "I'll do more research, see what else I can find out, but so far everyone I've talked to hasn't had a whole lot to say except what I already told you…well, except for one lady, but I think she might have been a little, you know, Woo-hoo." At the use of the word "Woo-hoo" he twirled one finger around in a circle by his ear.

"And who was this lady, pray tell?" Sadie said, setting her cup down on Jeremy's desk and receiving a scowl from the other. She retrieved a napkin from the coffee tray and delicately set it down and then placed her cup on top of it. Her partner smiled.

"She's a librarian in Rhinelander, Delores Schenker, I think her name is."

"Don't you take notes?" Jeremy said, and with an apologetic grin Corey took his notepad from his pocket, flipped through a few pages and then looked up triumphantly.

"Yes, Delores Schenker. She's been working at the Rhinelander public library for over forty years. Probably should retire if you ask me."

"No one asked you," Sadie said and then asked, "Why do you think that?"

"She sounded kind of nuts, well, what she told me anyway."

"The suspense is killing us," Jeremy griped. "Spill it."

"She told me that the citizens of Amber Hollow never leave."

"Never leave?"

"Her words, and I quote: they never leave."

"What does that mean?"

"I asked her that, too."

"What did she say?"

"She said that they are all born and raised there, and that no one ever moves away."

"Wait," Sadie said, trying to process it. "You mean to tell me this librarian thinks that no one in the village has moved away, like… *ever*? That's impossible."

"That's what I thought, and I told her as much. So, she invited me to come up to the library in Rhinelander, said I could look through some of their archived historical documents."

"Can't she fax them?"

"She said they're on microfilm. I'd have to go there in person."

"And what, exactly, is it regarding?"

"I asked her that too, and she said it involved any news that ever came from the vicinity of Amber Hollow."

"Came from the vicinity?"

"Yeah, that's what she said."

"So, none of this news actually came *from* Amber Hollow?"

"Nope. She said they had a local newspaper, and she has one on file, but that's it."

"Were these people Amish?" Sadie asked, only half-joking, but Corey answered her anyway:

"No ma'am, but by all accounts, it sounds like they could have been."

"And you know they weren't Amish how?" she said, and Corey looked at her quizzically.

"Um, because they had electricity?" he said, unable to refrain from making his statement sound like a question.

"He's got you there," Jeremy said when the phone on his desk rang. "Yeah?" He listened for a moment, mumbled a thank-you, and then hung up. For a moment he stared wordlessly at Sadie and Corey.

"What?" Sadie asked.

"One of the survivors in intensive care is cognizant enough to talk."

"The one in the coma?"

"Not that one. She's still in what they call a 'vegetative state,' but one of the others. According to Captain Martin he's awake, eating, and reading *People* magazine."

"What, this poor schlub doesn't get to watch TV either?" Sadie said, and Jeremy nodded.

"None of them do," he said. "The story is all over the news, and the less they know about it, the better."

"How come?"

"After what our first witness said, you actually have to ask?"

She regarded him silently a moment and then shrugged. "I suppose…" she grumbled, and Jeremy could have kicked himself.

"I'm sorry, I should have told you. That's on me."

"It's no big deal. I was just curious," she said, but her tone indicated quite clearly that she wanted to be informed of every decision made regarding this case, no matter how small.

"You have every right to know all the details," Jeremy said. "I'll keep you better informed next time. OK?"

"Sure."

"Shall we?"

"Let's roll." Sadie drank the rest of her coffee and then expertly tossed the cup three feet into the trash can. Jeremy whistled appreciatively.

"You ever consider trying out for the Bucks?"

"They wish."

"Can I come?" Corey asked and Jeremy shook his head.

"Not your department, bucko. You have research to do. We'll expect a full report when we get back."

"Yes, sir," Corey mumbled as the two exited the office, heading for the parking lot and the waiting cruiser outside.

CHAPTER 5

ANDREW LECARRE'S TESTIMONY

The survivor that Jeremy and Sadie were about to interview was recovering at St. Mary's hospital. Apparently, his condition was more suited for that of a trauma center than a psychiatric facility, as his injuries were more critical, and his brain appeared to be functioning normally.

We'll see about that, Sadie thought.

She experienced her usual malaise upon entering the antiseptic world of advanced medicine, but as it was the second hospital today, the feeling wasn't quite as strong. By the time they'd talked to all the survivors, she'd probably be over it entirely. Well, a girl could dream...

"Homicide investigators here to see Andrew LeCarre," Jeremy told the woman at the desk, showing his badge, and she nodded.

"Room two thirteen," she said curtly, then her phone rang, and she waved them on their way.

As they rode the elevator, Sadie considered the possibility that Sylvia Albright had fabricated a tall tale simply because her mind couldn't accept what really happened. It was entirely possible, especially if she'd seen something so horrible that she was unable to reckon with it until she received proper medication and psychiatric care. A disaster of that magnitude could unhinge even the stoutest person. She hoped the man they were about to question had a steady grasp on reality and could possibly fill in some blanks that desperately needed filling.

Exiting the elevator, Jeremy let Sadie lead the way down the brightly lit corridor. The sound of TV's came from some of the rooms, as well as the sounds of human misery; coughing, gasping, moaning, wheezing and the occasional fart. Yes, he thought, nothing like a hospital to bring it all out of you, physically and otherwise.

They approached the room, saw dim light spilling from the doorway. It was completely silent from within, thanks to the absence of a working TV, and to Sadie, it was somewhat eerie. She peeked inside, saw a heavily bandaged man sitting upright in his bed, reading the latest issue of *People* magazine with Matt Dillion on the cover as he shoveled eggs into his mouth through a hole in the gauze. Unlike their first witness, this man had sustained some serious external injuries and was hooked up to a vital signs monitor as well as IV fluids. Scorch marks ran up and down both sides of his neck, disappearing into the bandaging. The only part of his head that was visible was the top, revealing a bushy clump of dark black hair

"Good afternoon," Sadie greeted him amiably, and at the sound of her voice he started, his eyes growing wide.

"Who…who are you?" he stammered, his words garbled, his throat thick with phlegm. Sadie removed her badge, showed it to him.

"I'm Homicide Investigator Sadie Conrad, and this is my partner Jeremy LeFevre. We're here to talk to you about what happened on Sunday night."

He stared at them silently, his eggs now forgotten. "How come I can't watch TV?" he said. "I want to watch the news."

"Sorry, no television, doctor's orders."

"Bullshit."

"God's honest," Jeremy said, taking another step forward. "You mind if we come in?"

"Looks like you already are," he said, a touch defensively, yet Sadie could forgive him for that. He certainly appeared worse for wear, yet his eyes looked clear. She could only hope he wasn't doped up on pain meds; that would make getting to the truth that much harder, she suspected.

"Yes, I suppose so." She approached the bed, looking at him closely. "We really need to talk to you if you are up to it."

Jeremy stepped closer, studying the bandages covering his face, looking into his eyes to see if they revealed anything.

The windows to the soul, he thought abstractly. However, there was nothing there, nothing but a look of wary apprehension.

"What do you want to talk about?"

Sadie was struck with an overwhelming feeling of ennui. This man, like the other four survivors, had just witnessed an incomprehensible tragedy, and yet he seemed to take affront at their curiosity. Usually, when confronted by this attitude, she tended to think that the underlying reason was guilt, and most times she was right. Could this man have something to do with what happened?

If he did, he must be hooked up with the local chapter of the Milwaukee Mobsters…at least, according to Sylvia Albright.

"We'd like to know what happened on the night of Sunday, July 14," she said softly, and Jeremy nodded.

"They're all dead, you know," he said, and Sadie gave him a look which he duly noted but urged with a subtle raise of an eyebrow for her to go with.

"Am I the only one left?" he asked, and at this tiny utterance chills started at the base of Sadie's spine and worked their way up to her neck. She looked at her partner, and he nodded.

"We need you to tell us what happened," he said, ignoring the question, letting the man come to his own conclusion, just as they had with Sylvia. Hopefully it would work this time.

"I don't want to even think about it," Andrew said, his words slightly muffled by the gauze, and Sadie nodded sagely.

"Of course you don't, but we can't help you unless you help us."

"How can you help me?" His voice was a reedy, petulant whine, and a part of Jeremy—the masculine side—wanted to tell him to cut the crap and be a man about this, but because of his injuries he knew it would be imprudent, so instead he said:

"We can find out who did this so you'll be safe."

"I'll never be safe again," he said cryptically, returning his attention to the magazine. Sadie took a chair from the corner, slid it over near the bed and sat down.

"Yes, you will. Now, please sir, tell us what happened that night."

He sighed, ran a shaky hand over his unkempt shock of hair. His nails were ragged, chewed to the cuticles. He coughed without covering his mouth, and the sound was like a band saw cutting through an extremely thick piece of wood. Tears formed in his eyes from the force of his exertion, and then he hitched another big breath before looking from one to the other somberly.

"We never should have trusted him," he said, so quietly that Sadie had to lean closer.

"Trusted who?"

"Tony. Tony Guntram. This is all his fault you know."

Sadie and Jeremy exchanged another brief look, one of surprise. Why, if his story matched Sylvia's then they actually had something to go on, they could reach out to the Milwaukee County Police department and issue an all-points bulletin on any of their more notorious known mobsters.

"Who is Tony Guntram?" Jeremy said. To back up what he'd claimed, that this man was the only survivor, well, they certainly wouldn't know about this Guntram character, would they?

"He is, well, he *was*, the mayor. We elected him about twelve years ago, and everybody really liked him, but there was something about him that wasn't right."

At the uncanny similarity of his opening statement, Sadie felt a fleeting surge of hope. Maybe Sylvia wasn't completely crazy, not if this man backed up some of what she'd told them.

But, when he began to talk and his story unfolded, her hope withered and blew away like a plastic bag in a strong wind. Nothing in this world came easy, and this man would prove that with every passing sentence.

• • •

"We've always been a very private village, you know, we kept to ourselves. We never needed any outside help, and everyone who was born in Amber Hollow, stayed there. We were a self-sustaining community because of the gold mine. It offered us all we needed, so we didn't have to bring in strangers. It's been that way for over two hundred years.

"We progressed along with the rest of society, of course, with all the modern gadgets and what not. It wasn't like we were in the stone ages. But we kept to ourselves, that was the important part. We had to.

"Tony's ancestry can be traced back to the earliest settlers, in fact all of ours can. Our ancestors founded the village, and we kept it clean and pristine so generations to come could enjoy it. At least, until Sunday night. And we should have known that Tony was up to no good, should have seen that he was slowly going crazy, but none of us knew, not until it was too late.

"When we elected him for mayor, he was a real boon to the community. He was so smart, so thoughtful and kind. A good man, a real good man. In fact, Tony's family has always been in charge. For as far back as I remember they were always the elected officials who made all the important decisions, kept us all safe, kept us strong.

"But about five years ago that all began to change. He started getting paranoid, started instituting new rules that didn't make much sense. I mean, we were civilized people and out of the blue it was like he wanted us to be something we weren't. I don't know, it's hard to explain, because

the shift was sort of gradual. Only after so many changes had been implemented did we start seeing how crazy it was.

"He wanted certain families to mate with other families, you know? Said he was trying to start some kind of 'Super Lineage.' Why, all of sudden, no one got to choose anymore who they could be with, he chose for them. And then he wrote up a new village charter, and it was full of rules that forbid us to do things like watch football or wash our cars on Sunday or even to take a drink. And soon enough, those rules were in place for Saturday…and then every day.

"He had the LaCroix family back him up, they were his muscle. And there were a lot of them, those damn fools. And were they big? Why you bet your bottom dollar they were big boys, but not a lick of sense in any of their heads. Idiots. And when Tony didn't think they were enough to keep us all in line, he recruited the Arpin family too, and between you and me they were as inbred as puppy mill dogs and twice as mean. Bastards, every one of them. And they all just did what they were told, and pretty soon it became apparent what we'd become, and not a one of us liked it one bit.

"Why, for all practical purposes we'd become a cult! The whole town! You know, like Jim Jones? That fellah who made all of them people drink poison down in South America? That's what we were! And for the love of God we just couldn't stop him after it had gone too far. Don't ask me why, but it just was. He made us give up our guns, any of us that had them. I owned a thirty-ought six I used to hunt deer and the LaCroix boys took it from me. My wife of seventeen years owned a single barrel Remington shotgun, and they took that too. Took all of our guns, made us pray every day in the village square, and soon the prayer sessions took on an ominous new meaning.

"We started practicing, you see, for what Tony called the 'end of days.' I seen that Jim Jones movie, and it was just like that. We'd gather to pray, and he'd stand at this giant pulpit he made Charlie Olsen build. Charlie, why, he could build anything, and Tony made him construct him this huge monstrosity that he could preach from, like all of a sudden, he was a real preacher. We had a preacher—we had ourselves a normal church—but

Tony had de-frocked him and stripped him of his duties. He even made him have relations with a woman, and our preacher, why, he'd taken an oath of celibacy. He didn't want to, but Tony made him. And in front of the whole town too, made us all watch. My wife wanted to close her eyes—we all did—but we couldn't, they wouldn't let us.

"That was when we started plotting, started meeting in private. We had to do something, had to get Tony out of the way before things got too weird. I mean, things were already too weird, but you know, before he started getting a hankering for all of us to kill ourselves. And we couldn't have done it soon enough, because that was what he had in mind next, turned out.

"Every year we celebrated Bastille Days, to honor our French heritage, and that was when we planned to take our town back. Those secret meetings we had, well, we'd made ourselves some weapons, small knives we could hide easily in our pockets so they wouldn't be found. We were going to get Tony and his henchmen, kill them if we had to. And we had it all mapped out too, how we could distract them when we needed to, when the time was right.

"But it was as if Tony knew it, and he also had plans. When we gathered in the village square for the Bastille celebration the LaCroix boys, the Arpin family, and Tony's relatives had guns, and they made us all kneel before his pulpit. And up there next to him, mixed in one of those big metal garbage cans, was his poisonous punch. I don't know what was in it, but it would surely kill us all, of that I was certain. He had two of the LaCroix boys standing on either side of it, and they had ladles and all these little plastic Dixie cups, and he was chanting some nonsense, telling us it was time for us all to go and meet Jesus. Now, I'm certain I'll meet Jesus someday, but I'm going to do it on my own terms, you smell what I'm stepping in? No one is going to make that choice for me. No one.

"So, they were aimin' to have us kill ourselves, and did that sit well with us? You can bet your sweet ass it didn't—sorry about my language ma'am—and we were ready to fight, ready to do whatever we had to do to get out of there. We looked around at each other anxiously, everyone

knowing that this had gone way too far but not exactly sure how we were going to be able to initiate our counter attack. Some of us had been searched, our weapons taken, but some of the folks were smart enough to hide them where they couldn't be found, if you know what I mean. I sill had my knife, and my wife Bethany had hers. No one was going to make us drink that poison, not while I still had my dignity.

"He called up the Wellens family first, all twelve of them, and did they look scared? You bet they did, and I was frightened for them. Tony started reciting some nonsense about how God is all-powerful and how it was with great pleasure that he'd be helping us all on to our final reward, and those kids were just crying their eyes out, bawling to beat the devil. Broke my heart, and I held Bethany's hand tight in mine, ready to run whenever we got the chance.

"The first of the kids drank the punch at gunpoint, the man of the family hollerin' his head off about how it wasn't right, it wasn't fair, but then they made all of them drink it and the kids were convulsing and choking and turning all different kinds a colors. Made me sick, and for as long as I live, I'll forever hear those screams of terror and pain.

"That was when we decided it was enough, and we rebelled, all of us, while the Wellens family died up there on that pulpit we struck. My wife and I used our knives to hack our way through anyone hell-bent on stopping us, and other town folks that weren't struck dumb by what was happening did the same thing: we turned on our captors. It got real loud, everyone yelling their heads off, kids crying, women screaming, Tony screeching from that pulpit that the devil would open up a lake of fire beneath us if we didn't comply, if we didn't drink Christ's blood of everlasting salvation. And it was as if his prophecy came true, by God, because of what happened next.

"Danny Ansel had been the one who'd set up the fireworks, he was the one who did it every year. Kind of a firebug was Danny. But not in a bad way. We weren't afraid he was ever going to get an itch to burn the village down. But they'd got to him, got his weapon, and I could see he wasn't going to be able to set them off. That was our distraction, you see, how we were going to create confusion so that we could escape, and when I was sure he

couldn't, I knew that someone had to, so I figured it was my civic duty to set them off to save everyone.

"I told Bethany to run, to just skedaddle, but she said no, she wanted to stay with me. That will haunt me for the rest of my life; if I had made her run, she might be alive today, but instead I let her help me. Goddamn I'm an idiot, but what's done is done. She and I, we hit all the buttons on the control panel to set off all of the fireworks at once, and Danny had rigged it so that they wouldn't go straight up into the sky, no, he had them aimed at that damn giant pulpit. We hit all of them buttons, and in less than a minute it was like being in the middle of a fire fight, all of them exploding at once. But Danny had done it in haste, hadn't made all the right calculations, and the fireworks went everywhere, not just at the pulpit but into the crowd. People were hollerin' and screamin' fit to beat the band, and when I grabbed Bethany's hand to pull her away one of them rockets exploded and took her head right off…I was literally dripping my wife's brains off my chin, and then another went off a foot from me and the flash was blinding, and I could feel the skin boiling on my face. I screamed and fell down, rolling to try and put out the flames. It took some doing but I succeeded, even though I suspect I don't have much of a face left.

"The fire started almost instantly, and it spread fast too, because of the lousy rainfall we'd had all that spring and summer. Almost as dry as the summer of '89. Everything went up like kindling. And over all the commotion I could hear Tony screechin' like a loon, just howling his fool head off about Christ's eternal redemption. That bastard was simply bughouse crazy and there was nothing that was going to stop him.

"I escaped the village square and made it to an outlying part of town. I passed the Jensen place, and then the Horning's. I thought I was going to make it but then I heard the truck, an old Ford, the engine sounding like it was some beast out of a mythical story, chugging and belching and roaring, and next I heard the voices of the LaCroix brothers, hootin' and hollerin' like a bunch of hillbillies drunk on moonshine. When I heard the crack of a rifle shot, that's when I thought it was all over, I was going to join Bethany and my old coon dog Sunshine up in Heaven.

"I immediately started praying, just sent my request up to God—the real God—and asked him for forgiveness, but also asked him to help me, even though I didn't much want to live any more without Bethany. And I don't know what happened, maybe my prayers were answered, because I heard more gun shots fired, even felt a couple of them pass by me so close I could feel the breeze, but not a one of them hit me, and I ran and ran until I couldn't hear nothing but the crickets chirping and the wind blowing through the leaves in the apple orchard. Nothing but the hum of silence in a world that was blacked out by smoke and soot. I was so winded I stopped, trying to catch my breath, and then I don't know what happened. I must have passed out. And then I woke up here."

At this point the man stopped talking and asked for a drink of water. Detective Conrad poured him a cup from a pitcher on his nightstand, which he drank through a plastic straw with a bendable tip. He then claimed to be tired and said he needed to rest. The detectives decided to take their leave, determining it to be in their best interest to cross examine him at another time.

• • •

"He's a good story teller, I'll give him that," Jeremy said when they got in the cruiser, "but not only does that story sound like a bunch of baloney but it also contradicts the coroner's report."

"Once again, we have shots fired but no forensic confirmation nor shells or casings recovered," Sadie agreed, firing up the engine and putting the car into gear. "Anything else strike you as odd?" Her voice had a mischievous lilt to it, and her eyes reflected it. By God, she was actually quizzing him.

"Oh yeah," he said, "another inconsistency."

"Which was?"

"He said he set off the fireworks, and that was what started the fire."

"And why isn't that possible?" Her voice was playful, her eyes dancing merrily.

"Because of the report from the arson investigators," he said, matching her tone with one equally as cheery. "There were no traces of strontium, sulfur, or lithium on the scene, which as we both know are chemical compounds commonly found in fireworks."

"Glad to see you're paying attention." Sadie glanced at her watch. "Are we putting in overtime or should we resume our investigation in the morning?"

Jeremy looked at his watch, saw that it was just after five. Karen had been over at his house around noon to take Roxie out for a walk, but he hadn't asked her to come back for her dinner and a potty break. Not that he couldn't, as she was always reliable in a pinch, but he saw no need.

"Yeah, what the hell. Let's head back to the station, see if Corey dredged up any more information and then call it a day. My girl is waiting for me." He gave her a sly grin. "I'm sure your beau wouldn't mind seeing your smiling face for a couple hours this evening as well, hmm?"

Sadie blushed, looking away, and this tickled Jeremy to no end. She was so modest, so prudent. It was funny to watch her squirm whenever her love life was brought up.

"I think your girl appreciates you more than my guy appreciates me," she said, rolling away from the curb, and Jeremy chortled.

"There is no better affection than the love of a human and a dog."

"Hey, I didn't say Clayton wasn't a dog…"

This got the two of them laughing, and as she steered through the burgeoning evening traffic toward downtown Green Bay, Jeremy thought that she'd never looked prettier than she did right now, in her uniform, a grin splitting her face almost in half.

Best to keep that to yourself, cowboy…

"You better quit laughing and just watch the road missy," he said, "we don't need to have one of the Sheriff's deputies write you up for a moving violation."

"Duly noted," she said, wiping a tear from one eye, the other hand clamped around the wheel. "But my badge lets me get away with things the regular citizens don't."

"Ah, the abuse of power. God, I love that in a woman."

"You better shut your trap, or I'll abuse you!"

"Don't make promises you can't keep," he replied, and she shot him a wink, and it made his chest tighten momentarily before his heart lurched and did a lazy somersault. He looked away; it was now his turn to be embarrassed. How long had he been working with her, over five years? And on that note, how long had he been harboring feelings for her? Probably since he'd known her, but he'd kept a professional distance. There was nothing practical about falling in love with your coworker. "And just get us to the station in one piece."

"Can do," she said, weaving through the traffic on Webster with the ease of a New York cab driver while Jeremy stared out the window silently, watching the cars go by.

• • •

Corey wasn't at the station when they arrived, but he'd left a message for them at the front desk with the clerk on duty. To their utter surprise he'd decided to drive up to Rhinelander to talk to the librarian. The clerk told them that he promised he'd call this evening, and that he'd be staying at the Holiday Inn overnight.

"He should have told us he was going up there," Jeremy said, and Sadie shrugged.

"He's a big boy, he can handle it."

"I'm sure he can," Jeremy agreed, "but he should have told us first."

"He's bucking for a promotion, I think."

"Probably," Jeremy said, yet Sadie could tell it troubled him.

"You think he can't handle himself, or are you afraid he'll make us look bad?"

Jeremy smiled. "I suppose he'll look like a big city slicker to those hayseeds."

"Takes one to know one," she said, and he chuckled.

"I reckon."

Jeremy went to his desk, checked his desk phone's voice mail. There was a message from Calvin Lemory, the fire marshal. He spoke briefly, instructing him to boot up a file on his computer that would detail their latest findings. He fired up his Macintosh Classic Two, knowing it would take at least five minutes for the computer to warm up, if not ten. He certainly preferred it over his Mac Classic; this one was a lot faster and more streamlined. Ah, technology. Where would they be without it?

When the computer was up and running and he'd located and opened the file, he called Sadie.

She strolled over from where she'd gotten herself a cup of coffee (how she could drink the stuff after five always perplexed him. He'd be up half the night if he drank caffeine after three in the afternoon) and looked over his shoulder at his computer screen.

"What's up?"

"Latest report."

They both read in silence for a moment. It didn't take very long.

Sadie drained her cup and set it down on Jeremy's desk. This time he didn't notice or didn't care that she hadn't used a coaster.

"So, the bodies Allister has down in the morgue…those are it?"

"Apparently," Jeremy said, rereading what Calvin wrote. According to the report, no more bodies were found that had any meat on them; all further discoveries had been burned to a crisp.

"Allister will be relieved," Sadie said, and Jeremy shrugged.

"Maybe, maybe not. He's a sucker for a good mystery as much as you and I are. If he doesn't find anything on the bodies he's already got, I'm sure he wouldn't mind having the chance to take a poke at another."

"Should we check with him, see if he found anything else?"

"Nah. He'd let us know if he did." Jeremy looked over the report one more time, made a mental note to contact Calvin tomorrow to go over some of the particulars, and then he put his computer in sleep mode and turned to his partner. "Go on, get out of here. We have a lot to do tomorrow."

"Let me guess: more Loony Tunes from the survivors?"

"My, my, aren't you a bright one! Yes, dear, I suspect we'll want to hear all of their crackpot stories."

She nodded. "You sticking around?"

"No, I have to feed Roxie and take her for a walk. It doesn't look like there's anything left here for us to do, but answer your home phone in case anything comes up."

"I always do."

"And if you hear from Corey, let me know, huh? I'll do the same if he contacts me."

"Gotcha."

And then she departed, leaving Jeremy to his thoughts.

CHAPTER 6

A VISIT WITH DELORES SCHENKER

C orey's Toyota Corolla hummed along the two-lane highway as he listened to FM radio, tuned to a station that played current mainstream rock. He sang along to Guns N' Roses, Metallica, and Faith No More as the corn fields rushed by, not thinking much about anything, so much as the case. What he was doing, he was doing because he knew it was expected of him. Detectives LeFevre and Conrad were nice, but that would only take him so far. If he wanted to get ahead, he had to prove that he deserved a promotion. And what the hell, it got him out of the office. Let the rest of them fetch their own damn coffee.

He arrived in Rhinelander well before dark; according to the woman he spoke with on the phone, the library was open until eight, giving him plenty of time. After he parked, he gathered his notes, made sure he had a pen that worked, and ascended the large stone staircase to the double glass doors. He paused before going inside, taking a deep breath, feeling a momentary sensation of déjà vu. He was suddenly transported back in time, to the city where he'd grown up, to the library he'd once called home. The Rhinelander library was modern and cozy, but it wasn't this feature that made him think of the library in West DePere, the one he'd enjoyed in his youth before it was closed, the building sold and then reopened as a comedy club. He didn't know what it was, what nuance exactly, but he found himself thinking of the old stone and glass edifice, almost gothic in its design. He'd been entranced by that library because it was old, smelled of musty books, and had a paperback section filled with what he considered to be literary treasures. Novels by obscure authors sat side by side with the best sellers, and it was there that he'd discovered the endless plunder that kept his mind occupied when there was nothing else to do on a long, lazy August day. While other kids were outside playing baseball, soccer, or football, he preferred to be within the air-conditioned walls of the library, reading a book by Stephen King or Richard Laymon. The latter was a hack compared to the Master of Horror, but for a teenage boy the books were pure gold, with enough sex and violence to keep him turning pages until the calamitous ending. Laymon rarely disappointed. While King was an actual writer, Laymon simply did "gross for gross' sake," and Corey ate it up. He was certain that teenage boys were his biggest fans.

He entered and approached the main desk, taking a quick peek at his notepad to remind himself of the name of the woman he was here to see. Delores Schenker, his neat script told him, and he looked up and took a quick scan for a woman who looked like she belonged to such an outdated moniker. He could tell from her voice over the phone that she was old, so his eyes scanned the faces he saw, dismissing anyone whom he thought looked too young. After a moment, when no one appeared to be matching the description in his head, he decided to ask.

"Can I help you?" a young woman asked. She was pretty in an offhand way, like she only spent a few minutes in the morning getting ready, yet it was all the time she needed.

"Yes, please. My name is Corey Lindsley, and I work for the Brown County Sheriff's Department in Green Bay."

"Yes?"

"I'm looking for Delores Schenker. We spoke on the phone this morning and she told me if I needed any help with an ongoing investigation that I could come up here and see her."

"What are you investigating?" the woman asked, and for a moment Corey wanted to tell her it was official police business, but then he saw the slight smile play along her lips, and he realized without really knowing for sure that she was flirting with him. His natural instincts taking over, he smiled broadly, showing a nice set of teeth he brushed and flossed twice a day to look his best, and let himself be drawn in.

"Are you asking out of professional concern, or are you personally curious?"

"Would you tell me if I said, 'both'?"

"I sure would," he said, warming up to her quickly. Now that he really looked at her, he saw that his first reaction had been wrong. This woman obviously took a bit of time putting herself together in the morning so that it *looked* like it was slapdash. Despite the pair of large, ugly glasses she wore, she was gorgeous. "I'm here to read archived historical documents involving the village of Amber Hollow. Delores invited me up to look at some microfilm."

The woman's smile faltered only a little, when he uttered the words "Amber Hollow," but it passed quickly, and she recovered easily.

"Lucky you. Personally, I don't like viewing microfilm. The machine gives me a headache."

"Actually, me too, but I have a job to do," he confessed, and her smile grew.

"We're phasing those things out," she said matter-of-factly. "Computers are all the rage now. We're getting rid of the microfilm viewers and replacing them with Macs."

"The wave of the future," he agreed, deciding to politely refrain from telling her that the Green Bay central library already had a state-of-the-art computer lab, boasting over ten computers. Would the library in West DePere have a computer lab if it had stayed open? he wondered vaguely, the thought occurring to him and then passing on by like an eighteen-wheeler on a dark, two-lane highway. Probably not, he decided. There wasn't enough room.

"I don't know what she'd want to show you," she continued, "it might be some of Delores's secret stash." She looked at him closely, deciding whether or not she could share this with him and then determining she could. "She's been the head librarian for a long time. She's been around since they invented the Dewey Decimal System." This said as if she was talking about prehistoric times.

"Was that before or after the Civil War?" he joked, and when she laughed it was like the tinkling of angelic bells. Why, if he lived around here, he'd probably ask this woman if she'd like to go out to dinner with him. He figured she might say yes; he was a young looking twenty-three year old with a strong chin and handsome features. He was certain she could probably do a whole lot worse.

"She's in her office," the woman said when her laughter subsided. "Let me go get her."

"Thanks," he said, then before he could let her slip away, he held out his hand. "My name is Corey."

"You already told me," she said, but her smile was enchanting. She held out her hand in return. "I'm Keely."

They shook, their hands lingering a bit longer than a customary handshake, and Corey felt his pulse racing a little faster.

"Nice to meet you, I'm…uh…um…making an ass out of myself," he said lamely, yet she was unfazed.

"No worries," she said. "I'll be right back."

He watched her go, trying to keep his glance professional and above the waist, but he was a man after all, and his gaze slipped south for a moment to appreciate her behind before raising his eyes to instead look about him while he waited for Delores. This place was positively modern compared to the library in DePere, but the one in downtown Green Bay could give it a run for its money. Man, Corey loved libraries. What could be better than dating a librarian?

His thoughts were interrupted when he heard his name spoken, and when he turned, he saw a woman who actually looked older than her voice over the phone had insinuated. She shuffled over from the far side of the desk, walking slowly, with deliberate care. He appraised her briefly before offering a sincere, professional smile.

"Mrs. Schenker?"

"Please, call me Delores, Officer Lindsley. And it's miss, not missus."

"Certainly, Delores, and please call me Corey."

They shook hands, Corey trying not to but unable to resist looking over her shoulder to see if the other librarian would return. When she didn't make an immediate appearance, he decided it would be best to get down to business.

"We spoke on the phone about information regarding Amber Hollow."

"Yes, we did," she said, her gaze turning solemn. "That's quite a tragedy. I knew a few people who lived there. Not very well, mind you, they truly did keep to themselves, but still I can place a few names with their faces."

"I'm sorry if you lost anyone you knew."

"Of course, dear." She inspected him for a moment, deciding something. "Let's go into the sun room where we can talk. I don't want to disturb the readers in here."

"Sure," he agreed, and followed her into an adjoining room that lived up to the name she'd given it. The roof was glass, and the sun's rays splashed gaily down upon the racks of periodicals and news-papers. Several people were sprawled in chairs, reading the day's newspaper, Newsweek, or Time. A young man with long hair and a tie-dyed t-shirt that displayed the name "The Grateful Dead" sat reading a Mad magazine, and again, this took Corey back in time.

How he'd loved Mad magazine when he was growing up. It was another one of his favorite things about going to the library, besides the books by King and Laymon.

She motioned him to a table, where she pulled out a chair, sat down, and invited him to do the same. He did, making sure his pocket-sized notebook and pen were handy.

"How much do you know about Amber Hollow?" she asked him once he was seated, and he shook his head.

"Before this week, I'd never even heard of it."

"Where are you from?"

"East DePere, born and raised."

"You travel around Wisconsin much?"

"Somewhat," he said, making a pained face. "I've been to Milwaukee and Madison, and I worked a summer in Door County, in Fish Creek, but I really don't know much about the northern part of the state."

"Don't worry about it, son," she replied amiably, "because you wouldn't have heard about it unless you'd been, and most folks haven't. They didn't exactly advertise."

"So, what can you tell me?"

"There's not much more I can tell you that I didn't tell you over the phone," she said, and for a moment Corey wondered why he'd made the drive until she clarified: "You came here to learn a few things about Amber Hollow, correct?"

"Yes."

"Well, I can show you that if you like. I have information beyond their Chamber of Commerce piece. I'm correct in assuming you read that, hmm?"

"Yes, and that's the only information I could find about them." He frowned. "It's odd they made it known that they were a self-sustaining community because of a gold mine. According to a fact check, there are no prosperous gold mines in the state of Wisconsin.

Not that there aren't tourist traps where you can pan for gold, but nothing more than powder or flakes."

"You'll find that that's not the oddest thing you'll learn."

"So you said. The citizens of this town…they never left?"

"Some went away to receive an education, but they always returned. Born there and died there."

Corey felt this was a foolish question, simply because it had been posited at the station and he'd pooh-poohed it, but he couldn't help it: "Were they Amish, or some other kind of religion that forbid them from leaving?"

"Therein lies the mystery," Delores replied. "The people I knew who lived there, I knew because they made pilgrimages to Rhinelander, to this library. They were polite, respectful, but they had tight lips when it came to anything regarding their village."

"This information you have to show me: what is it in reference to?"

Delores appraised him for a moment with somber eyes, her lips shut primly, her eyes rheumy yet very clear, very sharp for a woman who appeared to be in her mid to late eighties.

"In a vault in the basement I have microfilm that pertains only to stories about Amber Hollow, weird stories. Are you a fan of mysteries or science fiction?"

"Now you're talking my language," Corey said, smiling. "But if the stories are as odd as you say, wouldn't I have read them already?"

She smiled in return, her eyes warming with it, the crinkles creating a bed for her baby blues.

"A central Wisconsinite such as yourself wouldn't have seen many of these articles, as they were published in either the Rhinelander Daily Reader or the Crandon Express. There aren't too many people outside of the area that have much interest in the news that comes from up here, unless it's something sensational, but even those stories tend to slip through the cracks for you big city folks. There is a lot of history in these little towns, and sometimes bizarre things occur, but no one but the neighboring communities are aware of it." She paused, thinking. "Well, if you are old enough to remember, there might have been a few stories that probably made the Green Bay Press Gazette or The Milwaukee Journal, but I think it's very likely you're too young."

"Fascinating," Corey said, and he wasn't joking. He'd minored in history at the University of Wisconsin at Green Bay.

She nodded, satisfied. "I can tell that you aren't just humoring me, and that will take you a long way."

"Yes, ma'am."

Her smile suddenly disappeared, in its place a look that suggested that play time was over, and now it was time to get down to the real business.

"The articles regarding Amber Hollow aren't for the faint of heart. They aren't your run-of-the-mill crime stories. They are a bit…unusual."

"Really?"

"Even though they kept to themselves, certain things happened over the last century that leaked out, strange things, perhaps even… unnatural things."

"Unnatural?" His curiosity was totally piqued now.

"Shall we go downstairs?"

"You had me at 'unnatural,'" he said, and this made her smile again.

"Follow me."

• • •

The basement of the library was like a catacomb, dark and full of cobwebs, and Corey couldn't help but feel right at home. He was glad he'd decided to come up here, if only for the personal experience. Well, and also for what he'd be able to report to the detectives. He'd show them he was worth more to them than just being a gopher.

Delores led him down a dimly lit corridor, large shelves holding books that appeared to be older than the library and his host combined. The spines displayed endless titles he'd never had the pleasure of reading, and he made a note to himself that if he did have time, perhaps on another visit to this library in the future, he'd ask to peruse these books, maybe even go a step further and get a date with the librarian upstairs. That would certainly make another trip up here from Green Bay worthwhile.

Shelves containing volumes of forgotten lore, the likes of which most folks would see no more, he thought, and this made him grin.

The corridor ended and opened up into a large room. Delores flicked toggles on a bank of switches and the room lit up as bright as Times Square on New Year's Eve.

"Follow me," she said, and another thought came to Corey, one inspired by a film he'd seen as a kid.

"Walk this way," Igor said, shambling away, and Dr. Frederick Frankenstein shambled after him, his leg pulling to one side. Again, a silly grin crossed his features, but when the elderly librarian turned to look at him, he erased it immediately. He didn't want her to think he was laughing at her.

"I keep the stories pertaining to the Hollow down here because I only show them to people upon request."

"Do many people ask to see them?"

"No dear, not very many."

She walked to a large metal safe and, after twisting the dial right, left and then right, she pulled a large lever and swung the door open. Searching around inside, she selected a canister of film, and held it up to the light.

"I transferred these articles from the newspapers to microfilm myself," she said proudly, and this time his smile was meant for her.

"Is it difficult?"

"Not really. You use a machine to make the transfer, but since the stories are so seldom read, it certainly is a labor of love."

"I see."

"Take a seat at that table," she said, indicating a lone table that sat beneath a bank of fluorescent lights. Corey had used a microfilm viewer before, but he couldn't say he was a big fan of the technology. Like the librarian upstairs *(Keely)* had said, the machine gave him a headache after a while. He preferred to read his news from a paper, possibly on his Macintosh Classic, but if this was the only way, so be it.

He took a seat at the table and tried to make himself comfy, which was a task indeed because the chair wasn't exactly designed for comfort. Delores opened the canister and then spooled the film into the machine. When she was finished, she turned on the viewer.

"The stories are in consecutive order as they appeared in print. They only go back about fifty years because I didn't start taking an interest in it until then." She smiled a coquettish grin. "I was just a young woman back then, I had other things to do."

"I'm sure you did," Corey replied, and in that moment, he could see that she'd long ago been a very pretty woman, maybe even prettier than the young librarian he'd had the pleasure of meeting.

"Very little information has ever leaked directly out of Amber Hollow; these stories are anecdotal, but I think you'll see what I mean when I say they're pertinent."

"I trust you."

"You know how to use one of these?"

"Yes, Ma'am," he said, yet she explained anyway:

"Use this dial right here to spool the film forward, and when you are done, you can just hit this switch on the side to shut it off and I'll put the film back later. If you finish before I return, can you find your way back upstairs OK?"

"Sure," Corey said, beaming at her like a little kid, "I left a trail of bread crumbs."

"That's the spirit." She smiled, but it didn't reach her eyes. "Happy viewing."

"Thank you," he said, and cued the film forward. Delores left the room so silently that he barely heard her shoes on the stone floor. And even if he could hear her, what he read took his attention away from her quickly. He read:

The Rhinelander Daily Reader, July 20, 1941
"Strange lights sighted over Amber Hollow, investigators baffled."
Over the course of last weekend, one replete with all the staples of a Wisconsin summer from picnic lunches to hiking through the maze of forests and swimming in the many freshwater lakes, there were several accounts of a curious incident on the evening of Saturday, July 14. Citizens of Crandon (a neighboring community to Amber Hollow), alerted the local authorities to report sightings of extremely bright, bizarre lights coming from the sky over the small, reclusive township. Crandon police officers dispatched to investigate the event the following day, however, could find nothing to back up the claims that there was a disturbance, and when Amber Hollow constabularies were asked to give testimony as to their own inquiry, Crandon authorities were astounded to discover that no examination had been made. Apparently, Amber Hollow investigators had no record regarding such activity, alleging they were unaware that anything had transpired. One of the witnesses from Crandon presented pictures he'd taken with a Kodak Box Camera, but they were later dismissed because the quality was poor due to the camera's lack of focus, and nothing could be clearly discerned from the photos.
"It's certainly odd," Crandon Police Chief Robert Mole said, "but if the folks in Amber Hollow can't offer any clues, nor are they in any way perplexed by this, there is nothing else we can do. It's a very small village, known for its secluded location and reclusive citizens. If they don't have anything to report, the case is closed."
Several sources for this story say that this isn't the first time weird occurrences have happened in the remote, unincorporated

village, claiming that either strange lights, noises, and/or unusual behavior have been reported over the course of several decades, most notably during the summer. Nevertheless, all claims have remained unsubstantiated, and members of the community haven't come forth to shed any light on investigations.

After Corey read the article, he read it again. It wasn't so much the content, although it was odd, but the date, July 14. Today was July 19, so the tragedy that had occurred last weekend coincided with the date of the incidence in the fifty-year-old article. He knew that it was the date of the storming of the French Bastille, which was what the townsfolk of Amber Hollow were purportedly celebrating, so it was possible that it could be much more than a coincidence. He scrolled the film forward and read the next article:

The Rhinelander Daily Reader, July 27, 1943
"Ghostly screams emanate from the forest surrounding Amber Hollow"

Said by one man to sound like discordant coyotes in mating season, by another to sound like the cries of starving wolves, eerie shrieking was reportedly heard by a team of government workers who were mapping out an unchartered section of forest in mid-July, around the fourteenth or fifteenth this month. The nature of their task required they camp in the woods from June 17 until July 20, and it was during a two-day stretch that they claimed to hear screams and cries of a most unsettling nature, accompanied by an un-forecast lightning storm, as well as winds reaching up to what they estimated to be nearly forty miles an hour. They gave their account to authorities of Crandon (the nearest town in addition to Amber Hollow where they were conducting their study) because attempts to report it to the local constabulary in the Hollow were met with indifference and denial.

"We know what we heard, and any one of us would testify under oath or take a polygraph test," David Sherman of the

National Park Service said in a prepared statement. "Something happened out there; however, what it was is simply a mystery."

Weather experts were consulted to weigh in their opinions and, using the most up-to-date technology, determined that there couldn't have been a lightning storm, or even rain, as Doppler readings showed nothing but clear skies over most of Northern Wisconsin during that time. Residents of Crandon were asked if they recalled a thunderstorm on the evening of July 14, and without exception they all concurred that the night had been clear and calm.

The members of the government team have been sent back to their home state of Washington D.C. and are undergoing psychiatric evaluations to determine their mental condition, as well as blood and urine testing for alcohol and/or drug dependency.

Corey stared at the screen, his mouth open, the date seeming to pulse and flicker before his eyes as if it were a neon sign. Per this article, the idea that this was a coincidence was rapidly fading from his mind, becoming more of a connection that it appeared no one else was seeing. Or were they but no one was saying? Either way, it was downright unsettling, and as he scrolled through more articles from successive years, he saw that in the majority of them the odd occurrences happened in the summer, in or around mid-July, a lot of them involving either noises, bizarre lights, strange weather, or mysterious figures that disappeared like smoke when approached. There were other articles that didn't correlate with the July dates, and some seemed to push the boundaries of what could or could not be connected to the little town, but a good deal of them were spot on, offering up a mystery as rich and disturbing as those created by his favorite horror writers. He couldn't believe his luck at being able to read these articles firsthand, his good fortune of finding a woman who'd chronicled the sordid history of a bucolic hamlet that seemed destined to be the epicenter of some terrifying event. He skimmed through a couple more articles, only halfway through the twentieth century, when he came across a story that held him captive from the moment he read the headline:

The Crandon Express, December 14, 1957
"Dismembered Jane Doe found in the woods outside of Amber Hollow"

On November 30 Loggers Joel McCready and Robert Cromarty, residents from the nearby township of Crandon, made a grisly discovery while working in a section of state-owned forest north of Amber Hollow, in Torrance County. They were in the process of removing fallen trees when they found the remains of an unidentified woman, partially buried in a shallow grave. A forensic investigator was brought in from Green Bay, and he noted that the body appeared to be recently deceased, judging by the nature of her decomposition. What made the find especially ghastly was that her hands and head had been removed. Following an autopsy performed by a pathologist from Milwaukee, it was asserted that the victim had suffered countless internal injuries, giving investigators the idea that she had very likely died an extremely brutal death before being dismembered and buried, but the cause of the injuries wasn't immediately obvious.

Attempts to identify the victim have been thwarted because of the lack of teeth and fingerprints, making the ongoing investiga-tion exceedingly difficult. Detectives from Milwaukee even went so far as to question Ed Gein, the notorious grave robber/murderer arrested only two weeks previous for the murders of Mary Hogan in 1954 and Bernice Worden on November 16 of this year, as well as numerous other atrocities related to cannibalism and body desecration. He passively yet convincingly denied the accusation, and it was later dismissed because he has been actively cooperating with the police, and the location of the body near Amber Hollow wasn't near in proximity to Plainfield.

As of this writing, no one has come forth to either report a missing person, nor claim the body. Detectives from Rhinelander and Crandon contacted authorities in Amber Hollow, but local officials offered no clues, avowing no knowledge that a crime was perpetrated as well as asserting that no one from their community was missing, although they said they would help in any way they could in trying to identify the woman and locate her family. The Chief of police in Crandon requested to see a recent census report from the Hollow, and when one was produced, he noted that the document appeared to be doctored. That said, there was no absolute proof of fraudulent activity. If anyone has any information that may further assist the authorities please contact either the Crandon or Rhinelander police departments.

Corey leaned back in the chair and rubbed his eyes. He had no idea when he decided to drive up to Rhinelander today that he'd be reading an article mentioning Ed Gein, and for personal reasons it gave him the chills. His father had a friend who worked as a security guard at the Mendota State Hospital, where Gein was serving a life sentence, and had offered him a chance to meet the notorious psycho, an offer his dad had straightforwardly refused. As a kid Corey thought that had been a mistake, to turn down meeting someone who'd become infamous for committing such dreadful deeds, but now he could understand why his father had passed up the opportunity. It just seemed so...*ghoulish.*

He thought about the article for a moment, wondering if it was a distraction from what had really happened to the victim; the date on the story had no correlation to anything he'd read so far, unlike the preceding articles. It could be pure speculation that it had anything to do with the little village. And if they'd found no proof of a missing person from Amber Hollow, all they had was a theory. He shook his head slightly, cueing the film forward again, looking at the dates of the forthcoming articles. He saw that there were dozens more.

He would be here all night if he read them all. He didn't know if his back or his eyes would give out first, but because of the eerie nature contained within, he felt compelled to push on, continuing to read in the silence of the basement of the Rhinelander library while the florescent lights hummed overhead.

• • •

Delores's hand on his shoulder was what alerted Corey to her presence. He started, uttering a low grunt.

"Sorry to sneak up on you," she said, and when he turned to face her, he saw she had a cup of coffee in one hand. "Here, take it. You could probably use it."

"Thanks," he said, accepting the cup and taking a sip.

"I take it you've found the articles interesting?"

"Yes, I'd say your assumption is correct." He took another sip and set the cup down on the table next to the microfilm viewer. "And given the nature of what I've been reading, it isn't very nice of you to sneak up on me." This he said with a crooked grin, belaboring the point that he was kidding, but she nodded solemnly.

"It isn't for the faint of heart, is it?"

"Definitely not." Corey rubbed his eyes and then placed a hand on the small of his back and grimaced. "I guess I'm done for the night. I don't think my back can take this chair anymore."

"Certainly, and it's late. The library is closed."

"I suppose I might as well get out of your hair." He stood, stretching his legs. "I truly appreciate you sharing these articles with me."

"Would you like to read the rest of them tomorrow?"

He considered it a moment and then nodded. "Actually, I would." The stories he'd read were a mixture of bizarre and fascinating, with a tantalizing hint of the macabre. How could he refuse? Besides, he hadn't even gotten to the most recent articles; they may actually contain clues as to what transpired in the isolated village on the night in question. "May I come in tomorrow when you open and continue my research?"

"Of course," she said. "Where are you staying?"

"The Holiday Inn on Main. Right next to the A & W Rootbeer stand."

"Nothing but the finest accommodations, hmm?" she said, removing the film from the viewer and returning it to its metal canister before shutting off the machine. She placed it in the vault, swinging the large metal door shut with a soft click before she turned off the overhead lights. Only the lights from the corridor remained on, and in the dark he could yet again visually erase the wrinkles from her face and see the pretty woman she'd once been many years ago. Man, she must have been a looker. Before she turned to go, she gestured toward the table.

"Please bring the cup with you," she said, and Corey picked up the mug, careful not to spill it. He wasn't one for coffee after five, nonetheless he'd sipped it to be polite. He didn't need the caffeine to keep him up. He knew reading the articles would take care of that for him.

"Since the Brown County Sheriff's Department is footing the bill, I have to keep it modest," he said in reply to her comment regarding his overnight lodging, to which she nodded approvingly.

"I'm sure you'll be comfortable."

At the top of the stairs she let him pass and then produced a ring of keys from origins unknown and locked the basement door. It was very dimly lit, only a bank of lights on over the main desk, yet it made the expansive room feel cozy and warm. In the diffuseness it was like a secret hiding place, containing treasures in the form of paper and words.

"We open at nine o'clock," she said, leading him to the front door. "I arrive around eight to get things ready, open the blinds, make the coffee, that sort of thing. Oh, let me take that." She took the cup from his hands, and when they reached the door, she opened it. A cold breeze blew in, making them both shiver. Even though it was summer, northern Wisconsin was always cool at night, the temperatures dropping into the low fifties.

"You should have brought a coat," she said, and he shrugged.

"I'll live," he said. "Thank you for everything. I'll see you in the morning."

"Pleasant dreams," she said, and he laughed.

"I can count on that," he replied and then turned and walked to his car.

• • •

Corey had just dozed off in front of the ten o'clock news when he heard a knock upon his door. At first, he wasn't sure if it was his door or not, but then he heard it again, a light tapping.

Gently tapping, tapping upon my chamber door…

He grinned at his silliness, getting up from the bed and using the remote to mute the TV.

"Yes?" he called, and was surprised to hear a female's voice in return. He placed his eye over the small spy hole, and when he saw who it was, his heart leapt mightily in his chest. With fumbling hands, he opened the door.

"Am I disturbing you?" she asked, her voice as soft and lilting as the song of an exotic bird. In the orange light of the outside fluorescents her eyes were a startling shade of green.

"Not at all," he said, unable to believe that the pretty, young librarian was here, at his door, at ten o'clock at night. "What can I do for you?" The question sounded stupid coming out of his mouth, but surely there was a reason for her being here other than the lurid fantasy that popped up in his mind when he'd first glanced at the silky strands of her fine red hair and saw the tiny smile flitter upon lips that looked like they begged to be kissed.

"May I come in?" The smile bowing upward until it reached her eyes. Eyes that contained a hint of playfulness, maybe something more.

"Of course, where are my manners?" He stepped back, allowing her room, and she slipped in as silently as the night breeze. She appraised the room briefly, noting his suitcase on the small aluminum stand, his sport coat draped over the back of a chair, a copy of Kurt Vonnegut's seminal novel *Slaughterhouse Five* on the nightstand next to a lamp that's shade was most likely not made out of human skin. Her glance then fell upon the bed and then returned to face him.

"I'd offer you something to drink but I'm afraid all I have is tap water. I could run and get a couple of sodas from the machine in the lobby..."

"I'm fine," she said, shrugging off the light jacket she wore and placing it on the back of the chair over his. Her eyes shone very brightly now, boring into his own, and he felt himself getting aroused. He knew he shouldn't be so foolish, thinking this woman was here to seduce him, yet why else was she here at this hour, grinning at him so suggestively? "I'm not thirsty, not for soda, anyway."

"OK."

She took a step closer. "Do you remember my name?"

He did, but it took him a moment. Something with a "K."

"Keely!" he said as it came to him, and this made the smile on her face grow.

"That's right." She took another step toward him, and then she was in his arms. She pressed against him, and at once he was at full attention, damn the torpedoes and all that happy horse crap. "My, my, someone is glad to see me."

"Sorry," he muttered, but he was anything but. Her face closed in on his own, and then her lips were upon his, and he could taste an earthy musk coming from her that was delightful and frightening at the same time. Her fragrance was pleasant, but it conjured images in his mind that were otherwise disturbing, ghastly visions of open graves with corpses spilling out, their mouths open and slack, tongues as swollen as waterlogged sponges, black and nasty, resting on lips cracked and crusted with dried blood. He tried dispelling the thought, sticking his tongue in her mouth to meet hers, and the force of hers pushing back nearly crippled him, buckling him at the knees. She pushed him toward the bed, fumbling with the buttons on his shirt, and he fell back, his mind an explosion of ecstasy that this was actually happening. He leaned forward and kissed her again, exploring her taste, and an odor arose from her, bringing back the images of the open graves. He opened his eyes and met hers and at once saw within their green confines something that made his heart lurch yet again, only this time in fear. She climbed on top of him and pinned him to the bed. She was astoundingly heavy; he couldn't believe that a woman with such a petite frame could weigh so much yet here she was, rendering him helpless. He struggled half-heartedly, his stiff member refusing to believe that this was taking a sinister turn.

"Hey, wait..." he said, and it would be the last thing he would ever say, besides surprised grunts and then horrifically pained exertions meant to be words.

Her hands closed around his throat, startlingly strong, and at once his air was cut off.

"You won't be leaving, I think," she said with astonishing ease for someone strangling the life out of another. "You'll stay here forever."

She laughed, baring enormous teeth that gleamed wetly. In a dim haze he realized that she was salivating, and one of his last thoughts was how inappropriate that was, given the situation, until she leaned in closer, removed her hands from his neck, and then savagely tore his throat out. The last thing he was aware of was her bathing her face in his arterial spray and then nothing more.

CHAPTER 7

SATURDAY, JULY 20

Jeremy arrived at the police station just before eight. He greeted the desk clerk on duty, asked if there were any messages from Corey.

"No, sir. He hasn't checked in yet this morning," the clerk said, his mouth half-full as he worked his way through an egg McMuffin.

"Although I see you are very busy, can you call the hotel he's staying at? Tell him to page me when he gets a chance."

"Can do," the other replied cheerily as a piece of bacon fell from his breakfast sandwich and landed on his ample belly. He picked it up and tossed it in his mouth, chewing noisily.

Jeremy nodded and then continued on to his desk. He wanted to see if there were any updates from Calvin Lemory, see if anything had changed. The last report he'd received detailed the progress of the Brown County clean-up crew, how they'd advanced further into the village, sifting through the ash and debris for any salvageable bodies. They'd found none. When his partner arrived, he'd debrief her on the day and then possibly they'd head over to St. Mary's and talk with the next survivor, see what cock and bull story they had to share. Given what they'd heard, he was sure it would be a doozy.

Placing his light jacket over the back of his desk chair, he sat down and booted up his computer. While he waited, he checked the voice mail on his desk phone; nothing of any importance there. He hoped Corey would dig up something they could use, anything really. At this juncture, a report of another survivor would be good news, even if they had another crackpot tale.

His phone rang, clanging like a school bell declaring him tardy, and he snatched it before it could ring a second time.

"Detective LeFevre."

"Good morning, detective, this is Agent Reginald Skelly, FBI."

"Yes? How can I help you?"

"We've received a detailed report regarding the Village of Amber Hollow in Northern Wisconsin and have been instructed to aid you in your investigation."

Jeremy sighed. He knew the red tape would arrive eventually, and here it was.

"Are you taking over?"

"No, nothing of that sort," Agent Skelly replied with a slight chuckle. "It's just that in cases like these, which involve a tragedy of this magnitude, we're required to provide assistance."

"I see…"

"My partner and I are going to fly up from Washington D.C. tomorrow and go over the testimony of the survivors. How are the interrogations…um, excuse me…the interviews going so far?"

"Not well, I'm afraid. We've talked to three of the five witnesses and so far, we have conflicting stories."

"Hmm, they don't wish to cooperate?"

"I don't think that's it, I think—" Jeremy cut himself off, wondering if this was something he should talk about on the phone. This, to him, was sensitive information. It would be best if they talked about it in person. "I think I'm dealing with some very confused people."

"I suppose, given the circumstances," Skelly said, but his voice betrayed his skepticism. "My partner and I will speak with them, see if we can't get those eggs to crack."

"Great," Jeremy said. What else could he say? He'd just been called a nincompoop by an FBI agent, a negligible achievement on any given day.

"Very good, we'll get in touch when we arrive tomorrow."

"Thanks," he said, but the other had already hung up. He replaced the phone on the cradle.

He was slogging through backlogged files when Sadie arrived.

"Good morning," he said, looking up from his computer and noticing she looked like she'd lost the battle of getting a good night's sleep. He'd planned to start by telling her that the FBI called, but judging by her weary demeanor that could wait. "Something keep you up last night?"

She shook her head, shrugged, and then nodded. "Yes, but it's none of your business." This said in a tone of voice that suggested it *was* his business, all he had to do was ask. He thought about how he'd recently accepted that he was carrying a torch for her, had been for some time, he'd just been hiding it and lying to himself. He wondered if that was an emotion he should put the kibosh on, like, immediately, but could not find within himself the ability to do so.

The heart wants what it wants...

So, instead, he decided to pursue his line of questioning, if only for the sake of their professional relationship.

"Let me guess: your beau and you got into a fight?"

"I told you, it's none of your business," she huffed, going to her desk and fairly throwing her purse down. She turned to face him. "That guy just doesn't know how a woman thinks. He's an idiot!"

"Whoa, whoa! What happened? He didn't want to stay the night?" He was only joking, but he did want to know what had her so upset. On the outs with the boyfriend? Well, that just might play out better for him in the long run.

Stop it man, just stop. There's no need to ruin a good thing, and it couldn't happen anyway, not in this lifetime, you know that...

She glared at him, irritated at his casual manner, but then realized he only meant well. Throughout the course of their partnership he'd always listened when she needed to vent, had always been a sympathetic audience. Sometimes she actually thought he might have a thing for her, but knowing how seriously he took his job, and how important a healthy working relationship was to him, she never pondered it too long, although she had to admit to herself that she was strangely attracted to him, why, she didn't know. He certainly was no Paul Newman in the looks department, but he was a bona fide good guy, of that she was sure, and he'd always been there for her. She took a deep breath, closed her eyes a second and then blew it out.

"He…he just doesn't understand that I have a duty to my profession. He makes light of it."

"Doesn't take you seriously, huh? Thinks you're just a woman?"

It really wasn't a difficult guess. He'd never met her boyfriend, but from what she'd told him he seemed like the old-fashioned 'women should be barefoot and pregnant in the kitchen' type. It wasn't uncommon, not in a small city like Green Bay, in the heart of the Midwest where white and blue-collar working-class values ran along the same lines as religion and family.

She nodded. "Yes, that, and he doesn't like that I work odd hours sometimes, thinks I don't spend enough time with him."

"We knocked off at five yesterday. What's to complain about?"

"You know as well as I do that we put in more than the average forty-hour work week."

"More like sixty if you ask me."

"Yeah, well, he doesn't like it." She paused, looked at him for a long moment that became almost uncomfortable. At last she continued: "And it's not just that, it…it's…well, it's also because of *you*."

Jeremy's heart did a little skip in his chest. Maybe it was the way she was looking at him, or maybe it was the way she said "you" in reference to himself.

"Me?"

"He's jealous, Jeremy, if you must know. He suggested that I like you more than him."

"You mean you don't?"

"Oh, shut up you pig—" she was saying when Jeremy's desk phone rang.

"Hold that thought," he said and then: "hello?"

"Just me, Detective," the desk clerk said. "I wanted to give you an update on Corey."

"Yes?"

"He checked into the Holiday Inn last night and went to his room, but he must have left really early this morning because he turned in his key and he's gone."

"Did you talk to the person whom he gave the room key to?"

"Uh, no, sir. Apparently, they have a window where you can just stick it in a slot and go about your business. No one there saw him leave."

"And the room is empty? All his stuff is gone?"

"Yes, sir, I told the hotel clerk it was official police business, and that I wanted them to check. He put me on hold and went and looked himself. He said the room was empty. The only thing he left behind was a dollar tip for the cleaning staff."

"Hmm," Jeremy said, perplexed. "Thanks." He hung up.

"What's up?" Sadie asked, appearing a little more relaxed now. She'd taken off her jacket and was sitting at her desk, checking her voice mail.

"Our amateur sleuth is already out doing more sleuthing, but he hasn't bothered to check in with us."

She looked at him closely, saw his anxious eyes and furrowed brow. "Why, are you worried?"

He nodded absentmindedly. "You know that boy as well as I do; he doesn't do anything without seeking our approval. Kind of strange that he went up there to research the town's history and hasn't bothered to let us know what he found, don't you think?"

"Yes, I suppose so. Why don't you page him?"

"He hasn't been issued one; he's too green around the gills."

"Who was he planning to meet?"

"He said he was meeting a librarian who had information about Amber Hollow. I don't recall her name, but she must be the one in charge."

Sadie picked up her phone, dialed 411 and asked for the Rhinelander Public Library. The operator connected her call, and after she listened to the message she hung up. "They open at nine." She glanced at her watch. "That's in fifteen minutes. I'll call at nine sharp."

"Sounds good," he said and then gave her a sly grin. "Are you sure you don't like me more than what's his name?"

"I'll never tell," she replied sweetly, and as far as Jeremy was concerned, it was the best answer he could get.

• • •

"No, he isn't here." The woman on the other end of the phone sounded puzzled. "Have you tried the hotel he's staying at?"

"That was my logical first choice," Sadie said dourly. "Has anyone seen him since last night?"

"I don't think he intended to come back, but I can check with my supervisor."

"Please do," Sadie said. "And who do I have the pleasure of speaking with?"

"My name is Keely, ma'am, and I'm going to put you on hold for a minute while I go and get Delores."

"Thank you." While Sadie waited, she thought about the fight she'd had with her boyfriend the previous night. She was getting sick of his jealousy issues, as well as his old-fashioned notions of what a woman could and should do with her life. When they'd began dating, he claimed to be turned on by her being a cop. Now, whenever they got together, he gave her the third degree, which in all actuality should be *her* job.

Her thoughts were interrupted when somebody took the line off hold.

"Can I help you?" a frail, female voice asked, and Sadie closed the door on her ruminations.

"Yes, please. I'm Detective Sadie Conrad, a homicide investigator for Brown County. One of my colleagues paid you a visit yesterday."

"Why, yes, of course, he was such a polite young man. I take it you needed him back in Green Bay."

"Excuse me?"

"He was supposed to meet me this morning, but he hasn't arrived yet. I was going to show him more articles pertaining to the Hollow."

"The Hollow?"

"I'm sorry, that's what some of us Old-timers call it up here. Don't dare saying that to a resident though; they don't like it much." She paused for a long moment, so long that Sadie thought that the connection had been broken, but then the woman spoke again: "I suppose there aren't really any more residents in Amber Hollow to offend, though."

"There are only five known survivors," Sadie concurred idly, her mind turning things over. "So…he was supposed to meet you this morning?"

"Yes, at nine. A man like that, well, I expected him to be early."

He would have been early, no doubt on that count, if he intended to show up. Sadie could have told the woman that, but it didn't matter. What mattered was where in the Sam Hill he was, which led her to another thought.

"Who was the woman I spoke with on the phone before you?"

"Hmm? Oh, that was Keely. She's new here, only been working at the library for about six months."

"She told me that he didn't intend to come back." This was a statement, but one presented as a question.

"I don't know how she would know something like that," Delores said. "The library was closed when he left last night, everyone was gone. That was when I made the offer."

"What offer was that?"

"For him to come back today." This said like Sadie had asked a very stupid question. And what the hell, maybe she had.

"Will you please do me a favor?"

"Why of course, dear."

"Will you take down my pager number and call me if he shows up, please? It's urgent that I speak with him."

"Anything I can do to help," the other replied, and Sadie gave her the number and then asked for the woman's name, writing it down carefully in her pocket notebook alongside "Rhinelander Public Library." She then thanked her and hung up the phone.

"Well?" Jeremy said, and Sadie jumped, startled.

"Cripes, I didn't know you were sitting there listening."

"What else would I be doing?"

"Work?"

"Bo—ring. So, what did she say?"

"He was supposed to come back this morning and he never showed up."

"OK, we now officially have a problem," Jeremy said, frowning. "With Corey's MO, I think it's safe to say he's missing."

"Aren't you jumping to conclusions?"

"Do you think I am?"

Sadie stared at him, honestly baffled. The more she considered it, the more it seemed that he was right. Corey didn't go to the bathroom without asking one of them for permission.

"No," she said at last, "I don't think you are." She looked at him thoughtfully. "What should we do?"

"Nothing we can do right now that we haven't already done, except to call the Rhinelander police and report a missing person." He glanced at the clock on the wall. "Only problem is he can't be considered missing until he hasn't been seen for at least twenty-four hours." He continued looking at the clock, thinking it over. He returned his gaze to Sadie. "What the hell, we'll get the ball rolling."

"I'll make the call," she said, picking up her phone.

"Make it snappy," he said, giving her a devil-may-care grin to show he was only ribbing her. "We have a date with another survivor at St. Mary's. I'm willing to bet an entire month's pay that what they have to say won't be remotely similar to anything we've heard so far."

"I'm not taking that bet," she said, grinning, and she placed the call.

CHAPTER 8

THE TOWER DRIVE BRIDGE

The call came when they were five blocks from St. Mary's, blaring from the radio in raucous a hiss of static that made both of them jump. Sadie looked at Jeremy; the confusion in her eyes would be almost comical if the situation wasn't so dire. He grabbed the handset on the radio, depressed the button.

"This is Detective Jeremy LeFevre. Please repeat the transmission."

"There is a ten fifty-six A in progress on the Tower Drive Bridge, I repeat a ten fifty-six A."

"We're two miles from that location," he said calmly, although his nerves suddenly felt as if they were live wires spitting enough electricity to power the entire city. "We're en route."

"Ten four," the dispatcher said, and Sadie flipped a switch on the dash that fired up the siren. She then grabbed the bubble next to her, rolled down her window, and tossed it onto the top of the car where the magnet on the bottom held it firmly in place. For some reason, she always felt like she was in an episode of *Starskey and Hutch* when she did that.

"You thinking what I'm thinking?" he asked his partner, but she looked at him only briefly, keeping her eyes fixed on the road. Traffic was light at this hour on this side of town, but she never forgot her training. Some idiot blasting their car stereo wouldn't hear them and could cause an undue car accident.

"What are you thinking?"

"I don't know, maybe I'm jumping to more conclusions, but somehow I think this is one call we need to take."

Turned out, he was right.

. . .

She was clinging to a support cable with both hands, in the center of the giant arch, the wind whipping her hospital gown around like a flag at full-mast. People had gathered, commuters on their way to work, housewives getting the day's grocery shopping done, families heading to Bay Beach to enjoy a picnic lunch and carnival rides. A man in faded jeans and a flannel shirt was shouting something at her, reaching out his hand, but the woman was oblivious. To Sadie's horror, there were actually a few people who were taking pictures; one man in fact had a large video camera and it was apparent he wasn't affiliated with any of the local news stations based on his attire of jammy-jam bottoms and a ripped Molly Hatchet T-shirt. She made a mental note to confiscate their devices once the situation was handled, *if* it was handled.

She pulled the car alongside the railing on the east side of the bridge, turning off the siren but leaving the flasher on. She and Jeremy got out, but they moved with deliberate caution, not wanting to frighten the woman any more than she already was.

"One of the survivors?" Sadie asked Jeremy, and he shrugged before nodding.

"Probably."

They reached the man in the flannel shirt, and Jeremy put a hand on his shoulder. He started, looking wildly at them, and they could see he was almost as scared as the woman standing on the ledge.

"Please stand down, sir," Jeremy said. "We're police. Let us handle this."

The man's eyes were practically bugging out of his head, his jaw working but no words coming out. Spittle had formed in the corners of his mouth, and he licked his lips with a tongue that was so dry it made a rasping sound.

"I was just driving by, and I saw that woman walking along the side there. People aren't allowed to walk on the bridge, ya know? No walkway."

Jeremy nodded. "Yes, of course. Now, please, let us do our job."

"I was just driving by in my truck when I saw her—"

"We understand, sir. Please."

The man nodded and backed away. Sadie stepped up to the rail, looked down at the roiling water below. The bridge connected the east and west sides of Green Bay at the mouth of the Fox River, and it had been used for suicide attempts in the past, although it wasn't quite high enough to be instantly fatal. Most suicide attempts from the bridge that were successful were due to the victim drowning. With this in mind, she removed her walkie-talkie from her belt and called for a police boat. "Heading that way, ma'am," she was told. "Ten four," she replied and replaced the walkie-talkie on her belt. Jeremy advanced toward the woman slowly, holding out one hand.

"My name is Detective Jeremy LeFevre, ma'am," he said calmly, his voice pitched low. One wrong word and all she had to do was let go of the cable, and the wind would whip her right off and into the bay.

"I'm not going back!" the woman screamed, her eyes rolling in terror. "You hear me? I'm never going back!"

"We understand," Sadie said, approaching carefully from the opposite side of her partner, although her reply couldn't have been farther from the truth. So far, she didn't understand anything; however, she knew for certain that this woman's passing wouldn't do them a damn bit of good at getting to the truth. They needed to keep her still so she wouldn't let go.

"We're here to help you," Jeremy said, "in fact, we were on our way to the hospital to visit you, to ask you some questions—"

"You have questions, you can ask Anthony Guntram! It's his fault, all his fault!"

"I'm afraid we can't do that, ma'am." He gazed down, saw a police boat approaching from the mouth of the river. Good timing. "Please, let us help you. Take my hand."

"I don't want your help!" she screamed, and in her exertion one of her feet slipped and she almost fell, the only thing keeping her from plunging over the side was her grip on the cable, which apparently was pretty tight. She was badly scared, obviously, but her mind hadn't been made up, not yet anyway. He had to try and keep it that way. "You can't help me, no one can!"

"Please let us try," he said, moving closer. He was five feet away from her now and closing. If he could keep her calm maybe he could get close enough to grab her before she made a decision that would put her in intensive care, if not outright kill her.

"You back up!" she roared with such ferocity that Jeremy stopped where he was, watching her carefully. "I told you: you can't help me, no one can! If God can't help me, there isn't a person on earth who can!"

Sadie flanked left, trying to get on her blind side. She regarded the woman judiciously, hoping that her partner could keep her distracted long enough for her to either grab the woman by her arm or at least get a hold of her gown and get her safely off the ledge. Even though the woman would very likely tell them a story that in no way concurred with the others, they needed her testimony, if only to keep bashing away at a case that was becoming increasingly complex. Her death wouldn't help anyone, most surely herself, but a person in the throes of suicidal mania didn't really see it that way, did they? No, they almost surely never did.

"What did Anthony Guntram do?" Jeremy asked. According to the other survivors, he'd either turned them into a suicide cult or he'd incurred the wrath of the mob. Whatever this woman believed he'd done, it was the only link any of their testimony had in common, and getting to the bottom of that would surely point them in the right direction, whatever direction that was.

"He doomed us all!" she shrieked, before gazing down and seeing the police boat. She let loose another wild scream that made the hair stand up on Sadie's neck, freezing her momentarily where she was, and that was when the woman at last let go of the cable that was the only thing tethering her to safety. The wind whipped up, a ferocious bellow that made her stagger, and Jeremy took one last look into her crazed eyes before she fluttered up like a discarded newspaper and then plummeted two hundred feet to the bay below. Jeremy ran to the edge, watched as she splashed into the water. The police boat was nearby, closing in on her, but after she sank below the chop, she didn't emerge. He grabbed his walkie-talkie.

"Get divers into the water immediately!" he yelled into the handset and then turned quickly to face his partner. "Let's go!"

Sadie stared at him blankly, the look on her face registering the shock of what they had just witnessed.

"Go?" she said through lips that felt numb. "Go where?"

This stunned utterance was what brought Jeremy back from whatever impulsive idea he'd had. Sadie was right: where could they go? The police boat and the divers were the only thing that could save the woman now. If they couldn't find her, there was nothing else they could do.

"OK," he said at last, putting his walkie-talkie away. "We'll let them take care of it. We should take statements from the witnesses."

He looked at her closely, saw that she was quickly pulling herself back together. It was what made her good at her job, her ability to compartmentalize events in a manner in which she could then use reason and deduction instead of panic to get to the bottom of things.

"You all right?"

"I'm fine," she said, running a hand through her thick, curly hair, turning away from the edge of the bridge. "I'm going to start with the people photographing it, most likely the guy with the video camera."

"Very good," he said. He intended to start with the man in the flannel shirt. Apparently, he'd had a front row seat to this theatre of mayhem from the git go. "Carry on."

• • •

The orderlies, nurses, and doctors they spoke with at St. Mary's had no idea how the woman had escaped. A nurse had gone to her room to bring her breakfast and found the bed empty. She wasn't alarmed at first, thinking that the woman with the wild eyes who spoke in broken sentences had probably just wandered off, and was taking a tour of the hospital unescorted. She'd had to rip out her IV lines to do this, but the nurse had seen stranger things during her time on the ward.

When the detective's interrogations were through, they had nothing more than they'd had this morning, only a missing woman whom they had to presume was dead until her body could be recovered.

It was no surprise to either of them that she hadn't been found once she'd sunk beneath the water. Given the nature of the case, it truly was an inevitability. Now all they had were a couple of wonky stories, a missing person, and a suicide. The only running thread to the whole case was a man by the name of Anthony Guntram who, by all accounts, was indeed a scoundrel, but since he wasn't available to talk to, it still felt like a dead end unless they could dig up some information about him. A birth record, police report, tax information from the IRS…anything to at least confirm he was who these people said he was. If a fingerprint could be found, Allister could possibly identify his body in the morgue, providing he was one of the stiffs on the slabs.

Jeremy and Sadie went back to the station, neither one of them saying much. What was to say? At a time like this, small talk was useless. When they arrived, they went to their desks, checked their desk phone's voice mail for any information regarding Corey. There was none. Jeremy let out a pent-up puff of breath, and glanced at his partner. He knew she was rattled by what had transpired, maybe not so much the death of the survivor but the lack of empathy from the onlookers. While he'd talked to the frantic man in the flannel shirt, she'd confiscated the cameras from those she could catch, the people who'd thoughtlessly filmed the event rather than do anything about it. What kind of ghouls were they? As he considered this, a thought came to him, one that felt totally out of the blue, but right at the same time.

"Maybe we should look at the footage on that video camera," he said, "and see if there is anything we can use."

"What? Are you kidding? The last thing I want to do is watch that woman jump off of the bridge again."

Although he agreed, he still felt the hunch burning inside of him, the feeling that the footage could shed some light on the case. He'd felt flummoxed before by cases that seemed impossible, but so far, this one was yielding nothing in the way of facts, just an increasingly complicated string of events that appeared to have no pattern...

"I think we should take a look. Can't hurt."

Sadie shrugged and got up from her desk. She'd set the video camera down next to the door when they'd returned, and now she picked it up and handed it to him without a word, simply a look on her face that aptly indicated her reluctance.

"Go ahead, take a look."

He studied the camera, saw that it was one of those new-fangled Panasonics that had a little screen for him to view the material. Searching for the right buttons, he rewound the tape until he found the beginning of the footage and pressed play. He watched the shaky video of the woman climbing up onto the ledge, grabbing a hold of a bridge cable. The person recording the event kept the camera trained on the woman, only losing her occasionally when vehicles passed. Many voices were shouting in the background, so he turned down the volume, tried to concentrate on the image, and that was when something strange happened.

"Whoa," he muttered, holding the camera closer to his face so that he could get a better look. The woman gave the impression that she was talking to someone who wasn't there, and it appeared that she was either pleading or arguing. Now he turned the volume back up, but it did nothing to capture the woman's voice, only made the background noise louder. The woman made wild gestures alternately with her arms, always keeping one hand on the cable, looking as if she was trying to push something away, and then, for just the briefest second, there was a blur of movement, almost indiscernible, but it caught his eye. It was only the tiniest flash, and then it was gone. He paused it and then slowly, frame by frame, he rewound it. He pressed play again, watching the screen raptly. There it was again: the woman seemed to be pushing something away from her, and there was the slightest hint of motion, something moving so fast the camera couldn't pick it up. Just a nanosecond and then gone.

"I think you need to see this," he said, and Sadie looked up from her computer.

"Oh God," she groaned, not wanting to, but she got up and stood behind him while he cued it back to the spot.

"What are we looking at?" she asked after he'd played it for her twice.

"I have no idea, but there's something there, don't you agree?" She grudgingly nodded her head, but she looked confused. "I don't understand how that is going to help us."

"To tell you the truth, I don't either, but it helped me to make up my mind."

"About what?"

He studied her closely, fixing his eyes on hers. She looked exhausted, totally wrung out, but he knew that she, like him, thrived on these cases. Solving this would make her feel a whole lot better, of that he was sure.

"I think it's time we take a little trip."

"Where to?"

"Where do you think?"

Her eyes widened, eyebrows arching, but then she nodded. "I suppose it's the logical next step."

"Glad to hear you're onboard." He picked up his desk phone, tucked it under his ear with his shoulder. "I'm going to call my pet sitter, see if she can stay with Roxie this evening. If you have any arrangements you need to make, now is a good time."

"You think we're going to spend the night?"

"You never know, we might."

"That's going to make you-know-who very unhappy."

"Screw him," he said and then laughed. "Maybe I should rephrase that…"

But this made her smile for the first time since this morning, when they'd received the call and watched the woman take a swan dive from the Tower Drive Bridge.

"In his dreams," she said. She picked up her own phone, made a call, and within the hour they were in a gassed-up cruiser, heading north.

PART TWO
THE INVESTIGATION

CHAPTER 9

A VISIT UP NORTH

The scenery passed by in a haze of corn and soybean fields, neither one of them saying much. The drive was uneventful; Jeremy played the radio quietly, listening to NPR. He couldn't stand the current state of rock-and-roll, he thought that all the popular singers were whiny adolescents who screeched instead of sang, juvenile songs that relied heavily on the 'car as a girl' metaphor, or comparing the female anatomy to food. Cherry Pie indeed. He wouldn't be surprised if heavy metal was a passing phase and that the music his partner preferred—hip-hop—would be more likely to stand the test of time. In the meantime, he preferred the droll voice of the speaker telling him how the economy was likely to stay stable over the next year, thanks to the presidency of George H. W. Bush. Well, they'd see about that, wouldn't they?

"You think we should have called the library, maybe let the woman know we're coming to see her?" Jeremy said, interrupting the relative quiet (as droll as the NPR speakers were, they very well could be listening to a recording of whale sounds to prelude a good night's sleep), and Sadie shook her head. She didn't know why, but she felt the element of surprise might be better. It wouldn't give anyone time to think of a cover story. She wasn't thinking of Delores specifically, but about what the other librarian had said, about Corey not returning when she couldn't have possibly known. Perhaps she knew something she wasn't telling.

"No, I think we're best showing up unannounced." She flashed a brazen smile. "You just think of what you want to say when we get there, big boy."

"Will do," he said, grinning. He liked it when she called him that. For obvious reasons it appealed to his male sensibilities. He returned his gaze to the passing farmer's fields and the occasional uninterrupted patch of forest.

In this part of Wisconsin, there wasn't much to see but the great outdoors. They were literally in the middle of nothing and nowhere. It was easy to understand how a village like Amber Hollow could be so isolated, especially in the winter months when roads were almost impassable, the snowplows working overtime yet barely making a dent in the continuous snowfall. While Green Bay would get roughly eighty inches of snow between November and April, it wasn't uncommon for northern Wisconsin to get upward to three hundred inches or more. It was why all the best skiing was up near Hurley, which sat on the border of Upper Michigan. Not to mention the hills were bigger, the runs longer. It wasn't exactly the Rockies, but for the people in the Midwest it gave them something to do a solid five months out of the year besides drinking themselves to death.

"Everything about that place is weird," Sadie said, hitting the switch to douse the windshield with cleaner to try and remove the plethora of dead bugs they'd picked up along the way. Her comment seemed random, but Jeremy knew she was just thinking aloud about the case. "How they could resist outsiders for so long is almost impossible."

"You're still not buying the story of the gold mine?"

"Do you?"

"Not for a second."

"Maybe the second survivor wasn't lying. Maybe they *were* a suicide cult."

"Only way we can find out is by doing a little old-fashioned investigating."

"I suppose so," she agreed, and they drove the rest of the way in silence.

• • •

The library was doing lackluster business for a Saturday afternoon. Sadie parked the cruiser near the front steps, put it in park.

"You want to play 'good cop, bad cop'?" Jeremy asked.

"Only if I get to be the bad cop," Sadie chortled. "You know I'm better at it than you are."

"You got it."

They exited the car, walking up the stairs as a brisk wind blew in from the east, making the American flag stand rigidly at attention. The pale blue sky overhead was strewn with clouds, obscuring the sun, and to Sadie it cast an ominous pall over the day. Jeremy held the door while a couple of giggling teenage girls exited with piles of CD's they were no doubt going to go home and tape on a cassette recorder. In Jeremy's day it had been vinyl records, and he'd recorded them using the Sears and Roebuck turntable/tape recorder he'd gotten for Christmas when he was ten. Stealing was still stealing; however, the method had changed.

The atmosphere inside was inviting, and both Sadie and Jeremy felt emotions similar to what their co-worker had felt, how the library felt so pleasant and cozy. Patrons sat reading newspapers and magazines while others perused shelves of hardcovers and paperbacks. During the winter months, the tables would no doubt be occupied by students cramming for the SATs or ACTs in the hopes of getting into a good school and breaking out of the confines of such a small town, but in July the attendance was light.

They approached the main desk, where a young woman was studying a computer screen with the rapt fascination one usually reserves for something illicit. Sadie cleared her throat loudly, a signal to her partner that she wasn't kidding about the routine they had performed hundreds of times.

"Can I help you?" the young woman asked, looking up from the screen.

"That depends," Sadie said. "Were you working here yesterday?"

"Um, no," the woman said, her eyes darting from Sadie to Jeremy. "Friday is my day off." The girl appeared slightly ruffled by the question, but Jeremy didn't detect that she was lying.

"Is Delores Schenker available?" Sadie continued, a frown creasing her otherwise pleasant face, and the woman nodded quickly.

"Yes, she's in the back." Now it was her turn to flex a little muscle. "May I ask who's looking for her?"

Jeremy pulled out his badge from an inside pocket of his sport coat.

"Detectives LeFevre and Conrad, Green Bay Homicide Division," he said curtly, but not too unkindly. He was, after all, the good cop. "May we please have a moment of her time?"

The girl looked at his badge and then Sadie's, and nodded again. "Of course. I'll go and get her."

She got up and disappeared behind the desk.

"Didn't you speak to a woman this morning that was here yesterday?"

"Yes, but apparently that isn't her."

Delores stepped out from the back a few minutes later, looking every bit the elderly matriarchal librarian. Perched at the very tip of a nose that had most likely felt the kiss of a million Kleenexes in its lifetime was a pair of glasses that had seen better days. On her face she wore a look of concern, one which Sadie duly noted and then dismissed. She wasn't going to give up her stern demeanor just yet; they could become best buddies later, after they'd learned everything they could about Corey.

"May I help you?" Delores asked, and Sadie nodded grimly.

"We spoke this morning. I'm Detective Conrad and this is my partner, Detective LeFevre."

"Why, of course," she said, nodding congenially. "Why don't you follow me to my office? We can talk in there."

"Thank you," Jeremy said, and the woman walked around the desk and led them to a small room near the children's section. She opened the door, allowed them to enter and then followed close behind.

She approached a coffee maker, took three mugs from a coffee cup "tree." She poured three cups without asking if either wanted any, which was fine because both Jeremy and Sadie needed the pick-me-up.

"Please, have a seat," she said after they each accepted the steaming beverage.

Cups in hand, they sat in two chairs facing her desk, a large, cluttered affair that felt like it belonged in this tidy little room, if only for the contradiction it presented.

"When did you last see officer Corey Lindsley?" Sadie asked, sipping from her mug, a cup that bore the library's logo: The Rhinelander Public Library...A World of Knowledge Awaits You.

How quaint...

"Last night, after he viewed some articles on microfilm. There are so many that he couldn't possibly read them all in one sitting, so he decided to go back to his hotel, and we made plans for him to return this morning."

"You have that many articles on microfilm pertaining to Amber Hollow?"

"Why, yes, several dozen. Your eyes get tired after only an hour or two looking at microfilm."

"What time did he arrive?"

"It must have been just after six, because I'd had my Cup O' Noodles and a sweetbread."

"What time did he leave?" Jeremy said, fixing the old woman with a look of sympathetic concern. It wasn't part of the routine. She seemed nice enough, and his radar wasn't going off. She didn't appear to be uncomfortable, and so far, her answers had been genuine.

"It was after the library had closed, so it may have been about eight-thirty, I think."

"The library closes at eight?" Sadie skipped the compassionate routine. She wanted Delores to know they meant business.

"Yes, on most weeknights, it does. On Wednesday, we close at five."

"Where was he in conjunction to the other patrons?" Sadie asked, and Jeremy aptly read her mind as to what she was angling at: was there anyone else that might have seen him? Delores's reply, however, ruled out another witness to their gopher's whereabouts.

"He was in the basement where I keep my personal archived microfilm."

"And all of the archived articles are strictly about Amber Hollow?"

"Why, yes, of course." She took a sip from her cup, gave them an odd, canted grin. "Strange things have been happening in or around that town since before I was a little girl. I saved articles from the paper and then transferred them to microfilm. It's long been a hobby of mine, even if computers are going to phase out that technology. Would you like to see them?"

"No, thank you," Jeremy said, setting his cup down on the desk, on top of a coaster he saw lying there. "Right now, we're more concerned with finding Officer Lindsley."

"I understand. He's a very nice man."

"Did anyone else see him leave, ma'am?" Sadie said, the old woman's apparent honesty starting to disarm her. While Jeremy was a human lie detector, she dealt more in emotions, and what she was getting from the librarian was nothing but concern for Corey's well-being.

"No, like I said, the library was closed. We were the last two people here."

For some reason, this innocuous statement set off Sadie's alarm. Something about how she said it, an emphasis on "people."

"As opposed to?" she blurted, and Delores looked at her curiously.

"Excuse me?" the elderly woman replied, honestly bewildered, and at once Sadie felt a trifle impolite. What did she mean, exactly? If there were no people, what else would that leave them, the librarian's cat?

"Nothing," she said, taking a sip of her coffee. Her instincts were sharp, but occasionally she chased shadows that weren't really there.

"Do you have surveillance cameras?" Jeremy said, nudging Sadie's knee lightly with his own, his indicator that he understood what she was talking about even if it came out poorly, and she cast him a slight smile.

"No," Delores replied, "we haven't had any reason to. No one steals from the library, everything is free. Why would someone want to steal from a place where everything is free?"

"No reason to, I guess," Jeremy said, the disappointment in his voice evident. Video footage would have made their job a little easier.

"Where is the woman I spoke with this morning? I believe she said her name was Keely?"

Delores returned her attention to Sadie. "Why, she worked a half-day and is probably halfway to East Troy by now."

"East Troy?"

"Yes. She has tickets to see a rock show at Alpine Valley. She and her girlfriends. I'm not too keen on what popular music is these days, but I do know it's too loud and they sure do shout and swear a lot." She grimaced. "In my day, music was something you enjoyed singing along to. Nowadays, these singers all sound like they're battling laryngitis. My throat hurts just hearing them."

Jeremy chuckled, as he'd been thinking the same thing on the drive up. Groups like Motley's Crue, Faith On Board and Metallic Finish gave him a headache. Sadie, however, continued her line of interrogation:

"Do you have any idea how she could have known that Officer Lindsley was staying at a hotel in town, or why she would assume that he wasn't going to return here in the morning?"

Delores flashed a grin that was coquettish, almost girlish. "He's a young man, is he not?"

"Yes," Sadie affirmed. "He is." She mentally noted that the librarian spoke of Corey in the present tense, which gave her more reason to doubt her suspicion only a moment ago. Guilty people generally spoke of a missing person in the past tense, as if to make them a part of the past would convince others to think the same. This woman was talking about Corey as if he was still alive, something she and her partner desperately hoped was so.

"When you meet Keely, you'll see that she is a young, attractive woman. I'd have to be blind not to see that they were flirting with one another."

Jeremy and Sadie exchanged a glance, but not much information was contained within, more puzzlement than anything.

"Are you suggesting that he told her he was staying in town?" Sadie said, and Delores nodded.

"I suppose I am. It's the only way she could have known. I didn't tell her. Why would I?"

For this, neither had an answer. It did make sense, after all. Corey was a single young man, and it was obvious to them that he liked women, although he didn't presently have a girlfriend. He was too consumed with his professional life at this point to find the time. However, a little flirting wasn't beyond him, and what did they know about him outside of the office, his proclivities toward the opposite sex when he could sandwich in the time, especially when he had an evening to himself? It sounded likely. Jeremy looked at Sadie, raised an eyebrow. She shrugged, briefly unsure.

"Is it conceivable that maybe your young co-worker might have decided he wanted to see a rock concert with some pretty young girls?" Delores said, her voice light, almost breathless. "Could it be possible that a man his age might shirk his duties and play hooky? Does that sound like a likely prospect?"

Sadie shook her head and was about to say no when Jeremy took her by surprise by saying "Yes, could be."

She looked at him and he shrugged. "For all we know, it is a possibility. He likes that noisy music, and it's obvious he likes girls."

"What? And not tell us? You know as well as I do that he comes in on his days off! I don't think he's ever taken a sick day unless we sent him home—"

"We'll talk about it in the car," Jeremy said, indicating with his eyes the woman sitting before them. To Delores he said: "She must be a real looker."

"She is, my dear boy, she is."

"For Corey to go AWOL she'd have to be a super model," Sadie grumbled, but she let it go. She'd find out what Jeremy was up to once they were back in the cruiser.

"Are there any other questions I can answer for you? I have a lot of work to do today. I'm in charge of the children's story telling hour, and I haven't picked out a suitable book yet."

"How about *The Little Engine That Could*?" Sadie muttered and Delores looked at her curiously.

"Excuse me?"

"Nothing."

"Anything else?" Jeremy asked Sadie, and after a moment she shook her head.

"No." She reached into her pocket, produced a business card. "This is my number at the Brown County Police Station. Below it is my pager number. If Officer Lindsley contacts you will you please call me and let me know? Or, better yet, tell him to call me."

"Why, of course, dear. Anything to help." She stood, gesturing toward the door. "If you are staying on in Rhinelander for the day, there are some great places to eat. Walley's serves a wonderful pot roast and mashed potato dinner. It's just up the road."

"Thank you," Jeremy said, standing as well. He looked at his partner quizzically and she reluctantly got up. "We appreciate your time."

"The pleasure is all mine."

"Oh, one more thing," Sadie said as they were walking toward the door.

"Yes?"

"When Keely gets back from East Troy, have her call us, OK? We need to question her as soon as possible."

"I'll be happy too. She's a very nice young woman. I think you'll like her."

"I'm sure we will," Jeremy agreed. "Have a good day."

"You as well," Delores said. "Enjoy our beautiful town."

"We will," Sadie said, but somehow, she doubted it.

• • •

"What do you think?" Sadie picked at her cheeseburger, removing the pickles and putting them in the paper bag it came in. They sat parked in the lot of a fast food burger chain, eschewing Delores recommendation for something they could get on the run. They hadn't said more than a couple words since leaving the library, and those words had pertained to food.

"I think we're no closer to anything solid then when we started." Jeremy wolfed down his burger, stuffing handfuls of fries in his mouth and chasing it with a soda. Although he wasn't terribly hungry, he could always eat. His ample gut was proof of that.

"So, Corey isn't at a rock concert with a bunch of half-naked girls singing along to songs sung by guys wearing more make-up than their girlfriends?"

"Probably not," he said, "but there was no use getting into it with the librarian. She doesn't know him like we do."

"What's the plan?" Disgusted by the soggy bun, Sadie dumped the remains of her early dinner back into the bag with the discarded pickles.

"Time to head to the source, I guess."

"Now?"

"No better time than the present."

He tucked the last of his burger in his cheeks, chewed, swallowed.

"Before we go running off, shouldn't we check in with the station clerk on duty, maybe give them a head's up?

"Good idea." He grinned. "You do it, my hands are dirty."

She wiped her hands clean with a flimsy napkin and retrieved the handset of the CB. She spoke briefly with the desk jockey, telling him their whereabouts as well as receiving some information from the other end. When she was finished, she said "Ten four" and returned the handset to the cradle.

She frowned, a puzzled look on her face creasing her forehead in a manner Jeremy found quite sexy. She looked at him, caught his doe-eyed glance and her frown deepened.

"What are you looking at?"

Scrambling quickly, he said: "Don't flatter yourself, cowboy, I was looking at your horse."

"What the hell is that supposed to mean?"

"Just tell me what the clerk said, I wasn't paying attention."

"I'll give you the gist, simply because he didn't come right out and say, but Allister wants us to pay him a visit as soon as we're back in town. He says it's urgent."

"But he didn't say what it is?"

"Nope, just said it's urgent."

"OK, we'll put that on our to-do list." He crumpled his fast food bag and tossed it on the floor of the car. "You done?"

"Yeah, that's about all the deep-fried crap I need for the week."

"Then let's roll. We may still have a little daylight to work with."

"Copy that." She started the cruiser and then headed for the town line and beyond.

CHAPTER 10

THE VILLAGE OF AMBER HOLLOW

Although Sadie hadn't seen it in person, the first thing she thought of when they arrived at Amber Hollow was the town of Barneveld, which had been leveled by a tornado in the early eighties. The F5 category storm had hit unexpectedly in the middle of the night, and it was a wonder there had been so few casualties because it had completely demolished the town. Her father had been allowed access because he had connections with the police department, and he'd described it in exquisite detail that had fascinated her as young woman. Although what they were looking at wasn't the scene of a *natural* disaster, it had the same vibe: desolation, destruction, and an overall sense of despair. One glaring omission the Amber Hollow death toll hadn't included was the animals, the companion pets and livestock. Thinking of that made Sadie's heart sick.

There was a blockade set up at the town line, and a bored looking sheriff's deputy regarded them warily when they pulled up.

"Town's closed," he said. "No one can enter without proper clearance."

Jeremy flashed his badge. "Brown County Sheriff's Department, Homicide Division," he said. "We're in charge of the case."

The patrolman looked at their badges, nodded and then took out his walkie-talkie. "I have to call the Sherriff. No one goes in without him knowing."

"Let him know," Jeremy instructed, and the other called it in. After a moment he walked over to one of the barricades, pulled it aside.

"You can go in, but he wants to meet you."

"Have him find us when he gets here," Sadie said, looking at his name on his uniform. "Thank you, Deputy Sanders."

She pulled the car forward. The tires squelched over charred, broken concrete and glass, as well as the usual (and unusual) detritus that accompanied a catastrophic disaster.

"I suppose clearing the rubble is the least of the Crandon police department's worries at this point," Jeremy observed as Sadie nosed the car slowly up the main road that led into the village.

"Assisting our guys with body removal is the top priority."

"Not many bodies to remove."

"Nope."

"I wonder where the clean-up crew is?"

"Knocked off for the day, I suspect. It is after five on a Saturday."

Jeremy glanced at his watch, saw it was six-forty-five. All things considered, they'd made pretty good time.

The early evening sky was littered with thick cumulonimbus clouds, allowing the sunshine to pour through like random spotlights. A beam of light shone down on the village square, the place where all the town folk had allegedly been gathered when the disaster happened. Sadie stopped the cruiser, put it in park. They were quiet for a moment, staring in amazement at the destruction before them. The fire had decimated the township, literally gutted it. What remained was charred ruins. Various items stood out among all the debris: a stop sign that had been mostly singed but still stood at a drunken angle, the metal pole melted. A shop sign lay on the ground like a wounded soldier, announcing CLEARANCE PRICES ALL DAY EVERY DAY framed in soot. The buildings were all gone, the only thing left of them was the foundations over the basements, which were filled with the structures that had once sat atop them.

It truly was a dreadful sight to behold, utterly gut-wrenching. The fire had ravaged most of the business district before the firemen had even arrived; there had been no chance of saving anything.

"Do you think they were trying to put out the fire? Do you suppose that's why there are only five survivors?" Sadie said.

"Maybe," Jeremy said, but without much conviction. "By the time the rescue crews arrived all but the five survivors were dead."

"What are we looking for?" Sadie asked, and for a long moment her partner was silent. What *were* they looking for, exactly? How would this help their investigation if the arson and forensic teams had yet to make any significant finds?

"I suppose we'll know when we find it," he answered at last, opening his car door. "Shall we take a walk?"

"What about the sheriff?"

"I'm sure he'll find us when he gets here. There isn't a whole lot to see."

"OK." Sadie switched off the ignition and opened her door, stepped out into the waning sunlight. At once a cloud covered the sun, and a chill swept through her. In the distance, she heard the baying of what could either be a wolf or a coyote, although she wasn't certain that either were native to this part of Wisconsin. She tracked people, not animals, so her knowledge on the matter was a bit limited. "You hear that?"

"What?"

She shook her head. "Nothing."

And they proceeded deeper into Amber Hollow.

• • •

As they walked through the barren wasteland that used to be a scenic, colonial village, neither one of them could get over the absolute devastation before them. The term ghost town certainly could have applied, if it was still a town. But this was just ruins, the aftermath of such destruction that it was like a giant pile of ashes and burned rubble had dropped from the sky and littered what had once been a corn field, if it had been sown with broken concrete. They walked from the village square deeper into the residential area, a walk that didn't take long, given the diminutive size of the settlement. The structures here were partially intact—unlike the downtown area which had been completely destroyed—allowing them to appreciate their architectural design, and they were surprised to see how old the dwellings were. They weren't just turn-of-the-century old, they looked more like relics from a fairy tale.

"Man, this is creepy," Jeremy said, and Sadie nodded. Since they'd left the village square, she'd had the feeling they were being watched, and the feeling was strong. She wanted to ask Jeremy if he felt it too, but she figured if he did, he would say. He wasn't shy about anything, and if something was tripping his meter, he'd spill it.

Jeremy walked up to the remains of a home, a structure that looked more like a log cabin than a house.

"This reminds me of Heritage Hill," Sadie said, and Jeremy nodded. It certainly did seem like the quaint little old-time village in Allouez where people in period dress pretended to churn butter and milk cows, some fat oaf (ostensibly the town drunk) locked in shackles, hoping no one took it in their mind to creep up behind them and mete out their own form of crude justice. Meanwhile, a man pretending to be a doctor explained how if the leeches didn't cure you of your ails, the bloodletting device would. Jeremy loved the place, and he visited it at least once a year.

"It's a wonder they had electricity, TV even," he said.

"Yes, it is." The thought that the villagers may have practiced a religion that eschewed modern comforts struck Sadie yet again, and maybe it had something to do with the wonky stories they'd had to sit through. Something had definitely been afoot here in Amber Hollow but trying to find it in this mess was going to be like finding Waldo in a sea of clones.

Sadie stepped closer to the remnants of the house and then reached out and placed one hand on a scorched wooden beam, for what reason she wasn't sure. At once she felt the wood pulse like a living thing, and she pulled her hand away in surprise, uttering a small cry.

"What?" Jeremy said, and she shook her head.

"I don't know," she replied, her face an ashen gray.

The clouds grew thicker above them, and the occasional beams of sunlight disappeared. Very quickly, the sky turned a leaden color, and a brisk breeze whisked up, driving swirling piles of ashes around in a frenzy. Thunder erupted with such a crash that they both started, clutching one another fearfully. It was followed by a bolt of lightning that sizzled as it streaked through the air, and the smell of cordite was strong. Drops of rain began to fall, slowly at first and then increasingly heavy, becoming a near white out.

"Come on," Jeremy said, taking Sadie's hand, and he led her into the shell of the house, entering through the fire-ravaged door and into darkness. They both stumbled over the doorstep, nearly falling, the clamor from the storm deafening. However, once inside, the noise vanished, as if they were entering a soundproof chamber, and the stillness was unsettling. In the near total darkness, Sadie saw a flickering spark reflect within Jeremy's eyes, and he in turn saw the same inside hers, and then blackness overtook the light, washing over them like foul water.

"Jeremy?" Sadie called, and to her partner, it sounded like her voice came from far away.

"Sadie!" he hollered back, but the word was ripped from his mouth as if it was wrenched out by a giant fishing hook, and then there was the sense of falling, as if a trap door had opened beneath him, and consciousness left him then.

• • •

The first things that Sadie registered were whispered voices overlapping one another and swirling around like mist in a strong breeze, that and the scent of the air around her. She smelled wood smoke and cooking meat; she detected the aroma of pine trees and fragrant flowers. The air seemed to throb, to physically direct her, and as she regained her vision from the terrifying blackness, the sounds of chirping birds and buzzing insects arose, and within the tantalizing effects of all of these scents and sounds she sensed a disconnected feeling she couldn't place, a sensation that her mind and body had separated; she was conscious, but she had no control over her movements.

"Here now, young lass!" a strident voice chastised her. "Quit your day dreaming and finish your chores! We have much to do tonight after supper! 'Tis the Bastille celebration and we'll not be caught unprepared!"

"What?" Sadie said, her eyes lifting from the dirt canopy of the forest floor to behold the sight of an angry old woman before her. She wore clothing that looked like a costume circa the seventeen hundreds, and her hair hung in damp, ugly strands, framing a face that was smudged with mud. Her eyes shone irately above round cheeks, her mouth curved in a sneer. In her gnarled, arthritic hands she clutched a crude broomstick.

"You dasn't back talk me girl, or I'll see to it you spend the evening cleaning the animal pens," the elderly woman said, and Sadie had no reason to doubt her.

"Sorry," she muttered, her mind spinning frantically, trying to grasp the reality of what was happening to her, but was unable to comprehend how this could be tangible.

"I'll show you sorry!" the woman shrieked, raising the broom over her head and preparing to strike her with it when another voice cut through the air like an arrow.

"Leave the young lass alone!" someone said, and Sadie turned her head to get a glimpse of her savior and saw that it was a handsome young man. He sat atop a horse, and his clothing were finer than the rags that she and the woman wore; indeed, they appeared to be of royal quality. "Drop the broom and back away, old crone!"

The woman swore under her breath and spat on the ground, but she did as she was told.

"Ye can't tell me how to discipline my own blood, my Lord," she said, leaning the broom in the crook of a tree. "She needs to know her place if only to grow-up to be a proper lady."

"She'll become one without the stinging kiss of the lash," he countered, clicking his tongue, regarding the old woman with a jaundiced eye. He leaned toward Sadie, holding out his hand.

"Come with me," he invited. "We'll take a gallop through the fields."

Sadie couldn't help herself, she saw her hand lift from her side to take his. His large, gloved hand enveloped hers, and with such strength that she couldn't fathom she was whisked off of her feet and onto the back of the horse. He dug his heels into the mare's sides, uttering a small yip of encouragement, and the animal leapt forward.

"Ye can't keep her from her chores forever, my Lord!" the appropriately labeled crone called after them. "Mark my words!"

Her voice soon disappeared behind them as the horse trotted away, Sadie clinging to the man tightly as they picked up speed. He smelled of tobacco smoke and lavender, and his back and shoulders were muscled from years of heavy toil.

"I'll take you to my special place," he said, grinning at her over his shoulder, and she smiled in return, his voice comforting her, a feeling of security emanating from him like a heady cologne. She rested her head against his back and closed her eyes, tranquility settling over her as they rode away from the terrible old lady and her broom.

• • •

The first sensation Jeremy was aware of was of moving very fast, the second was small hands wrapped around his waist, clutching him tightly. He heard the steady clop-clop-clop of what had to be horse hooves, and as he breathed deep, he felt the air pass over him in aromatic waves, inviting and pleasant. He next realized his hands were covered in heavy leather gloves, these holding the reins that led to the neck and mouth piece of the horse he was atop of. Glancing behind him, he saw he was transporting a young girl, one who appeared to be no more than ten or eleven years old. Her head was resting against his back, and he felt a rush of pleasure shoot through him, one he found familiar but confusing at the same time. Surely she was much too young for him to have these sorts of feelings, but the body his mind was trapped within insisted otherwise, and he felt his turgid member pressing urgently against his pants, throbbing with the motion of the horse's stride. But it wasn't sexual lust he felt, no, it was something darker. It felt violent, an unappealing appetite for something beyond carnal, in its stead was something ultimately more sinister.

Going through motions he had no control over, he watched as he led the horse through a sunlight dappled prairie and then into a dense tangle of woods. When they came upon another clearing, he pulled on the reins, bringing the horse to a halt.

"Come, young lass," he said, the words erupting from his lips upon their own accord. "We shall take a walk."

The young girl looked at him sweetly, her green eyes like liquid jewels, her fine red hair fairly shimmering in the late afternoon sunshine. The urgency from his trousers overwhelmed him, and he felt his heart beat faster, his hands trembling ever so slightly.

"Whatever my Lord desires," she said in a voice as silky as churned butter, and after he was upon the ground, he took her in both hands, helping her down. Her hand clutched his tightly as he led her deeper into the woods, and he sensed more than he actually knew what he was going to do, whether he wanted to or not. This feeling, this free-floating awareness was completely beyond him; he could only watch as he went through the motions this body (in whatever temporal vortex he was caught within) was commanding him to do. He took her to a large overturned tree, sat down and then invited her to sit next to him. She did so, and when she smiled he admired the light spattering of freckles that dotted her milky white cheeks.

"You are content with your lot in life, are you not?"

"Yes, my Lord," she replied sweetly, and he nodded approvingly.

"I daresay that is indeed what I thought," the lips on this foreign face said, and as they left his mouth Jeremy felt a ponderous dread streak through him like the clamoring of an enormous bell. "However, you are an abomination, and this charade has gone on far too long."

And then he shoved her cruelly to the ground, and the look of trust and complacency left the girl's eyes at once. She stiffened, tried to creep away on all fours from him.

"I...I don't understand..." she said, and he felt coldness rise up within him, a sense of power that would not be denied. He knew it was time, long past actually, to do what he was compelled to do.

"It is time for me to finish this," he gushed in a hot whisper, flinging himself upon her where she lay, and that was when she started to struggle harder, tried to pull away from him, making mewling noises like a pig before slaughter. Anger coursed through him, a fiery bolt of righteousness that he would do what he came here to do and everything else be damned. He shook her and then spat in her face.

"You'll lie still, wench! You're only making this harder for yourself!"

"No, please," she gasped. "You're hurting me!"

He slapped her with such force her head rocked on her fragile shoulders.

"You be a good lass and silence those screams," he said, and just as he was wrapping his glove-clad hands upon her throat he heard something, some shrill noise coming from far away, and his vision began to swim as if his eyes were full of tears, and he felt a sensation of being picked up by a hurricane force gale and being flung into the outer reaches of the sky.

· · ·

Sadie fought against her savior turned captor, his gloved hands seeking her throat. She understood she was too young and small to stop him, that he was going to do what he intended whether she liked it or not. His breath was hot against her face as his hands took hold of her neck, and when they clamped down like steel bands, her heart beat calamitously in her frail chest. She struggled, but he was much too strong. Her breathing grew labored, the fear within her total, and when his grip loosened momentarily, she opened her mouth and issued a cry that was nearly overpowering. It shook her with its force, and suddenly the reality around her began to change, to undulate, and she felt the opposite of what she'd felt before, that sense of falling was now an impression of being picked up by a giant hand and being forced into the heavy air of the night sky.

Then emptiness, and nothing more.

CHAPTER 11

SHERIFF CARTER CONROY

The sound was like an air raid alert, its piercing blast an urgent call to arms, and it was this sound that broke the spell that held Sadie and Jeremy in its grasp. It whooped and twanged, and as consciousness returned to the detectives, they both recognized it for what it really was: the siren of a police car.

Jeremy could make out motes of sunlight penetrating the holes in the roof above them, could see Sadie getting to her feet from where she had apparently fallen. He reached for her, took her hand in his own, and at first, she cringed, trying to draw away from him until he spoke her name.

"Jeremy?" she said, and there was a palpable note of fear in her voice.

"Yes, it's me. Let me help you."

Once she was on her feet, she looked around them, the look on her face a disoriented mixture of anxiety and relief.

"What…what happened?"

"I don't know, but let's get out of here, huh? This place is giving me a first-class case of the willies."

They stepped out into the fading light of a brilliant sunset, and that was when they saw the police cruiser approaching. There was no evidence that there had been any rain; undeniably everything was dry, hardly a ruffle in the air from a light summer breeze. The police car drove up slowly, and when the driver saw them, he cut the siren but left the flashers on. He stopped, put it in park and got out.

"Detectives LeFevre and Conrad, I presume?" a police officer said amiably, and as quickly as the two could gather themselves, they nodded.

"Are you the sheriff of Crandon?" Sadie said, and the man nodded, extended his hand.

"Sheriff Carter Conroy at your service." They shook hands, first Sadie and then Jeremy while the other appraised them thoughtfully, a smile upon his lips. "You two look like you've seen a ghost," he said, and to Sadie's ear there was no real surprise in his voice. "Taking the grand tour, hmm?" He gazed around at the ramshackle homes, eyeing the one from which they'd emerged. "I been looking for you for about twenty minutes. I put on the siren to flush you out."

"It worked," Jeremy said, his mind struggling to recall what it was that had just occurred to him and his partner, but it was rapidly slipping away, like the last vestige of a dream you have just before waking. He glanced at Sadie, saw a similar look of bewilderment on her face as well. "We, um…we were doing some investigating."

"Find anything interesting?" This asked with genuine curiosity, his eyes darting back and forth from Jeremy's to Sadie's. Jeremy shrugged, apparently not ready to share anything with a total stranger, so Sadie felt compelled to reply.

"We…we don't know…" she said, and this response perplexed her as much as it did her partner. She wasn't the type to be uncertain about things. In her world, all questions could be summed up with a yes or no answer, no matter what the circumstances. Yet, the more she thought about it, the less it made sense. What *had* happened? The more time went by, the further it slipped away, leaving her with only the fleeting realization that an event had truly occurred, but what it was, well, that was disappearing off into the strata and beyond. She looked at Jeremy to see if there was anything he could offer, but the look on his face mirrored hers, and it was with dawning regret that she understood that whatever had happened, it was lost to them now.

"You'd be surprised how often I hear that," Sheriff Conroy said. "Well, heard it, I suppose."

"What do you mean?" Sadie said, casting a glance behind her at the house, which appeared to glare back at her, the broken front windows angry eyes, the crooked, rotting door a sneering mouth.

"You two could probably use a cup of coffee." He looked up at the ever-darkening sky, grimaced for the first time. He actually looked as if he felt uneasy about the oncoming night. "Why don't you come down to the station with me, have a cup and talk about a few things."

"We're looking for a missing officer," Jeremy felt obliged to explain. "He went to Rhinelander yesterday to do some research and we haven't heard from him since. We figured we'd come out here, have a look around."

"I'd be lying if I said I'd never heard that one either." He took off his hat, mopped his brow with a handkerchief that had seen better days. "Hop in, huh? I'll give you a ride back to your car."

Jeremy and Sadie nodded gratefully, even though it couldn't have been more than a quarter of a mile away. Right now, they wanted to get as far away from this place as they could.

The three of them got into the car, the sheriff politely holding the door for his two guests, and then drove back to the village square.

• • •

"As long as I've lived here, there have always been strange things happening in or around Amber Hollow," Sheriff Conroy said, pouring them coffee and settling back behind his desk. He put his feet up, took off his hat, eyeing them thoughtfully. "I'll bet, before all this, you'd never even heard of the place."

"You got us there," Sadie said, sipping her joe, appreciating the warmth from the cup. She couldn't help it, she was still shivering slightly from their encounter, even though it was all a distant blur now. "I've never heard of Crandon either."

The sheriff nodded, expecting that. The sixty-mile drive from the Hollow to Crandon had passed by quickly for him, but he was certain that it had seemed a lot longer to his newfound friends, especially after their encounter in the decrepit little village.

"I was born in Rhinelander, grew up there, and as long as I can remember there were always weird stories coming from out of the Hollow, well, from the neighboring communities anyway. When I went into law enforcement, I pictured myself working in Green Bay, maybe even Milwaukee, but when there was an opening in Crandon, I jumped at it because I had me a young wife pregnant with a child who would turn out to be my first-born son. The thought of dodging gangbanger bullets suddenly didn't seem like that much fun to me."

"I can understand that." Sadie had never wanted to have anything to do with Milwaukee, in fact, was overjoyed that she was able to rise within the ranks in Green Bay. The differences between the two port towns was night and day. While Milwaukee had local chapters of the Crips and Bloods shooting up neighborhoods with unhinged abandon, the majority of the crimes that the Brown County Swat Team dealt with were for domestic disturbances. When the Packers lost at home to a divisional rival (or on any major holiday), some addled paper mill worker (or slaughterhouse, tannery, warehouse laborer, etc.) would go bonkers and take his family hostage with a hunting rifle or buck knife, almost always with non-lethal results. Most times, he or she (mostly "he") could be talked out without too much fuss, but obviously there were some exceptions. Overall, though, Green Bay was the safer place to put your neck on the line, given that the yearly average murder rate was between four to six people.

"I got to be honest with you: I ain't exactly surprised that something of this nature happened, and judging by how you two looked when I found you, you must have seen something while you were there."

His candor was refreshing, although neither Jeremy nor Sadie could exactly confirm nor deny his assumption. Whatever it was they had witnessed, it had completely slipped away from both of them. All either of them could now recall was the weather turning sour and seeking shelter in a house that had given them a scare.

At length, Jeremy spoke, fielding the question for both of them. "Something did happen," he said, "although neither one of us can remember what it was."

"Again, doesn't surprise me, given the reputation of that place and all the strange things that have happened over the years."

"Were they Amish, or some kind of religion that forbid them modern comforts?"

"Nope, they had cable TV and all the accoutrements of a modern society, but I know what you mean. Looking at those houses, you'd think they was living in *Little House on The Prairie* times."

"What about the story of the goldmine?" Sadie asked, genuinely curious. That right there had to be one of the biggest cock and bull stories regarding the town.

"This is going to come as a surprise, but that story is actually true. Don't ask me how, because it's a geographical impossibility, but I've seen it myself."

"There is actually a prosperous goldmine that kept the village financially secure all these years?"

"As incredible as it seems, yes. Again, don't ask me how, I'm not an expert on such things, but if one were so inclined, they used to offer guided tours."

"Why, I wonder?"

"That question is worth all the money in the big sweepstakes jackpot, but if I was to hazard a guess, I'd say it's because they didn't want anyone to dig around in their business. Claiming to be self-sustaining is one thing, proving it is another. I'd say it was to keep people satisfied enough to refrain from prying any further into their business."

"But why?" Sadie was trying hard, but she simply couldn't get a handle on this assumption. "Why would they care?"

"People generally care when they have something to hide. A village like Amber Hollow, I suspect there was some doozy of a reason. Given the outcome, wouldn't you agree with that?"

Neither Sadie nor Jeremy could deny such simple logic. It did indeed make the most sense.

"So, what were they hiding?"

Sheriff Conroy laughed. "Why, you figure that out and you've solved the case." He eyed them inquisitively. "And if you could remember what it was that raised your dander, you might be one step closer to finding out what it was."

Jeremy smiled. This small-town sheriff and his irrefutable lucidity was a welcome breath of fresh air.

"Yes, I suppose you're right about that one." He looked at Sadie. "Is there anything you'd like to add?"

"We still have a missing person, and no leads as to where he's gone." She studied the sheriff for a moment and then blurted: "Is there any reason we should be suspicious of the head librarian at the Rhinelander Library?"

The sheriff laughed again, a wheezing bark that suggested a fondness for unfiltered cigarettes. "Delores? I don't see why. She's been the chief historian regarding matters of the unusual in Amber Hollow since I was a little boy. If anything, she'd be the best source to help you."

"Do you know anything about the other librarians? Possibly a young woman named Keely?"

"Hmm, never met her. I guess she might be new. Can't say either way."

"OK." Jeremy drained the last of his coffee and then stood. "Thank you for all of your help sheriff. I suppose we should be on our way. We have a bit of a drive ahead of us."

"Heading back to the big city tonight, huh?"

"I suppose so. There's nothing more we can do here."

The sheriff stood, offered his hand one more time. "Well, drive safe, and if you need anything you just give me a holler."

"Will do, thanks," Sadie said, and they exited the station and out into the ever-darkening night.

• • •

Neither said very much on the drive back to Green Bay, both of them lost in their own thoughts. Sadie struggled to recall what had frightened her, as did her partner, but neither of them could remember anything from when they entered the house.

"Maybe there was a gas leak," Sadie exclaimed, her voice startling Jeremy after a lengthy silence.

"A gas leak?"

"That would explain why we became disoriented, why we can't remember anything."

Jeremy pondered this for a moment, chewing on his bottom lip distractedly. "Maybe," he said.

"Do you think it's a possibility?"

He looked at Sadie in the darkness of the car, the stars above offering very little light. She looked beautiful in the dimness, and as before something stirred within him.

"Yes, it could be. And if there *is* a gas leak, the best thing would be for someone to find it. A stray match tossed by a deputy and the place would blow sky high." He smiled at her appreciatively. "You might be on to something. We might actually have a lead."

"I'll call Sheriff Conroy in the morning," Sadie said, blushing slightly. The way he was looking at her made her feel vulnerable, like there was more between them than just being co-workers. Something in his expression, as if he were appraising her with lover's eyes. She looked away, training her gaze on the road, not quite sure how she felt about that.

"And don't forget, we need to talk to Allister first thing too." Jeremy said, looking away from her and out his window. "Whatever he wants to tell us, he didn't trust to the desk clerk. It might be pretty good."

"We can only hope," Sadie said, and they drove the rest of the way not talking, just the sound of the tires on the pavement below them.

CHAPTER 12

SUNDAY, JULY 21

The cold air in the morgue was a pleasant departure from the summer's characteristic humidity, but that was about the only thing one could consider pleasant when visiting Allister, well, that and his dry wit and charm. Sadie supposed that had to make up for the rest of the experience, especially with this case.

"Good morning, Allister," Jeremy said, approaching the coroner where he stood over a table frowning. "You have news that might help?"

"No," the other replied, shaking his head. "I have news that is going to perplex you, more than anything. Me, I'm flummoxed."

"What is it?" Sadie asked, and he gestured to the table. At first glance she didn't know what she was looking at, as there wasn't much to see.

"What does it look like?"

Jeremy studied the debris that sat atop the autopsy table. "Did the janitor decide to use one of your tables to empty his dust pan?"

Allister sighed. "Nope. What you are looking at is the body of one of the victims of the Amber Hollow fire."

Sadie and Jeremy assessed the remains on the table with more interest this time, only it was simply too confusing. Jeremy shrugged. "It's just dust."

"Yep, that was my initial evaluation of it too."

"So, what is it?"

"I took a sample and after a thorough examination I've discovered it is in fact the remains of a human being."

"That's impossible," Jeremy said, feeling as if Allister was having some cruel fun at their expense. "Did one of your assistants put it in the incinerator?"

"Would you like to see the forensic report, or should I just tell you?"

"Please," Jeremy said, "just tell us what we're looking at."

"OK, according to my findings, these are the remains of a body I just examined on Thursday, and in less than two days it turned into the pile of dust you see." He waited for the inevitable questions, but when they said nothing he continued. "Sending it to the lab for a second-hand verification confirmed what I already knew to be true, but they also carbon dated it."

"And?"

"It's over two hundred years old."

Both Sadie and Jeremy stared at him blankly, unable to come up with a suitable reply. What he was saying wasn't possible, it couldn't be.

"Yes, I know you're thinking what I was thinking, so let me show you the other bodies. This might convince you."

He walked over to another table, pulled back a sheet and showed them another pile of dust, although this one had bone fragments in it. They were partials, none of them whole, but clearly bones. He waved his hands like a magician over the remains before dropping the covering. He then walked to another table, pulled back the sheet, and there was a larger pile still, this one with the visible features of a person, but instead of the usual putrefaction it was charred, ashen. Sadie wasn't sure she wanted to see the last one, but when he walked to the table and pulled back the covering, she didn't look away. This body was still wholly intact, but it was actually disintegrating as they looked on, as if they were watching a time lapse video. The flesh was melting, becoming liquid that then turned into dust. The detectives stood there, their mouths agape, witnessing something that in their collective experience they couldn't even begin to explain.

"How is this happening?" Jeremy watched as the flesh ran in little pools that flowed like tiny tributaries away from the mound of flesh. Black smoke arose from the pools, thick and acrid, before burning into ash.

"If I could tell you that I'd probably win a Nobel Prize," Allister said, covering the body. He scrubbed his face with the back of one liver-spotted hand. "I have no idea what is going on, but you better get one of those survivors to start telling you the truth." He shot them a sour look, one that suggested he was exhausted. "You want to know the strangest thing? The bodies are disintegrating in the order that I autopsied them. This was the last one," he said, pointing at the table. "I watched two of the other bodies do the same thing this morning."

"And you're telling us that the forensic report dated the remains as being two hundred years old?" Sadie said, and the coroner's scowl deepened.

"*Over* two hundred years old," Allister corrected. "As much as this seems like an impossibility, those are the facts."

Sadie wanted to repeat what her partner said and say this was impossible, but she refrained. Her mind then turned to the episode she and Jeremy experienced the day before, and a feeling of incredulity filled her, that and a persistent surge of dread, of what, she had no idea.

"We were thinking that maybe there was a gas leak in the village, that perhaps that had something to do with the fire," she said, addressing Allister before briefly appraising Jeremy. "I think we can officially disregard that theory."

"Yeah, I guess we can," Jeremy said. "I think what we should do is take blood samples from the survivors, see if there is anything we can determine from that. Is it possible that this has something to do with a contagion and we're not looking in the right direction?"

The coroner grinned. "Now you're thinking like a pathologist. I better watch out, you might come gunning for my job."

"Not on your life—" Jeremy was saying when his pager beeped. He removed it from his belt, glanced at the number. "May I use your phone?"

"By all means."

He walked to the phone on the wall behind the coroner, picked it up and punched in the number.

"This is Detective LeFevre." He listened, the expression on his face changing from casual to all-business. "We're on our way." He hung up. "We have to go." He nodded to the coroner. "Thank you, Allister, keep us posted on anything else you find."

"Will do."

"What's going on?" Sadie asked, but he gently took her by the arm, leading her toward the door.

"I'll tell you on the way," he said, and she knew that whatever it was, she wasn't going to like it. She was right.

• • •

The FBI agents were waiting for them in their office, and by the looks of it they were making themselves right at home. One of them was sitting in Jeremy's chair, his feet on the desk, while the other was going through their files, letting them form a sloppy pile as he discarded them indiscriminately on Sadie's desk.

"Can we help you gentlemen?" Jeremy said, trying but failing to keep a note of impatience out of his voice. Their presence was an intrusion, one he and Sadie didn't need. He didn't believe for a second they could possibly help; they would only impede their efforts while the unusual "clues" piled up. He mentally dared them to prove him wrong.

"Of course," the agent sitting behind his desk said. He made no effort to stand, nor extend his hand. "Agent Reginald Skelly, at your service." He nodded at the man going through the files. "That's Agent Trevor McAvoy."

"'Sup," the other said, barely casting a look in their direction, and Sadie felt a vein throb in her forehead. She opened her mouth to say something about their apparent lack of manners when she felt Jeremy's hand close over her bicep, his fingers locking strongly around her meaty arm. She knew with that gesture that he wished her to be silent, so she held her tongue.

"You boys are early," Jeremy ventured, his hand remaining locked on his partners arm.

"Ah, what the heck," Skelly said. "Since you two don't have any useful leads, we figured the sooner we got here, the better. We got supervisors breathing down our necks wanting to know what, exactly, is going on up here." He fixed Jeremy with a snide grin. "You *don't* know what's going on, do you?"

Jeremy felt his bile curl, could feel his arms tensing, longing to punch the agent in his sneering face, but he took a deep breath, accepted who he was dealing with, and shook his head.

"No, sir, I do not."

"And your partner?"

"She doesn't."

"Can't she talk?"

"Yes, sir."

"Then let me hear it from her."

"No, sir, we do not," Sadie said, understanding that she should accept this with humility, like a passive Hindu allowing a sacred cow to pass by unfettered, but right now she wanted nothing more than to claw out their freaking eyeballs with her nails and use them for a spirited game of Ping-Pong.

"That's why we're here," Skelly said with a gruff laugh. "The cavalry has arrived to vanquish the Indians!"

Personally, Sadie didn't like his choice of words. Although she was certain the FBI agents were unaware, the Oneida Indian Reservation was a part of their jurisdiction, and the local sentiment wasn't on the Indians' side. The citizens of Green Bay still made cruel jokes about the Indians and their intolerance to "firewater," among other things. Unfortunately, the cops saw a lot of activity at the White Eagle (the Oneida Indians local watering hole) on Fridays and Saturdays, so it was hard to make a case for their sobriety, but still…

"What's on your agenda?" Jeremy asked as civilly as he could muster, and the other regarded him idly.

"We'll start by doing successfully what you two botched: taking correct statements from the survivors."

"Yeah? Have at it then."

"We will." The agent stood, the expression on his face revealing his distaste at Jeremy's apparent insubordination. "But first we'll need all of the files pertaining to this case, as well as any notes disclosing relevant information."

It was, at last, Jeremy's turn to make the others feel like something the cat dragged in.

"Just how up to speed on everything are you?" he said, thinking of the experience he and Sadie just had in Amber Hollow, the conversation they'd had with the sheriff of Crandon, and the fact that all the corpses in the morgue had recently turned (or were turning) into dust. Not to mention that forensics dated the dust as being over two hundred years old. In Jeremy's humble opinion, he didn't think these two dipshits would find jack, not with both hands, a flashlight and a video tutorial.

"Trust me," Agent Skelly said, "as soon as we see the files, we'll be light years ahead of you two."

"If you say so." Jeremy turned to Sadie. "Hand over everything we've compiled on this case to the two agents, Detective Conrad." One of his eyes twitched visibly as he said it, but only Sadie caught on.

"Yes sir, can do." She replied, moving forward into the cramped room and absently taking a couple of files from the pile on her desk. She didn't attempt to hand them to either agent, instead she dropped them on the floor. "Happy hunting," she said before swiveling on one heel and departing. Jeremy watched her go, feeling a swell of pride.

"You heard the lady: have fun." Jeremy winked at Skelly and followed Sadie out of the office, successfully refraining from laughing as he did so.

• • •

"How can they come here and just take over?" Sadie clutched her beer so firmly that Jeremy was afraid she was going to break the bottle. He wanted to console her, but he knew that it was out of their hands. Federal jurisdiction took precedence over local investigations every time.

"Because they can," he said, sipping his scotch, and possibly to sound poignant, he repeated himself: "because they can."

"Well, I think it's a bunch of crap! Those arrogant bastards don't know what they're up against!"

"No, they don't," Jeremy said, his voice calm, quiet, trying to get her to follow suit. The bar they were sitting in on Broadway didn't currently have a lot of patrons, since it was just before noon (actually kind of suprising for a Sunday), but still he didn't want anyone to get the impression that they didn't have everything totally under control. "And they'll run into all the problems we did and then some."

"So, what do we do?"

"As far as I'm concerned, we're doing it."

"Drinking on the job?"

"Precisely." He took another belt of scotch. Man, but that was smooth.

Sadie took a drink of her beer and then set the bottle down. She wiped her mouth with the back of one hand, a dainty gesture that didn't go unnoticed by her partner, and examined him with eyes that fairly gleamed with exhaustion, exasperation, and fear.

"What *are* we up against, Jeremy?" she whispered, her voice cracking slightly with the weight of emotion. Her eyes searched his, deep brown pools that were nearly iridescent in the diffuse lighting. "I can't even begin to decipher what happened yesterday, and now today, in the morgue…" Her voice trailed off, her confusion total but her energy spent.

"I don't know," he said, but he wished he could offer her more, desperately wished he could. Right now, they were staring down the barrel of a situation that was out of their hands, and the only thing he could think of to do was to get drunk. If the FBI guys knew where they were, they'd be laughing their asses off. Well, to hell with them and whatever they thought. Let them chase some ghosts around for a couple of days until they got sick of it and crawled back to D.C. where they belonged. If they actually stumbled upon some concrete evidence, Jeremy would personally buy both of them a drink of their choice, right before he told them to screw themselves. He took another sip of his scotch, let the liquid roll around in his mouth a second before swallowing.

"Drink up, honey. I'm getting us another round."

"Are you sure we should be doing this?" she said, but he could tell she wasn't going to turn down another beer.

"We most definitely shouldn't, but what are they going to do, fire us?"

"I'd like to see them try."

"That's the spirit." He waved at the bartender. "Two more over here, please."

The guy with the ponytail nodded and brought them more drinks, and the afternoon passed by quickly for the two detectives as one lightly flirted with the other and she pretended it irritated her when actually she didn't mind, not one bit.

CHAPTER 13

MONDAY, JULY 22

S adie and Jeremy stood before Captain Martin's desk, the two of them looking at the floor. They were both so hung over that they were wearing sunglasses, and this enraged their superior officer.

"Take those damn sunglasses off," he growled, "and sit down."

They both did as they were told, removing their sunglasses and taking a seat. Jeremy could feel his blood pressure raging from all the scotch he'd consumed, and was slightly dizzy. Sadie was embarrassed about a vomit stain on one of her boots. After eight beers, she couldn't really recount what had happened, but she was sure there were chili fries involved at some point, judging by the color of the offending substance.

"Look at me when I'm talking to you," their superior officer said, and when they did, he snorted derisive laughter. "Jeez-Louise, your eyes look like piss-holes in a snowbank! What the hell were you two thinking?"

"They undermined our authority, sir," Sadie said, trying to contain a belch but failing. At least she covered her mouth with her hand, but damn, was her breath nasty! It tasted like she'd brushed her teeth with a toilet brush, and maybe she had. She certainly wouldn't be surprised. One thing she *was* sure of, though, was that even with all of Jeremy's flirting, he'd been a gentleman. She'd awoken at her house, alone in her bed, with chili sauce all over her face. He'd called her at the crack of dawn to make sure she was all right, in fact, the ringing of the phone was what got her out of bed on time. She didn't indulge in liquor all that often, and what with the aftermath, it was no wonder why. It was a good thing Sunday was Clayton's bowling league night, as she would have had a hard time explaining this to him.

"That's your excuse?"

"It's not an excuse, sir," Jeremy said, "it's a fact. Those two blow-hards barged in here and treated us like hayseeds."

Captain Martin rolled his eyes. "Well no kidding! That's their job! Your job is to take it like men…um…" he looked briefly dis-comfited, eyeing Sadie. "Like *professionals*. And did you? No, you went and got wasted!"

"There was really nothing else for us to do, sir," Sadie said, but she knew that wasn't true. Corey was still missing; boozing it up didn't help find him, only another trip to the Rhinelander library would, where she and Jeremy could talk to their prime witness (and possible suspect), Keely whatever-the-hell-the-rest-of-her-name was. In fact, it was what they should be doing right now instead of going back and forth with the captain. What with all the time they squandered, he could be dead by now.

(dead…)

That didn't bode well with Sadie, the thought that she and Jeremy might never see Corey again, but it was an eventuality that they had to prepare themselves for.

"No, what you need to do is assist the federal agents with any and every aspect of their investigation. At the very least, you could help them find their way around town."

"I believe that's what a road map is for, sir," Jeremy said, but not impolitely. He wasn't trying to be facetious, he was just stating a fact.

"You can do one better than that and escort them wherever they need to go."

"They didn't ask for any assistance, sir," Jeremy said. "In fact, they made it quite clear that they wanted us out of the way."

"That's not what they told me," Captain Martin said, his anger gradually relenting. The two sitting before him had been a reliable team for as long as they'd been here, had never done anything but their jobs to the best of their ability and had the track record to prove it. If it came down to a matter of he said/she said, he'd believe these two in a heartbeat over two federal suits. Nonetheless, there was an investigation underway that hadn't gained any traction, so it was best to keep all the players on the same team.

"They told you they wanted our help?" Jeremy said, surprised, and the captain nodded.

"Not in so many words," he said, smiling a genuine smile at last. "Maybe they were suggesting that they wanted you to get them coffee, run out for sandwiches, that kind of thing."

"I'll be damned—" Sadie declared but was silenced by the captain's laughter.

"I'm pulling your leg, honey, cool down."

"So, what do you want us to do?" Jeremy asked, lightly massaging his temples.

"OK, I'll level with you," Captain Martin said. "They're both a couple of jerks, I get it. Those federal knuckleheads always think they're better than the local law enforcement, I've seen it many times." He gestured over his shoulder, pointed to a plaque on the wall. "I did some training at the Quantico FBI academy, in Virginia. I was one of only two people from Wisconsin picked to train there in 1985. Did either of you know that?"

Sadie and Jeremy shook their heads.

"No, I didn't think so. It was an honor, I'll tell you that, an experience of a lifetime. But I'll let you in on something: those federal boys, the ones who answer to the highest office, they don't give a ripe fart in a strong breeze about anyone who isn't in the same league as them, you get me? We may have been hand-picked to receive training at their official base, but that didn't mean they had any respect for us, our hometowns, or our families." He fixed them with a stare that was slightly perplexed. "I could never figure out what the problem was until I overheard a couple of them in the restroom. While I was copping a squat two federal boys were talking at the urinals, didn't even know I was there. They laughed at how seriously we were taking the program, how after it was all over, we'd crawl back to our little towns and all we'd have to show for it was a plaque we could frame and a photo of ourselves shaking hands with the head of the FBI." He shook his head, the memory clearly rattling him. "I'll tell you, that really chapped my hide, that they thought so little of us, and I was lucky it was near the end of my training or it would have soured what had been up until that point a great experience. Luckily enough, it was during the last week, and I made it through, got my diploma, shook hands with the director of the FBI, who was actually a really nice guy. And then it was over, I went home. After a couple weeks back on the job, back to the grind, I began to think those feds were right. I never would be a federal officer, I'd just be a big fish in a little pond. However, the more I thought about it, I realized they were essentially wrong. That training was a valuable learning tool I later applied to many facets of my job. I'm honored that I got to be a part of that, got to learn something that very few people do. And I've never had a problem being a big fish, and I love this little pond I call home. And my job? Never better. I wouldn't trade it for the world." He squinted at the two of them thoughtfully. "Do you understand what I am getting at?"

Jeremy nodded, and after a long moment Sadie did too. They may have been tucked away into a tiny little corner of the world, but it was *their* tiny corner and the people who inhabited it were just as important as anyone else, thank you very much. And in short order, the suits would dry up and blow away back to their corner of the world, and life would roll on.

"Yes, sir," Jeremy said, and Sadie echoed him.

"Good," Captain Martin said, satisfied, when a deputy stuck his head in the door, rapping lightly on the doorframe.

"Captain?"

"Yes?"

"Phone call for you on line two, sir. It's the principal from your son's school."

"For the love of God..." Captain Martin groaned. "What'd he do?"

"Um..." he said, glancing at the detectives.

"Just say it, we don't have any secrets."

"They caught him smoking marijuana, sir."

"Ah, crap." He returned his attention to Sadie and Jeremy. "So, you two know what you need to be doing, right?"

"Yes, sir," Jeremy replied, and the captain nodded.

"All right then, get out of here and do it."

"Thank you, sir," Sadie said, and they exited his office, but not before they heard their superior officer hitch an exasperated sigh and mumble "Jesus Christ" under his breath before punching a button on the phone and taking the call.

• • •

For several minutes, neither one said anything to the other. Maybe it was the ringing in their ears as their blood surged behind eyes so bloodshot that Visine was required to maintain their alleged sobriety, or maybe it was because anger is a rough mistress, and getting rid of the green-eyed monster can be harder than one could ever imagine. Whatever the case, it was finally Sadie who broke the silence, speaking quietly because her head was throbbing miserably.

"You told the captain we knew what we had to do," she said, and her partner grunted in affirmation.

"Yes, one thing we forgot about while we were nursing our wounds was Corey." He gave her a plaintive look. "We should have controlled our anger and gone back to Rhinelander to talk to that librarian, Keely."

"Yeah, I know," she said, "but we still can. Let's check in with the suits, see if they need anything, and when they blow us off, we'll take a road trip."

"In this case, I think we should just call instead."

"Why? Don't we want the element of surprise?"

"I'm afraid not," Jeremy said. "We don't have time to spare for the drive. We might be needed here."

"You really believe that?"

"No, but for the captain's sake—and our jobs—it might be better if we stuck around."

"So…?"

"One of us will get in touch with the feds, the other will call the library. You have a preference?"

"I'll call the library," Sadie said, and Jeremy grinned.

"Yeah, I thought so." He stood up and cracked his back and then sat back down and picked up his desk phone. "You know what to say?"

"Does the pope crap in the woods?" Sadie chuckled. "Do your job and I'll do mine."

"Righty-ho," Jeremy said, took a breath, and pulled the card from his inside jacket pocket of one Agent Reginald Skelly. He glanced at the number, scowled and then dialed. "If I'm lucky, they won't be near their car phone."

Sadie watched him for a moment, and when the phone was indeed answered and he addressed the caller on the other end, she picked up her phone as well. She pulled out her notepad, found the number and then dialed. It rang twice before it was answered.

"Rhinelander public library, can I help you?"

For an instant, Sadie wasn't sure who she should ask for. Did she ask for the head librarian or take a shot at requesting Keely to come to the phone? Did it matter? No, probably not. The best place to start was at the top and work her way down.

"Yes," she said at last, "may I please speak with Delores Schenker?"

"Certainly," the other person on the line, a woman, said. "May I ask who's calling?"

"Of course, this is Detective Sadie Conrad, Brown County Homicide Division."

There was a brief pause, hardly more than a couple of seconds and then the other said: "Sure, let me get her. Please hold."

The soothing strains of James Taylor's "You've got a Friend" began playing in her ear, and this caused her to glance up at her partner, who was frowning into his phone, listening to some half-assed BS from the fed on the other side, no doubt, and she smiled.

I believe I do have a friend...

She was on hold for no more than a minute when Delores got on the line.

"Hello, Detective Conrad," Delores said pleasantly, but there was a hint of reservation in her voice, something less than the congeniality that the woman had shown during their visit. Or maybe Sadie was imagining it, she couldn't immediately tell. "Can I help you?"

"I hope you can," Sadie began, wondering if the old woman suffered from early onset Alzheimer's. Surely, she couldn't have forgotten about Corey, about their investigation. "I'm calling to find out if Keely is there and, if so, may I speak with her regarding Corey Lindsley."

"Oh yes, the nice policeman that came to see me the other day. Have you heard from him?"

"Not yet, hence my call." Sadie felt a surge of irrational anger bolt through her, yet she kept calm, focused on what she had to say. "Is Keely working today?"

"Why, it's the strangest thing," Delores said, and damned if she didn't sound as if she was lying. "She hasn't shown up for work in two days, and that just isn't like her. Even though she's only been here for six months, she's as reliable as they come, even covers shifts for other librarians when they're sick. I'm starting to get worried."

Welcome to my world…

"She never came back from East Troy?"

"I don't know about that, but she hasn't been to work in two days."

"She didn't call you, tell you she was sick?"

"Nope, not a word. No one here has heard from her."

"Have you contacted the local police, filed a missing person's report?"

This time the pause on the line was so long that Sadie thought the connection had been broken, but then the elderly woman cleared her throat and coughed.

"No, no," she said, "I don't think she's missing, she just hasn't been to work."

"Has anyone tried calling her?"

"My, you certainly do have a lot of questions, don't you?" Delores said, and this remark caused Sadie to experience a brief flash of déjà vu. The way she talked, she sounded like someone else she'd spoken to recently, but for the moment she couldn't put her finger on it. "What Keely chooses to do with her time isn't my business, but if you must know I had one of the other librarians call her and leave a message on her answering machine."

"OK," Sadie said, feeling as if this conversation was going nowhere and wanting to end it as soon as possible. "When and if you hear from her, please call me right away. Will you do that for me?"

"Why, certainly, dear." Her voice was lighter now, as if relieved that Sadie was ceasing and desisting her line of questioning. "I'll be happy to call you when I speak to her again."

Sadie knew what she was going to say next was pointless, nonetheless she said it anyway: "And if you hear from Corey Lindsley—"

"I'll let you know," the elderly librarian said, cutting her off. "I have to go now, thanks for the call, have a nice day!"

And then the phone went dead in Sadie's ear. She sat there, listening to the silence until the phone began squawking it's "Receiver off the hook" sound, so she hung up. She thought about what the woman said, her tone of voice, how it reminded her of something she'd heard recently. She rubbed her temples, not so much to soothe her headache (which, thankfully, was subsiding to a dull roar) but to think, to try and remember. Who did the librarian sound like? What was it in her inflection or her words that made her think of something she'd encountered recently? She rubbed harder, trying to clear her mind of the images that would be with her forever, the woman jumping off the Tower Drive Bridge, the decimated village with its turn-of-the-century houses, the strange event that had transpired while visiting said village...

And then it came to her, in a rush, so clear that it made her suck her breath in sharply. She glanced up, saw that Jeremy was still on the phone, his face a barely controlled mask of loathing. She looked down at her desk, studying the files and notes lying there.

Delores Schenker sounded like the survivors. She sounded irritated that someone was meddling...

Could that be right? And if so, why?

Corey Lindsley disappeared after visiting her library, after flirting with a woman who knew more than she was telling. Delores could be covering for her.

Again, what did that have to do with the price of ice in Antarctica? She didn't know, but it was her job to find out. She looked up, saw that Jeremy was off the phone.

"Well?" she said, and he looked at her with eyes as murky as the Mississippi. He wore a sneer on his face like a scar, and it was only with great effort that he drew his lips back in the semblance of a grin.

"We have to meet the FBI agents. They want to talk to us."

"How are their interrogations going?"

"I suppose we're about to find out, but my money is on 'not well.'" He shut down his computer, the screen abruptly going blank. "Did you get in touch with her?"

"If by 'her' you mean the woman we want to talk to, no. But I did just speak with Delores Schenker, and according to her Keely hasn't been to work since she left to see the concert in East Troy."

"Hmm," Jeremy said thoughtfully, picking up a pencil and chewing on the eraser. "What did she say exactly?"

"Pretty much what I told you, but I'll be honest: I'm not sure if I believe her."

"What? Why?"

"There was something in her tone, I don't know...she didn't sound like she was telling the truth."

"Why would she lie?"

"You got me, but it sort of seems like she's in cahoots."

Jeremy laughed, a resounding belly laugh that took Sadie by surprise. "Did I just say something funny?"

"I guess you did, because I'm laughing."

"You don't think it's possible that she could be in on this, on Corey's disappearance?"

Jeremy's laughter subsided, and he regarded her frankly. "I suppose anything is possible, but after meeting her I honestly think she was telling the truth." He leaned back in his chair, put his feet up on the desk, closed his eyes, and hitched a giant sigh. "It's hard to tell over the phone. When we get done babysitting the Feds, we'll take another trip up there and talk to her in person. How does that sound?"

"Sounds about right."

"OK." He swung his feet off the desk, stood up. "Let's go and get this over."

CHAPTER 14

THE FEDS INVESTIGATION

Krohls' was doing pretty good business for a Monday afternoon, even with Lambeau Field mostly deserted for the summer. The restaurant sat in the shadow of the iconic football stadium, but it had been many years since the Packers had brought home the highly coveted Lombardi Trophy. In fact, they hadn't since 1967, when Vince Lombardi was the coach and Bart Star the quarterback. In Sadie's opinion, they were long overdue, but Dan Majkowski didn't seem like the quarterback that could take them all the way. What they needed was someone new, someone with an arm like a cannon and accuracy to boot, but she doubted they'd find a guy like that anytime soon.

The Feds were sitting at a booth near the front windows, and it was Jeremy's impression that the two wanted to keep the front of the place in their sights so no one could sneak up on them.

It had been Jeremy who suggested they meet at the restaurant. He figured the place's laid-back atmosphere and good food would disarm the Feds, at least subdue their blatant lack of respect for the local authority. He could be wrong, though.

"Agent Skelly, Agent McAvoy," he said as he and Sadie approached. The two were perusing menus, and they both had cold bottles of Pabst sweating on the table in front of them. Gleaning the awkwardness of the seating situation, McAvoy got up and sat down on the bench next to his partner so that Sadie and Jeremy could sit across from them. As they sat, Sadie felt a nauseous ripple in her guts just looking at the beer.

"Hey," Skelly said. "You want a beer?"

"No, thanks," Jeremy said, and Sadie shook her head. She'd had enough alcohol to last her for quite a while. "So…things not going as smoothly as you expected?"

Skelly grimaced but his partner kept a poker face, remaining noncommittal.

"You could say that, I guess." His voice was reproachful, as if, somehow, this was the fault of the two detectives. "They're all full of crap." Skelly took a swig of his beer, licked his lips. "Except the little girl, but she didn't give us much." He reached into his suit coat, produced a pack of cigarettes, tapped one out and lit up. The reek of the smoke made Sadie feel nauseous again, and she wished that it was illegal to smoke inside, however, like the Packers and their Superbowl absence, it was something she might not see in her lifetime.

"She's suffering from a head injury," Sadie said, trying but failing not to match his tone.

"What did they tell you?" Jeremy asked.

"Well, the woman—"

"Sylvia Albright," Sadie supplied, and the other nodded.

"Yeah. She gave us a load of baloney about some mobsters from Milwaukee shooting the place up and starting the fire." He took another drink of his beer, puffed grandiosely on his cigarette. "She had all the classic traits of someone who wasn't telling the truth."

Sadie and Jeremy exchanged a glance. At least the woman was consistent with her story.

"And LeCarre?"

"The guy in the bandages?"

"Yes, him."

Skelly shook his head and then tilted the bottle back and drained it in a long swallow. He belched lightly, waving his hand for the waitress to bring him another. Sadie raised an eyebrow and Jeremy nodded his head, albeit barely perceptibly.

"He's nuttier than she is," he said as a waitress approached and took the empty bottle, placing a new one in front of him. She looked at McAvoy, who was still working on his, and he shook his head. She moved on. "He told us that the mayor of the town turned them into a cult and that they were all sacrificed to Jesus." He took one last drag and crushed the smoke out in a glass ashtray.

"His words?" Jeremy asked. If so, they had an inconsistency in the telling of the tale. But the agent shook his head as he upended his second (as far as Sadie was counting) beer.

"No, he didn't say that, I'm paraphrasing."

Jeremy leaned back in the booth, unable to keep from displaying an almost triumphant grin. The all-hallowed FBI agents had achieved no more than he and his partner had, and all they had was local law enforcement training. How about those apples? he was about to say, when the other agent, McAvoy, said something that put a hold on his would-be celebration.

"The chick in the coma told us an even weirder story."

Sadie looked at him sharply. "The patient in the coma woke up? When?"

The two agents exchanged a glance before erupting in gales of snide laughter.

"She woke up just in time for her interrogation," Skelly said, tipping his bottle at his partner, who lifted his and saluted the other.

"How," Sadie said, unbelievingly, "did she do that?"

"Ve haf vays of making zem talk," Skelly said, and for one regrettable moment Jeremy felt like strangling him.

"What does that mean?" he said instead, but received no reply.

The FBI agent's laughter finally subsided, but it took some doing. In the meantime, the waitress approached, wanted to know if they were ready to order.

"I am," Sadie said, and ordered a butter burger with a side of onion rings. Jeremy ordered the same, but asked for cheese on his. The agents chose to stick with their beer, and ordered another round.

"You should try the burgers," Jeremy said, trying to be friendly even though his tone was icy. "They're a regional specialty."

Skelly affixed him with a stare that said he'd been the world over and there wasn't a burger he hadn't tried, but after a moment he relented. Possibly the beer was getting the better of him. His partner stuck to his guns, however, and refused anything but liquid sustenance.

"So," Jeremy said, after their order had been placed. "How did you get the survivor to wake up from a coma and tell you their story?"

"It was pretty simple, really," Skelly said. "Oldest trick in the book."

"Used a popper," McAvoy said, and this got the two of them laughing again.

"Amyl nitrate?" Sadie gasped, unable to comprehend something so devious.

"No, ammonium nitrate," McAvoy clarified. "A trick out of the book of Rocky."

"You used smelling salts on a coma patient, and it worked?" Jeremy said, unconvinced. "That's not only messed up, it's unethical!"

"Now, that's where you're wrong," Skelly said, shaking his head as he drank more beer. "Technically, she was faking the coma, so we don't consider what we did unscrupulous."

"How did you know she was faking?" Sadie said. "Is it possible to *fake* a coma? How the hell does someone do that?"

"You'd have to ask her, but once we held the popper under her nose long enough, she sat up and gasped for air."

"Ok, ok," Jeremy said, not wanting these two dimwits to go into a detailed explanation of such barbaric cruelty. "What did she tell you?"

"Another bogus story, that's for damn tootin'," Skelly said, and his partner nodded.

"What was it?" Sadie asked as the waitress arrived with their food. After what they'd just learned, Sadie didn't feel much like eating anymore, but after smelling the burger her stomach changed her mind for her. Greasy food on top of a hangover was just what the doctor ordered.

"You want to hear it?" McAvoy teased, and Jeremy rolled his eyes.

"Of course, we do. Tell us!"

"Don't have to," Skelly said. "She can." He pulled a tape recorder from another one of his inside jacket pockets and set it on the table. It was a new, compact model that used tiny cassettes like an answering machine. Jeremy had been meaning to get one of those. The agent pressed play, and they all stopped talking to listen.

"My head feels funny. What was that you were holding under my nose?"

Skelly: "An ammonium nitrate popper."

"What? What's that? I'm tired, I want to go back to sleep."

"Tell us what happened on the night of July fourteenth."

"Tell you what? I'm tired, leave me alone."

"Afraid we can't do that."

"Who are you?"

"We're FBI agents, ma'am, investigating what happened to the village of Amber Hollow on the night of July fourteenth."

"The FBI? Well, I can't tell you anything, I don't know what happened."

"Lying to federal agents is a felony offence, ma'am. We can arrest you if you choose not to cooperate."

A brief pause and then:

"Well, maybe I know something, but then I need to rest. This is all Andy Guntram's fault. Do you know him? Anthony Guntram?

"Is it Andy or Anthony?"

"I said Andy? I meant Anthony, that's what I said, didn't I? I'm so tired. I can only talk for a little bit and then I need to rest…"

"Tell us what you know, and we'll let you go back to sleep."

"OK, I suppose I can do that…We've always been a very private community, didn't have much use for outsiders. We were lucky that we had a prosperous goldmine. It kept us afloat when there were droughts…Now, we've long kept the outside world from getting to us, and we had good reason for it. You want to know why? Sure, you do. But you can't go and tell everybody I said this. And before I do, I have to know…am I the only one?"

"Excuse me?"

"You know, am I the only one who survived? Is there anyone left?"

"We can't discuss that with you ma'am. Please, just answer the questions."

"Why not?"

"Just tell us what you know, and we'll leave you alone."

"All right…We were a secret society, you know, like the Illuminati? We had ties that went back centuries to very famous and powerful people. It was how our village was founded. Was what funded us. We sailed here on a magnificent ship, stocked with everything we'd need to make the journey…our ancestors, I mean, not actually us…"

The confusion in the woman's voice was evident, the fear and uncertainty, and it was only with a very concentrated will of effort that Sadie didn't punch these two laughing jack-asses in the kisser apiece. How was that for awful, using smelling salts on a woman in a coma? Of course, if the popper did wake her up, she wasn't really in a coma…the logistics of the situation didn't make much sense as it stood, and only a doctor's explanation would make this right for her, but in the present moment, listening to this woman speak was painful, the ridiculous story putting the whole thing right over the edge. However, she was intrigued that all the survivors thought to ask that particular question, of whether or not they were the only survivor of the tragedy. All of them except for the little girl, that is. She hadn't asked them any questions, just stated the facts of what she knew before she'd become upset and needed to rest.

"We were related to royalty, French royalty. We had connections to Napoléon, the Marquise De Sade, even King Henry VIII. There was no one in power that we weren't connected to in some way. Did I tell you this was Andy's fault? I mean, Anthony, it was all Anthony's fault—"

Sadie reached over and turned off the tape recorder. "I can't listen to this."

Jeremy looked at her, the perplexed expression on his face almost comical, but when she returned his stare and he saw the hollow look in her eyes he understood.

"Besides this absurd story," he said to the FBI agents, "did she give you any real information?"

"This is evidence!" Skelly said, his tone half reproachful, half mocking. "What, your partner doesn't have the stomach for this?"

"We've listened to their crazy stories," Jeremy said, feeling the muscles in his arms tense up as his blood boiled. "We know they're all full of crap, and there has to be an underlying reason for it. We don't need to sit here and listen to this, we need to be doing something about it."

"Like what?" McAvoy said, and Jeremy turned his powerful gaze on him until the other lost his nerve and looked away.

"We have an officer missing," he said carefully, stressing each word. "We could be looking for him right now instead of wasting our time hashing this over with you two."

This sobered the agents, the two of them leveling their gazes on him.

"Missing cop?" Skelly said. "When did that happen?"

"Didn't you read the files we gave you?"

"You didn't give us any files," McAvoy grumbled. "She threw a couple of folders at us containing Wisconsin homicide statistics from 1990."

Jeremy's anger was at a dangerous point, one in which he felt the floodgates were fighting but were not going to be able to restrain the deluge of bitterness that was beginning to spill over the top. He opened his mouth, was about to let fly with a torrential spew of words when Sadie put her hand on his arm.

"Stop," she said. "This is going nowhere. If we're going to work together, we all have to be on the same page."

"We're not working on this together," Skelly said. "We're just trying to do our jobs without interference from you two. We thought we were doing you a favor by keeping you up to speed."

This made Sadie bristle, and that was when she decided lunch was over. Even though her burger was only half-eaten (and it really was delicious), she threw her napkin down and glared at Jeremy until he got the point and slid out so she could as well.

"I think that will be all for now, gentlemen," she said, her voice a grating mixture of anger and disgust. "If you need us, give us a call, but for now we have to do some real police work."

"Real police work?" Skelly said. "We woke a patient up from a coma and got her to talk! How's that for real police work?"

But Sadie wasn't listening, and neither was Jeremy. They hastily made their way to the door of the restaurant and into the brilliant yet waning sunshine of the late afternoon.

• • •

Static crackling from the radio was the only sound in the cruiser as the two of them fumed over what they'd just learned. Another day was passing, and they were still no closer then when they started. They both knew that a trip to Rhinelander wasn't on the docket today; that trip would have to be made tomorrow, if the captain would allow them to leave town for a few hours.

"We have to speak to Captain Martin," Sadie said, breaking the stillness in the car, and when Jeremy didn't reply she persisted. "Don't you agree?"

"Yes, we'll need him to green-light our little excursion tomorrow."

"It's the only way we'll know for sure."

"Hey, you're preaching to the choir. We'll give him the hard sell."

They didn't speak for the remainder of the drive. Sadie was thinking about what could have befallen Officer Lindsley, while Jeremy was wondering if his dog walker could do two walks for Roxie tomorrow, possibly feed her dinner. Ah, what the heck, he thought. He might as well check with her and see if she was available to pet sit. That way he wouldn't have to worry about Roxie in case they needed to stay the night. He decided he'd call her first thing when they arrived back at the station. And that's what he did.

CHAPTER 15

AN INTERESTING DIVERSION

Sadie didn't normally listen to news in the morning on her drive to work, she preferred listening to WIXX. The station played all the latest hit songs. However, what she especially liked was that they didn't play that heavy metal garbage the kids listened to. The music was so juvenile and asinine, the singers self-destructive drug addicts. It certainly wasn't her cup of tea. She preferred the new soul singers and R&B groups like Mariah Carey, Whitney Houston, Color Me Badd, Luther Vandross, En Vogue, artists like that. Now, that was *real* music. The DJ had just played an old favorite of hers by Donna Summers when the programming was interrupted for a news break, a rare occurrence indeed for her bubble gum pop station.

"Breaking news today," the DJ said, and Sadie turned up the volume. "In what is being considered the most gruesome homicide investigation in Wisconsin history, with the exception, of course, of the tragedy that took place last week in Amber Hollow, investiga-tors are revealing what they describe to be an actual chamber of horrors."

Sadie's ears perked up at the mention of the Hollow, and she turned up the volume a little more.

"Milwaukee police officers were alerted to an attempted homicide last night around midnight, when a naked and bleeding man approached two policemen and told them that a Caucasian male by the name of Jeffery Dahmer had invited him to his apartment for a drink, and then handcuffed him and told him he was going to kill him. The victim somehow managed to escape, and as proof he showed the cops a handcuff linked around one of his wrists. The officers were skeptical at first, but they accompanied him back to the apartment where the alleged suspect calmly addressed the attending officers, saying the victim was his boyfriend and they'd had a fight. The police sensed something amiss and a cursory search produced Polaroids of what appeared to be dismembered human bodies, so they took Mr. Dahmer into custody. A further exploration of the apartment revealed a grisly scene straight out of a horror movie. Human remains were found in pans on the stove as well as in the refrigerator, and a giant plastic barrel was discovered which contained hydrochloric acid, presumably used to dissolve the body parts he didn't wish to save as souvenirs. Milwaukee Police say they've never seen such a horrific scene, and an extensive investigation is underway. We'll bring you more on this story as it develops."

The DJ then cued up the song "Eat It" by Weird Al Yankovic, and Sadie savagely twisted the dial and turned it off. She liked the station, but that was just too macabre, even for her.

She drove the rest of the way to the station with the music off, wondering if this would impact their investigation in any way, and also wondering how humanity could produce such repulsive deviants.

• • •

When Sadie arrived, Jeremy was already there, as well as the FBI agents. They were having a spirited discussion when she entered the office, and paused only briefly to note her arrival before continuing their conversation. Sadie noticed that Jeremy didn't seem upset. What she'd taken as heated was actually excitement.

"Looks like you two can have this case all to yourselves, for the time being," Skelly was saying, a smirk on his acne-scarred face. "We're being called down to Milwaukee to interrogate this Dahmer guy." He looked at Sadie. "You watch the news last night?"

"I heard about it on the radio," she said, removing her purse from her shoulder and setting it on her desk. "Multiple homicides, body parts in the refrigerator."

"Not only that," Skelly said with obvious glee, "looks like he was a cannibal too. There were body parts in a pot on the stove. I guess he liked his Rice-A-Roni with a side of testicles."

"Yum-yum," McAvoy said, and Sadie grimaced. Jeremy's face never changed, however, and she knew that this news was pleasing him to no end. With the FBI agents out of the way, they were free to handle the Amber Hollow case any way they chose, without federal interference. She couldn't help but agree; it did sound win/win all the way around.

"We want you to keep us apprised of your findings on this case," Skelly said, buttoning his suit coat and smoothing his tie. "Any evidence you turn up, you float by us, you hear me?"

"Of course," Jeremy said, but Sadie knew he'd do no such thing.

"Very good," Skelly said. "Now if you'll excuse us, we have a plane to catch at your quaint little airport Boston Strudel—"

"Austin Straubel," Sadie corrected absently, and Skelly shrugged.

"Whatever." He looked at his partner. "You ready?"

"Born ready."

"Let's go talk to this freak." He shot a twisted smile at Sadie. "If we can bring someone out of a coma, I think we can wrangle a confession out of Ed Gein."

"Certainly," she agreed. "Let us know how it goes."

"Oh, you'll know all right. You'll be hearing about it on the news. Ciao."

And then they were gone. Sadie and Jeremy looked at each other for a long moment before they both smiled.

"Did you know about this before you came in?"

"Yeah," Jeremy said, taking a seat behind his desk and shuffling some papers. "I wasn't sleeping very well so I got up early. I saw it on the five AM news."

"This has been one hell of a week."

"You're telling me—"

Jeremy's desk phone rang, and he picked it up.

"Detective LeFevre, homicide department." His face suddenly changed, the joviality gone, replaced by true concern. "When did it happen?" He listened and then: "What's being done about it?"

Sadie watched him, wondering what news he could possibly be receiving now. There certainly had been a lot of excitement already this morning. When he hung up the phone and stood, she looked at him expectantly.

"We have to go," he said, putting his jacket on.

"What's wrong?"

"I'll tell you on the way," he said and, grabbing her purse, she followed him out to the car.

• • •

"The little girl is missing?" Sadie said as they raced to Bellin Hospital. They had the siren and the flashers on, but she took care to slow down at all the red lights. Several years ago, she had been in pursuit of a perp whom they suspected had killed his wife with a circular saw, and even though she'd taken all the precautions, a woman had pulled out of a drive-in bank and caused a head-on collision that put Sadie in the hospital while the woman had walked away without a scratch. From then on, she knew that the lights and the noise could only do so much, you always had to factor in the unexpected, much like this assignment.

"A nurse went in with her breakfast and she wasn't there. A search of the hospital hasn't turned up anything yet."

"Sounds like we've heard this story before," Sadie said, and Jeremy grunted.

"Let's just hope she doesn't wind up on the Tower Drive Bridge." Static squawked from the CB and Jeremy picked it up. "Detective LeFevre." His expression turned from a frown into a scowl, one that contorted his face almost comically, if one could laugh, given the situation. Sadie listened, getting the gist "OK," he said, "we'll be there shortly." He replaced the handset, shaking his head. "This is going to be a long day."

"She isn't the only one missing?"

"Nope. You better step on it."

"Done," she said, pushing the accelerator to the boards, screeching around a corner and flying out into the middle of an intersection, just barely missing a city bus.

"I think it would be best if we arrive in one piece," Jeremy said, but he was smiling a little.

"You want to drive?"

"No," he said. "Keep up the good work."

· · ·

Nurses were assembled at the front desk, each of them strenuously denying that they were responsible for the missing patients. A couple of doctors were in their midst, rolling their eyes furiously at what surely had to be a flagrant breach of protocol. Jeremy and Sadie approached them, badges in hand, but that wasn't necessary, the staff knew who they were.

"When was the last time anybody saw them in their rooms?" Sadie asked, and after much arguing it was determined that the patients had been checked on during the night at varying intervals, but approximately four hours before it was noticed that they were missing.

"We have to spread out and search the hospital!" Jeremy shouted over the din. "Who's in charge of the security cameras? Have them start looking at the footage from last night!"

One of the doctors took charge of the nurses, directing them each to separate floors. He then called the head of hospital security, had him start searching the video surveillance tape. After he did all that, he looked at the detectives expectantly.

"What now?"

"Tend to your patients, doc, we've got this," Jeremy said. "We better give them a hand, Sadie. Why don't you start on this floor and work your way up, and I'll start at the top."

"OK."

They parted, but not without each of them feeling a small twinge of displeasure at having to do so. Jeremy turned and looked at Sadie as she headed down the hallway, and just as he was about to turn away, she swiveled her head to glance at him as well. Their eyes met, locked on each other briefly, a wordless message shared between them.

Be careful...

And then they both went their separate ways.

• • •

The search wasn't underway more than fifteen minutes when Jeremy received a call from Sadie on his walkie-talkie.

"One of the orderlies found a body. It appears to be one of the janitors."

"I'll be right there."

He took the elevator down from the fourth floor, his mind spinning furiously. Why they hadn't thought to assign the survivors security guards was beyond him, especially after one of them took a swan dive off the Tower Drive Bridge, but that was past history now, wasn't it? He supposed he could blame it on the federal intrusion, the fact that those two took over and he and Sadie essentially dropped the case for a day when they should have tightened the screws, but he knew that to be untrue. No sense assigning culpability when it was presently a moot point. The elevator reached the first floor, and as the doors opened, bedlam ensued. He waded through the people, a mixture of staff members and patients. Apparently, the news had spread very quickly.

"Where is it?"

"The janitor's closet," an orderly said. He was unshaven, and his eyes were bloodshot, typical of a man who probably drank his breakfast after waking up with a hangover the size of Texas.

"Take me there."

He followed the disheveled man down a corridor, and when they got close, he saw a large splash of blood congealing on the ground, droplets dotting the far wall like an artistic mosaic. Following the splatter, they eventually reached Sadie, who was standing outside of the tiny chamber, her hand over her mouth, sweat dotting her brow. In their time working together, they had seen many bodies in various stages of putrefaction. The way she looked, however, indicated that what she'd just seen was so awful it made them all pale in comparison.

"In there…" she gasped, and he noticed that she'd vomited; her mouth and the back of her hand were slimy with it. He took his handkerchief from his back pocket and gave it to her, reaching out with his other hand to give her shoulder a reassuring squeeze. He took a deep breath, braced himself and then peered inside the room.

"Oh my God," he croaked, an icy band of terror streaking through him like an errant bolt of lightning. This man hadn't merely been murdered, he'd been ripped apart, and not only that…

"Someone fucking ate him," Sadie said, and had this been under other circumstances, he would have been surprised at her use of profanity, but indeed this was a situation where it could be used with impunity. He felt his gorge rise as well, and he covered his nose and mouth with one hand while his mind tried to accept what he was seeing. It was nearly inconceivable, but the hospital janitor was lying in a large wash of blood, his face and neck savagely mutilated, revealing the muscle and gristle beneath. His stomach was torn open, large loops of intestines draped over him like uncoiled snakes. Jeremy noted that the entrails had also been masticated, and judging by the size of the teeth marks and bite radius they were definitely human. The walls were spattered with gore, even the lone lightbulb that swung by a single cord was dripping with blood. He abruptly turned away, nearly knocking Sadie over because he hadn't noticed that she'd stepped up beside him. He took her in his arms, hugged her tightly, whispered something comforting yet unintelligible in her ear and then let her go. He took his walkie-talkie from his belt, called the front desk at the Sherriff's department and told them to send some cops and forensic experts stat. He then gently pushed Sadie away from the door so that he could close it.

"That was David," the orderly said, his face ashen, his voice barely a whisper. "I just went bowling with him and his wife."

"I'm very sorry for your loss," Jeremy said, "but we have to see the surveillance footage, now."

"Good idea," Sadie said, struggling to regain her composure, and was surprised at her ability to quickly detach herself from it. Of all the things she'd seen in the line of duty, this had to be the most horrific. This...*atrocity*...was well beyond anything she'd ever witnessed. To have the capacity to compartmentalize the grotesque was a professional trait she'd learned during her many years on the force. "Let's go."

"Can you take us there?" Jeremy asked the orderly, who was still staring at the closed door.

"Huh?" The expression on his face was one of numb confusion, and if Jeremy were inclined to think in terms of old Disney movies, this would be the point where the orderly would reach inside his pocket, remove the flask he'd been nipping from and toss it over his shoulder, after rubbing his eyes, of course.

"Can you take us to where the surveillance video is viewed?"

"Oh, yeah, sure." With deliberate effort he pulled it together, shaking his head wonderingly, but failing to produce a bottle or flask that he wished to toss. "This way."

And they followed him back down the corridor while the sounds of sirens grew louder outside.

CHAPTER 16

A DIRE WARNING

The room was too small for all of them to fit inside, so Jeremy thanked the orderly for his help and dismissed him. He walked away like a man in a dream, his eyes rheumy, his gait unsteady. Sadie certainly couldn't blame him.

The person in charge of the surveillance footage was a portly, cantankerous man who looked like his hair hadn't enjoyed the cleansing touch of shampoo since last summer, perhaps even longer. The stench that came off of him was possibly more stomach-churning than the body they'd just viewed, but Sadie and Jeremy crowded into the room with him nonetheless.

"Have you found anything?" Jeremy asked, and the other nodded.

"Yah, I seen some stuff. Strangest Goddamn thing." He punched some buttons, cued up the footage. "I been tru it already, I'll show ya what I just seen."

Jeremy and Sadie leaned in to take a closer look, and Jeremy was glad to see that his partner had recovered from the shock. She appeared to be more or less her usual self, the look on her face almost making him forget the terror he'd seen there only ten minutes ago. Not that he hadn't felt it himself. It's not every day that you saw a body that's been cannibalized, especially not in Green Bay. Chicago maybe, but up in this neck of the woods if they found a body that was eaten, it had been done by wild animals. He suddenly thought about the cannibal in Milwaukee, Jeffery Dahmer. A shiver passed through him. He was glad the FBI agents had already left; this turn of events might have quite possibly kept them in town, knowing there was a local man-eater to contend with.

"What are we looking at?" Sadie said. The footage was grainy, the cameras long in need of being replaced. It was in color, but it was a washed out, tri-color hue that left a lot to the imagination. It reminded Sadie of the old Zenith TV her family had when she was a girl.

"Right dere, watch dat door at da end of da hall."

A door opened, and a young woman stepped inside. Even though the picture was crap, they could tell she was remarkably pretty, her long auburn hair swept back and arranged in a tight bun. She wore large sunglasses accompanied by a white doctor's coat. She looked about her before furtively darting down the hallway and disappearing from the screen.

"Where did she go?"

"Keep yer damn pants on, Charlie," the video operator groused, "I got it." He punched more buttons and an additional camera angle appeared on another screen. "Dere she is."

The woman approached from down another corridor and then entered a room. A minute passed, and then the woman exited. She had the little girl in tow, holding her hand. She led her down the corridor back the way she came. The little girl wasn't struggling, in fact she was going with her as if...

"It's like she knows her," Sadie said, and Jeremy had to agree that it indeed did seem so.

"Who is she?" he wondered aloud, and on the tail of that: "You think she's the one who ate the orderly?"

The camera operator nodded while in the process of shoving a donut in his mouth. "We'll git to dat," he said, crumbs spraying from his robust lips.

They crowded closer toward the screen.

"Did we get a description of that woman from the library?" Sadie said, and Jeremy shook his head.

"No, but we should have." He squinted at the screen. "Do you know where she went next?"

"Oh yah, dey went out dere." He pointed at another monitor; this shot was from a camera mounted above one of the side exits. The woman exited with the little girl, walking her toward a large, windowless van and then helping her inside. The girl didn't appear to be in distress, in fact, in this last shot, she actually smiled at the woman as she helped her buckle her seat belt, an innocent smile that aptly portrayed the virtue of youth. Sadie felt a ripple of revulsion clench her guts, the idea that this woman had presumably murdered someone to get this girl out of the hospital and the kid looked like she was in the company of a trusted friend.

"Cue up the footage of her taking the other survivor."

"Sure, but I'll warn ya, dis one ain't so good."

He punched more buttons and an image popped up on another screen. According to the time stamp on the bottom, this had taken place five minutes after the little girl had been led outside to the van. The camera angles showed the same thing: the woman entering the hospital, walking down a corridor, only this time she encountered the janitor, who they saw questioning her but couldn't hear anything regarding their exchange because of the absence of sound. She tried to get past him, he attempted to stop her, and in a moment so quick it was animalistic, she lunged forward and bit his neck, tearing out his throat in an enormous spray of arterial blood. The man dropped to his knees, clutching his throat with both hands, and that's when she dragged him toward the closet by the collar of his shirt, opened the door, and took him inside. The time stamp on the bottom of the screen showed four minutes pass, and then she exited, her white doctors coat spattered with gore, rivulets of blood running down her face in garish streaks.

"Dat's when she ate him," the surveillance operator narrated pointlessly, and was ignored. He grunted in indignant dissatisfaction and cued the camera to the next angle. Creeping down the corridor now, the woman jumped into an open doorway when two nurses accompanying a patient in a wheel chair went past, and once they were out of sight she exited, walking very slowly before entering anther room. Hardly a minute passed when she next came out, only this time the person she escorted wasn't going willingly, instead appeared to be struggling in vain against the other. It was no wonder, what with her gore-streaked appearance, but there was something more, like the survivor *knew* her.

"Dat dame don't look like she wanted to go," the operator said, and for this he received two sour looks.

"You think?" Sadie said before returning her attention to the screen. She and Jeremy watched as the woman (who looked like she could be a model if she were so inclined) effortlessly ushered Sylvia Albright out of the hospital and, finally, opened the side door of the van and tossed her in. She walked around the other side and disappeared from the camera's view, and several seconds later, black exhaust erupted from the tailpipe. Then something odd (odder) happened. The woman came around the vehicle and then stared directly into the camera. She stood there for a moment, a crazy smile canted on her otherwise beautiful face, blood smeared around her mouth, her teeth stained crimson, and then she raised one hand and gestured to them, curling her finger.

(Come and get me....)

She then walked around the vehicle and out of sight, and a few seconds later she drove away. The time stamp on the screen at the moment of her getaway was 4:13 that morning. Jeremy looked at his watch, remembered what the nurses had told him. The two survivors were long gone by the time the nurses did their eight o'clock morning rounds, giving their captor almost a four-hour head start.

"What now?"

"We have to check on the other two survivors at St. Mary's."

"OK."

The two departed the room without a word, the surveillance operator staring after them with his mouth agape.

"Yer freakin' welcome!" he yelled, his powdered sugar coated mouth curved in a sneer, but he received no reply. "Ta hell wit ya, anyways," he mumbled, and went back to working his way through the box of donuts.

• • •

Sadie and Jeremy received the news from St. Mary's before they even reached the front door of Bellin. Sadie took the call at the front desk while Jeremy fidgeted beside her. After a moment of yeses and uh-huhs, she hung up and then thanked the nurse on duty for the use of her desk phone.

"Hospital efficiency certainly isn't one of St. Mary's strong suits."

"What's up?"

"The other two are gone as well."

"I wish I could say I was surprised."

"What do we do?"

"Let's send some deputies over there, have them check the surveillance footage and get back to us. Right now, we have four people who are in need of rescue."

"You mean three?" Sadie said pointedly, and for a moment Jeremy just looked at her before nodding.

"I suppose so."

"The question remains: what do *we* do?"

Jeremy rubbed his chin thoughtfully. "I think this changes things." He stared at her so long that Sadie began to feel uncomfortable.

"What?" she demanded.

"One of us needs to go look for them, and one of us needs to stay here."

"Come again?"

"Captain Martin would want one of us to stay here to investigate the homicide. Both of us can't leave town until a report is made."

"So, who's going to go and look for them?"

"You know the answer to that one."

Sadie shook her head defiantly.

"No way, Jose," she said. "You're not going up there by yourself. It's too dangerous."

"I'm a trained detective, I can handle it."

"It's not just that," she said, lowering her voice as nurses and other hospital personnel passed by, going about their business. "You can't cut me out of the case like this. We're a team."

"I'm not cutting you out—"

"Don't give me that crap. That woman is dangerous, and this is *our* case. I'm coming too."

"It's because she's dangerous that you should stay here. We have no idea what we're getting into."

"That's our job, remember? To track down killers and put them behind bars. I wouldn't be in this line of work if I didn't think I could handle it."

"Sadie," he said, measuring his words carefully, "I don't know if I can protect you."

"Protect me? I'm a big girl, I can take care of myself."

"Shit," he sighed, shaking his head. He hadn't known how this case was going to turn out, but this was the exact thing he feared the most. He could see that he was getting nowhere with his argument, and one of them should stay here because they needed to adhere to protocol, but she was stubborn as a bull and twice as mean if she didn't get her way. He didn't know what else he could say, and if he tried to bring the captain in on it to convince her to stay, even he might wonder why Jeremy would leave her behind, standard procedure be damned. If she was determined to come, she would, and that was that.

"I'm going too, end of story." She folded her arms, stared at him with a look that said, "Try and stop me."

He sighed again, this time with less resignation and more humor. "Okay then, saddle up."

Sadie nodded, satisfied. "I already told Clayton he's on his own tonight. Is Karen going to take care of Roxie?"

"I talked to her last night. She's got my girl covered."

"What are we waiting for, then?"

"Nothing, I guess. Let's roll."

Following Sadie's lead, they headed to the parking lot to get the cruiser.

CHAPTER 17

ANOTHER TRIP UP NORTH

"**W**hat are the facts of this case so far?" Sadie said as the car hummed along the nearly deserted highway. Occasionally a vehicle passed them going the other way, mostly pick-up trucks with gun racks, driven by rednecks wearing John Deere baseball caps. Nothing unusual in this neck of the woods. In the back seat sat two overnight bags, one for each of them. "List everything that we know to be true regarding this case, to the best of our knowledge."

Jeremy consulted his notebook, ticked them off one by one. "First, we have an episode of what may or may not be mass hysteria; unexplained event, everyone but five people in a secluded village die horribly, the place burns to the ground."

"OK."

"Of the five survivors, we talked to three of them, all of them with a different story to tell."

"The little girl didn't really tell us much of anything."

"So that's her story."

"All right."

"The coroner can't find any evidence to corroborate either of their stories and then Corey goes up to investigate, he disappears." Jeremy waited for a response, and when she nodded, he continued. "One of the survivors commits suicide, we go and talk with the last person who saw Corey alive, we visit the town, something weird happens."

Sadie glanced at him again. Since the incident happened, the two of them hadn't talked about it; in fact, have been avoiding it altogether. The subject made them both uncomfortable because as detectives, they were so rooted in facts and forensic evidence that the idea of something so...*otherworldly*...just didn't make any sense. The suggestion of a gas leak made them both feel much better, even though that theory had already been scrapped.

"And?"

"The bodies in the morgue all turn into two-hundred-year-old ash and then the Feds show up to try and steal our case, only to be diverted by a serial killer in Milwaukee. Then some crazy lady takes off with the survivors, but not before killing—"

"*Eating.*"

"Yes, killing *and* eating a hospital janitor."

"And we think it's the librarian from Rhinelander?"

"Yes, I think we do."

Their conversation came to an abrupt halt, Jeremy's words hanging in the air as if they were balloons neither one of them dared to pop. The road passed along beneath them as the car ate up the miles. A minute passed and then another, the sound of the tires on the pavement overly loud. The day was dark, no sun just a thick covering of clouds that ate the light as if it was

(Human...)

on the verge of a celestial black hole. Another pick-up truck passed them, and then a tractor driven by a grizzled old farmer. He lifted a hand and waved and Sadie waved back. On either side of the highway there were cornfields stretching as far as the eye could see.

"So," Sadie said at last, "are we going to visit the librarian, the sheriff of Crandon...what?"

Jeremy considered the question. The librarian would make the most sense. In his pocket, he had a still photo of the woman who kidnapped the survivors, printed from the surveillance footage. If the head librarian, Delores, recognized the woman in the photo, confirmed she was indeed a librarian employed at the Rhinelander Public Library, then they'd have an identity, could update the APB to include who this mystery woman was. If she didn't, they could rule her out, if Delores Schenker was telling the truth, which Sadie didn't think she was. Of course, in the meantime, they still had four missing people.

"At this juncture, it isn't important who the woman is, only that she's committed a crime. We can figure out her identity later. I think we should head for Crandon and then Amber Hollow."

"Why Amber Hollow and not Rhinelander?"

"Because, my dear, that is most likely where the librarian is taking them."

"You think so?"

"There is nothing else that we *can* think," he said. "You saw what I saw, what else could you make of that?"

Sadie thought of the expression on the woman's face, saw in her mind's eye how she raised her hand and gestured, beckoning them.

"You're right," she agreed. "So, is there any reason we aren't calling ahead to let the sheriff know we're coming?"

"Yes," Jeremy said, picking up a bottle of water from the holder next to him and taking a drink. "You know there is."

"You think they're all in cahoots?"

"What else could I think? Add everything up, see what you get."

Sadie did so. She thought of everything that had transpired so far, thought of how neatly everything fell into place. This little village and its late inhabitants found a way to stay off the grid for so long…how could they do that without a little help from neighboring communities? She supposed it wouldn't be impossible, but a little help from your friends was always a good thing, no matter how you sliced it.

"If what you think is true, he'll know we're coming, anyway."

Jeremy tapped his nose, as if they were playing a game of charades. "Bingo." He tipped her a wink. "Besides, he'd know anyway because of the statewide alert that was issued, at least, I'm sure he'd make that conclusion eventually."

"You know how we're going to approach this then?"

Jeremy sighed, a genuine exhalation of breath that expressed his every thought.

"No, I don't. We're going to have to play this by the seat of our pants."

"Great," she said, but she was smiling. "I knew you'd know exactly what to do."

"Who loves you, baby?" he said, doing his best Teddy Sevalis, and her smile turned into a grimace.

"Don't quit your day job," she said, and they both laughed, the sound almost startling in the otherwise stillness. When it subsided, they both remained silent for the rest of the drive, watching the scenery as it passed by.

• • •

"Why, Detectives Conrad and LeFevre," Sheriff Conroy greeted them as they entered his office. "What can I do for you?"

Sadie watched the man carefully, observed the lack of surprise in his voice. Jeremy had been right. He knew they were coming even though they hadn't called, and now he was playing dumb, as if he had no idea that there were four people missing and a statewide alert had been issued.

"Don't check your faxes much, do you?" Jeremy said, walking into the office and pulling out a chair without being invited. He sat, crossed his legs, and leaned back. "You telling me you don't know what's going on?"

The expression on the sheriff's face remained still, but Sadie saw his left eye twitch, a casual tell that he knew full well what was going on. He shook his head. "Don't know what you are talking about. I just got in about ten minutes ago."

"And no one in the station let you know that the survivors are missing?"

"Did you see anyone in the station when you came in?"

Jeremy paused, swiveled in his chair and looked out the door. In their hurry to speak with him, he'd paid no attention to the fact that the place was deserted. Maybe they'd thought the deputy was in the can, the secretary out getting coffee…

"No one mans the station when you're out?"

"Why would they? I have my walkie-talkie on me at all times." He leaned forward in his chair, smiled at the other as if he were a young boy in need of learning a lesson. "I don't know if you noticed, but not much happens up around these parts. Sure, every now and then someone wrecks their car, and there are the occasional hunting accidents. In the winter, I help jump start a lot of dead batteries, but otherwise it's pretty quiet up here, not like down in the big city."

His reference to Green Bay being a big city was almost funny, if the man hadn't been dead serious, which he appeared to be.

"The survivors are missing?" he said, sitting back in his chair and scratching his head. "When did that happen?"

"Don't play stupid with us, sheriff," Sadie said brusquely. "You know what's going on."

"What are you talking about?" He looked at Jeremy with a 'Women…can't live with 'em, can't shoot 'em' expression. "You want to rein in your partner there, detective. It ain't nice to be disrespectful on somebody else's turf."

"She's just trying to get to the bottom of this, sheriff."

"There's nothing to get to the bottom of—"

"Can the act, Conroy," Sadie interrupted. She was sick of not knowing what the hell was going on. In her gut she was certain this man had information he wasn't sharing, was in on something that had eluded them thus far. She wanted answers, and she wanted them now. "Why don't you start by telling us everything you know?"

"Your partner sure has got a mouth on her, doesn't she?" Conroy said, and Jeremy had to reach out and hold Sadie's arm, afraid that she'd take a swing at the sheriff.

"Why don't we all try and get along?" Jeremy said, and at this Sadie stiffened.

"I'm not the one lying to cover for somebody."

Jeremy sensed that the situation was beginning to slip out of his control, that soon enough it would be an all-out war if he didn't intervene. He knew he had to change tactics, had to try and convince Sadie once again that she was needed elsewhere. He'd meant what he'd said to her at the hospital, that he wasn't sure he could protect her. He had to try one more time, if only for her continued safety.

"I have an idea, sheriff," Jeremy said, nudging Sadie with his elbow. "Detective Conrad here will take our cruiser and go to Rhinelander to speak with Delores Schenker, see if she can dredge up any more information from her. Meanwhile, you and I will take your car and head to Amber Hollow, see if there is anything we can find. Sound like a plan?"

Sheriff Conroy nodded. "Yes, I believe that would be alright with me—"

"The hell it is!" Sadie interjected, glaring at Jeremy. "Why are you trying to cut me out of this case? We're partners, and we're not splitting up!"

"Sadie," Jeremy said, "one of us should go and speak with the librarian, see if she can positively identify the woman from the photo—"

"We already agreed that didn't matter! Why are you doing this?"

"Doing what?"

"Arguing with me in front of this idiot!"

Sheriff Conroy watched them from his chair, his head swiveling back and forth like he was watching a tennis match, a cocky grin on his unshaven face.

"I'm not arguing, I'm just saying—"

"To hell with what you're saying," Sadie said, shaking her head defiantly. "We're going to take a ride, the three of us."

"Yeah?" Sheriff Conroy said. "Just like that, huh?"

"Just like that," she said, daring Jeremy to override her decision. He fidgeted in his seat but said nothing. If she was determined to go, then so be it.

"Where to?" the sheriff asked, and Sadie blew a disgusted raspberry.

"You know the answer to that," she said. She stepped around his desk, took him by the arm, and hoisted him to his feet. He looked down at her hand and for a second she saw real violence in his eyes, a desire to grab her hand and twist it in his own, but then it passed, and he offered a sheepish grin.

"Why, all you had to do was ask politely," he said quietly. "Let's get going then, see what we find."

"After you," she said, letting him go, and she could tell he was resisting the urge to rub his arm where she'd clenched it.

"Ladies first," he countered, and Sadie rolled her eyes. She grabbed him by the arm again.

"Let's go."

They exited the station, getting into the unmarked cruiser and heading toward Amber Hollow.

. . .

The drive didn't take long, just under an hour, but it felt like a lifetime to Sadie. Sheriff Conroy didn't say a word, not even an attempt at pleasantries after their tiff in his office. Sadie didn't like that, it was disconcerting. The sky grew darker the closer they got, and she could taste the rain in the air, tangy and unpleasant that left a bad aftertaste. She didn't know why, but she felt the first pangs of fear when they approached a sign announcing the town.

It was leaning at an obscene angle, the writing in an old-fashioned script. It reminded her of ghost towns in the movies, of places best left alone. She couldn't recall seeing it last time, but that didn't matter now, did it? It was neither here nor there. And when they approached the barricades, she felt the pang turn into an out and out flurry, her heart beating faster in her chest for some crazy, unknown reason.

"Where's your deputy?" Jeremy said, pointing to the spot where the man had been the other day, guarding the entrance of the village, and Conroy shrugged.

"Don't know," he said. "Maybe he decided to go fishing." He leered at Sadie, ran a tongue as white as paper over his bottom lip. She watched him in the rearview mirror, revulsion filling her. There was something wrong with this man, *seriously* wrong, yet for the moment she didn't understand what it was, didn't know what it possibly could be.

"He picked a lousy time to go," she said, trying to remain in control of the situation, and this got him to look away, making her feel slightly less uncomfortable. She stopped the car at the barrier, put it in park. She raised an eyebrow at Jeremy, and his expression in reply aptly conveyed something he'd said in the car earlier. He didn't know what to do either.

"Shut off the car," he said to Sadie before addressing the sheriff. "We're going to take a walk."

"A little exercise sounds good," Conroy said, "but I don't know what you expect to find."

"Hopefully the people who are missing," Sadie said. The wisps of fear she'd felt fluttering within her became stronger, some nameless thing that tugged at her like invisible strings. She contemplated the village apprehensively; it looked repulsive, the ruins appearing like some prehistoric creature that's been killed and left to rot while the insects and animals devoured it. She didn't know why, but her fear was growing into terror, and she could tell Jeremy felt uneasy too. The air had an oppressive feel to it, the quiet unsettling. "Can we at least agree that that is what we've come here to do?"

"I suppose we can, detective," Conroy said, his grin turning into an obscene caricature of itself. "That's assuming they're here, of course. Could be we're barking up the wrong tree."

"Any suggestions where they might be then?" Sadie said, her heart now banging away in her chest like the Liberty Bell but the expression on her face as serene as a Tibetan monk. "Seems to me you don't want us here. You have something to hide, sheriff?"

This sobered Conroy, in fact, his expression of smug good humor turned into one of grim reality. He shook his head, his eyes rolling inside their sockets like loose ball bearings.

"No," he said at last. "I don't." He swung his gaze from Sadie to Jeremy, apparently deciding to share something with them at last. "If you must know, this place gives me the freakin' creeps. Always has." His countenance changed to one of unnerved disquiet. "This town...it ain't right, never has been. I'd rather be anywhere but here."

His "confession" was what finally pissed Sadie off. She yanked on her door handle violently, got out, and opened his door. She pulled the sheriff out of the backseat like he was a ragdoll and shook him back and forth, his head bobbling comically on his shoulders.

"You can't scare us with some crazy, backwoods bullshit!" she roared, her nostrils flaring. She turned him around, facing the barricade, the entrance to the village. "Now be a good boy and march!" She shoved him forward and he almost fell, but by some grace of God kept on his feet. He swiveled his head on slumped shoulders, a surprised expression on his face.

"Easy now," he said. "I'm breaking in new boots..."

"March!" she yelled, and he nodded politely.

"OK," he said. "I'll be good."

Jeremy watched this interaction with a look of amusement on his face, but he said nothing. The air was silent; there were literally no sounds at all. No birds, no crickets, no wind blowing through the dense foliage of trees...nothing. The barricade loomed before them, looking like a prop in some old horror movie, and beyond that was the scorched remains of a township so mysterious it wasn't on any map, at least not one manufactured outside of the county it resided within. Sadie arrived at the barrier first, reaching out to touch it with one trembling hand. It was unusually warm, and for a moment, it felt to her like it throbbed, pulsating like a snake uncoiling, and she quickly retracted her hand, a look of puzzled terror etched on her face.

"What?" Jeremy said, and she shook her head, unable to answer. She looked at Sheriff Conroy, and he, too, was looking beyond the barricade and into the village, where the light was receding fast, darkness creeping toward them like a shadow, erasing the daylight an inch at a time as it lurked ever closer.

"You sure you want to do this?" was the last thing that Conroy said. "Yes," was the last thing Sadie said. Jeremy had no last words, for he didn't say anything. They passed by the barricade, and then all sound, light, and sensation ceased being, as if they had been swallowed by the darkness.

Truth be told...they had.

PART THREE
AMBER HOLLOW

CHAPTER 18

CELEBRATION OF THE SECOND BASTILLE DAY

The first thing that Sadie was aware of after everything went dark was sound; gradually increasing in volume, as if emanating from some hidden speaker, she heard the chirping of birds and then the wind blowing through the leaves of what must have been very large trees. Color began to return, and as it did, her vision swirled, as if she were looking through a kaleidoscope. Voices then arose to greet her ears, softly murmuring and then progressively becoming louder. This sensation wasn't new to her, as this had happened to her when she'd last been in the Hollow, but the feeling was unsettling, the loss of control more than anything, as she wasn't one who liked her destiny steered by anything else than her own will. She felt dizzy, as if the world was spinning much too fast, and as her senses came to recognize that what she was experiencing was real, panic filled her, the fear of the unknown. She tried to speak, to articulate any sound, but was rendered unable. She swooned, reached out to steady herself, and felt a hand grasp her shoulder, callused and strong.

"I daresay, young lass," someone said, their accent unfamiliar to her but the cadence measured and calm, "you need to get more rest."

For a moment, Sadie stood poised between two worlds; as her sight returned, she could see that she was standing in the center of the village square of Amber Hollow, and what she saw only increased her vertigo. On one level, she could see the decimated ruins of the village, the burned and gutted buildings, the debris strewn about by the fire. On another, deeper level, she could see a village overlapping it, one that had been sheltered from time. It reminded her of a drawing from a book of fairy tales, a story from which sprang a wolf in an old woman's shawl, ready to attract the attention of a little girl with the intention of eating her. This old-time village swayed before her eyes like a mirage and then slowly enveloped the other, becoming more solidified, more real. She could clearly feel the hand that clutched her shoulder, could feel the warmth of it through her clothes.

"Have you eaten today, young lass?"

Sadie lifted her head, saw first the hand that was upon her, her gaze following it up to the arm and then to the person's face. It was an old man, his face seamed and liver spotted, but his expression was of kind concern. He was wearing clothes from another century, and again she was reminded of the fables she'd read as a girl. She wanted to shake her head, to tell him that there must be some mistake, that this couldn't be happening and that she must be suffering from a delusion, but her mouth had other plans for her.

"Yes, good sir, I've breakfasted quite early so I can make preparations for the celebration tonight."

Like her last experience, she was marionette, a meat puppet that would do the bidding of some other force. She'd been hijacked and could only watch as her body was made to go through the motions the illusion required of her.

"I say you look a might peaked," he said, removing his hand now that she appeared steady on her feet. "You might rest a spell before you continue your labors."

"I may do that, good sir, but I have much to do."

"As do we all," he agreed. She now saw that he had an axe over one shoulder, one of very crude design, although she had no doubt it could do the job intended for it. "Sit down for a few minutes and collect your wits, young lass. Tonight, we shall dispel the gloom the past year has wrought." He fell silent, a memory halting his speech as he let it unravel in his mind. She watched his eyes as he blinked once and then twice until he appeared to gather himself. "Rest, and then get back to work."

"Yes, good sir," she said, and he nodded courteously.

"Good day."

As he strode purposefully away, her gaze chanced upon a fallen log, so she sat upon it, observing her surroundings. The sky above radiated an amazing glow, the sunlight brighter than she'd ever seen it. The woods around her were a wonderous display of timeless beauty, and as she took in the dwellings, she marveled at how realistic this hallucination was. The little houses stood out in stark relief against the backdrop of the forest, and she admired their rudimentary yet sturdy design. She tried to concentrate for a moment, to take in all she was seeing with her rational mind so she could dissect it, but in an instant she found that was going to be impossible; the vision had other plans for her, and she realized that it wanted to show her something, something that she must participate in if she were to fully grasp it. Her thoughts were interrupted by the presence of another, and from that moment the skit she'd been cast into began, and all she could do was watch and unwillingly partake as it unfolded before her.

● ● ●

"After the fire is ready, you'll need to slaughter one of the pig-glings…are you listening to me? Where is your mind today girl?"

"I'm sorry, dear mother, I felt dizzy for a moment."

"Well, gather yourself, young lady, we have a lot to do today." The woman studied Sadie closely, an expression of distaste marring her bland features. "Have you lain with one of the young hunters, lass? You aren't in a motherly way, are you?"

"No, mother, you know I'm not."

"I should say I know nothing of the kind, but I suppose we'll know in time. You wouldn't want what happened to young Maria to happen to you, would you?"

"No, mother," Sadie replied, "I surely wouldn't."

"God didn't want her to have that child because she was too young to care for it. He took it back to Heaven where it belonged."

"Yes, mother."

"Now go and get more firewood, but don't stray too far into the woods. No one knows what happened to Isaac but the forest and the wild animals. You don't want to be a feast for the wolves, do you?"

"No, mother."

"Then don't dally. Get the wood and come back at once."

"Yes, mother."

Sadie walked away from the small cottage in the clearing and into the dark of the surrounding wood. She could feel something heavy in the air, some oppressive force that played tug-of-war with her spirit. Memories came to her, not her own, but true just the same, recollections of the plagues that had beset the village since the past summer solstice. Countless babies had emerged from the womb stillborn, wild game had become scarce in the neighboring woods, and numerous bizarre tragedies had befallen the village. A group of men had gone missing during a routine hunt, and their bodies were found several weeks later, the flesh eaten from their bones. The elders of the village blamed it on the savages, even though their presence had been all but eliminated during the previous decade thanks to the noble hunters. Nonetheless, a party was assembled to rid themselves of a potential native scourge, but there were no tribes to be found, nor any rogue barbarians hiding out in encampments nearby.

And when fall came and it was time to harvest, the villagers found that the crops had died overnight, the source of the blight a mystery to even the keenest of the lot. Yes, bad luck had impinged upon the village, and Sadie couldn't help but think that it had something to do with what had transpired the year before, on the eve of the first Bastille celebration. Could it just be coincidence, or could it be that the collective actions of the townsfolk and the elders had brought this upon them? She didn't have an answer for that, but in her heart, there was the conviction that everything would be all right because what they'd done had been sanctioned by God. At least, that was what Master Guntram had assured everyone, he and the preacher who taught them the words of the Old Testament in the confines of the tiny church. And following the black deeds that occurred on that dreadful day, his son, Lord Guntram, had been made to toil harder than he'd ever had in his life, his punishment for his dastardly conduct. Lord Guntram was not happy with this assignment, but there was little he could do about it, if he wished to succeed his father when the time came and take the reins of the village.

After she'd gathered as much wood as she could carry, she returned to the tiny cottage, and by that time the sun was in the western hemisphere of the sky. The villagers had been scurrying about all day to make their preparations, and soon the celebration would be upon them. And this year, it would count, for there would be nothing to interrupt them. This year, they could drink and dance and be merry and not worry about a disturbance that would rob them of their reveling spirit. This she hoped for very dearly.

"Come hither, young lass, for the celebration is soon to start."

Sadie looked up from her toiling, saw the smiling face of a chivalrous young man. She knew him well, for he was a prominent man about the village. He'd nearly fallen in disfavor with the Master and his family for his insubordination the previous summer, but with everything that had happened over the course of the past year it had practically been forgotten.

"I'm almost ready."

"Will you accept my hand for a dance?"

She smiled. "I shall accept your hand for a dance, and nothing more."

"That is all I ask, my lady." He bowed courteously then offered his hand. "Come. Escort me to the village square."

She felt heat rise in her cheeks as she reached out and took his work-worn hand. She noticed how clean his nails were, and this made her smile inside as it was a measure of vanity that was common to women, but not to men. He had other funny traits, fastidious as he was in his appearance; nevertheless, she had to admit it made him more appealing. Hand in hand, they walked to the village square, one smiling impishly, the other sensing an imminent foreboding she couldn't place, only a vague awareness that the village as they knew it would be forever altered after the events that would transpire that night. However, for that single moment in time, they were happy, a moment that would pass as quickly as a fine meal, the embrace of a loved one, the smile from a favored child. Hence forward, Sadie knew (but didn't know *why*) the course of their lives would be irreversibly altered, and there was not a thing they could do about it.

• • •

The band played a lively tune while the villagers feasted on roasted duck, wild pig, salmon, and venison. Children played a game that involved chasing a rat. The winner would be the child who caught and killed it. Fermented beverages were imbibed as chatter and laughter merged to create a steady din, and as the sun set, it could be reasonably attained that everyone was content, happy with their lot despite the hardships they'd suffered throughout the course of that year.

Master Guntram sat at the head of his table, his son at his left elbow drinking from a flagon of ale. Lord Guntram wore a somber expression, for over the course of the past year, his role in the village had been reassigned. He was no longer the reckless divergent he'd once been; for now, he'd have to curtail such activities if he was to regain the favor of his father, for it was no secret that the elder blamed his son in part for the hard year they'd had. Even though God was merciful in his wisdom, there were certain crimes against humanity that couldn't go unpunished, even if they were committed upon a commoner. The good book said so, and until all was made right in their little borough, Lord Guntram would have to atone for his sins.

Sadie danced merrily with the energetic young man, and she knew without being told that his name was Jeremiah. His smile brought her joy, and she could feel something stirring within her, a hidden longing that was as timeless as the valley around them. He twirled her about, his gait somewhat clumsy, but his enthusiasm made up for it. As the music rose to a crashing crescendo, she sensed a feeling of safety emanating from him, why, she didn't know, but she was glad he was by her side. He said something but she couldn't hear him, merely saw his lips moving and his tongue dancing behind teeth that appeared well cared for. She leaned closer to hear him better when an obstreperous clamor arose, overtaking all other sound. It ascended in volume like a great wind flanked by bitter rain, and at once the citizens of the village craned their necks to look into the night sky as a source of light grew brighter on the horizon.

"I daresay..." Jeremiah muttered haltingly, the words catching in his throat. His hand unwittingly clamped down harder on Sadie's, and she uttered a pained cry. An explosion of deep purple luminescence filled the sky above them, radiating outward in an octagon of oscillating clouds that roiled like thunderheads, although the sky had been completely clear only a moment before. Voices cried out in fear and surprise as this alien, luminous mist enveloped them, and when the wind grew to a near fever pitch, the villagers ran to take cover, chaos ensuing among them. Children were trampled by adult men seeking to get away from this encroaching doom, while women fought one another to get to safety.

With the wind there came the sound of a voice, like a Gregorian chant, a low, guttural humming that was tuneless and overpowering. It rose in pitch and volume, the sound filling in the spaces where the light could not penetrate, and the villagers clasped their hands over their ears as it became a piercing wail. To Sadie, it sounded like the cry of a young girl screaming in fear and torment from some unimaginably horrific act. She couldn't help herself: she screamed along with it, falling to her knees. Jeremiah fell to the ground beside her, his arms over his head, and that was when the atonal rasping hum became a voice, one that reeked of the gallows. It shifted from a scream to that of primal laughter, cackling like a demented wraith, furious that it was trapped between worlds.

"You shall kneel before me!" the voice shrieked in three separate octaves, from low to high, a feat that was impossible for a mere mortal, but this indeed was not human. "You shall all pay for the sins you've committed!"

Master Guntram stared from his position at the head of the table, his mouth agape. His son, the lousy coward, hid beneath, clutching a table leg. The master struggled to make sense of what he was seeing, and as the light and the mist swirled and eddied, a face emerged from the smoke, one he knew all too well. He swallowed, terror possessing him, for wasn't this what he'd feared when the first child had been delivered stillborn, when his prized pig had conceived a two-headed monster, and the river's clear, cold water became overrun with crimson algae? Hadn't this been the thing he'd feared the most? Yes, it was clear that it was, and to his feverish mind there was only one way to settle this, to make it right. He rose to his feet, his knees shaking like twigs in a hurricane force gale, clutching the table with his old, arthritic hands to steady himself.

"What is this price you would have us pay?" he asked boldly, his voice cracking on the last word, betraying him.

"You know who it is I seek!" the voice replied as the enormous visage rippled and distorted like a flag in high wind. "Bring him to me!"

Relief stole through the old man, for with this request, he understood that the retribution would fall upon the shoulders of his son. He did not feel craven in this respite, no, for it was his son's own doing that had brought this upon him.

"He is here with me," Master Guntram said, pointing beneath the table. "Take him, take him, and spare the lot of us!"

The table flew upward into the night sky, revealing Lord Guntram cowering underneath, and a giant hand reached out of the mist, a hand as gnarled as a thousand-year-old oak, and within this unearthly palm it took him, shrieking fretfully, tossing him high into the sky over the village. He hung there, his mouth choking out the most horrendous of screams as invisible bands pulled his limbs in four different directions. For a brief moment, he looked like the Savior on the cross, but for only a second before there came a rending tear as his arms and legs were separated from their sockets, the grinding rasp of bone snapping in half, followed by a geyser of blood as his head exploded into a million tiny fragments as if a bomb had been detonated within. The villagers watched in horror as his limbs danced and cavorted, free of his body, spinning around and around, held aloft by a rogue cyclone. His blood and liquefied remains rained down upon them, his nose, mouth and moustache landing at the feet of his father, who gasped and clutched his chest. The mouth smiled at him and then pursed as if to give him a kiss, and then Master Guntram was airborne, his screams echoing like that of his son's as the wind and the light eviscerated him.

One by one, each member of the royal family was taken into the air and turned into human jelly, their remains alighting upon the earth at the feet of the villagers in grotesque gelatinous plops. The entire village square became littered with their waste, and it was only when they'd all been liquefied that the air grew still, the light beginning to dim.

"You all belong to me," the voice said, this time in only one octave, that of an old woman. "From this day forward, you shall all be sacrificed, over and over again, for as long as the sands of time turn. That is my promise to all of you, one I made in blood, as yours shall follow. Look."

The gnarled hand appeared again, pointing at the ground. The mounds and pools of congealed flesh began to quiver and dance, to prance gaily in the strobing purple light. Pools ran toward one another and connected with the gobs of flesh, reattaching themselves, becoming solid. As the mounds grew in size, a terrible racket arose from each, the screams of the souls trapped inside crying in unimaginable agony. The mounds ascended into the air and swirled about, legs growing out of strings of skin, arms, hands and faces reappearing where they had once been reduced to fluid. Slowly, agonizingly slowly, the body parts reattached themselves, producing whole the beings they had once been. And when they had been returned to their human form, they were dropped to the ground carelessly, like discarded dolls. Master Guntram opened and closed his eyes, blinking unsteadily in the waning light. Beside him lay his wife and son, and they too were disoriented, their looks those of collective disbelief. The pain he'd just experienced was so acute that to think of it was like living through it again, but it hadn't merely been physical pain; the plain of existence in which he'd just been was one of madness, of excruciating mental torture. His memory of it was fading quickly, but it was someplace he never wanted to go again.

Slowly, with great care, they took to their feet, watching as the purple mist began to retreat, the specter's hoary visage becoming faint, nearly iridescent.

"From this day forth, you shall live forever to die over and over again to pay for your sins against the innocent," the voice said as the light crept away like water swirling down a drain. "You belong to me, you belong to this village, and this is where you shall stay forever, to be punished for eternity..."

The mist and the light receded, and in seconds the starry night sky was once more above them. The villagers were quiet, watching the royal family as they clutched one another, unashamed to openly weep before the town folk. A light rain began to fall, from where was anybody's best guess for the sky above them was clear. When she'd regained her footing, Sadie stood with Jeremiah's hand clamped firmly in her own, watching the sky where the menace had come from. She turned to her partner, saw within his eyes a knowledge she'd never known to be there, a realization that this was real, this was no fantasy. She opened her mouth to speak, to ask him what he knew, when suddenly she saw him fading away, felt herself being sucked down into the ground as her vision began to fail her.

And then she was wrapped inside the darkness once more.

CHAPTER 19

THREE AGAINST ONE

S adie opened her eyes, saw that she was lying on the ground. Like the hallucination she just experienced, sound gradually returned to her, the low burbling of voices. She looked up and saw Jeremy and Conroy standing nearby, deliberating something.

"Holy crap…" she muttered, looking around her, noticing it was still light outside and then glanced at her watch. It was four o'clock in the afternoon, roughly five minutes from when they'd arrived. What she'd just experienced seemed like an eternity.

An eternity…

"Did you just see what I saw?" she said as she gathered her bearings and sluggishly got to her feet. "Am I going crazy?" She looked at the village, saw nothing but the decimated remains it had been reduced to from the fire. "I think I just had another out of body experience." She glanced at the sheriff. "Did you see it too?"

Sheriff Conroy just stared at her, a look of uncertainty on his face.

"I don't know what I saw," he said, unable to hold either of their eyes with his own.

"I saw it," Jeremy said, reaching forward and rubbing Sadie's back reassuringly, "and I'm going to ask you one more time: why don't you go to Rhinelander and talk to the librarian and let the sheriff and I handle this? I think it would be the best thing for you to do at this point."

"What the hell are you talking about? I'm your partner, we're a team!" She scowled at Jeremy, then at Conroy. "This place," she ventured, the words feeling strange in her mouth, but no other explanation could clarify it, "it's cursed, or haunted, or…something. If the survivors *are* here, we have to find them as soon as possible."

Jeremy nodded, taking his hand off her back and smoothing his unkempt hair. He took a deep breath, and then another, fiddling with an invisible wrinkle on his shirt. To Sadie, he appeared to be making a decision, one he wasn't very pleased with. He eyed Conroy speculatively.

"Well, sheriff, you think it's time to do our job?"

The sheriff locked eyes with Jeremy for a long moment, and to Sadie it seemed as if some secret passed between them. She studied them, puzzled. At length the sheriff nodded, but the look on his face remained ambiguous.

"I suppose so," he agreed and then said to Sadie: "We better get to it. Lord knows what might happen to those folks if we don't find them before dark."

"Copy that. Should we split up, Jeremy? Make it go faster?"

He returned her glance, something in his eyes she couldn't read.

"You want to walk around here alone?" he said, and a scrap of the vision returned to her, the enormous face in the sky with teeth as black as old crankcase oil, wrinkles cutting grooves through her flesh like furrows.

"God, no!" she blurted, and this made him laugh. Even the sheriff uttered a guffaw.

"OK, good, because I don't want to wander around here alone either. How about you, sheriff?"

"Me?" Conroy said. "Nope, I say we stick together."

"Good enough," Jeremy said and, taking the lead, they walked further into the village of Amber Hollow.

• • •

At first glance it didn't seem to Sadie that it would take very long to search the ruins, but as the three of them passed from the village square and into downtown, she realized that no matter how small, there were still a lot of places to explore. They had to be thorough, and as the sheriff had suggested, it didn't seem wise to be here long after dark, which gave them about four hours. Sadie stopped in front of the rubble of what might have been a hardware store.

"We have to search all of these buildings," she sighed, wiping sweat from her forehead. "All of the houses too. I don't know if we'll beat the sunset."

"We might not," Jeremy said, but it didn't seem to bother him. In fact, the further they walked into the village, the more his demeanor changed. It wasn't just his words, he appeared to undergo a physical transformation. Although he was alert, he no longer seemed afraid. Sadie regarded him curiously.

"What do we do if we don't find them by then?"

"I'm sure something will present itself," he replied in an aloof manner that was uncharacteristic of him, and for a second Sadie thought he was joking, until she realized he wasn't. He was staring vacantly at the ruins, a detached expression on his face.

"Are you OK?"

He smiled at her dreamily. "Never better."

"You don't seem better," she said, and his countenance changed, the look on his face something she'd never seen before. It was as if there was something that now came between them, and whatever it was, it put their relationship in jeopardy.

"I asked you not to come here, Sadie," he said, but there was no menace in his voice, just something akin to exasperation. "I told you that I might not be able to protect you."

"What are you talking about?" she said, but he ignored her. Instead he stared at the sheriff, and again the two looked at each other in a manner that alluded they were more familiar with one another than they were saying, and this caused Sadie to bristle.

"Is there something you boys know that I don't?"

"Maybe we do," Sheriff Conroy said, "and she does too." He pointed toward the near distance, and when Sadie looked in the direction he was indicating, she saw the shadowy figure of a woman emerge from behind one of the crumbling buildings. She walked with deliberate leisureliness, like a cat stalking a mouse, her eyes peering at them from behind limp strands of auburn hair. As she drew closer, Sadie could see she was streaked with gore; it had dried to a brown color, covering her face and bare arms like tribal tattoos. Her dress was spattered with it, dark against the cottony white. Sadie drew her weapon at once.

"Freeze!" she said, training her gun on the other, and the woman stopped, assessing them curiously. She nodded at Sheriff Conroy and then Jeremy, exchanging a look with them that Sadie couldn't decipher, although once again it appeared information was passed along that she was left out of. The woman nodded once more and then resumed walking forward.

"I said 'freeze'!" Sadie's finger touched the trigger, the memory of the cannibalized body very fresh in her mind. This woman, she was either a part of this cursed place or she was psychotic, and neither one sat well with her at this juncture. "Stop right where you are!"

"Sadie," Jeremy said softly, "put the gun down."

"Are you nuts? She ate somebody!" Sadie never took her eyes off the woman, who continued her slow approach. "What about 'freeze' do you not understand?"

"It would be best if you put the gun down, detective," Conroy said, and this unnerved her enough that she finally took her eyes off the woman to glower at them, and when she did, she was shocked by what she saw.

"What the hell is going on?"

Conroy had his gun out, aimed at her. Jeremy had his hand on the butt of his gun, but it remained in his holster.

"Sadie," Jeremy said, "there are a lot of things you don't understand, things that even if I explained them, you'd have trouble grasping. Now, please, put the gun down."

"You're in on this?" she said incredulously. "You're with these people?"

"It's a lot to digest, but if you just listen to me, it will be OK."

Sadie couldn't believe it, after all they had been through together over the last five years on the job. This made no sense, she thought she knew Jeremy, had actually thought he had a thing for her. This betrayal was more than she could comprehend, even more so than whatever it was that held this village in its grasp and controlled it. She shook her head, began to back away.

"No," she said, "I will not put the gun down. That woman ate someone, and we know it, we saw it on the video surveillance feed. There is no way I'm letting her walk out of here." She studied him closely for a second, her mouth set resolutely. "And I won't let you leave either, or the sheriff. Uh-uh, not gonna happen."

"Sadie," Jeremy said, his voice soft, his eyes boring into hers with an intensity she'd never seen. "There are forces at work here that are bigger than all of us. Like I said, I can't expect you to understand, but you have to trust me—"

"Trust you? Ha! That's a good one." She took two steps back and then another. She now swung the gun back and forth from the approaching woman to Conroy. She wondered when Jeremy would pull his piece and she'd have three people to contend with. She knew she couldn't shoot them all before someone shot her, so she took yet another step back. "I don't think I can do that anymore."

"Sadie," he said, his expression one of deep of sorrow. "I didn't want it to go down like this."

"I'm sure you didn't," she said, even though she had no idea what he meant. Right now, in her humble opinion, it was time to get away from these people immediately. She could hide, call for back-up. If she was lucky, she could get a couple of state patrol officers out here before the sun set. She saw the woman getting steadily closer, the tiny smile that played along her lips widening. She had a large caliber handgun; her hands had been behind her back, and when she brought them forth, Sadie saw the woman was holding it loosely in one hand. There was matted blood in her hair, flecks of it in the corners of her mouth. If there was ever a time to flee, this was it.

"Just stay back," she said, moving away from them, hastily glancing over her shoulder to get a read on where she would go. At this point, she understood she'd have to evade gunfire, and she'd have to move very quickly to do that. "I'll shoot anyone that makes a move for me."

She continued retreating, her eyes darting from Conroy, to Jeremy, to the woman, and then back. "I'm sure I'm a better shot than you are sheriff, so don't get any funny ideas. And you," she called to the woman, "don't even try it. You'll be on the ground with a bullet in your forehead faster than you can say, 'Bon appetite' got it? Everyone just stay the hell back!"

She now had a good twenty yards between herself and the others and knew that if she could sprint behind one of the gutted buildings, she'd have a chance to find cover before they could open fire.

"Sadie, don't do this."

"Consider it done, Jeremy."

And then she went for it, she turned and dashed away as quickly as she could. A gun shot rang out, and a piece of wood splintered near her head. Another shot was fired, and she could feel it pass her left ear, missing her by mere inches.

"Hold your fire!" Jeremy yelled, but yet another gunshot obliterated the stillness of the afternoon. Sadie made the corner of one building, out of sight of them, and then took a hard left to flank around the other side in an attempt to do something unexpected. She ran as fast as her stout legs would take her, trying not to trip over the rubble and debris that littered the ground, and still she could hear them coming for her. She made a quick decision, one based on survivalist instinct: she saw a doorway to a building that looked like it could provide a place to hide and she dove for it. Once inside, she could barricade herself long enough to make an emergency call, from then, well, she didn't know what would happen, but she had to make the effort. Four people's lives counted on it. Actually, five, counting herself.

She reached the charred, splintered door and entered quickly, not knowing if they'd seen her or not. She could hear their voices getting closer, but she couldn't make out what they were saying. Stepping in, she studied her surroundings, and saw a door that led to the basement. She peered down the stairs into almost total darkness and then took her flashlight from her belt and flicked it on. The light was dim, and she wondered when she'd last changed the batteries, but realized that it didn't matter now, escape was essential. Taking a deep breath, she placed one boot-clad foot on the top stair and tested her weight on it. It held. She took another step, and then another, negotiating the stairs cautiously to the dirt floor of the basement, hoping she'd have time to do what she needed to do.

• • •

Jeremy was the first around the corner. He saw a flicker of movement in a doorway, a brief flash, but enough to know that it was where Sadie had gone. He didn't, however, have to share that with the two others, not if they didn't already know. There was nothing his partner could do, nowhere she could go that they wouldn't eventually find and subdue her. He stopped, waited for the other two to catch up.

"You didn't have to shoot at her," he said.

"Did you see where she went?" Conroy asked, ignoring the admonition. As far as he was concerned, they had a job to do and results were all that mattered. Keely came up behind him, her weapon in both hands, held chest high.

"No," he said, and Keely frowned, lowering the gun.

"You know you can't protect her forever, Jeremy. This has to end, and the sooner the better."

"I'm aware of that," he said, and truly he was, but he didn't want to deceive the woman he'd been working with for the last five years, one whom he'd become quite fond of. "There's nowhere she can go. Let her hide out for a bit while we take care of the preparations. There's no harm in that, is there?"

The other two gave it some thought, and in short order they tucked their guns away. Keely's expression changed to one of compassion.

"We can't screw this up," she said, "and we don't need any loose ends."

"She isn't a loose end, trust me. Just let her hide." He scrubbed his face with one hand, scratched the stubble. It felt like a million years since he'd last shaved, although it had been this morning. Still, it felt like a lifetime ago. "Everyone present and accounted for?"

"I have them secured in the basement of the Bougie's house. They aren't going anywhere."

"Excellent." He took a last, inconspicuous peek toward the building where Sadie had gone, bid her a silent farewell. He wasn't sure exactly what would transpire over the next day, if he could keep Sadie safe. The three of them had a sworn duty they needed to fulfill. Nothing could stand in their way, not even his beloved partner. He'd try to keep her out of harm's way, but he couldn't promise, not at this stage. "Let's go. Please lead the way."

Keely nodded and then turned and headed for the far side of town, the two men following close behind her.

• • •

Once secreted inside the remnants of the building, Sadie removed her walkie-talkie from her utility belt. It would emit a burst of static when she turned it on and then intermittent bursts while she radi-oed this in, but she had to take the chance. She twisted the dial on top, set it to an emergency frequency. It squawked in her hand as she had expected before she pressed the button.

"This is Detective Sadie Conrad," she said as quietly yet as clearly as she could, "calling for back-up in Amber Hollow. There is a two oh seven and a four one seven in progress, and I need back-up from any officers in the area. I repeat, this is Detective Sadie Conrad of the Brown County Sheriff's Department, and I am in Amber Hollow where there is a two oh seven and a four one seven in progress. Please reply or send help as soon as possible."

She took her finger off the button, waited for an answer, but there was nothing, just the hiss of static. She repeated the mes-sage again, this time with more urgency, yet for all her attempts it seemed her call was going nowhere. She tried once more before giving up, twisting the dial to quiet the walkie-talkie however keep-ing it turned on. She didn't want to miss a return call, that was for damn sure, but she had a feeling that her request for help wasn't going anywhere, that something was stopping her from making the transmission.

For eternity…

At once, she knew what it was: it was this place. This creepy village was keeping her from contacting anyone. She didn't know for sure, but based on the hallucination she'd had (which was fad-ing in her memory now), there were evil forces at work here, why, she didn't know, but the reason wasn't important right now. All that mattered was getting the survivors out of here safely, if she could.

She twisted the knob on the walkie-talkie, sent the message again and waited. When a reply wasn't forthcoming, she squatted down on her haunches, trying to think things through. She stayed like that for a long time, while the light grew dimmer outside.

CHAPTER 20

AMBEREEN GATHERS HER STRENGTH

The house had been completely undamaged by the fire, a fact that none of the three found odd. Even though it sat between two houses that were completely destroyed, among a whole village that was in rubble, it was untouched, not so much as a singe mark on the outside. Keely walked up the porch steps, took a key from her dress pocket and unlocked the door. She swung it open and from within they could hear the hiss of an air conditioner blowing from a mounted window unit. How this house could have power was another mystery, although it didn't even register on their collective radar.

"Feels good in here," Conroy said, taking out a handkerchief and mopping his sweat-dotted brow. "Damn humidity out there sucks."

It was no lie, the summer humidity in Northern Wisconsin was as legendary as the billions of mosquitoes that drained the blood of its innocent residents. A common joke was that these insects were the state bird. Because of this one-two punch, many folks preferred the winter months, even though the snow started falling in October and could continue all the way until May.

"Take a seat and cool down for a moment, boys," Keely said, walking to the kitchen where there was a coffee maker. "Care for a cup?"

"Please," Jeremy said, and Conroy grunted in affirmation. She poured cups for all of them then returned, handed them out. She then took a seat on an overstuffed chair and crossed her long, attractive legs. Even though she was spattered with dried blood, she was gorgeous. Time hadn't touched her smooth, pretty skin, as it hadn't for Jeremy and Conroy, although the sheriff had a face the texture of a well-worn catcher's mitt and Jeremy's the hint of a constant five o'clock shadow.

"How is the girl?" Conroy asked, and Keely smiled radiantly.

"Ask her yourself."

The little girl emerged from a bedroom, a grin on her youthful face. She was wearing a bright pastel dress, and her hair was in pigtails. In one hand she held a doll with porcelain eyes.

"Hello, Ambereen," Conroy said.

"Hi, Sheriff," she replied sweetly, and Jeremy felt his heart tug at her simple beauty and innocence. Of course, she wasn't completely innocent, hadn't been for a long time, but that would end soon, and all of them would be released. Jeremy wasn't sure how he felt about that, personally, but for the girl, it was absolutely the best thing. He'd known it couldn't last forever, hadn't *wanted* it to last that long, but now that he could see a light at the end of the tunnel, he was filled with mixed emotions.

"It's nice to see you again," he said, and she turned her sunny smile on him.

"It's nice to see you too, Jeremiah." Her face clouded suddenly, a pout forming on her lips. "Why did you let the other detective go?"

Jeremy wasn't surprised that she knew this, for Ambereen knew everything that went on in the Hollow, but he hoped that she would understand, could grasp why he'd done what he did.

"She isn't a threat to you," he said, sipping his coffee. "She isn't a threat to any of us."

"She's trying to call for help," Ambereen replied. "She thinks the people downstairs need to be saved."

"Well, we know differently, don't we?"

"Yes," she said, "but I'll need some time to get my strength back. I've been gone too long."

Again, this was something that Jeremy had known, and it was why the others were disappointed in him. The deed they'd come here to do couldn't be done just yet, not if it were to be done right. The girl had to recover from being away from the village. It was a wonder she'd survived outside of it as long as she had.

"How do you feel?" Keely asked her, and the girl came forward, wrapping her arms around the other's shoulders.

"I'm tired, I'm really, really tired."

"You poor thing," she soothed, stroking the girl's hair. She drained her cup and set it down on the table next to her. "We'll take you to the goldmine. And since Jeremy decided to make this game a little more challenging, I think one of us needs to stay here to keep guard."

"I'm not trying to make this harder than it already is, it's, it's just..."

"Jeremiah is in love with her," the girl said, and she giggled into her fist. Keely looked at him in surprise.

"You know how such a love will end, don't you, Jeremy? You aren't doing that poor woman any good by loving her."

He sighed, taking a last sip of his coffee and placing the cup on the table before him.

"I know," he said, "but I can't help it. It just happened."

"Is that why you brought her here, because of this love?"

"No," he said, a note of sadness in his voice. "I tried to talk her into staying in Green Bay, but she wouldn't listen. You don't know her, she would have come here anyway, and I wouldn't have been able to stop her."

"But you know we have to stop her *now*, right?" Ambereen said, and Jeremy nodded.

"Yes," he said, "I do." He truly loved Sadie, but his love for Ambereen eclipsed it. She had been his charge since the day he'd stepped forward to help, and this was the most important thing he'd ever been responsible for in his entire life, which was saying a lot, given the circumstances. The dire actions of the villagers had granted them a reprieve, and to let it slip away was insanity. Here was their opportunity to end it, and anything that got in the way of that was not in their favor. As of this moment, he realized he either had to convince Sadie of the severity of their deed or he had to let her go; there was no other way.

"I'll take care of her," he said, and the girl sensed the sincerity in his words.

"Good," she beamed. "I know you will." She stroked Keely's cheek with one small hand. "Can we go now? I'm so tired."

"Yes, honey." Keely appraised the men. "Who would like to guard the survivors?"

"I'll stay," Conroy volunteered. "I'm kinda pooped. I think I'll just set here and rest a spell."

"If Sadie comes to the house, don't shoot her," Jeremy said, rising to his feet. "Tie her up with the others but keep her alive, is that clear?"

Conroy grinned. "Still chapped, huh? I wasn't shooting to hit her—"

"You could have fooled me."

"Hey, we haven't come this far for me to disappoint you at the end, good buddy. I'll make sure she's all right."

"Thank you," Jeremy said. "OK, let's go."

Taking Ambereen's hand and then Keely's, they walked out into the early evening sunshine.

• • •

Sadie waited for over a half hour for a reply on the walkie-talkie, and when she didn't receive one, she turned it off. The shadows were growing longer outside, this she could see from a little window with a cracked pane of glass. There was no sign of the other three, and she was starting to get antsy. She couldn't just hide down here while there were people in distress, she had to do something. She paced the length of the basement, trying to sort out her thoughts, and the only thing that made sense was to go and look for the survivors. She was stunned that her partner of five years was involved in this, but what this was, well, that was still a mystery. How could he be connected to those people, to this place? Just what the hell had he got himself involved in that it required he stab her in the back for people who were purportedly strangers? Homicidal *cannibalistic* strangers.

Unless they weren't strangers, maybe she was the stranger, the interloper in some secret world where nothing made sense, where one could be transported to some alternate reality where your body pantomimed a performance put on by people hundreds of years ago. What had that vision been trying to tell her? She could only hold on to small bits and pieces, but of what she saw, she knew that some terrible power was in control here, but what Jeremy and the others' position in the scheme of things was, she couldn't even guess. She couldn't imagine him working for the forces of evil, yet if it wasn't that, what was it?

She was damned if she knew, but she was also damned if she was going to just sit here and do nothing. She looked out the window again, saw naught but the abandoned town. She made up her mind: she wasn't going to hide anymore, she had to do what she'd intended to do all along, even if it put her in danger.

Even if it kills me…

For that was her job, wasn't it? To protect and to serve. And that's just what she'd do, even if the odds were greatly stacked against her.

Steeling herself against the inevitable, she ascended the stairs and into the muted light above.

• • •

They had just reached the mine when Ambereen stopped, raised her head, listened. She stood quite still for some time, her head tilted, reminding Jeremy of the dog in the old RCA ad, and after a long while, she nodded.

"I don't hear anything," she said. "I think it's safe."

"Wonderful," Keely said. "I'll accompany you inside. Why don't you wait here, Jeremy? I'll be out in a bit."

"Sure."

The two disappeared into the mouth of the mine, and as Jeremy waited, he thought about poor Sadie. He wasn't sure what would become of her when this was finished, wasn't sure he wanted to know. None of this was scripted, and he and the others had no idea how it would turn out. They could only hope that the little girl would find peace, and if that was attainable, that was good enough for him. He craned his neck, enjoying the rays of the fading daylight. All they had to do was keep the remaining villagers locked up overnight, and in the morning, they could perform the final ritual and be finished with this, be free. At least, that was what they were all hoping. If he was a praying man, possibly he'd put in his request, but he knew that wasn't a solution, just wishful thinking. If anything could break the hold on Ambereen, this was the only resolution that made sense. In a matter of time, they would know. Until then, he could only watch and wait.

• • •

When she rounded the corner of the first building, she let her gun take the lead. Very slowly, she peered around the other side, looking from left to right in a wide sweep. Nothing there. Where were they? she wondered. Were they looking for her or tending to their own business? She didn't know, and this uncertainty caused her to move very cautiously. She was the last link to safety for the poor people trapped here, and getting herself killed was like signing their death certificates herself. Could she live with that on her conscience? She really didn't think so.

She didn't want to expose herself, but as she moved out into the open, she did so very deliberately, scrutinizing every shadow, jumping at stray leaves blowing in the wind. It was so quiet here. As she'd noticed earlier, there were no other sounds of life, just the blustering of an endless wind, some odd weather pattern that began at the Amber Hollow town line and probably ended on the other side where Highway 29 stretched further into the isolation of Torrance County. And what was on the other side but woods? Infinite miles of forest without end, knitting seamlessly together to become part of Upper Michigan. She didn't want to think of what else might be out there, but she figured if there was anything to fear, it was right here, not out there in all that wilderness. No, the monster was here, and she had to do something about it. The gun she held in her hands wouldn't do much good if she encountered something that wasn't of this world, but it comforted her nonetheless. It wasn't going back in her holster, and there would be nothing stopping her from using it should the occasion arise.

And that's what almost happened: a figure appeared a ways down the road, a silhouette with the diminishing sunlight behind him, walking very slowly. A closer look showed it was a man, and he had a gun drawn too. Holding her .45 in both hands, one eye squinted to sight down the barrel, she approached him as silently as possible, keeping him in her cross hairs. As she got closer, she realized she recognized him, but she couldn't recall from where. It didn't matter, though, for she had to take anyone into her custody before they could turn a weapon on her. She was almost upon him when he saw her, and he uttered a short yelp and fell back a step. His mouth hung open for a moment, but then his expression turned to one of relief.

"Oh, thank Christ it's you." He lowered his weapon, inspected her carefully. When she didn't put her gun down, he cleared his throat and grinned. "Uh, don't shoot." 203

Sadie recognized him now: he was the deputy who'd been standing guard at the barrier when she and Jeremy had first come here, and judging by the look on his face, he certainly didn't appear to be gunning for her. But she didn't know that, not yet anyway, and she wasn't taking any chances.

"What are you doing here?" She kept the gun trained on him, and she could see it was starting to unnerve him.

"I...I honestly don't know." He flashed a sheepish smile, and Sadie detected sincerity in his voice. "I have the day off today. I wasn't even supposed to put on the uniform but for some reason I felt compelled to do it." He shrugged. "Pretty weird, huh?"

"Are you in cahoots with Sheriff Conroy?"

"What do you mean? I work for him."

"Well, he's gone nuts, him and my partner and some crazy woman who I think is a librarian from Rhinelander. They tried to take my gun away and then they shot at me." She gestured to the gun he held in his hand. "You mind dropping that and kicking it over here?"

"Why?"

"I want to know if you're on my side."

He laughed, but then he did what she asked, bending over to place it on the ground at his feet before kicking it toward her.

"That's got to be the strangest thing I've ever heard," he said. "How can I be on your side over that of my commanding officer?"

"I told you: he's gone nuts. Would you believe me if I put my gun away?"

"I think that would certainly help."

Sadie lowered her gun and placed it in her holster, although she didn't snap the clasp. She wanted it ready, just in case. She bent over and retrieved his, but held it pointed down.

"What's your name?"

"Deputy Sanders," he said, extending his hand but she ignored it.

"Do you know what's going on here?"

"Detective," he said, his grin returning, "I don't even know what I'm doing here. This place gives me the creeps." He glanced around, actually shivered visibly. "I had the pick-up truck loaded, you know? The fishing poles, bait, a ham and swiss sandwich on a French roll and a six-pack of Buckhorn in the cooler. I was gonna go out on the lake, maybe catch me a trout or some perch even though I was hoping for a Muskie, and the next thing I knew I was back in the house, changing clothes. Then I was in the squad car." His smile dissolved, a perplexed expression replacing it. "It was like I had no choice, I had to come here."

Sadie examined him as he spoke; she could see the genuineness on his face, hear the frank bewilderment in his vocal cadence. What he was saying was odd, but what could one consider bizarre, here? It seemed one checked normalcy at the town line.

"How long have you been working for the Crandon Police Department?"

"About four years, why?"

"How long has Sheriff Conroy been working for them?"

"Hell, I don't know, but most likely forever. It's like they built the building around him because he was already there."

His answers seemed honest, and Sadie made a quick decision, one she hoped she wouldn't regret, but she decided to trust him. She took a step closer to him, and he in turn took a step toward her. He didn't look very threatening, but then again, she hadn't perceived a threat from her partner of five years either. It was best to be safe, but the read she was getting from this man seemed OK. She took an even bigger chance and held his gun out to him. He looked at it, looked at her, and when she nodded, he took it and placed it in his holster.

"Are you from Crandon?"

"No, ma'am, Crivitz born and raised."

"How much do you know about this town?"

"Not much but what the people in Crandon say about it: the folks here are weird." He shrugged, a gesture he appeared very good at. "*Were* weird."

"Weird how?"

"Well, here's a tidbit you may or may not know: none of them ever leave, they're born here, they die and are buried here."

"And you know this how?"

"Why, I suppose I just grew up hearing the stories, like about the gold mine, and how come they never had to invite any outsiders in because they could make do for themselves."

"Anything else?"

"Yeah, there's another thing."

"What?"

"This place," he said, looking around to see if anyone was listening, "it's cursed. There's something really strange going on around here."

Sadie laughed, an honest-to-God belly laugh. "Deputy," she said, smirking, "tell me something I don't know."

CHAPTER 21

FREEING THE SURVIVORS

When Keely emerged from the mouth of the mine, the expression on her face was puzzling. She looked uneasy, and to Jeremy that spelled trouble.

"What's wrong?" he said, and she tried to smile but failed.

"The poor girl," she said, "she's wiped out from being out of the Hollow for so long. I wonder if one night in the mine will restore her to full strength."

"If it doesn't, we'll just have to wait until she does. None of us are going anywhere until this is over."

"She never should have gone."

"She had to, you know that. There was no telling what any of the survivors would have done, and there was no guarantee we would have been able to get them back here."

"But I did," she said, drawing closer. "I got them all back."

"Yes, but we were lucky. If it hadn't been for that serial killer's arrest in Milwaukee, we'd still have the FBI to contend with." He appraised her for a moment, looking past the dried blood and seeing the beautiful, intelligent woman before him. "Will you be all right, you know, after what you had to do to Corey, and to the hospital janitor?"

She looked away, shuddering momentarily, and then returned her gaze upon him, her eyes fiercely alight with grim resolve. They appeared moist, but there were no impending tears.

"I didn't have a choice so I can't really feel bad, can I? We're all playing out the roles that have been assigned to us." She studied him in return, gave him a small smile. "Besides, it's not like I haven't had to do that in the past, you either, for that matter."

He nodded. "I know, and I don't like it, I never did."

What any of them did, they did because they were commanded to. They may have had some free will, but not all. What the old woman had put in motion had been ordained a long time ago and they had to go along, like it or not. They'd given up their freedom of choice the second they'd stood up for her and Ambereen, but there was no way they could have known that then. For their compassion, they'd been awarded both a gift and a curse. The only thing that made it better was recognizing what was at stake, although the methodology was less than desired. From the moment Jeremy had learned that Corey had gone to Rhinelander he knew he'd never see him again, that anyone who meddled would invoke retribution...he'd known that every day since this had all began. Everything he'd done to look for him had been for Sadie's benefit only, and believe it or not it broke his heart. The kid had only been trying to be useful and for his trouble the curse had claimed him. And for what it was worth, it wasn't his fault or Keely's, it was simply the luck of the draw in a game with unbreakable rules.

"We're not monsters."

"I know that, but I'm sure I didn't exactly look like a saint on the video footage from the hospital."

"Don't think about it. It's done now."

"What I wonder is how you will deal with your partner. We can't let her stop us...so where does that leave us?"

Jeremy didn't hesitate when he replied: "I'll do whatever I need to do to ensure Ambereen's safety, you know that."

"Do I?"

"You should."

"I won't hesitate to kill her if that becomes necessary," she said, and he gave her a look that neither accepted nor rejected her statement.

"I know you will," he said, "and that's what you're supposed to do. We're Ambereen's guardians."

Keely smiled, a beautiful, ageless smile that made Jeremy almost forget about Sadie for a moment, but only a moment. Keely and he had been lovers a long time ago, but that was the past, the very distant past, and ever since they'd been inseparable partners, locked together within a puzzle that wasn't of either of their design.

"Do you still think I'm pretty?"

"Are you crazy? You look just as good as the day I met you." ·

"How can you remember that far back?"

"I remember more than you'd ever know."

"I don't doubt that."

She reached out, took his hand. "Come on, let's take a walk."

"Are you trying to seduce me?" Jeremy said, and she laughed, a husky, titillating sound.

"No, you goof, not anymore. Let's just take a walk. I could use some fresh air."

"What about the survivors?"

"I think Conroy has it handled, don't you?"

Jeremy nodded. "Yeah, I don't think they're going anywhere."

"Good enough. Come on. Let's go to the river. Maybe you might want to take a swim."

"Only if you go swimming too."

"You know I will, I look like a fright. I have to wash the blood off."

He reached forward with one free hand and brushed a stray lock of her hair over one ear, leaned close and kissed her on the forehead.

"I love you," he said, and the smile she gave him was one of deep sorrow.

"I know," she said. "I love you too."

The two set off for the river, leaving the girl alone in the gold mine to rest and to heal herself before the next phase of their plan could begin.

• • •

As they walked along, Sadie nearly had the desire to take the deputy's hand. Her rational mind knew it was stupid, but for a moment, she wanted the reassurance of another's touch, something to keep her connected to reality. She shook it off though because someone had to be in charge, and in this case it certainly wasn't going to be him, so by default that was her job. She did step a bit closer to him as they crept along, and that made her feel a little better.

With every step deeper into the village, Sadie felt the tension ratcheted to a near fevered pitch, with the constant sound of the mysterious wind blowing overhead countered by the pointed absence of any other noises, her nerves felt frayed. As they passed from the downtown and into the residential section, she pondered the possibility that there was nothing here left alive, that the fire had killed every living thing. But the lack of any other sound than the wind…it was an incongruity that deeply disturbed her, as well as the knowledge that Jeremy and the others could be hidden anywhere, waiting to make an ambush.

"So, we find the survivors, and then what?" Deputy Sanders asked, and to this Sade had no immediate reply.

"We have to get them to safety," she said at length, but she wasn't exactly sure what that would entail. Dusk was upon them, and out here, when darkness fell, it would be near total, for there were no lights to guide them through the dark save for their flashlights, and Sadie's was already running low on juice.

"They could be in any one of these houses," he said, pointing at the derelict structures. "How come we're passing them by?"

"They don't feel right," she said, not exactly knowing what she meant but knowing it was correct. Jeremy and the others had to have them somewhere that escape was impossible, and these dwellings didn't look very secure. She didn't know *exactly* what they intended to do with them, but she had a good idea, given that they'd shot at her, but a bigger question was one regarding their motive. That was the hardest thing she was struggling with, the *why*. That really had her stymied.

She glanced at the deputy, watched him almost trip trying to swat at a mosquito buzzing around his head, and despite her fear, she grinned. He may have been a lock stock and barrel goofball, but right now she was glad he was with her, for she couldn't imagine having to do this alone. And his action also proved that not everything was dead; the mosquito population had hardly been deterred.

"How are they supposed to feel?"

"I don't know, but I'll know when I find it."

They walked without talking as the shadows grew longer, and as they were reaching the outskirts of the residential section Sadie stopped abruptly, staring straight ahead, and the deputy, who hadn't been watching, bumped into her.

"Watch it," she said, but there was no menace in her voice.

"Sorry."

"There," she said, and the deputy followed her finger to where she was pointing, saw an anomaly that didn't make any sense.

"Now, how in hell did that happen?"

"You got me, but if they were going to be anywhere, that sure looks like it would be the place."

He had to agree it did. What they were looking at was a house that was completely intact, not so much as a burn mark marring what looked like birch logs. The lawn, too, hadn't been touched, and to Sadie it emanated an aura of evil. The last thing she wanted to do was go inside, but she knew there was no choice. They had to.

She ducked back, behind the ruins of a nearby house, grabbing the deputy by one arm and dragging him with her.

"If the survivors are in there, we have to assume someone is guarding them."

"What do we do?"

Sadie studied the house carefully, planning their strategy. The front door wouldn't work, as that would be too obvious, but there must be a back way, maybe a window they could crawl through.

"Follow me."

She went around the adjacent cottage, crouched down, moving as silently as possible. The deputy did his best to keep up with her, but he was clumsy, and crouch-walking wasn't his forte, so he resorted to crawling. Seeing him like that was funny, and maybe she would have laughed had it been another place and time, but she was too frightened to do so. When they reached the rear of the neighboring house, she knelt down, deliberating her next move. She saw a porch that led to a back entrance, but she figured that entry would be guarded as well, so she kept looking until her eyes alighted on a basement window. It was small, and possibly locked, but she figured they could both fit through it. She'd break it if she had to, but she hoped it wouldn't come to that.

"We have to get to that window as quickly and quietly as possible."

"I don't like this."

"Neither do I, but we have to do something and that looks like our only choice." She saw the uncertainty on his face. "You can stay here if you want to, but I could really use your help. It's three against two."

"Who are we up against, really?" he asked, his voice betraying his fear. "Sheriff Conroy couldn't be behind this."

"Well, he is, and so is my partner and a librarian from Rhinelander. I don't know why, but they're all in on this together."

"Maybe there's a reasonable explanation—"

"They shot at me, deputy. There is no reasonable explanation for that."

"OK, but this sucks."

"You think I don't know that? Now, follow my lead and stay behind me."

Sadie surveyed the yard surrounding the house, and when she felt reasonably sure it was clear, she made a quick dash for the window, the deputy right on her heels. Squatting, she saw that the opening was so old-fashioned that it merely had two metal hook clasps. These she undid, raising it slowly to avoid any noise it might make.

"I'll climb in, and when I see if it's safe you come in next."

"All right," he said, but he sounded unsure.

"Don't you flake out on me," she hissed, "I need you to back me up."

"I will," he said, and this time she believed he would do as she asked.

"Hang tight, and I'll let you know in a minute."

And then she disappeared through the small window.

•   •   •

Sheriff Conroy sat in a Lazy-boy, reading a book. He'd read it before, but he had nothing better to do while he waited for Jeremy and Keely's return. Besides, it was a classic he'd enjoyed since he'd been a kid. Even though he knew how it ended, he simply loved the way the author teased the reader with little clues that eventually led to the surprise ending.

A half hour earlier, he'd looked in on the survivors, reassured himself that they were all present and accounted for. They'd looked at him with pleading, desperate eyes, and damn straight. They knew what fate awaited them, and they didn't like it one bit. He'd say he couldn't blame them, but he did. All of this was their fault, and in doing what they'd done, they'd also condemned him to this situation.

If it hadn't been for them, his life would have turned out a hell of a lot different than this, that was sure as shootin'. Had he been a cruel man, he could have knocked them around a bit, made them suffer a little more than they were going to eventually. However, he wasn't such a person. He knew that when the reckoning was delivered, it would be all the torture they could get and then some. The worst thing he did was hand feed them a few sips of water and a couple of stale Ritz crackers as sustenance when he could have been a better host and offered sandwiches. That ought to teach 'em.

He turned the page to start the next chapter when he heard something from the basement, a voice grunting in surprise. He got to his feet, dropping the book on the seat of the chair and listening. He could hear the incessant wind blowing, could almost make out the distant sound of the Iron River lapping at the banks, but from below him there was now nothing but silence. Maybe one of them sneezed, or coughed, maybe groaned in pain from being in restraints for so long. He stood there for several minutes, waiting to hear it again, and when another sound wasn't forthcoming, he returned to his chair, picked up the book and sat back down, trying to find his page. He was just finishing chapter twelve when another noise came from downstairs, and this one was unmistakable, for it was the sound of footsteps on the stairs.

"Not on my watch," he said, removing his .357 from its holster and heading for the basement door. "Not on my Goddamn watch."

He approached the door slowly, his gun cocked and ready, his hand reaching for the handle when it suddenly flew open, striking him in the forehead and knocking him to the floor. Simultaneously the gun sprang from his hand, skittering well out of reach. Sadie stood there on the top step, and he could see the survivors behind her, clutching one another in fear.

"Stop, woman!" he bellowed. "Whatever you think, you're wrong! They need to stay down there, they aren't who you think they are!"

Sadie paid no heed; she stepped up and walked over the threshold, ushering the survivors toward the front door of the house. She kept her gun aimed at Conroy's head.

"You stay out of my way, sheriff and I won't shoot you, I promise." She appraised the survivors, Andrew LeCarre, his face covered in bandages, Sylvia Albright, and the woman whose name she didn't remember, the one who'd somehow faked a coma. "Go on, get out of here and I'll be right behind you."

LeCarre looked out the door uncertainly, checking to see if the coast was clear, while the other two huddled closely behind him, clinging to his broad shoulders. They'd all been tightly bound, and the welts on their skin showed ample evidence of this. Sadie had had to use her knife to cut the ropes that'd restrained them, rough pieces of hemp she'd left on the basement's dirt floor.

"I have no idea why you would do this," Sadie said, stepping around Conroy, trying to keep several feet between he and her, "but I have to assume it's illegal, whatever it is. I'm going to get these people back to the hospital where they belong."

"You don't understand, Detective Conrad," Conroy said, getting to his feet with an agility she wouldn't have dreamed he'd possess for a man his age. "I can explain it to you, but we need to get them back downstairs and tie them up first." He offered a plaintive look that appeared genuine, but Sadie couldn't trust it, couldn't trust anything but her instincts at this point.

"No dice, sheriff. You just stay back and—"

"You put that gun down nice and slow, missy," the deputy said from behind her, and Sadie could have kicked herself in the ass. Why she had allowed him to take the rear, she didn't know, but it was surely her undoing. She turned around, saw he had his gun pointed at her.

"Don't you worry, sheriff, I got her. You go ahead and get your gun."

"So, you're in on this with them?" she said, and he stared at her blankly.

"I don't know what you're talking about, but he's the sheriff of Crandon and I take my orders from him, not you." The deputy grinned as he said this, and Sadie realized he'd played her all along. He may have been a bigger hayseed than she, but he'd duped her fair and square. The only thing he'd probably told the truth about was his dislike for this place, and she assumed that would be anyone's reaction.

Sheriff Conroy retrieved his gun, aiming it at the survivors. "You all just stay right there with your hands where I can see them. I'm going to get you back downstairs where you belong and we're going to end this. Hasn't this gone on long enough?"

LeCarre stared at the sheriff and his gun defiantly.

"We tried to end it," he said, his voice muffled by the bandages, "but it doesn't seem like it will ever be over."

"It will, LeCarre, trust me," Conroy said. "Now, I want you all to walk over toward the basement door real slow."

LeCarre didn't move, he just stared back with hard, unforgiving eyes.

"I'm not doing it, Conroy, you can't make me."

"Now, you know I can't shoot you, but I want you to listen to me: you brought this on yourselves so you might as well be good and just let this whole thing play itself out." He looked at Sadie, saw the confusion on her face, and he couldn't blame her. Without knowing the whole story, there was no way she could understand everything that had transpired to bring them to this point. And he meant what he'd said to Jeremy; there was no way he was going to disappoint him by doing something stupid. He wanted to reassure her, but words couldn't articulate what they were experiencing, not without him sounding crazy.

"I'm getting them out of here, sheriff," Sadie said, her stance unchanged despite the deputy's gun on her. "That's my job, to protect and serve. That's your job too, in case you forgot."

"I *do* protect and serve," he replied calmly, "more so than you would ever know."

"Then stand down and let me get them to safety."

"I can't do that."

"Then I guess you'll have to shoot me, or I'll have to shoot you. Which one is it going to be?"

"I'm not going to shoot you, woman. I made a promise and I aim to keep it."

"A promise to whom?"

"Your partner," he said, lowering his gun slightly. "He doesn't want you to get hurt, so I don't want that either."

"I'll take care of her, sheriff," Deputy Sanders said, "then we'll get these bastards back downstairs."

"Stand down, deputy, I have this under control."

"It doesn't look that way to me," Sadie said, pulling back the hammer on her gun. "Now call off your boy."

"Stand down, deputy," Conroy ordered, but Sanders ignored him.

"Maybe you made a promise, sheriff, but I didn't. I'll be happy to blow her head off right now."

"Put the damn gun away and stand down, Sanders!"

"Consider the bitch toast." The deputy cocked his pistol, his eyes gleaming sadistically. Conroy tried to warn her, but the deputy was too quick. His finger was on the trigger when Sheriff Conroy did the only thing he could do: he took aim and fired his weapon.

The report was extremely loud within the confines of the small cottage, and when Sadie heard it, she reacted by discharging her weapon as well, hitting Sheriff Conroy in the chest and knocking him flat off of his feet.

"Oh my God..." she said, turning to look at the deputy. He had a small hole in his forehead where the bullet had gone in, the back of his head splattered on the wall behind him. His eyes were wide, shocked, and she knew without checking his pulse that he was dead.

"What the hell is going on here?" she asked the survivors, and was amazed to see the lack of emotion on their faces. They didn't even appear relieved that their captors were down. She didn't know what to think of that, but she didn't have time to give it much more thought because of the next distraction.

"I can't let you leave here with them, Sadie."

She turned, saw Sheriff Conroy struggling to sit up. The bullet hole in his chest was shrinking, the blood returning to the site of the shot and reentering his body, as if she were watching a film played backward. Her eyes bulged, her mouth slack. What she was seeing was impossible, couldn't be happening, not in a thousand lifetimes...

"We better get gone, honey," LeCarre said, "before he recovers himself and stops us."

Sadie took several steps back, her eyes never leaving the sheriff, who appeared to be feeling better by the second. His eyes shone with a brilliant light as his body miraculously repaired itself, but what she also couldn't believe was that he'd shot his own deputy to protect her. And the expression on his face...it appeared to be one of compassion, not of loathing, definitely not fear. At least, he didn't fear *her*, of that she was certain. He reached out a hand to her and for a moment she felt compelled to take it, but in her terror, she stumbled backward and bumped into one of the survivors, and the woman took hold of Sadie's arm, dragging her out the door and into the dusky evening. Sadie could hear the sheriff grunting strenuously, getting to his feet, the air whistling in and out of his lungs laboriously as he struggled to come after them.

"Do you have a plan, dear?" the woman who'd faked the coma asked, and Sadie didn't know how to respond, in all honesty didn't know what to do. LeCarre stepped forward, took her by her other arm.

"You think about that while we get out of here," he said, and they headed for the outskirts of town and the dense woods beyond.

CHAPTER 22

THE SURVIVORS' STORY

The sunset was a brilliant display of orange, purple and gold, and for the first time in a very long time, Jeremy felt at peace. Being back in Amber Hollow gave him an overwhelming sense of calm, even in its decimated state, for this had been his home for a long time. The position he'd taken with the Brown County Sheriff's Department had been required of him; like Sheriff Conroy, he'd been assigned a vigilant post, in the event that the villagers attempted a coup. It was no surprise that it turned out to be a good idea.

He'd enjoyed his time in Green Bay, though, and he felt bad that he'd lied to Sadie, but she would understand before too long, and he suspected that would make everything better. The ending, however, wouldn't be pretty, but that was the fire they had to walk through before they could move on to whatever was next. He wondered if he'd ever get to see his dog, Roxie, again, and his heart lurched with a sick thud, sensing that he probably never would.

Keely stood in the water up to her knees, her dress hiked up in her hands as she waded. She leaned over and splashed water on her face and arms, washing away the blood, and Jeremy thought she looked stunning in the fading light. His love for her was purely platonic, nonetheless, he appreciated her charm and infinite intellect. She exuded an aura of worldly mystique with even the most casual gesture.

"Are you going to just stand there or are you coming in?"

He stared at her, mixed feelings running through him that he couldn't immediately identify. For a second, he wished he could spend the rest of eternity living in this precise moment, however foolish that may seem. The sky was so rich with the fading sun, the light reflecting off of the water making it appear as ageless as young Ambereen. The beauty of everything around him made him want to burst into irrational tears that were neither of sorrow nor happiness but some mythical place in-between. He smiled at Keely and then sat down and took off his shoes and socks. Rolling up his pants, he carefully navigated the stones and waded into the river beside her. She reached out her hand and he took it, and the two of them watched as the sun set.

"What do you think is going to happen when this is all over?" she said, and he turned to her, giving her his most sincere smile.

"I don't know, but I think we'll finally get to take a day off."

Her laughter was genuine, and it made him feel good. He wanted to kiss her, and he couldn't see why that would be a bad thing, so he did, gently, on her cheek. She blushed, and it made her look even prettier.

"What a romantic you are," she said.

"Yes, I suppose I am."

"There's nothing wrong with that, you know." She glanced at him sidelong. "And there's nothing wrong with loving Sadie."

"I guess, but there's nothing I can do about it."

"You don't know that, maybe you can."

He didn't look at her, he kept his eyes on the horizon. He didn't say anything for several minutes, and when he did speak, it was deeply heartfelt.

"If there was some way to be with her, I would. But you know as well as I do that after we're done here, we're done. Aren't you relieved for that?"

"I didn't think this was ever going to be over, so yes, I suppose I will be relieved." She bent down, reached into the water and picked up a handful of stones. She then began to skip them across the surface, and Jeremy decided to join her. He reached down and picked up a handful of stones as well, and the two laughed as they watched them skimming over the surface.

. . .

Passing from a clearing and into dense foliage, Sadie was surprised at the dexterity of the survivors. It would seem logical that because of their injuries, they would have trouble navigating the forest in the growing darkness, but they were able to move faster than she was. Indeed, it was she who was trying to keep up with them. She was still trying to process what happened at the house, the logic defying, miraculous recovery of sheriff Conroy and the death of his erstwhile deputy, but that didn't keep her feet from moving, didn't keep her from wanting to put as much distance between themselves and him as she could.

He wasn't afraid of me, but he is afraid of them...

She paused for a moment to catch her breath, and she couldn't help but see Conroy's face in her mind's eye, how calm he appeared as his skin stitched itself back together and spit the shell casing out onto the pine floor with a metallic pinging sound.

He shot his own deputy. Why would he spare her life over that of his deputy?

Her thoughts were interrupted when she heard the sound of laughter coming from just east of them. She stopped so she could listen better, and when she did, she immediately recognized it; it was Jeremy and the cannibal librarian.

"Everybody stay quiet," she said, but that wasn't necessary. The three were practically holding their breath.

"The river is in that direction," LeCarre whispered. "We need to go the other way." He pointed toward the darkening forest.

"Where's the goldmine?" Sadie said, thinking frantically. "Could we hide there?"

"God, no," Sylvia blurted and then put a hand over her mouth to shush herself. Sadie looked at her questioningly. "That's the last place we want to go," the woman explained. "In fact, we want to go as far as we can from there."

"What's wrong with the goldmine?"

"Later," LeCarre interjected. "I know where we can go, just follow me."

Conroy didn't shoot me because Jeremy told him not to...am I backing the wrong pony?

"What's going on here?" Sadie said, keeping her voice as low as possible.

"When we get to a safe place, I'll tell you, and then you can decide what you think we should do."

"Sheriff Conroy knew you by name," Sadie said to LeCarre. "How does he know you?"

LeCarre looked discomfited, but he answered without hesitation. "Let's just say that he and I have a history."

"What do they want from you?"

"I'll tell you, but we can't do it here." LeCarre looked past her, toward the river where Jeremy was giggling with his girlfriend.

Facts are facts: that woman killed and ate somebody and now Jeremy and Sheriff Conroy are working with her. Whatever these people did, it couldn't be worse than that, could it?

"OK," Sadie said, making up her mind at last. She didn't feel threatened by these people, in fact, they looked so cowed she was certain she could take on all of them at once, should that become necessary. She'd listen to what they had to say, and then make a decision. Following LeCarre, they crept deeper into the ever-darkening woods.

• • •

Moving as quickly as he could, Conroy dragged the deputy's body behind the house and covered it with a sheet he stripped from one of the beds. He was sorry that he had to shoot the kid, because he hadn't done anything wrong except try and protect him, but he couldn't let him shoot the detective and he'd had no other choice. If he had shot to wound him, the deputy might have fired another round, and that hadn't been a chance he'd been willing to take. Why he had even come here, Conroy didn't know. He'd given him the day off to keep him out of the way, but it was no surprise that he somehow turned up. In Amber Hollow, bad things just happened, no matter what you did to protect yourself from them.

Once he was done, he headed toward the river, figuring that Jeremy and Keely might be there. He knew it was a favorite spot of theirs, and that once, in another lifetime, they'd been sweet on each other. This thing that held them in its grip, it had robbed them of everything, the most important thing being love. It was tragic, but there it was. Sometimes, there are things in this world and beyond that are more important, no matter how unsatisfying that might be.

Walking as fast as he could, he made his way toward the river in the dying light.

• • •

Leading them through near dark, LeCarre brought them to a clearing that to Sadie felt as if it must be at least two or three miles outside of the village. By the time he stopped, they were all breathing hard, and he pointed them to a fallen tree where they sat down. Darkness and silence settled over them in tandem.

Sadie sat still for a moment, taking deep breaths. She noticed that they didn't seem as winded as she was, and yet they had all been recently hospitalized. She stared hard at LeCarre, straining to look him in the eyes in the dark. It was time to hear their story, that was for damn sure. He fidgeted with his bandages as she stared him down, his fingers crawling like spiders over his indistinguishable face. The gauze was starting to come loose, and he tried continuously to keep it in place as it became more shredded at the edges, but the tape was losing its stickiness.

"Everything you told me was a lie," she said. "You have to tell me the truth now. It's the only way I can help you."

"Telling you the truth *won't* help us," Sylvia said, "but I suppose you deserve to know what really happened."

"What's that supposed to mean?"

"Why, detective, you sound as if you are angry with us," LeCarre said. "I thought you were here to save us."

"What the hell happened back there? Conroy just killed his deputy and then pulled a Lazarus, and none of you seem to be the least bit surprised."

"We're not," LeCarre said. "Feel better?"

"No." Sadie looked from one face to the next, her gaze settling on the woman who'd been in the coma. "I haven't had the pleasure of meeting you."

"I'm Helen LaCroix." The woman offered her hand and Sadie shook it. Her palm was completely smooth, like she'd never done a day of work in her life, and her skin ice cold.

"Were you faking a coma? The FBI agents said they woke you up using smelling salts."

"I have no memory of anything until talking to them. The last thing I remember was being here before everything went dark."

Sadie didn't trust the honesty of the woman's reply, but she let it go. For the time being, they had more important things to deal with. She returned her attention to the other two.

"Why did you lie to me when I first talked to you? Why did you two tell me a different story?"

"I don't want to sound like Jack Nicholson from that movie," LeCarre said, "but we didn't think you could handle the truth."

"You'd be surprised at what I can handle."

LeCarre chuckled. "Maybe, maybe not."

"What happened to the sheriff back there? That...that's impossible."

"Nothing is impossible here; in fact, *anything* is possible here, thanks to that little girl."

"I don't get it."

"Just listen, and maybe you will. I'll tell you what's really going on, but I have to warn you, it isn't a nice story."

"Can the crap and just tell me," Sadie said, irritated by the cryptic nature of the man's tone. She'd had enough of that to last her a lifetime at this point. "We haven't got all day."

"No, I guess we don't," he agreed, settling back on the log and crossing his legs. "This story goes back quite a ways, over two hundred years to be exact."

The look on Sadie's face made him chuckle again, for it was one he'd expected.

"This is going to be a lot for you to take in, I suspect."

"Could be," Sadie said, "but I'm all ears.

"The village was founded in 1774, and there were about seven hundred of us when we got off the boats, but we were down to just over six hundred before too long. My wife perished during the first winter, as well as one of my sons—"

"This isn't going to work if you're going to keep lying to me," Sadie said. "Even though Sheriff Conroy miraculously healed himself of a gunshot wound and you people don't think it's a big deal, I still find it hard to believe that I'm talking to someone who came over on the freakin' Mayflower."

"You're just going to have to listen with an open mind, honey," Sylvia said. "What Andrew is telling you is real, and it will give you an idea of what we are up against."

Sadie stared at them with angry, disbelieving eyes, but when she thought of everything that had occurred up until this very minute, well, there had to be some over-the-rainbow wacked out explanation because nothing else in the natural world made sense. There was a cannibalistic librarian who stole her partner from her, the aforementioned self-healing sheriff, two out-of-body experiences she could catalog on her own behalf, as well as a whole town demolished by a fire that had yet to be explained. What the hell, the crazier the man's story, the more likely it was to be true.

"OK, I'll listen," she said, and Andrew nodded satisfactorily.

"That would make this a whole lot easier."

"Go on," she said, so he did.

• • •

"*One thing none of us lied about was Anthony Guntram being to blame; he's the reason for all our trouble. He was a teenager when we settled here, just a few years younger than me, but I could tell a rotten egg when I smelled one. There are some folks who are born bad, and I think Guntram was one, just crazy as an outhouse rat, but what came later sure didn't help.*

"*When we arrived and met the local inhabitants, saw how primitive and godless they were, we took it upon ourselves to try and convert these savages to Christianity. It was what the Good Book told us to do. When they refused, and took up arms against us, we had to thin their ranks to show them who was in charge. That was when his personality changed for the worse, for young Guntram took great pleasure in their conversion, murdering and mutilating any that he saw fit with a biblical fervor. It was during the first three years that he went from being a rebellious kid to a homicidal maniac driven insane from bloodlust. He became toxic, like a diseased animal.*

"*It was upon his eighteenth birthday that he desired to take a wife, but most of the women wouldn't have him, despite his lineage. His family, you see, were the ones who helped us to escape the tyranny of the French ruler who prohibited us to practice our religion and live how we chose. The Guntram family was very wealthy, but in France they had no political power. In the colonies, that could be different, so they financed the ships and provisions that brought us here. Because of Anthony's financial advantage, it was easier for us to look the other way while he committed these atrocities, but when it came to the woman he wanted, well, that's when things got out of hand. There was one girl who was attracted to him, Cassandra Bougie. However, her mother forbid her from seeing him. She recognized pure evil when she saw it.*

"Cassandra was only sixteen years old, very awkward and unsocial, so she played right along to his affections. Because of her mother's disapproval, he abducted her and escaped into the woods where they disappeared for well over a fortnight. A search party was dispatched to find them, but they'd vanished like smoke. Eventually, he returned with her to the village, depositing Cassandra at her mother's hovel, telling her he was through with her. Lord knows what happened out in those woods, what terrible things he did to her, for the girl was weak and emaciated, sick from malnutrition and exposure.

"A month passed, and it became apparent that Cassandra was with child. Her mother was furious because it was obvious the poor girl had been taken against her will. She petitioned the Guntram family to take action against Anthony, but because she was a mere peasant, her cries for justice were ignored. She pleaded with them, even made threats, but eventually her insubordination led to her banishment from the village. We tried to help the disgraced woman, to speak on her behalf, but there was nothing we could do because Anthony wouldn't allow it, nor could Master Guntram be persuaded. The impregnated child never spoke a word on either her own or her mother's behalf, and for this reason she was allowed to stay, much to the disdain of the condemned woman.

"Nine months later, Cassandra had the child, a baby girl, but she died during childbirth. Some thought it was a fitting end for the poor thing; this way she didn't have to live with what was wrought from Guntram's loins, but the question arose as to who would care for the baby. Who could possibly want it?

"A pretty young lady came forth and offered to raise the child, and Anthony accepted under the condition that she live with him, in the royal domicile. She was an outcast in the village; even though she was beautiful,

she harbored a strangeness that kept folks at bay. You've met her, she's the librarian, she's the one who became the baby's nanny. She moved into the Guntram's home and raised the child as her own. She had a lover too, and you know him as well. He is...was...your partner. Lord Guntram also had a henchman, a guy who did his dirty work, and that's Sheriff Conroy. Together, they were all protectors of the child so that none of us good folks could interfere.

"About three weeks after the baby was born, Cassandra's mother came back for her grandchild, but she quickly discovered that wasn't an option. She was heartbroken to learn that her daughter had died, and that her own flesh and blood was being raised by scoundrels, but there was nothing she could do. Master Guntram sent her packing once more, this time with the threat of death by stoning if she ever set foot in the village again. She left, but not without a warning that one day she would return, and either the child came with her or there would be hell to pay. No one took her seriously, and why should they? She'd been in the woods for so long it was apparent she'd gone mad.

"As the child got older, her behavior became erratic. She was oddly sadistic, cruel to the other children and disrespectful to her elders. This conduct was tolerated because of her family lineage, but we didn't like it. She was creepy, like some God-awful insect. She took delight in hurting the other children. And her eyes...they were like black holes, as if she'd stared too long at the sun. You've met that girl too, she's the little one who was rescued from the fire. She's evil but she acts sweet as pie. You can't trust anything they tell you about her.

"On the eve of the celebration of the storming of the French Bastille, ten years after the old woman had been banished from the village, she returned, again seeking her granddaughter. The years out in the woods hadn't been kind to her; Lord knows what she'd been doing over the last decade. She made a scene during the ceremony, demanding the child, and damned if Master Guntram didn't make good on his word and called for her stoning while her granddaughter looked on with impassive eyes. The child didn't know the old woman, had never before met her so she didn't *know what the old lady meant to her. Although the girl didn't partake in the woman's punishment, neither did she stand up for the old crone when the villagers threw the first handfuls of rocks.*

"The old woman squawked like a wounded crow and retreated quickly with Master Guntram's men giving chase. They felled her once near the town line, but she managed to get up and escape into the woods. That was the last time any of us saw her alive, but it wasn't the last time we saw her. Those years out in the forest, she'd been communing with demons...maybe even the Devil himself. Utilizing her knowledge of the dark arts, she took out her rage at Master Guntram by cursing the whole village.

"It started gradually, little things here and there. Our crops died after a summer of exceptional rainfall. Crimson algae overran the banks of the river, and mosquitoes and deer flies infected the villagers with the diseases they carried. Babies emerged from the womb stillborn; pox and malaria swept through the village and further devastated our inhabitants. The graveyard grew bigger as our populace grew smaller. But they were the lucky ones, those who died, because for those of us who lived, there was a fate awaiting us that no one could have ever imagined, nor did we deserve. Because that old woman couldn't have her granddaughter, and because Master Guntram had banished her from the village—almost killing her—she exacted a revenge upon us that she must have sold her soul to attain. A year later, yet again on the eve of the celebration of the storming of the French Bastille, she came to us, but not in human form, no, she'd left this life as we know it and had become a demonic force, a being entirely unnatural in the human realm, with powers we couldn't fathom. I couldn't tell you how she did it, all I know is the consequences: she used her powers to enslave us all. She summoned up a curse that stuck our village in time, made us immortal. If you could see my face under these bandages you would never believe I'm over two hundred and thirty years old, but it's true. All of us, we've been here since the storming of the French Bastille in 1789, since before that even. She cursed us so that we could never move on from this form of existence, that we have to live here in Amber Hollow forever, dying over and over again every year during the celebration of the Bastille.

And it's painful, my God you have no idea how it feels to be eviscerated every year only to be resurrected so that it can be repeated in perpetuity. It's no way to live, and I'll say it again: we don't deserve it. We, the villagers, were made to pay for sins committed by others, but the curse allowed the girl and anyone she favored to be spared. They are trapped here as well, but as our prison guards. And not only that, they have powers, terrible powers. You saw Conroy heal himself; you should see what the little girl is capable of. They were not only granted immortality, but limitless strength to keep the rest of us imprisoned.

"I can tell you are having a hard time believing me, but that's OK. The only thing you need to trust is that we are the ones who need your help. Your partner and the people with him are the enemy, them and that little girl. We tried to end it ourselves, tried to break the curse. That's what happened the night of the fire, that was us trying to escape. We set the town on fire at Anthony Guntram's suggestion, at the stroke of midnight during the Bastille celebration. And it almost worked, except for us who lived. We're still here and it can't be over until every last soul has passed over to the other side. At least, that's how we think it works. Except maybe if you can get us out of here, get us past the townline. Perhaps time will resume for us in a normal fashion and we can then grow old and die naturally. There's no way of knowing unless we try. And if you can't get help us escape, maybe you can do us the favor of killing us yourself. It'd be mighty neighborly of you.

"We don't know if they can be killed, or if they'll ever stop hunting us down, but that is what we are up against, and you have to decide whether or not you believe us and want to help. Our fate, detective, is in your hands."

CHAPTER 23

FINDING THE REAL GUNTRAM

Jeremy heard Conroy's yells from afar, and as quickly as he could, he dried his feet and slipped back into his shoes.

"They got away," Keely said flatly, drying her feet with the hem of her dress before slipping on her sandals. "Your partner must have found them and overpowered Conroy." She didn't sound angry because of this, just resigned to the fact that there was more work in front of them.

"They won't get past the town line, the curse won't let them," Jeremy said, reaching out to take her hand. She looked at him skeptically and shrugged. He knew no such thing, but his demeanor was convincing. "And I have faith in Sadie's distrustful nature enough to know that without proof she won't make a decision. I'm sure they're laying it on thick right now, telling her they're innocent, but they have nothing to back up their claim." He smiled. "We do. Now come on, let's make sure Conroy is all right."

"OK," she said, and they headed toward the sound of the sheriff's voice.

• • •

When Andrew was done talking, the four of them sat quietly for several minutes, the darkness enveloping them. What he'd just told her, well, hadn't she thought that the stranger the story, the more likely it was to be true? She couldn't vouch entirely for its credibility, for it certainly did ring of something you might see on the late-night horror show, but she had to admit to herself that there had to be something to it, for why else did her partner turn on her and side with a woman whom she knew was responsible for a grisly murder? Not to mention the sheriff's miraculous recovery from what had to be a terminal gunshot wound. But immortality? A cursed village? With night falling, it certainly was enough to lend the story credence, at least until morning. In the light of day, things that were scary had a way of seeming silly, even if they were deadly serious.

However, to her trained detective's ear, the story had several incongruities that the teller seemed to realize as he was speaking, which in all her years working in law enforcement indicated deliberate fabrication. In layman's terms, he was lying. He appeared sincere during parts, so *some* of it may be true, but she'd listened to enough hogwash in her life to know when someone was deviating from the truth in order to vindicate their own actions. Someway, he and these women were involved in a manner in which he wasn't saying, and the only way she would discover the truth would be watching the whole thing play itself out. The catch-22 was that was what she was hoping to avoid.

"That's a lot to take in," Sadie said at last. "I'm a homicide detective, not a paranormal expert."

"You don't believe me?" Andrew said, fiddling with his bandages again. They were becoming increasingly frayed and he was having trouble keeping them in place.

"I didn't say that, but it does sound like a pretty tall tale," she said, swatting a mosquito buzzing around her head. "However, right now, I can't think of any other explanation, so I guess that will have to do until a better one comes along."

"What should we do?" Helen said, and to Sadie it was a damn good question. Night had fallen and in the darkness she could barely make out their faces. The woods seemed to take on a life of their own, the wildlife stirring and prowling around them. Where there was once an absence of sounds, just the constant wind that blew in the trees overhead, there was now the noises of living

(Dead...)

things stalking the woods nearby, rustling the underbrush, stirring like restless spirits.

"We have to stay here," Sadie decided. "It's too dark for us to do anything else. We should wait here until morning."

"What if they find us?" Andrew said, "They'll try to take us. If we keep moving north, maybe we could find a logging camp—"

"We're not going anywhere, not in the dark. And they won't take you because I won't let that happen." She took her gun from its holster, held it tightly in her right hand. "I'll keep watch if any of you want to get some rest."

"I can't sleep," Sylvia said, shuddering as a howl arose from somewhere to the east of them. "There's wolves out here, big ones."

"If you are what you say you are," Sadie said, "then I think the least of your problems are the wolves."

"You got us there," Andrew agreed, watching as Sadie slapped at the mosquitoes that buzzed around her head. He and the others had no such thing to worry about. It was as if the insects didn't even know they were there.

"Tell me about the goldmine," Sadie said. "Why can't we hide there?"

"We just can't," Helen said, and when she didn't elaborate, Sadie persisted.

"Why not?"

"All right, I agree with you. We should stay here," Andrew said, shooting a quick look at Helen. "We're fine where we are."

"Is there something wrong with the goldmine?"

"No, nothing wrong, except it would be a real bitch to get there in the dark." He looked at her gravely. "There are bogs around here, quicksand even. The last thing we need is to get stuck in the mud. We'd be sitting ducks."

"OK," Sadie said, hoping she sounded reasonably satisfied, but what he didn't know was that the woman's abrupt reply and his sudden change of heart had started her wheels spinning. First, he wanted to leave to find a logging camp, and now there were bogs and quicksand? And they not only didn't want to go to the gold-mine, but they actually seemed afraid of it…why was that? She suspected it was all tied in with the story he'd just told, one that he'd verbally redacted to protect the guilty. "We'll just sit here and wait for the sunrise."

To this no one replied, and in the absence of conversation they listened to the sounds of the forest. Sadie's analytical mind digested everything, considering the contradictions of what she'd been told, which she figured she could dismiss for the moment because the biggest question at this point was would they make it until sunrise or would Jeremy and his band of merry men find them first? If they did, what would she do? So many questions, yet an even bigger one was how could she possibly protect these people if the others were immune to gunfire? What chance did she have?

"I need to know," she said, choosing her words carefully, "how you want to deal with this."

She studied them closely, tried to find their eyes in the dark. "You said the only way I could save you was by getting you out of here or killing you myself." She slapped at another mosquito. "If they find us before sunrise, which is it going to be?"

The three of them said nothing for several minutes, and just when Sadie thought she had to repeat the question, Andrew answered her.

"We want to try and get out of here," he said. "If they catch us, well…then we would ask you to please take it into consideration that death by gunshot in our humble opinion's is much better than what they have planned for us." He paused, looked at the two women for confirmation. At length, they both nodded. "OK?"

"I don't know, can you be killed? Conroy didn't die."

"They're different from us, I told you that. Everyone in the village, they're all gone, killed by the fire. If they can die, we can too," Andrew said, and that seemed to settle the matter. Sadie shivered against the chill of the night, wishing she'd brought a jacket, but she couldn't have known she was going to be spending it roughing it in the great outdoors. She'd just have to tough it out. And if Jeremy and the others found them, well, she supposed she'd find out if Andrew's theory was true or not.

And so, they waited there, listening, not talking, watching as the stars started peeking out in the sky above them and the moon arose from the north, bathing them in a pale, silvery light.

• • •

They sat in the living room of the only undamaged house in the village while Conroy recounted what happened. While he talked, Keely made coffee.

"I don't know why he took it in his mind to come out here," Conroy said, accepting a cup from Keely and blowing on it before taking a small sip. "This place has always given him the willies. I'm just as surprised as you are."

"Strange things have always happened here," Jeremy said, taking a cup from Keely, nodding his thanks. "He probably wasn't even aware of what he was doing."

"Could be," Conroy said because, what the hell, what else could it be? That boy loved his days off, getting drunk and pissing away his time in his beat-up old boat with a Mercury engine that was falling apart two nuts and a bolt at a time. He didn't even care if he caught any fish, he just liked being on the water. "I sure wish I didn't have to kill him though."

"I appreciate you not hurting Sadie," Jeremy said, and the other nodded.

"Of course. I wouldn't let anything happen to her, not unless it was necessary."

"You sacrificed your deputy for her."

"What are friends for?"

What went unspoken was the fact that Conroy had taken a bullet and yet here he was, sipping his coffee, oblivious to the dried blood stains on his shirt. With everything they'd been through throughout the course of their lives, that was simply a given.

"So, what do we do?" Keely wondered, and when the two men looked at her, she could see they were just as puzzled as she. From the time that the citizens of Amber Hollow had started the suicidal blaze they had hoped would end the curse, the three of them had been playing this by the seat of their pants. There was no script, no instruction manual on how they should proceed in the event that the villagers tried to escape their fate. All they really knew was that the power was in the hands of Ambereen, and they had to protect her until she was ready.

"Nothing we can do, I suspect, but wait until the girl is at full strength," Conroy said, and Jeremy nodded.

"They're going to try to get as far away from here as they can, but they aren't going to do it at night. It's too dark."

"Shouldn't we at least try and look for them, in case that isn't what they have planned?"

Jeremy considered this for a moment, wondered if Sadie could be persuaded to push on in the dead of night through a forest full of unimaginable terrors. He knew her very well, and in a situation like this, she would first and foremost think like a cop, and a cop would want to get the victims to safety, even at her own peril.

"I suppose it beats sitting here." He lifted the cup to his mouth, drank the last of the coffee. "Even if we can't finish them without the girl, we should at least make sure they aren't going anywhere. We would be doing her a great disservice if we let them get away."

"What are you going to do about your partner?" Keely asked, and when Jeremy opened his mouth to speak, he had no idea what was going to come out. What could he do? After all, none of this was up to him, he had no say at the ultimate outcome.

"It isn't my decision to make," he said resolutely, not liking it, but knowing that it was the only way. "Whatever Ambereen decides to do, I'll have to be OK with that. I don't have a choice."

Conroy nodded, as did Keely. They knew how he felt about her, knew that if it was demanded she be sacrificed, he would understand it was the best thing for all of them, but essentially for the girl. All of this, it was for her. They were merely bit-players in the movie that was Ambereen's "life." He was about to say something to that effect, when suddenly a brilliant luminescence poured in through the front window, so bright it was as if someone had trained a dozen spotlights on them.

"What the hell is that?" Conroy sputtered as Jeremy got quickly to his feet, dashing to the window. Keely moved swiftly to his side, and together they saw something that took their collective breath away.

"Oh my God..." she said, and instinctively took Jeremy's hand. "What is it?"

"I have no idea," he said, his heart beating in his chest thunderously. From the light, solid forms began to emerge, one by one, in pairs, in groups, until the house was surrounded in the sickly light, pulsating and strobing. The three of them watched wordlessly, helpless in their fear, when at last a voice spoke, telling them what it wanted, telling them what it had to do.

• • •

Warm drowsiness had overtaken her when suddenly she heard the sharp crack of tree limbs snapping as a strong wind whipped up around them, and when she looked up, she was astonished to see a brilliant light on the horizon, moving in their direction. She was on her feet in an instant, her gun drawn. She was about to warn the others when she saw that they, too, had arisen.

"What is it?" she said, and if she could see better, she'd see that her companions suddenly looked hopeful.

"We got us some help," Andrew said, the relief in his voice palpable. "I can't believe our luck."

"What?" Sadie gasped. "Who?"

"You'll see."

"So...we're just going to stay here?"

"No sense trying to run. They won't hurt us."

"How do you know that?"

Andrew turned toward her, and through the fraying bandages she could see a crooked smile on his face. "One always knows his own," he said, and before Sadie could reply, she heard the voices, whispering, swirling around her head like the incessant clouds of mosquitoes. The voices rose and fell, rose and fell, eddying in the dark, murmuring unintelligibly while growing gradually louder, progressively closer. Her fear was like a living thing inside her, her stomach twisting and roiling maddeningly. Her hand that clutched the gun was slick with sweat, and she transferred it to her other hand so she could wipe her palm on her pants before switching it back. She looked at the others, saw Sylvia and Helen's appreciative expressions, welcoming whatever was heading for them. Judging by the looks on their faces, you'd think the cavalry was coming to save them.

"What's going on?" she asked again but the three survivors ignored her, watching the distance expectantly. A moment later it didn't matter, for the light was so bright she could barely see, the voices so loud they echoed inside her head. The words were jumbled, chaotic, but occasionally the voices would merge and become one unified voice before overlapping once again and then separating. Within this pandemonium, Sadie thought she would go absolutely crazy if it didn't stop, she would simply lose the ability to make any reasonable decisions. "Tell me what's going on!" she screamed over the cacophony, but she could hardly hear her own voice.

"We're saved, you stupid bitch" Andrew said, "and it means we won't be needing your help after all." His hand slipped into the left back pocket of his pants, grasped a secreted object and held it tightly in his fist. "If that's the case I'm awful sorry, but we have to look out for our own and we don't need you in the way."

He tested the heft of the hammer he'd taken from the basement of the Bougie house after the cop had cut him loose, clutched it tight, knowing that he might only get one chance to get it right. He raised it above his head as he stepped closer to her, ready to bash her brains in, when a vociferous command came forth, spoken by someone he knew very well.

"Stop!" A figure emerged from the light, his body shimmering like an image on a movie screen. "Put it down, Guntram!"

Andrew's jaw dropped practically to his knees when he saw who walked among them.

"I...I don't get it..." he gasped, and Sadie, seeing the hammer, struck his hand with her own and knocked it to the forest floor. In his amazement, he barely appeared to notice. "What are *they* doing with you?"

From within the ranks of the citizens of Amber Hollow—the *ghosts* of the citizens of Amber Hollow—walked Jeremy, Keely, and Sheriff Conroy. They trailed close behind the man who'd issued the command, and Sadie saw he had a kind, compassionate face. He offered her a smile of unadulterated benevolence, and she could feel power emanating from him, like heat from a fire.

"We're ending this, Guntram, once and for all," the real Andrew LeCarre (and once acting mayor of Amber Hollow) said, his spectral image rippling like smooth water that has been disturbed by a stone. "It's time for you to give up so that we can all be free."

• • •

Sadie looked in awe at the specters of Amber Hollow, and then glared at the man who'd just about clobbered her over the head with a hammer, the one calling himself Andrew LeCarre. She noted the look of fear in his eyes at the sight of all his dead comrades. Well, *deader*, she supposed.

"*You're* Anthony Guntram?" she said, but there wasn't a lot of surprise in her voice, as that was mostly beyond her now. The ghosts, lit up like they were infused with radiation, watched somberly, their expressions those of fools who have been betrayed.

"Yes, he is," Sheriff Conroy said. "He tricked us with those bandages on his face, but it's him, all right. Why don't you shed those wrappings and let us take a good look at your ugly mug?"

"The hell with you," the man who'd been going by the name of Andrew LeCarre said, but he sounded uncertain now. He fidgeted, looking from face to face to face and then he did the unexpected: he reached up with one hand and unwound the bandages, removing them completely. His skin was scorched in places, but otherwise intact. His large moustache had burned unevenly, but it still covered his upper lip like a demented caterpillar. Once his face was bared, he sneered and then spat on the ground. "The hell with you," he said again, but his words carried no weight. Although he tried to look tough, it was clear that the tables had most definitely turned.

"You screwed us while we were alive and then dead-alive, and now dead," Mayor Andrew LeCarre said. "It seems you just can't get enough of that."

"I did no such thing!" Guntram exclaimed, but he faltered, couldn't even back up his own claim. "I helped you to escape the curse!"

"It's because of *you* that we're cursed," Andrew said. "And it isn't over until Ambereen has her justice. With the help of her guardians, we can finally put an end to this for good."

"Nobody is going to touch me," Guntram said, backing away, but as he did the group advanced. His female companions cowered behind him, their facial expressions revealing their growing lack of faith in the man they'd chosen to follow.

"Come with us now, Guntram, and take your punishment like a man," LeCarre said, floating ever closer, his hand out.

"Wait!" Sadie said, stepping between the mayor and Guntram. Even though he'd just tried to attack her with a hammer she was still a police officer, and that meant she wanted answers. "No one is going anywhere until I find out what's going on here!"

Jeremy smiled, because that was exactly what he knew she would say and do. She followed the law to the letter (within reason; she'd always been sympathetic of women who'd resorted to violence during domestic disturbances with chronically abusive husbands) and Sadie wouldn't let anything bad happen to someone unless she knew for sure they were guilty. In this moment, like many others preceding it, he was glad he knew her, was happy that he'd had the pleasure of working with her for the past five years. He came forward, an empathetic, open smile on his face. He nodded to her courteously, silently bade her to stand her ground.

Sadie faltered as she felt a wave of warmth wash over her, felt all her fear melt away beneath his gaze. At once she realized, *truly* realized, that she loved this man, and that there was never any reason to doubt him.

"Can you offer the detective proof," he said to Guntram, "that you haven't done what you are accused of? If so, I'm sure she'd be happy to listen."

Guntram scowled, looking from Jeremy, to the dead citizens, to Sadie, and back. It was apparent that he couldn't understand how they could be against him, how they could have sided with the guardians of the girl, but all evil men must admit at some point that those they deceive will eventually side with whoever has their best interests in mind.

"*You tricked us into burning ourselves alive,*" the ghosts said in one communal voice. "*You tricked us so that you could escape and survive.*"

"I did no such thing! I don't know how I survived, I was supposed to die too!"

"*You tricked us to try and save yourself. Ambereen must have her justice...*"

"Like her grandmother had her justice?" Guntram countered. "None of this is fair, and I won't stand for it!"

A lone figure emerged from the group, a diminutive woman whose head was bowed in supplication, yet when she looked up, her eyes were filled with venom.

"*None of us can escape,*" she said, her voice a watery gurgle. "*I thought death was an escape, yet here I am...*"

"Doreen?" he sputtered, unable to comprehend her presence, and when she smiled water gushed from between her lips.

"*My body may be resting at the bottom of the Green Bay, but my spirit shall always be in Amber Hollow.*"

Squinting, Sadie suddenly recognized her: she was the woman who'd jumped off of the Tower Drive Bridge.

And then another figure emerged, and when it did, Sadie had to hold back a startled gasp and an involuntary impulse to weep.

"*I too have been claimed by the Hollow,*" the man said, and at once Sadie wanted to rush to him, to take him in her arms. She could literally feel her heart pounding with the strain.

"Corey?" she said, and he smiled.

"*I realize that my place is here, it has* always *been here,*" he said, and she believed she saw sincerity in his ghostly, fragmented eyes. A tear trickled down her face and then another, and she used her free hand to swipe at her nose. She then saw the janitor from the hospital, and beside him was Deputy Sanders. They'd all been claimed by the cursed village. Seeing this, she made up her mind. She raised her weapon, aimed it at Guntram's head.

"It looks like they have you by the short and curlies," she said, smiling coldly. "So, did you want me to help you cross over to the other side?"

The expression on Guntram's face gave her the answer she wanted. No, he'd never wanted her to shoot him, he'd wanted to escape all along, even if it appeared to be impossible.

"Now tell me, Guntram," Sadie said, relishing his expression of fear, "what proof do you have that they are lying and that you are telling the truth? Whatever you got, I think now's the time to spill it."

Guntram looked at her indecisively. His mouth worked but no words came forth.

"Anything?" Sadie asked again, when Jeremy went to her, put his hand on her arm and directed her to put down her weapon.

"He has nothing, Sadie. He's lied to everyone and now he has no one to save him." He reached out and took her hand, held it tightly in his own. "It's time that you learned the truth about Amber Hollow."

"Are you ready to tell me what's going on here, Jeremy?" she inquired softly, her voice husky with emotion.

"I can't tell you, but I can show you, and then you'll understand." He smiled, and within his gaze she felt an outpouring of emotion that made her chest hitch as another sob tore through her. "Do you want me to show you?"

She brushed tears from her eyes, her heart overflowing with love for him. How she could have doubted him was beyond her, but sometimes we can only see what our eyes perceive, even when our hearts are telling us a different story.

"Please," she said, and he held out his other hand so that she could take it as well. Both their hands linked, he looked into her eyes and she felt herself begin to swoon, felt the ground give way below her as if it had opened up and swallowed her. Everything fell away from her rapidly and she was immersed in total darkness...and then the truth revealed itself to her.

CHAPTER 24

AMBEREEN BOUGIE HOLLOWAY

Sunlight dappled the ground, filtered through the thick needles of the enormous pine trees and firs. A young girl knelt by a slow-moving river, filling first one bucket and then two with the clear, cold water. She hummed as she worked, a religious hymn about the glory of God, but she did so absent-mindedly, her thoughts elsewhere. Tonight, the village would celebrate the storming of the French Bastille, a festivity the townsfolk had been planning since early spring, when a fur trapper had visited to trade furs for food and supplies and told them about the insurgence during a French rebellion the summer before. He gleefully informed them a group of revolutionaries stormed the tower for gun powder, releasing the prisoners within and killing the Bastille's governor. He then told them that the tower (which had been a symbol of French oppression for centuries) had been torn down, and that the French revolution had begun. As a Protestant community, this brought them much joy, as they had escaped their home land to avoid religious tyranny, and so from the day they'd learned of this victory, they intended to celebrate it. The little girl thought this would be grand, as there would be music and dancing and eating, all of which were very favorable to her.

"Here there, young lass!" a strident voice cried from behind a stand of firs, and when she looked up, she saw her grandmother approaching, a look of scorn on her wrinkled, bland face. She gazed at her benefactor with an expression of supplication, for one thing she dared not do was raise the woman's ire, if only to escape a beating. "Quit your day dreaming and get those buckets of water to the fire. We have much work to do!"

"Yes, grandmum," the girl said, taking the handles in her tiny hands and hurrying along the path back to their hovel, where a large fire burned unattended. She poured the contents into a large pot and then dashed back along the path to fill them once more. When she repeated this task, she then forayed into the woods for more firewood. Upon her return, she dumped what she'd gathered on the pile and then placed a few of the larger sticks in the fire. Once she finished that, she stared into the flames, a dreamy look on her pretty, dirt-smudged face.

"Enough of your dallying about!" her grandmother scolded, a woman whose mood was either enraged or sour, there was no in-between, and for good reason. It had been her job to raise the child, which wasn't easy, given the peculiar nature of the girl's birth. A decade prior, the girl's mother conceived her out of wedlock, and with the wealthiest, most powerful man in the village. Their tryst had been cleverly disguised, and the pregnancy hidden until the child was born, at which point it could no longer remain a secret for the community was much too small. When the baby was discovered and there was no clear indication of who the father was, the woman was tortured until she confessed the child was Anthony Guntram's, the son of the village elder and heir to his legacy.

Initially, he declared that she was a liar; however, the child bore a striking resemblance to him so his assertions were suspected. It was genuinely uncanny, this similarity, so he changed his story and claimed that she was a sorceress and that she had used her evil witchery to seduce him. His conviction was such that the village ruled in his favor, (his wealth and power readily brought about this decision) and after a speedy trial, the girl's mother was lashed at a stake and burned to death in the village square. Her ashes were then scattered in the outer lying area of the forest surrounding the township, and the matter was spoken of no more. Still, there remained the girl, and it was only by the extemporaneous decision of the wealthy father that she be allowed to live with her grandmother, with no knowledge of her lineage.

The girl's grandmother didn't yell at the poor girl because she disliked her; indeed, she loved the child immensely. Nevertheless, she felt it best not to spoil her, and by never sparing the rod she would learn her place in the village, and understand that she was a mere peasant, that life was toil, and happiness fleeting. Had the poor girl known about her mother it would surely crush her, so under a cloak of indifference the old crone raised her, the love she harbored buried away deeply in her heart. Her exterior may have been cold, but inside was a soul almost pure in its essence. And she detested Anthony Guntram; make no bones, she wanted nothing to do with the man who'd sired the girl and murdered her mother. He was a monster for what he had done, yet this he concealed with acts of outward munificence, tenderness toward the girl that he'd borne yet did nothing to relieve her of a life of hard work and poverty.

"I'm sorry, grandmum," the girl said, looking away from the flames and at once gathering more wood to put on the fire. "I'll make sure to get my chores done."

"I should say you will, or there will be no celebration for you, tonight." The old woman's voice took on a convivial tone, fetching a sigh as deep as the river that flowed through the center of the village. Dash it all, she loved the girl, but what would eventually become of her when she started asking questions about her mother or father, queries she no doubt would begin making once she was old to enough to understand? What would she tell her?

The clop-clop-clop of horse hooves interrupted them, and looking up at the approaching rider, they saw it was none other than the scoundrel Anthony Guntram. He was dressed in his riding gear, his thick mustache combed with pig fat to make it shine, his long hair swept over his brow and cascading down the back of his head, cinched in a tight knot with a leather strap.

"Good morning, ladies," he addressed them in a clipped tone, and the girl could hardly contain herself, uttering a squeal of delight. For reasons unknown to her, she felt drawn to this man, and he did nothing to diminish her affection, instead encouraging it. "Making preparations for the celebration tonight?"

"Yes, my lord," the girl said, while her grandmother scowled. If looks could kill, he would have dropped dead where he sat in the saddle, but instead he favored them with a cherished gaze, rubbing his gloved hands together as if to keep them warm.

"Perhaps your chores can wait and you'd like to take a ride with me?" he said, not looking at the old woman, only the girl, but she answered on her granddaughter's behalf.

"There will be no riding today, my lord. We have much work to do to before this evening's festivities."

"Of course, where are my manners?" He clucked his tongue at the old woman while keeping his eyes on the girl. "A little gallop through the forest wouldn't spoil your whole day now, would it?"

"No, my lord," the girl said over the protests of her caretaker, and when he reached one hand down for hers, she took it, and he lifted her easily off of the ground and swung her onto the saddle behind him.

"I daresay, my lord, we have much to do—"

"We shan't be gone for long, old crone. Do continue your toiling and we shall be back by the noon's repast."

And with this announcement he nudged the side of his horse with one knee-high boot and they trotted away in a cloud of dust, leaving the old woman to wordlessly watch them go. Something tugged inside of her, some nameless fear, but there was nothing she could do, for she was a common peasant and he a man of royal blood. She watched them go until they were out of sight and then turned around and stoked the fire, stirring the pot of boiling water with a large birch stick stripped of its bark. She continued with her chores until lunch, and when the girl hadn't returned, she worked into the afternoon. Only when night fell and the celebration had commenced did she seek out the man who had born her a granddaughter, for what she'd learned would forever change the village in ways they never dared to imagine.

· · ·

The horse moved at a fine trot, and the girl giggled as she bounced along behind the man whom she held in such high regard, clutching him tightly around his muscled middle with her miniscule, delicate hands. Even though she'd been toiling since she was merely a toddler, her hands were still pretty, not rough and gnarled like her grandmother's. She had no idea they would stay that way forever, would never get callused and work-worn.

They passed through a sunny meadow, the horse seeming to know the way without encouragement, and after they passed through a darkened stand of thick firs, they entered into another clearing, where the rider brought the horse to a stop. He dismounted first and then assisted the girl out of the saddle and onto the ground next to him. He stood two full heads taller than the girl, and he stared down at her with an indecipherable expression until she looked away in embarrassment.

"I say," he said softly, his voice lilting like a lullaby, "shall we take a seat over yonder on the fallen log, my lass? You look as if you need some rest."

"Yes, my lord."

She followed him to the resting spot, took a seat next to him. He smiled a strange smile, a faraway look in his dark eyes. Something had changed within him, she could see it upon his tanned, handsome face.

"Are you content with your life, young lass?" he said after a long moment, and the girl furrowed her brow, considering the question.

"Yes, my lord," she said after only a slight pause, for it was impolite not to answer a question from one in higher standing. Her answer was honest, to the best of her knowledge, and this made the man's smile deepen.

"As I thought," he said, swinging his gaze around to meet hers. "But I think I've let this charade go on for too long."

The girl frowned, unsure of what he was saying.

"What do you mean?" she asked, her eyes growing wider as his demeanor continued to darken. He reached out with one gloved hand and stroked her shoulder, gently at first and then a bit rougher.

"You are an abomination, and it is time for you to move on to the next world, for it is what God wants."

To the girl this made no sense; she felt cold dread send a chill down her spine. He grasped her arm around her bicep, forcefully now.

"You're hurting me..."

He pulled her off the log and tossed her to the ground. His eyes radiated a malevolent sheen, sweat standing on his brow as a frown creased his face in half.

"You are an evil girl, and it must end this way. Do you understand?"

"No, my lord," she said, but she could barely spit the words out. Her arm ached where he'd clutched it, and as he drew closer fear ignited inside of her. He drew back one booted foot and swung it hard, kicking her in the side. She screamed, a wretched wail that caused a flock of birds to uproot from a branch overhead and flutter into the late morning sky.

"Silence, wench!" he grunted and then kneeled over her and backhanded her bluntly, rocking her head on her slight shoulders. He hit her again, and again, grunting with his exertions.

"This is what God wants," he said, settling upon her and holding her down on the cold, unforgiving ground. "And he shall have this sacrifice, wench, he shall have it in all His glory."

"I…I don't understand…" She now wondered if she would ever leave this clearing, if she would ever see her grandmother again. She began to weep, bitter tears she could not hold back.

"Stop your blathering," he spat at her, striking her yet again. The black look in his eyes brought to her a realization: if she didn't fight back, she would indeed never leave this place. She now knew exactly what it was he intended to do. When he leaned back to smooth his long, black flowing hair with one gloved hand, she did what her grandmother had instructed her to do should a man try to hurt her, doing it so instinctively that it took him completely by surprise. Drawing one leg back, she jettisoned it forward in one quick motion, her foot landing squarely in the center of his crotch.

"Ahhh!" he roared, falling off of her, and she scrambled to her feet as fast as she could, backing away. She then turned and ran, but in her fear, she headed away from the village and further into the woods.

"Come back here!" he shouted, his voice filled with such fury, she knew that if he caught her it would be the end of her for sure.

She ran without stopping for as long as she could, and when she paused to catch her breath, she could hear the hooves of his horse tearing up the damp forest floor. The terror that possessed her commanded her to keep moving. She sprinted off, but not before hearing the whinnying of the horse behind her, very close.

"Stop, wench!" Lord Guntram yelled, and her mind raced as fast as her heart, as fast as her little feet. She jumped over rock outcroppings and fallen trees, over a tiny brook babbling quietly in the late morning sunshine. All these things she catalogued as she passed them, clues for her as to how to get back to the village once she lost her pursuer.

Yet, onward he came, and no matter how far ahead she got, he was always right behind her and closing. Her breath was coming out in ragged pants, her legs feeling wobbly. She chanced a quick look over her shoulder, saw that he was closing the distance between them rapidly. He had his dagger drawn, a large implement of violence that she'd only seen him polish, never actually use. And the look on his face was pure madness, his lips drawn back, his teeth bared, his eyes burning fiercely in their sockets with a rage that was unlike anything she'd ever seen.

"You are a vile creature!" he roared, his voice low and guttural. "You never should have been born, I should have killed you the second you peeked from your mother's womb!"

At the mention of her mother the little girl stopped, turned, and stared at him more closely than she ever had in her life. She knew she should keep running, but curiosity got the best of her.

"What do you know of my mother?" she said, the terror subsiding to make way for a fiery anger of her own. He pulled the horse to a stop only a few yards from her, and the bucking mare almost reared over on her backside and toppled him off, yet he clung to her valiantly, keeping his bottom firmly planted in the saddle.

"I know more about your mother than anyone," he hissed as he trotted slowly around her, keeping her off balance. "I know who your father is as well."

"Who, my lord? Who is my father?" Totally fearless now, her inquisitiveness overwhelming her, she was no longer concerned with immediate escape. She desperately wanted to know who it was who had helped conceive her, for her grandmother had never told. Once he told her she could flee, but right now her fury eclipsed all other emotions, held her in place before him.

Lord Guntram stopped the horse, the dagger clutched in one gloved hand while the other held the reins. His eyes shone with maniacal glee, spittle encrusting the corners of his lips. His finely combed moustache was in disarray. The girl was certain that he was completely mad, that the man she had trusted for so long had been a lunatic in disguise, but this no longer troubled her, not if she could get the answer to her question.

"Who," she asked again, "is my father?"

"If I tell you, will you be a good lass and not run?"

"Perhaps, if you were to drop the knife, my lord."

"Consider it done," he said, and he tossed the knife into a patch of overgrown weeds. He held up his gloved hands as if in surrender. "Will you come back to the village with me willingly if I share what I know?"

"I shall," she lied easily. "Tell me." Once she learned what she wanted, she would sprint as fast as a rabbit into the safety of the woods, and when she returned to the village, she would tell everyone what he'd tried to do.

He nodded serenely, and in one fluid motion he jumped from the horse, standing before her in the mist enshrouded clearing. He strode toward her purposefully, stopping when he was a few feet away.

"The old crone has not told you anything about your birth parents?" His voice was soft now, almost kind. His eyes were still unfocused; indeed, it was as if he was staring right through her.

"I know nothing of them, my lord."

"I can tell you," he said, "but the answer may shock you."

"Tell me, please."

"It may bring you pain."

"I'll be all right."

"Perhaps…"

He paused, looking at the ground as if searching for something there, stroking his moustache with one gloved hand while he contemplated the matter. He appeared to be deep in thought, when he suddenly reached for her and she flinched, tried to dash away, but he was too quick, and his hand clamped tightly around her arm.

"My lord," she stammered, and at once she knew he'd tricked her. Her chance to escape had passed and now she was at his mercy. He removed another knife from within his cloak and deftly slashed her dress, slicing it open to reveal her flat, sexless chest, and she cried out piercingly, but she knew no one would hear her, not out here. He studied her with cold, fathomless eyes as she tried to wriggle out of his grasp, but he held her fast.

"Let me go!" Tears spilled down her face, her curiosity gone, replaced by terror at what he might do.

The sounds of the forest whooshed and chittered around them, the wind picking up and blowing leaves around in swirling cyclones. He raised the knife, his eyes locked on hers, and then thrust it forward with a speed and precision that was ethereal. In a moment as quick as the blink of an eye, he carved a hole from which to excavate her heart. He'd had a lot of practice at this, for it was what he'd done to dozens upon dozens of hapless squaws and vanquished warriors. With the meticulousness of a surgeon, he excised her still beating heart from her tiny, fragile body, and held it before her very eyes.

"It is I, young lass. It is I who sired you…"

And then he bit savagely into the steaming organ, blood splashing his face, later to congeal in his moustache. His teeth gnashed as he masticated her living essence, the sound of his chewing louder than all the other sounds from the forest combined. She saw this for only mere seconds before she collapsed to her knees and then went face down into the mud. Barely another minute passed, and then she was gone.

• • •

The old crone kept at her work, only taking a brief respite to eat a small lunch. Lord Guntram had not yet returned with her granddaughter, and there was no fooling herself that she wasn't concerned. She never should have allowed him to take the girl for a trot, but what could she do? She was a peasant and Lord Guntram was royalty. Shielded beneath the umbrella of his family, he could do whatever he pleased.

As the shadows grew long, her toiling for the evening's festivities almost complete, she felt a trickling of fear steal through her, a supposition that something bad had happened to the child. What, she wasn't sure, but her absence was now hanging heavily in her heart. There was no good reason for Lord Guntram to be keeping her this long; what could have become of them?

The sun was entering the lower half of the western sky when she decided to go looking for them, traveling in the direction they'd gone. She was very familiar with the forests around the village, and knew them extremely well for someone of her age and disposition. The reasons for this were known only to her and her late daughter, something which if the others found out, they would reason that Lord Guntram had been right all along in his accusation. For even though it was well known among the villagers that Lord Guntram was crazy, and having the little girl's mother burned at the stake for witchcraft was a sham, there was some truth to his assertions, although he was unaware.

The old crone knew these woods well because it was within them that she could practice the rituals she'd been taught as a girl by her own mother, spells and incantations that were mostly innocuous, but they yielded genuine results when times were dire. The old woman was powerfully in tune with the earth, and so these spells pertained to plentiful rain, fertile ground for their crops, abundant game, and fair weather come spring after a long, harsh winter. She'd never used them for any other purpose than that, even when her poor daughter's life was on the line. It wasn't her predilection to use them for evil, the intention was to reduce harm and to increase their chances of survival.

She walked along the horse path, following the freshest set of horse hooves. Their village was so small, so remote, that they had very few horses, and only those of noble heritage were allowed their use. So, it was with certainty that she followed the tracks, sure in her heart that they were that of Lord Guntram. She passed through a quiet meadow as the sun streaked ever downward toward the horizon, the sound of crickets playing nature's symphony as the day dwindled away, the light growing dim. She passed a clearing and then walked through a dense stand of fir trees only to emerge at another shaded glade where she paused to rest. The ground here was disturbed; it looked as if a tussle had occurred. As her eyes searched the forest floor, they at last lit upon a set of small footprints, these followed by horse tracks. They lead deeper into the woods, and so she tracked them until she came upon another clearing, and stopped when her eyes came to rest upon a sight that made her gasp involuntarily. There was no mistaking what she saw: it was blood, a lot of it.

She followed the trail with her eyes, and saw the drag marks that led still deeper into the forest. After her initial shock, she composed herself, steeling herself against a fate she knew she didn't want to witness, but was certain she'd find. Ever forward she walked, slowly, this moment in time stretching out as if minutes had become hours, hours had become days. She knew what she would see at the end of this trail, her mind accepting it before her eyes made it real, but she was in no hurry to make the discovery, no rush to learn the truth. Along she walked, her eyes following the trail of blood, the matted floor of the forest, until at last she saw something that proved to her inexorably that her fear was real: a fragment of the girl's dress, caught in a patch of prickly brambles. It waved limply in the light breeze that blew down from the north, and like the earth beneath it, the cloth too was blood stained. She drew in a deep breath, let it out slowly.

The old woman had made the dress herself, from fabric she'd bought at a trading post near the port of Green Bay seven years ago. She'd sewn it over the course of a frigid January when the snow had them holed up, and she and the girl had been living off of elk meat and jarred tomatoes. As she stared at the material, she felt something give inside of her, some small part of her essence took flight like a songbird and soared off into the darkening sky. She took another step forward, and then another, and when she passed the prickly brambles and stepped into the shadows of the woods, she saw the mound of dirt.

"Dear God," she whispered in a hoarse voice, and the sound of her own words now caused her to hurry. She scrambled to the dirt mound and began digging with her hands. It took at least twenty minutes before she touched the silky hair of the little girl, felt her cold skin beneath her callused hands. Brushing the dirt from her face, she at first didn't know what she was looking at, and when she realized what she was seeing, her fear and sorrow were replaced by anger.

"You bastard," she said, her words rasping from her throat. "You filthy, unrepentant bastard!"

No longer hurrying now, she carefully removed the girl from the shallow grave, picked her up in her work-muscled arms and carried her back to the village.

• • •

The festivities were in full swing when the old woman stepped out from the darkness of the woods. Her arms were aching from carrying the girl so far, for in her anger she didn't stop to rest; she couldn't, not until she found the man responsible for this atrocity. She'd heard the music from at least a mile away, coupled with the voices of the revelers. And it was a celebration to be merry about, for that there was no doubt. The French revolution would free the people of France from the tyranny of the oppressive regime, and even though their village was free, it was still a wonderful thing to know that the tides had turned. The old woman had supposed it was something she'd never see in her lifetime, so for that she should be glad, but right now her mind churned with a deeply burning rage, and the idea of a celebration was far and away from her current thoughts. For now, all she thought of was revenge.

When she reached the village square, she could smell the odor of fermented beverages, could tell by the coarse laughter and the gait of many of the villagers that they were drunk. She didn't feel disdain for them, but it maddened her watching them rejoice so wantonly while her granddaughter was dead. Not that they were aware of this, but they soon would be.

She strode through their midst, and when she trundled past the villagers and they saw the burden in her arms their laughter died on their tongues. They drew away from her, their eyes wide, their mouths showing expressions of shock and horror, for she'd done nothing to cover the girl, she was exposed before them in exactly the manner that the maniac had left her.

"Where is Lord Guntram?" the old woman yelled at the very top of her voice to be heard over the music. "Where is the man who killed my granddaughter?"

The lute player was the first to stop, eyeing the woman from the stage set up in the center of the square. Next was the mandolin player, followed by the fiddler. They stared in open-mouthed surprise at the woman and the bundle she carried, for it was a horrific sight, beyond ghastly, nearly beyond belief. A woman shrieked, and then several more. They drew away from the old woman as if she were bringing them the Black Plague gift wrapped in a box topped with a bow.

"Where is Lord Guntram?" she yelled again, her voice carrying much further now that the music had stopped. No one stepped forward to help her, for they all knew who she was: the mother of the witch they'd burned at the stake over a decade ago. For all they knew, she was a witch as well, and her granddaughter a pariah that should be shunned at all costs.

The crowd fell ever away from her until they revealed the Master and his family sitting at the grandest table, a feast before them of suckling pig, duck, and venison. Lord Guntram sat next to his father, who sat at the head of the table next to his wife, flanked by their many servants.

"Who dares call for my son?" Master Guntram said indignantly, his face suffused with blood from the many flagons of ale he'd consumed. There was a large napkin tucked under his chin, and pig grease bathed his face below his sneering mouth. "Who is the commoner that dares to interrupt my family while we are feasting?"

"I dare to, Master Guntram!" the old woman declared. "I am Alicia Bougie, mother of Cassandra, the woman you have wrongly slain, and grandmother to Ambereen, whom I now present to thee!"

Master Guntram stared agape at the old woman as she strode closer. When he saw what she carried in her arms, he gasped, spitting out a mouthful of duck and placing a handkerchief over his mouth.

"Good lord..." he sputtered, for the sight of the child was nearly beyond comprehension.

"Yes!" she cried, "look upon the child and see what Lord Guntram has done to her! He is a monster that should have been stopped years ago, yet you haven't the stones to cry for his head! Look! Look at what he has done!"

She held up the girl so that the light of a nearby torch could illuminate her better, and in the firelight, what was revealed made even the stoutest heart cringe.

"He has killed and eaten her! Look! Look upon the face of his wickedness!"

The young girl's cheeks were mottled with blood, but it was clear that her flesh had been eaten. And where her eyes had once been, there were now only two empty sockets that cried dual runners of thick gore. She was naked, save for a torn undergarment that barely concealed her budding womanhood, her nearly non-existent breasts savagely masticated. A hole rimmed with matted blood showed that where her heart once was, there was now only an empty cavity.

"And not only that, the deranged lunatic ate her heart! He treated her like a savage and ate her still-beating heart!"

Lord Guntram got to his feet, a carafe of ale clenched in one ring-clad hand.

"I have done no such thing!" he countered, his lips curved in a grimace his moustache barely concealed. "The old woman is crazy. I would never do such a thing to the girl. Surely, she was beset by wild animals—"

"Lord Guntram came to our hovel this morning and bade young Ambereen to ride with him through the meadow. When she didn't return, I went in search of her, and this is what I found! Lord Guntram killed her and feasted upon her flesh, can you not see that?"

An angry roar rose among the crowd, and fearing insurrection was near, Master Guntram took to his feet.

"Silence!" he cried over the din. "Silence or I shall have the lot of you hanged!"

The crowd began to settle down at the threat of punishment, but this did little to assuage their fear at the horrific sight.

"You are a liar, old crone! Why do you accuse my son of such an atrocious deed? Is it money you seek, perhaps retribution for your witch-daughter? Well, you shall have neither as long as I command the throne!"

"Look at him closer, Master Guntram, for I can see it from here by the light of the torch and the moon." The old woman set the girl down on the ground before her and pointed at Lord Guntram's jacket. "Look, can you not see the blood that has spattered his fine garments? Look, all of you, look!"

The Master's gaze turned to his son, and indeed the old crone was right: there was blood on the younger man's sleeves, dried and dark. Closer scrutiny revealed splotchy gore within his mammoth moustache.

"I daresay," Lord Guntram said, "I have pig blood on my sleeves from an early slaughter. Is that a crime?"

"Since when does an elder of our village slaughter his own pig?" the old woman refuted, looking now at the villagers around her. The expressions on their faces were turning from horror to pity, as well as a dawning realization that the old woman could be right. Lord Guntram had made quite a name for himself over the years, and his deeds were well known within their ranks. He hunted and slaughtered the natives of this land in a fashion that was considered cruel by some, outright bestial by others. Not a one of them forgot the terrible night when the old crone's daughter had been burned at the stake following his accusation that she was a witch, and it was well known the girl she had sired was his. If he had done what the old woman claimed, then he was more than just a monster, he was a demon who should be banished from the village forever.

A furor rose among the people again, angry shouts from the bravest men that an injustice had occurred, women calling for the Lord's head. The Master watched this revolt with mounting unease bordering on alarm, for if they were to rise and rebel, it would be all over for him and his family. There was nothing else he could do. He had to stop them before it got out of control.

"Silence!" he roared, his voice carrying loud and strong. "You shall all be respectful in the presence of your superiors!" His tone carried a conviction his eyes did not. Fortunately for him, though, they were peasants, and were used to doing what they were told.

"The old woman is clearly suffering from delusions, possibly wrought from her dealings with the dark arts!" He clapped his hands. "Come forth medicine man! Come forth and examine the body of this young girl and tell us what it was that killed her!"

A small man with a stooped walk came forth from the crowd. He wore the clothes of a peasant even though he was the only doctor in the village, for he was not of noble blood. He approached the old woman, gave her a pitying look.

"May I?" he said to her, his voice nearly indiscernible, paper-thin. "May I examine her?"

"Yes," she said, and at last a sob escaped her, tears welling up in her eyes. Her anger wasn't gone, but sorrow was having its way with her now and she could fight it back no more.

He knelt down over the girl's body, took in what he could with his eyes before he touched her. When he did, he was very careful, as if she was still alive. He noted the blood that coated her pale, cream-colored skin, the gaping cavity in her chest where her heart had once been, as well as the gnawed flesh that remained on her tiny frame. In a moment, he knew that the old woman had not been wrong, and it was clear how she had died, but he also knew where his loyalties lie. He glanced at the old woman, shook his head sadly and then got to his feet.

"It appears she died a violent death, but it isn't quite clear to me how…" He felt bad for saying this, but he wanted no part in upsetting Master Guntram and his family. If it hadn't been for them, the lot of them would still be in France, fighting for the revolution.

"You are a liar!" the old woman screeched, and he had to move quickly to get out of her way as she tried to strike him. "I see it in his eyes, he is lying!"

"Guards!" Master Guntram shouted. "Come hither and subdue this woman!"

Several stout men appeared at his behest, and they surrounded the old woman, but the look of rage on her face kept them at bay.

"Don't you touch me!" she said, kneeling to pick up the body and then backing away. "Is there no one in this village who will accept that this man is a blood-crazed cannibal? Will you all turn away from the evil he has done?"

Everyone grew quiet, the sounds of the night growing louder around them. No one spoke, no one made a sound. Truly, they could no longer take the sight of the wretched old woman and the slain girl, so it was at their feet they stared as she looked on with contempt.

"No one?" she said again, and the villagers began to retreat, knowing what they had to do in order to preserve their standing in the community. It was clear that something foul had taken place, but was it fair for them to judge a peasant's word over that of royal blood?

And then from their ranks a young woman strode forward, an expression of resolve on her pretty, timeless face. She cast a compassionate glance upon the old woman and the murdered girl before addressing Master Guntram.

"We've looked away for the last time," she declared. "We cannot let that animal get away with this again!"

The old woman looked at her gratefully, knowing what courage it took for her to speak so freely. A young man stepped forward from the crowd as well, and then another, accompanied by an elderly woman whom he helped along.

"This has gone on long enough!" the first man to approach said, his eyes darting from the Master's table to the citizens gathered around. "How can we continue to bear witness to this man's evil deeds when we can stop him right here, right now? Isn't this what our fellow countrymen have done across the sea, laid waste to their oppressors in a revolution from which we ran away? Do we want to continue to be cowards in the face of tyranny, or shall we stand up and fight for what we know is right?"

The crowd fell silent, and the old woman could see they were listening to what this man had to say. They exchanged puzzled looks with one another, but their uncertainty was what truly guided them, and she knew that in the end tyranny would win. It almost always did. She glanced at the other three gathered by the man who had spoken, saw them challenge the crowd with their eyes. The moment was almost magic, a hush so quiet upon them that nothing could be heard but the flickering of the torch flames in the light breeze. Until Master Guntram ended it, his reedy voice as piercing as an arrow.

"I told you to seize her!" Master Guntram said, and the guards drew closer but the woman stopped them with a cold glare. "And if you sympathizers wish to be punished as well, please do continue to stand tall before me. I'll take five heads as gladly as I'll take one!"

The old woman looked to the four villagers who stepped forth, gratitude shining in her eyes. She smiled at them and then shook her head sadly. She gestured for them to step back into the crowd. She was grateful for their entreaty, however, she instructed them to save themselves.

"Spare them, Master Guntram, and if your guards will back away, I shall go," she said, a note of resignation in her voice. "Let me take my granddaughter and you shall never see me again."

He stared at her from his place at the table, considering his options. He had to appear strong before the villagers but imprisoning this woman would only make them resentful in the long run, and possibly make them insolent come the winter months when food was scarce. If he showed mercy, he would be perceived as benevolent, and sometimes respect worked more in your favor than fear. At length he nodded his head.

"Step down and take your place among the crowd and I shall forgive your defiance," he told the four who'd come forward and then turned to the old woman.

"Take the child and go," he said, scowling at his son. For in his heart, he knew that the old crone's accusations could very well be true, as his son was prone to vicious deeds, but that could wait. He'd deal with him later, but for now, during the celebration of the liberation of the Bastille, he'd appear to be a kind ruler, if only for the greater good. "Take her and be gone from this village at once. And if you return, I shall not hesitate to punish you for the allegations you've made on this night."

The old woman nodded vigorously, making shooing motions at the sympathizers, backing away with the girl clutched tight against her breast. Their expressions readily articulated their reluctance, but at last they stepped back, accepting the old woman's plea on their behalf.

"Thank you, Master Guntram, and many blessings upon you and your family." She cast one last hateful glance at Lord Guntram, but his eyes were like chips of ice. A man like him felt no remorse, for that was beneath him. And that is when he came forward, bending down to pick up a stone from the ground, a large chunk of granite he unearthed with the tip of one boot.

"This woman shan't leave here upon her own accord," he professed in a loud, strong voice. "I don't take these accusations lightly, not from her, not from anyone."

He glared at the villagers, tossing the rock up and down in his hand. "If you are with me you must do the right thing."

"I daresay..." Master Guntram gaped, swallowing spittle that felt like a sodden lump. "The old crone is taking her leave..."

"She is a liar, and if she is allowed to leave then it is I who appear to be in foul standing." He glared at his father, daring him to stop him, but the elderly man didn't know what to do, and in the minutes that passed he knew that a power struggle between him and his son in front of the entire village would hold negative ramifications as to who was truly in command. He did not want to comply, but the moment was drawing on too long, so he merely bent over to pick up a stone as well. He cast a look at his son, nodded gravely, allowing consent.

"We shall send this woman on her way with the kiss of stones," Lord Guntram avowed, and he flung the rock, hard, and it struck the woman on her forehead, the force of the blow staggering her. She was too shocked to cry out, but she kept a hold of the girl in her arms, continuing to back away. At Lord Guntram's urging, the villagers then followed suit, picking up stones. She watched with lidded eyes as they armed themselves, knowing she'd have to flee as fast as her legs could carry her. She turned to run when the next stone hit her, and then the next. In a flurry as tumultuous as a driving rain, the rocks came down, pelting her head, neck and back. The pain was immediate, intense, and their shouts arose clamorously as their bloodlust drove them on. She ran as fast as her arthritic legs could carry her, absorbing the blows with a fortitude brought upon by her hatred.

She turned once more and examined their faces, taking another rock to the chin so she could see the indifference that brought upon this terrible act. They would all pay for what they'd done to her, for what had been done to Ambereen, with the exception of those who'd spoken on her behalf. They wouldn't be made to suffer, she'd make sure of it.

She fled quickly from the village square, the stones driving her on, knowing exactly what she must do. She'd never harbored evil in her heart, but now it was time to unleash a wrath the likes of which these simple fools had never known.

• • •

When the old woman arrived at her hovel, she placed Ambereen's body inside on a wolf pelt and then went to her oak chest where she kept the ancient books that had been passed down to her by her mother, and from her grandmother before her. She'd only used them for good, but she knew the power within them, and was aware that they could be used for ill intent as well. She resurrected the antique tomes and then packed a hemp sack with everything she was going to need.

"Don't worry, my dear, I'll see to it that they regret this decision for the rest of eternity."

Once she'd gathered everything she needed, she hastily constructed a handcart to carry the girl and her supplies. She knew she had to hurry now, because if she wanted the spell to be at its peak potency, the girl had to be less than twenty-four hours dead. Time was now passing by rapidly, she had to make haste.

Her preparations made, she bid her hovel farewell and stole off into the murky night.

• • •

She followed the trail she'd tracked mere hours before, only the pale light from the moon guiding her way. Her burden was heavy, and she was old and stiff, but her determination was such that the physical labor was nothing compared to her mental anguish. This was a deed that needed to be done under the cloak of night, and as quickly as possible.

Lord Guntram's horse tracks led her deep into the woods, to the clearing, and then to the shallow grave. It was here that she stopped, studying the landscape around her. Her eyes searched for what she'd need, and when they alighted on the mound of earth, she knew this was the place.

When they'd settled in this location, the men had to clear out the natives that dwelled there, half-naked colored men and women who spoke a strange tongue, and worshiped not the true God but some deity that defied their Christian values. When reasoning did little to rid them of their presence, they'd mercilessly slaughtered them until the remaining few chose to flee. They left behind their villages, their homes, but what they could not take with them was their dead. The old crone hadn't personally viewed their presence as an affront; she'd rather admired the way they communed with the spirits of the earth. It was during this purge that Lord Guntram proved what a vile creature he was, indiscriminately butchering any and all, young and old.

She contemplated the large earthen pile before her, the resting place of the savages' dead, and nodded her head, satisfied. It would be here that she would perform her ritual, because it was here that it would work the best. For what she planned to summon needed to be seeded with the pain of others, needed to be a tribute to the holocaust they had visited on the natives, for it was only in this environment that it would be its most prevailing. Setting down the cart, she attacked the mound with a shovel she'd made herself of wood and stone. She sank it into the rich soil and dug until her arms were aching and then dug some more. She tossed aside the bones of the dead, but not too far as she would later return them. The moon was in the fourth quarter of the sky when at last the hole was deep enough, and so she set the tool aside and went to the cart to prepare for the ceremony she needed to complete before the sun came up. She would have to make quick work of it, but in her anger and sorrow, she knew it was something she could complete—*had to complete*—if only to make everything right again.

In the waning light of a sliver moon, she took sacred items from the sack and positioned them within easy reach. She then placed Ambereen in the hole, arranging her limbs carefully. And last, she removed the old books and opened them to the pages she needed. The spell she was preparing to cast wasn't familiar to her, but she did not doubt its power. Her grandmother had been crazy as a loon by the time of her death, but she never doubted that the magic she spoke of was real, that the spells she cast had every possibility of coming true.

So feverishly she labored, long after the moon had passed from sight and the glow from the sun appeared on the horizon, and at last, as the fiery glow of a new day was nigh, the old woman's work was almost complete. She kissed the sacred tomes before she placed them once more in the sack and then crawled inside the hole next to young Ambereen, lying down beside her and placing an arm around her. There was one last step, the final offering that would finalize the spell and ensure its efficacy. She had no fear, for without

Ambereen, without the safety of the village, there was nothing more for her.

She took the knife from a pocket in her dress, felt the edge with the ball of one old, knotted thumb. It sliced through her flesh easily, and she nodded to herself as the sun poked its head over the horizon. Holding it to her throat, she skillfully slashed the skin under her chin and hot blood spurted over her hand as a sharp pain stole through her.

"This is for you, young Ambereen Bougie Holloway," she croaked, gurgling on the blood as it poured copiously from the wound. "My life for you, so that you may live again…"

As the sun made its way up into the sky, the old woman's life ran out of her, and as it did something began to stir within the confines of the small cave she'd dug, something that was not human, something more, a terrible thing that would hold sway over the town and entrap it in its grip for eternity. She'd doomed them, doomed them one and all…except for those who had tried to help. They would be summoned and given the job of protecting Ambereen from anything or anyone that tried to break the curse. It was their gift, the least she could do for them. As the thing inside the cave came to life, and a new day awoke upon the village, it would prove to be be one that they would remember for all time.

CHAPTER 25

THE BASTILLE CELEBRATION, JULY 14, 1991
(What Really Happened)

Like the sunrise greeting the new day, light returned to Sadie's eyes, the glowing of the wretched damned as they hovered despairingly amid the tall pines. She first looked at Jeremy, saw within his eyes a question: Did she now understand?

"Yes," she whispered, looking from him to the dead villagers of Amber Hollow. "No one is innocent," she said. "You are all guilty as charged."

"Now wait a minute," Anthony Guntram said, continuing to back away. "I don't know what he just did, or what he told you, but it isn't true."

For everyone except Sadie, barely a minute had passed from when Jeremy linked hands with her and showed her the vision. Guntram barely had enough time to hitch up his pants, much less run.

"It *is* you," Sadie said. "You are the man who killed and ate the child, the one who threw the first stone at the old woman." Something occurred to her, the realization that all along, the truth had been dangling just beyond her reach. "You actually blamed *yourself* in all the stories you told because it's much easier to lie when you base your fabrications on the truth. I don't know if you actually feel any remorse, but this is all your fault, and these people have had to pay for your sin."

"These people," Guntram seethed, "are nothing but common peasants. No one cares what happens to them, the least of all I." He stared at her defiantly, for it was all he had left. The ghosts of the village floated motionlessly, their eyes swirling vortexes of brilliant colors. Keely stood with Sheriff Conroy, alert and ready for Guntram to try and escape.

"Yes, I suppose that's what I would expect from you," Jeremy said, stepping away from Sadie and toward the erstwhile nobleman. "It's time for you to pay the price for your crimes, you and the two others with you. You tricked these people into killing themselves so that you could try and escape the curse, but now it's time for you to pay the piper so that their souls may rest in peace."

Jeremy appraised the specters sympathetically. "Even though you contributed to the indifference of the child's murder and the outward misery of the old woman, you have no other crime on your souls. Possibly the curse will offer leniency upon you." He then turned to Guntram, smiling smugly. "When young Ambereen is ready, she'll exact the ultimate revenge that has been a long time coming for you, Guntram. There's nowhere else you can hide."

Anthony stared hard at the other, longing for something he could say to make Jeremy shut his filthy mouth, but he had nothing. In the end, he was a very stupid man, one who could perpetrate hateful deeds but could not back them up with logic. He scowled, opened his mouth to give them a piece of his rotten mind, when suddenly the ground began to shake, the trees around them uprooting, the sound of an enormous explosion bellowing forth.

"What's that?" Jeremy barely spit out before the trees began collapsing around them. He reached for Sadie, but when he tried to take her hand, he found this time it went right through hers. He looked at himself, and saw that he was beginning to fade. "Keely!" he shouted. "What's going on?"

Keely shook her head, trying to grasp Conroy's arm, but found the same thing happening to her: she was becoming transparent, like a ground fog that is slowly burned away by the first rays of the sun.

"Jeremy!" Keely wailed, one last desolate sound before she abruptly disappeared. Sadie watched as first she, Conroy, and then Jeremy vanished, as well as the citizens of Amber Hollow; they all shimmered and rippled, their outlines growing weak and dim, and then at once they were all gone, leaving nothing but darkness in their wake, that and the mighty force of nature that was ripping up the ground below her, toppling the trees. She dove out of the way of a giant pine, then another, when she saw a glimpse of movement. Plucking her flashlight from her utility belt, she flicked it on, and it shone dimly in the blackness, the battery still charged enough to allow her some visibility.

"You stupid bitch!" Guntram gloated as the light fell upon him. Before him was the most beautiful of opportunities. He had no idea why, but Amber Hollow was self-destructing. He'd be able to escape with both his life and away from the curse that had plagued him since the fateful summer of 1789.

"Wait!" Sadie yelled, alone now with the three people who she'd thought needed her help. They were gathering themselves as the quake that erupted so suddenly subsided, looking to Guntram to show them out of the forest, to get them some place safe.

"You'll have to catch me," Guntram said, and to the surprise of his companions, he left them to fend for themselves as he fled around Sadie, heading for the heart of the once proud but now decimated little town.

. . .

Sadie didn't waste a moment; the second he took to his feet, she dashed after him, ignoring the other two. She now knew that they were his henchmen. They had contributed to his black deed, and they belonged with him at the very end, but right now that didn't matter. The only thing that did was catching Guntram before he could make it to the town line.

She hurdled over fallen trees, running as fast as her legs could carry her, but she soon lost sight of him in the dark when the batteries in her flashlight at last died. She replaced it on her belt and retrieved her gun, blindly firing several shots in his direction, knowing full well that she was wasting ammo but not caring. After all that had happened, she couldn't let him get away. She simply couldn't allow it after everything Jeremy and the others had endured to contain him. What had just happened to offer the rotten bastard this last-ditch chance to escape? It wouldn't be the least bit fair, not after what he'd done.

She forced herself to move faster, and soon she could see the silhouette of the village before her against the diffuse starlight. She passed from the forest and into the devastated residential area, running by the one house that still stood untouched by the fire.

The Bougie House…the home of young Ambereen…

Her legs aching, she kept running until she made it to the town square, and once there she thought she saw something, someone, heading toward the barricade that separated the town from the large unincorporated tract of land between it and Crandon. Could it be that if he made it out of the village, he'd be free? Could that be how this worked? If he evaded his punishment, would that doom the rest of the villagers to a spectral eternity?

"Stop!" she screamed uselessly, slowing down, her legs giving out on her. She'd never been the fastest runner, and she'd somewhat let herself go over the years, enjoying more than the occasional deep-fried cheese curd while watching the Packers on TV, snuggling with a boyfriend whom she could now see was nothing but a louse. He may not have been an Anthony Guntram, but he was no Jeremy, that was for sure.

She had to stop, bending over and putting her hands on her knees, trying to catch her breath. He was gone, of that she was certain. The lousy son of a bitch had managed to escape.

Standing there, gasping, she at last heard something, and when she turned to look, she was astonished at what she saw.

"What do you two want?" she snarled. "How come you aren't running away?"

The older of the two women, Sylvia, came forward, put her hand on Sadie's back and stroked her gently.

"We have nowhere to go," she said softly. "There is nowhere for him to run either. This needs to be over, the sooner the better. I'm ready to pay the full price for my crime."

"I am too," Helen said, her eyes revealing an ardent entreaty. "Please, take us to the goldmine so that we can all be free—"

Suddenly, lights splashed down the highway, headlights. Sadie looked with genuine puzzlement, for who would be coming here at this hour? No one even knew they were here.

The three women stood there, watching, waiting, and finally the car slowed, edged past the barrier, and drove up to them. It was Jeremy and Sadie's unmarked police car, and what did that say about her trained detective's eye? She hadn't even noticed it was gone. The thought of turning in her badge suddenly occurred to her. This case had worn her out...maybe she just wasn't fit for this line of work anymore. The driver killed the lights, and when the door opened Sadie couldn't believe who got out.

"Hello," the old woman said, and as Sadie struggled to remember her name, she offered it: "I'm Delores Schenker, the librarian from Rhinelander. We met once, remember?"

Sadie nodded, gulping mutely. The other two simply looked at her, for they possibly knew that she hadn't been accounted for, and had most likely been waiting all along for her to arrive.

When Sadie caught her breath, she shook her head sadly. "He's gone," she said, her guilt enormous, for she had been the one to free him. "I let him get away."

"No, my dear, you've done no such thing," Delores said, smiling. She opened her door so that the light came on inside the car, and when Sadie saw what the woman wanted her to see, she almost laughed.

"The idiot was hitchhiking," Delores said, a musical tinkling in her voice that reverberated with merriment. "Who would be driving around out here at this hour?" She eyed the other judiciously. "Fortunately for your unmarked cruiser, he had no idea he was getting into a police car. No handles on the doors; he's locked inside."

Now Sadie did laugh, a great big whooping sound, and the other women joined her, the doomed friends of Guntram, who sat stolidly in the back of the car watching everyone reproachfully.

"You can't hold me," he huffed, his eyes betraying his fear. "If anyone tries to touch me, I'll chew their hand off."

"Spoken like a true cannibal," Delores said. "Don't worry, none of us has any plans for you, although there is a certain someone who would like to have a moment of your time."

Delores curtsied to Sadie and Guntram's henchwomen and then sat behind the wheel of the cruiser, turning the headlights on once more. She was lucky the metal cage separated her from her passenger, for if he could, he would have surely reached over the seat and throttled her without hesitation.

"Follow me, ladies, I'll drive slow. It won't take very long."

"OK," Sadie replied and, walking much slower now, she followed the car back into the ruins of Amber Hollow.

• • •

The partially collapsed entrance to the goldmine was draped in shadows, concealing the cavernous space beyond. Large chunks of earth and stone lay scattered as if strewn about by giant hands, and Delores looked on with an expression of relief.

"This was where it all started," she said in a hushed tone, gazing at it reverentially, "and this is where it's going to end."

"It looks like it's caving in," Sadie said, and the librarian nodded.

"Yes, it is. The quake you felt? That was Ambereen, and it means she's nearly ready."

"Jeremy and the others disappeared..." Sadie said. "Are they OK?"

"Under Ambereen's watchful care, I'm sure they'll be fine."

"What do we do now?" Sadie looked into the mouth expectantly, hardly able to suppress a shudder.

"We wait for her to emerge."

"Is she all right?"

"She lost a good deal of strength when she left the Hollow to keep an eye on the survivors," she said, glancing at Sadie with an air of mischief. "But I think it's safe to say she's all better now. I think it will still be a bit before she's completely ready, so in the meantime, would you like to know what happened the night of the fire, and what transpired to bring us here in the first place?"

Sadie nodded. "I would."

Delores looked at the two women. Helen had taken a seat on the forest floor while Sylvia stood by the entrance, watching anxiously.

"I believe the most appropriate person to tell it would be one of the survivors," she said, frowning in the direction of Guntram. "And since we'd like to hear the truth—the whole truth—I don't think we want him to tell the story."

"I'll tell it," Sylvia volunteered, and Delores nodded, a smile upon her old, wrinkled face.

"Please do us the honor," she said, and the woman favored her with a sad smile in return, and then began the tale.

• • •

"We'd been suffering for over two hundred years from the curse of young Ambereen, placed upon us by her Grandmother Alicia Bougie, brought upon us by the awful deeds perpetrated by Anthony Guntram. This life we were living...it's no life. By now, I believe you know all this. I'm honestly

not sure if the old woman's curse would have gone on forever if we didn't try to free ourselves, but of course, that's where Anthony Guntram comes in again, always with a suggestion that is wicked in design, cruel in its intentions.

"He came to us first, his trusted aides, and told us what he wanted to do. We were both his lovers, you see, Helen and I, and the woman who killed herself—Doreen—she was his hand maiden. We did his bidding, made sure he was satisfied in every way. That is our part in this. If you want to consider us his 'henchwomen,' so be it. I suppose that is what we were. We took no part in his evil schemes, but we didn't try to stop him.

"He had no idea if his plan would work or not, but that was of no matter. He said we had to do something, even if we took the chance of making it worse. What he proposed, well, as usual it was self-serving, but we could see his logic, could tell that he was trying to appease the spirit of Ambereen while attempting to release ourselves. You have to understand, this made sense to us then, but now I realize it was a folly. There really is no breaking free, except maybe now, but only as Ambereen wishes.

"Anthony explained to us how we'd do it, and God help us we agreed. We thought that if we offered the spirit all those souls at once, it wouldn't miss a measly four. But that was an understatement, of course, because how could the spirit be satiated when the one man responsible for all of this was trying to get out of fulfilling his part of the bargain?

"The week before the Bastille Celebration—it's funny to call it that, because it has been our call to arms for the last two hundred years— Anthony gathered everyone in the village square for a meeting. Don't get the idea that he was in charge; Andrew LeCarre had been acting Mayor of Amber Hollow since the curse was enacted, but Guntram was a good public speaker and could be very persuasive. He could probably lull a rabid wolf into slumber by crooning it a sweet lullaby. And that's what he did that week: sang everyone a cradlesong to get them to show up, even though he'd had been stripped of his power after what he'd done to the child. He still lived in the royal domicile—we were all in residence with him—but he had no political positioning within the community. All he possessed was his silver tongue, and he wielded it mightily.

"With everyone gathered in the village square, he declared that enough was enough, it was high time we did something about the curse. The villagers erupted in a fury, because it seemed to them that there could be no end in sight for their misery. Anthony had long ago lost their trust, so it was no small feat for him to talk them into what would be his most insidious plot yet. And talk them into it he did, because a week later, on the eve of the Bastille, everyone was ready.

"He could have chosen any method, I suppose, but over the course of the previous week he'd made up his mind that there could be only one way, no matter what we said to counter him. It just sounded so...awful. But no one could tell Anthony anything, not even us. He only listened to one person, and that was himself. He couldn't have known if it would work, he was just guessing. Over the course of two hundred years, people had attempted suicide, only to find death unattainable. They always came back, the same as they'd been before. It was different with Doreen, but after what happened, I assume everything would be different. I've never quite understood it; I suppose it simply is what it is.

Anthony's logic, ultimately, did involve a bit of genius: we were all truly alive on the eve of the Bastille. If there was one time when we were vulnerable to mortality, that was surely it. That was the gamble, anyway. And it worked, it actually worked.

"We organized the Bastille celebration as if it was just like any other year: the band was playing, fireworks were set up, we had booths with food and carnival games...nothing was unlike any preceding year. The only difference was all the gas cans. Every family had two. Were we afraid? You bet we were, because we had no idea how it would turn out. But I'll tell you, after everything we'd been through, I was ready to try anything. The curse was...is...cruel and unusual. We believed we'd paid our debt, had given our lives enough times to satisfy the old crone. If this could be the last time, then it didn't matter how painful it was, it would be a relief just to have it over. Of course, it's hypocritical of me to say that, seeing as

Guntram's plan would allow us exemption from the final agony, but just the same...

"Anyway, the celebration dragged on excruciatingly slow, everyone acting as if it was just another year. For one thing about the curse of Amber Hollow: with the exception of the culmination of the evening, we never saw the spirit, she never came alive at any other time. Besides the fact that we didn't age, that we were trapped in this little town for centuries while the world progressed around us, it was as if there was nothing keeping us here. But if anyone did try to leave...well, they were always brought back. Either by the guardians of Ambereen's crypt or by some other method. No one, and I repeat no one, has ever escaped this village or the curse.

"When it was nearing midnight, the time when the spirit of Amber Hollow would come out and do its bidding, Anthony acted quickly, assembling everyone. He jumped up onto the stage after whisking the band off, addressing us all.

"It's time!" he cried, raising his gas can, but he had water in it, as did I and my sister and Doreen. I am so Goddamned ashamed of myself for this, because we were setting them all up to die so we could live, hoping to purge the village and escape while the chaos ensued.

"Anthony poured the contents of his can over himself and then dramatically showed everyone his Zippo. He'd splashed gas on the stage ahead of time, and to make them think he'd set himself ablaze, he set that part on fire, near his feet. And then they did it, like lemmings to the sea, they poured the gasoline all over themselves. While it was happening, I couldn't believe it, like a part of me knew it was so terrible that I didn't want to bear witness but I was helpless to look away. I watched as the Wellens family first poured the gasoline on their children, and then themselves before using a cigarette to set themselves on fire. I watched as dozens of families did this. And did they scream? Oh my God, yes. Screamed right up to the heavens and all they got for their pains were seared throats. And the smell...have you ever roasted a whole pig over an open fire, skin and all? It smelled kind of like that, a sweet, sickly aroma, like boiling lard.

"My sister and I hurried to where Anthony was cowering from the fire as it enveloped the stage. We actually had to save his sorry ass; he'd spilled gas all around and had fairly painted himself in, so to speak. We grabbed him and pulled him off while all around us, every citizen in town was running helter-skelter engulfed in flames. And as they flailed around in their misery, they set fire to the town, and soon everything was ablaze. That had been part of the plan as well. All week the four of us had been secretly hiding bottles of gasoline and grain alcohol around the village, so that when the time came, these Molotov cocktails would help spread the fire far and wide. We put them anywhere we thought they wouldn't be detected, and we did a good job too. Explosions shook the ground as cars detonated, propane tanks blew sky high, and gas lines ruptured...all according to Anthony's design, to physically remove the village of Amber Hollow from the face of the earth.

"Master Guntram came running up to us; how he found us in the chaos I don't know, but the skin was melting off of his face, his cheek bones showing through, and I swear on my life his eyes were boiling in his sockets like eggs. He was screaming, mostly nonsensical ramblings, but I knew what he was trying to say. He was condemning Anthony for what he'd done, for everything he'd ever done. And the bastard deserved it. We all did, but Anthony couldn't be bothered by the man who had sired him, he only saw him as an impediment to his escape. He kicked Master Guntram in the chest, knocking him down and then stomped on his head with one boot-clad foot, crushing his skull. I don't know, maybe Anthony took pity on his father, possibly it was his idea of helping him... but I don't think so. I think he just wanted him out of the way.

"The smoke was getting thicker, something I don't think Anthony had even thought of. We were trying to get away from the center of the village, trying to get past all of the people who were literally dying at our feet, when we heard the sound we always heard at this time of night, at this time of year. It was Ambereen, emerging from her cave, the goldmine, coming for us.

"The noise always started out like a shriek of pain, or like an especially high wind blowing through a dense stand of trees. It would whip itself into a frenzy, picking up random items that weren't nailed down and sucking them into a central vortex, and then she...it...would appear. It's hard to describe to you what we'd see, for it's beyond my limited vocabulary, but it was downright awful, all-encompassing, and it would suck us into its greedy mouth and do terrible things to us.

"But this time, it was different, of course, because of the fire. The vengeful wrath of Ambereen blew in like a cyclone but what it greeted was the flaming agony of every last citizen, save for us. We'd made it almost to the town line, and we could hear it bearing down. We felt the hot wind of her breath on our backs, hotter than the frenzied flames. Then I could hear the timbre of the people's screams...change...and it was because Ambereen was taking them like she did every year, only they were burning alive while she did so. They had to endure a death that was twice as miserable as what they'd been accustomed to, and it wasn't fair...it simply wasn't fair.

"That was when the smoke inhalation finally got to me, got to my sister too. I'd lost track of Doreen at this point, didn't know if she was still alive. We dropped to the ground, gasping for breath, and like the coward he was—always will be, I guess—he ran for the town line for all he was worth. Right before he abandoned us, I saw the fear etched on his face like script on a tombstone. From the ground, we watched as he made it almost to the welcome sign when his feet left the ground and he was sucked up into the sky, but he wasn't up there long, not this time. He was held aloft for only a few seconds, and not too high, maybe only ten feet in the air, before he came down, landing awkwardly. But that lousy son of a bitch has the luck of the devil, and he was on his feet in seconds and running again. And that's the last I know. Next thing, I heard the sound of a helicopter, and there were these people squatting over me, poking me with needles, shoving a tube down my throat. I could feel that I'd been burned pretty bad, and the smoke made my sinuses feel as if they'd been packed with burning coal, but then I realized: I'm alive! The triumph I felt in that moment was beautiful, I can't describe it in any other way. I felt as if I'd passed through the eye of a hurricane and I came out intact on the other side. I don't know much after that, I passed out. When I woke up next, I was in the hospital *in Green Bay, covered in bandages. In a daze, I must have told the rescuers about Ambereen and the curse, that's probably why I was transferred to the psychiatric ward. Who in their right mind would believe that? And when Jeremiah and his partner came to question me, I knew it wasn't over, it could never be over.*

"I lied about what happened because I didn't know what else to do. I told the truth that it was Anthony Guntram's fault—it was why I asked if I was the only survivor—but because of my uncertainty, I made something up, I can't even remember what it was now, and I suppose it doesn't matter. I remember thinking that the longer I stayed in that hospital bed, the safer I'd be. But then Keely came for us, and I knew it was time to pay for what we'd done.

"I suppose it doesn't help anything to say I'm sorry, because it's just a word and it probably doesn't mean anything. But I am, you know, I'm so sorry that I had anything to do with this, and I'm sorry I did that to all of those innocent people. They all got swept up into this and they didn't deserve it, and then they died the most gruesome death you can imagine. I pray they find freedom at last.

"That's my piece, that's what happened on the night of the last Bastille Celebration in Amber Hollow. I hope that Ambereen's justice will be swift when she comes to take us, I really do. And if there is an afterlife, I hope Anthony Guntram isn't there, because I never want to see his sorry ass again. I don't think it's asking a whole lot."

CHAPTER 26

AMBEREEN'S JUSTICE

Sadie didn't know what to say as the woman spoke the last words of the story. She wasn't certain if she required a response. What she did know was that she was glad she wasn't her, nor the other woman, nor Guntram, for it was certain that whatever they had coming, it was going to be worse than anything they'd ever known. Night was beginning to fade now, the earliest rays of sun peeking over the far horizon. The crumbled mouth of the cave was dark, and Delores sat near it, every so often casting a glance inside.

"Do you feel better having told us?" the old woman asked Sylvia, and the other sat silent for a moment, an indecipherable expression on her face. At length she nodded, running a trembling hand through her hair.

"Maybe," she said, whisper quiet. Her eyes told another tale, one that would haunt Sadie for the rest of her life. The fear that clouded her vision was truly a thing to behold, and it was so profound that Sadie felt it too, a strangling, unhinged terror that roiled inside her, even though her calm, rational mind told her she had nothing to be afraid of.

Or did she?

She didn't know, but she supposed she would soon. The librarian got to her feet as the dawn stole over them, and Sadie realized that whatever was to unfold, it was soon to happen.

"Delores," she began, when a thin shriek issued from the entrance of the goldmine, gradually growing louder, and a wind picked up, blowing the tops of the tall pine trees and sending down nettles like a winter snow storm. The shriek built in intensity, and the two women who served Guntram, Sylvia and Helen, stood up. Sadie turned to look inside the police car, saw Guntram desperately trying to get the door open, and when he couldn't do that, he began to pound on the glass.

"Let me out of here!" he yelled furiously, although his voice betrayed his terror. He pounded harder, and soon his fists were bleeding and smearing bloody handprints all over the glass. Delores watched him from the mouth of the disintegrating goldmine, a tiny smile playing along the corners of her mouth. The noise from the mine increased, becoming so high-pitched that it hurt Sadie's ears. She clamped her hands over them, almost falling to her knees, the agony was so acute.

"You might not want to watch this!" Delores hollered over the din, using one hand to hold down the hem of her dress as it fluttered around her knees. "She may have once been an innocent little girl, but that's long passed!"

Sadie couldn't find the voice to reply. The noise was becoming so fever-pitched it was dreadful, and as leaves and debris blew around her feet, she wondered if she should take the old woman's advice. This wasn't something she needed to see, was it? Was there any reason for her to witness this?

Guntram's terrified screams pulled her from her reverie, and it was this that decided it for her. Yes, this was something she needed to be a part of, for this was truly history in the making. Suddenly, the wind died down and everything became calm once more.

And then, from the ruins of the mine, came Ambereen.

• • •

The sunlight highlighted the streaks of gold and red in the girl's hair, and her solemn expression quickly gave way to a smile when she saw Delores. She walked toward her, holding out her hand, and the elderly librarian took it.

Sadie was amazed at how vibrant the girl looked, much different from how she'd looked at the hospital, her eyes dull, her hair a dirty clump atop a forehead as white as porcelain. She was beautiful, this child, so beautiful that it was ethereal. She felt a chill pass through her, and when the girl turned her gaze upon her, she froze, hardly able to breath.

"Sadie…" the child spoke, but it didn't appear as if she'd even opened her mouth. Sadie stood there, paralyzed, unable to make a sound.

"Have no fear, Sadie, you are safe here," the girl said without moving her lips, "I know your heart is pure, and within you, you harbor only love…"

This broke her paralysis.

"I love him," she said and then burst into tears. She felt ashamed to carry on like this, but she couldn't help it. The tears came forth, unbidden, hot and salty, and there was nothing she could do to stop them. She swiped at her face, tried to compose herself, but she couldn't. "Dear God," she whispered, her words taken from her mouth and swept away on a random breeze that brought with it the cold winds of vengeance. "I'll always love him."

"I know…"

At once the girl's face clouded over and the sky, which had slowly brightened to reveal the new day, darkened as thunderheads gathered above them. Sadie felt another chill run through her, but she was no longer afraid, not for herself anyway.

Delores let go of Ambereen's hand and stepped away, moving close to Sadie. She reached out, took her hand.

"Remember what I said," she whispered, and Sadie nodded mutely.

An ominous noise emanated from the mine, initially sounding like the drone of a Gregorian chant before becoming much more sinister, deeper in timbre. It was followed by an animalistic screech that Sadie's rational mind had no way of cataloging. She clutched the old woman's hand tighter, her breath caught in her throat. She didn't want to see this, but she knew she'd come too far not to. It wouldn't be fair to her, or the memory of Jeremy, wherever it was he'd gone. Her heart issued a lonely pang at the thought of him, his impish smile, his carelessly mussed hair, his constantly half-tucked shirt and the belly that rebelled against it. She hitched a sob, felt tears fall anew upon her cheeks, but then the time for sorrow was over as Ambereen prepared to give birth to the final terror that would consume the guilty like the flames of Perdition they'd brought down upon their fellow villagers and, ultimately, themselves. May she have mercy on their souls.

• • •

For an instant, time stood absolutely still. Sadie could see the frozen faces standing out in stark relief against the once brightening day that was now turning dark. Their expressions solemn, the two women united to hold one another's hand. Guntram struggled in vain to break the cruiser's window, his lips pulled back in a snarl of rage and fear. Delores had a curious look on her face, one that insinuated that this was something she'd never seen before, despite everything else she'd been through during her lifetime. If Sadie could see herself, she was certain that she'd see a woman with crud caked in the corners of her lips—her mouth was so dry—one whose eyes were wide, nostrils flaring, eyebrows arched into dual peaks. Everything was calm, the eye of the storm, awaiting a reckoning that would ignite at any time...

When it did, it happened so quickly that Sadie wasn't exactly sure what had transpired; in fact, she would later have trouble trying to put all the errant pieces of her memory back together. But at the time, this is what she saw:

Ambereen's expression turned from one of childish innocence into a severe look that presaged the ominous events to come. Her brow furrowed, and her lips withdrew from her teeth to form a scowl that rapidly erased her seemingly virtuous exterior. The wind suddenly resumed, whipping her long, red hair around like bicycle streamers as her eyes inexplicably widened. Darkness filled them like spilled ink, becoming black holes with a single pinpoint of light in the center that shined as piercing as lasers. Contrary to any probability dictated by the routine laws of nature, the girl metamorphosized. Accompanied by what sounded like a fleet of fighter jets ripping the sky to shreds at Mach speed, she blew up like a hot air balloon, her body mass expanding until she was as big as a house, then bigger, and then bigger still. Ambereen, now bloated and horrifying, filled the entirety of Sadie's vision, eclipsing the rest of the world, and in her terror, she fell to the ground on her butt, her legs splayed out before her, her mouth hanging open.

Competing gales from all directions combined into a funnel cloud, becoming two and then three, until there were several tornados converging around the spot where the monstrous girl stood. Out of this chaos, she continued to grow. Sadie raised her hands, wanting to cover her eyes, but she forced them back to her sides and made herself witness what was surely a miracle, something far beyond anything in the natural world.

Ambereen swelled up until she abruptly burst in a torrential rain of blood and body parts, the little girl facade detonated, exposing the demonic force that she'd become. She/it was monolithic, something that Sadie's rational mind couldn't comprehend. The oblong body was an indecipherable mass of reptilian skin from which sprouted thousands of firehose-sized fleshy, squiggly strands, and its scales radiated an ever-changing light show of kaleidoscopic colors, so bright that Sadie had to squint her eyes. Violet mist enshrouded the creature, seeping from it like exhaust from a car's tailpipe while the gargantuan appendages writhed in frenzied motion. Once the conversion was complete, it became airborne.

Hovering above them in the sky, the creature twisted and wriggled, its skin undulating and rippling, creating an obstreperous noise that buzzed like a band saw in Sadie's head. She followed the body of the creature up and up and up, until she saw perched atop it—like a pumpkin on a scarecrow—the thing's head, and its juxtaposition to the rest of the body made no physical sense. Attached to the malformed thorax was a humanoid, bulbus skull that showcased an enormous maw filled with jagged, tombstone-sized teeth. The mouth worked furiously, dripping dark saliva as thick as Jell-O while the fangs gnashed against each other. From its throat emanated another sound, this one worse than any they'd experienced thus far. It sounded like the screams of terror from millions of haunted souls as the ground opened up beneath them and swallowed them whole.

The creature blotted out everything. To Sadie, there was nothing left of the world save for what was before her, as if there had never been anything else but this one moment in time. It stretched unto eternity, this moment, until at last it launched into motion the actions it had come to execute.

It turned toward the two women, and when Sadie saw its eyes—two giant, glowing prisms—she felt as if the world tilted and she was sitting on the edge of an enormous chasm. The dizziness was overwhelming, and while she fought to retain consciousness, the colossal oculus swirled and sparkled, alighting upon her briefly and conveying a message, another assurance that she not be afraid, and suddenly her fear was replaced by a gentle tranquility. She got it now, she completely understood. The energy this thing emitted may have been wrought by a magic spell, but its aims were not driven by evil, no, they were the higher purpose of someone who had been denied the right to live life on their own terms. It was righteous in its imminent actions; it may have been repulsive, but its intentions were pure.

Sylvia and Helen understood as well, and with their hands clutched tightly together they ascended into the sky, their feet hanging limply below them, one of Sylvia's sandals falling off to land carelessly on the ground below her. They were suspended in place like insects pinned to corkboard while the creature's all-knowing, penetrating eyes appraised them, and when its tongue came out—an enormous slab of meat the size of an SUV—Sadie saw it was covered with bumps that were undulating grotesquely. The lumps rose and fell, pressing against the fleshy barrier, fighting it, and from them came the sound of delirious screaming, and she realized that they were people, they were the trapped souls of Amber Hollow. They were contained within this gigantic thing, straining to escape but the rubbery flesh sucked them back in.

Dozens of the squiggly, membranous cords darted out from the beast, entwining the women, separating them. The appendages were covered in wriggling clumps of worms, and as they moved back and forth, the larvae rained down from the sky in clusters. When they hit the ground, they writhed directionlessly at first, but then Sadie saw them squirming toward the police cruiser. When Guntram saw them, he renewed his escape efforts, issuing choppy barks of desperate horror. He was a sitting duck. Whatever this being had planned for him, it was going to happen, like it or not.

The women were shrieking, both in pain and fear, and the thing that had been a little girl brought them up to her hideous face, the slavering fangs mere inches away. Its vortex eyes glared at them with a fury that could never be satiated, except maybe in this moment.

"I'm so sorry!" Helen screamed, her voice barely audible over the catastrophic din, and to Sadie's surprise she saw the look in the creature's eyes change, albeit briefly. They softened, taking on a hue of commiseration. A voice issued from the repugnant mouth, human, a little girl's voice.

"You are merely pawns in a wicked game of a madman's design," she said mournfully. "You've been duped by a man who has fooled many, and *for that I cannot condemn you to his fate. You may join the other villagers to haunt this forest forever, but rest well with the knowledge that you have been spared from the eternity that awaits Guntram."*

"Thank you," Sylvia blubbered. "Thank you so much…"

Then its eyes grew darker, the blackness within swirling hypnotically. The tentacles raised the women high up into the sky, and with a pulsing squeeze, they were both popped like balloons; indeed, they were once there, and a second later they were nothing but gooey remains that showered down from the sky in jellylike clumps. Sadie screamed, but the noise was so loud she couldn't hear it, she could only feel her voice reverberating in her chest. It then turned its attention to Guntram, the manifold feelers squirming and writhing with a thick, liquid sound, the mouth opening wider in a sadistic grin. The worms now covered the car, enveloping it within their wriggling mass, and Sadie saw that they'd made entrance and were covering Guntram like a living blanket. He screamed with leather-lunged terror, and as the worms crawled inside his mouth the noises he made became watery and choked.

Another voice came from the creature, this time that of an old woman's, and Sadie briefly recalled the visage of the old crone in the sky from one of the hallucinations she'd had. The voice was haggard, screechy, and it hurt to hear it.

"For what you've done, there is only one punishment that fits the crime," she/it said, and then it was overtaken by a hurricane force gale that was centralized to the surrounding area of the monster and her captive. Sadie could see and feel the magnitude of the tempest, yet she was on the fringe of it, safe, some invisible barrier keeping it at bay. Suddenly, everything was whited out, like a heavy rain falling so hard that for several minutes you can't see anything at all. And in the blankness, sound ceased to exist.

• • •

Anthony heard the chirping of birds and the whinnying of horse, but he couldn't see anything, the world around him dark. He recognized the timbre of the neighing, and at once he knew it was his horse, the mare he'd owned when he first came to this land and basked in the pleasure of brutally slaying the savages for sport. But that wasn't possible, for that was over two hundred years ago, the horse long dead. She hadn't been held responsible for his criminal deeds; none of the animals had, only the villagers. Their beasts of burden and companion animals had succumbed to the ravages of time, released from the village in death.

When his vision returned, he saw he was dressed in his nobleman's finery, and he was standing in a forest clearing he undeniably knew very well. Gazing about him, he saw the fallen log where he'd brought many young wenches to have his way, and as he continued to look, his mare stepped into view.

"Saints be damned," he muttered, his heart hammering in his chest.

Sitting atop his noble steed was the little girl, Ambereen Bougie Holloway. She looked radiant in the early morning light, her hair streaked with orange, red and gold. She was smiling a beautiful, innocent smile, and it made the dimples in her cheeks deepen. At once, his mouth went dry as dread filled him, for what reason, he did not know.

"Hello, Father," Ambereen said, her voice light, merry. "It certainly is a wonderful day, isn't it?"

He stared at her, unable to comprehend what this was, or what was required of him. Should he dare to speak? Would that help him at all?

"You needn't say a word, dear sir, for it is I who shall impart the final bit of information upon you." The horse whinnied and trotted in place, as if momentarily disturbed by some unseen force, and then settled down. She stroked its mane delicately with her small, child's hands. "You know how this has to end, right? Surely you don't think I'll let you off as easily as the others?"

Anger arose within him, the thought of a little girl, his own daughter no less, trying to intimidate him…preposterous! He felt his bile curdle, the vile words rushing out of his mouth before he could even think to stop them.

"I should thank you not to address me as such, young wench, unless you'd like another taste of the medicine I meted out for you lo these last two hundred years!"

She laughed, a joyous sound that rankled his sour mood. "You never fail to disappoint me, Father. Even in the face of your condemnation, you still think you have the upper hand. How I pity you."

He clenched his hands into fists and menacingly strode forward two steps, but Ambereen appeared not to notice. "I daresay you shall not speak to your elder disrespectfully!"

Her face scrunched up suddenly, folded into itself, became a blank slate and then reappeared, only now it was the visage of the old crone.

"How brave you are," she cackled, "to talk to us as if you have any power. You are a beaten man, Guntram, and I thought it just to bring you here, the place of your foulest deed, to enlighten you as to your future."

"Future?" he sputtered. "Surely there is no future, for there can only be death. Are you saying you can do worse than to kill me? I think not, old crone."

Her laughter was the opposite of young Ambereen's; it was like the sound of fingernails on a chalkboard, a boisterous declaration that intoned the weight of many years, and promised an eternity of torture.

"I shall spare you your death, Anthony, for it is only you that I wish to keep alive."

Her words gave him pause, and at once he felt fading turpitude, replaced by ice-cold fear.

"Alive?" he croaked. "What do you mean?"

"For what you've done, you shall take Ambereen's place within her crypt in perpetuity, only I have to warn you: you won't be alone."

Now he was silent, digesting this news. The fear inside him blossomed into full-blown terror as the ground commenced to tremble at his feet and the earth began to move. He could feel it throbbing beneath him, as if there was an army under the soles of his knee-high riding boots, clawing their way to the surface.

And then from behind her, an enormous mound of dirt exploded from the ground, growing ever larger in size. From it came the vocalizations of hoots and war-cries, the blaring voices steeped in homicidal rage. The mound grew and grew, the dirt creating an avalanche that cascaded down upon the horse, upon young Ambereen with the old crone's face. And from within the dirt, he saw skeletal hands with ringlets of tattered flesh clawing at the air, struggling to break free.

A scream froze in his throat as he saw the savages emerge from the soil, their bodies rotted, covered in skin as mottled as peeling wallpaper. Even though their faces were decayed and worm-riddled, he could see the wrath burning within their eyes like embers of fiery coal. These inferno-fueled ocular orbs bored into his own, their mouths working feverishly, from them spilling a chant that grew louder, ever louder. He couldn't understand the words, as it was in their heathen tongue, but he knew what it meant, and felt their unchained lunacy fill the air like rancid smoke.

"These shall be your companions until the end of the world, dear Father," the child's placid voice sighed, replacing that of the old crone. "These poor, innocent people who only wanted to defend their land, they shall be your cellmates in the prison of my heart." She smiled, but it was a sad smile. "Oh, that reminds me...."

Guntram suddenly felt his stomach clench as nausea overtook him. He leaned over to vomit, though what came out was like nothing he ever would have expected. Into his gloved hands, he regurgitated a heart, a still-beating heart. The thumps were loud in his ears, pounding like tribal war drums. His blood smeared mouth opened and closed soundlessly as he looked up one last time at the girl whose mother he had condemned to burn at the stake, whose life he had taken, whose grandmother he'd banished from the village by stoning. She looked happy, content at long last.

"I believe that's mine," Ambereen said, and the object flew from his hands and into her ever-widening mouth. Once it passed her lips it was gone, and the last thing he saw was it beating robustly in her chest.

And then the savages were upon him, their bony hands encircling his own, and he could not resist them, for they were too strong. They smelled worse than flyblown carcasses rotting in the sun, the touch of their putrefying hands deliriously repulsive. They dragged him toward the mound *of dirt, which he saw was now a living thing, for it had grown a mouth with teeth as large as tombstones and pointed as spears. Toward this he was hauled, and at last the scream that had been bottled up within him was released, a desperate, dismal cry of one who finally has to confront the foulness of his very own soul, and in so doing has gone completely insane in the extremity of his horror.*

"Goddamn you!" he bellowed, the last earthly sound he would ever make.

Into the mound of dirt they pulled him, the mouth stripping him of his nobleman's finery as the teeth bore down upon him...

• • •

The whiteout lasted only a few seconds. Like the sun banishing the night, the air cleared and Sadie could see once more. She felt as if something had just happened, but what it was she didn't know. She could only perceive what her eyes and ears told her, and this is what she then saw:

The police cruiser shot up into the sky, Guntram's terrified face barely discernable behind the larvae and smeared blood on the glass. Sadie couldn't hear anything now but the shrieking wail of the wind and the raucous noise the creature made, so beneath all this she couldn't hear the man's petrified screams. But make no doubt, he was screaming, and to Sadie's amazement she saw that he'd actually cracked the glass on the window. Not that it would matter, of course, because to stop this thing wasn't going to happen, not today, not in a million lifetimes, but it drew the very real certainty that within the margins of Guntram's fear, he'd almost found the strength to escape the car. The cruiser went up into the air until it was hovering in front of the creature's face, and the mouth opened wide as half a dozen tentacles gripped the cruiser, demolishing it in one swift move that cast Guntram into the maelstrom. He hung in the air, completely exposed, his body sheathed in the large, horrible looking worms, and then the rubbery, scaly appendages took hold of him, gripping him around his legs and torso, bringing him ever closer to the yawning maw. Finally, the noise the creature made relented enough so that Guntram's screams could at last ring forth, and to Sadie they were the most horrified, piteous cries she'd ever heard. But in her heart, she felt no empathy, not for him.

"Goddamn you!" Sadie heard him bellow before the giant teeth chomped down on his head, bursting it like a grape, his blood staining the teeth in all its crimson glory. It then devoured him in a single gulp, his body disappearing into the cavernous throat as a spray of gore jetted into the air. It chewed vociferously, masticating him like a dog would a treat, his last words reverberating loudly in Sadie's ears, and then he was gone.

And that was when Sadie could finally take no more, and this time she fainted dead away as the wind, at last, began to die down.

Epilogue

She was out for no more than a couple of minutes, maybe five tops, when her eyes popped open. It was quiet now, very quiet, just the soothing sound of a gentle breeze blowing through the trees. From where she lay, she looked around her, and saw the sunlight streaming gloriously upon the forest floor. She could taste the humid bite of the sodden, early morning air. A mosquito buzzed around her ear, and then another, so sitting up, she slapped at it. And then she saw him.

His being emitted a bright, neon light, as well as Keely's, Conroy's, Delores', and the little girl's.

Ambereen...

They were standing in front of an enormous mound of dirt, and Sadie knew without being told that it was the remains of the goldmine, Ambereen's tomb. It was completely collapsed, gone.

"Jeremy?" she said uncertainly, and he smiled, and in his smile, she could sense a satisfaction that was so incredibly profound, it was like no other experience of pleasure one could possibly enjoy. He looked as if he was home, at peace.

"It's over, Sadie," he said, only like the little girl his mouth didn't move to make the words, she simply heard them in her head. "We can all rest now, our watch is over."

"Good," she said. After two hundred years, it had to be a relief to finally escape the immortality that had ensnared them. She looked from face to face, all as serene as angels, and for all Sadie knew, maybe they were. She knew she wasn't looking at mortals, and if their time here was done, what else could they be? "I'm very happy for all of you."

Ambereen stood placidly between them, and Sadie couldn't help but admire how beautiful she was yet again, so stunning, so innocent. How someone could have done something so terrible to a child so pure, well, they certainly had no business existing in this world. If there was a Hell, truly Anthony Guntram was making acquittances with his new cellmates, and she was sure they'd give him a greeting he'd never forget.

"We'll escort you to the edge of town," Jeremy said, again his lips never moving. "From there, you'll have to walk to Crandon to call it in."

"What should I say?" She truly was at a loss, for none of this would be easily explained in a police report, if indeed it could be explained at all. They'd lock her up is what they would do. Captain Martin would look at her sympathetically before he called the doctors at the Bellin Health psychiatric ward and told them to come on down and get her, and don't forget the straight jacket, please, thank you very much.

"You'll know what to say when the time comes," Jeremy said, and his words rushed over her like cool water, allaying her fears. Yes, she would know what to say, and in that story there would be truth, but there would be a whole lot of lies as well, if only so she could keep her job, if only to keep her from getting locked up.

"Come on," Jeremy said, "let's go."

And the five of them walked slowly toward the town line of Amber Hollow, one of them with their feet planted firmly on ground, four others hovering beside her.

. . .

The day came on bright and hot, and the closer they got to the town line and the barricade the more translucent her escorts became. She could see right through them now, and to Sadie that was a good thing, except, of course, that she'd most likely never see Jeremy again. The walk went quickly, and soon there they were, at the end of the line.

"Jeremy," Sadie said, when he came forward and placed an arm on her shoulder. She could barely feel it, just the slightest sensation that there was pressure there, but that was all. His eyes shone the brightest as his physical form began to disappear.

"Don't be sad," he said, and the voice in her mind was clear and strong, as if he was discussing a case with her, not a spiritual being whose time here on earth was almost finished.

"I love you," she said, and in her heart, it was the purest, most simple truth. "I always have…"

"I always loved you too, Sadie." His eyes held her in place, kept her feet solidly planted before the barrier, that once she crossed it, he would be no more. She wasn't ready for that. She didn't think she ever could be ready for that, but she knew that like any moment, it had to end eventually, like everything else in life. She wanted to hold on to it forever, to encapsulate it in her mind so that whenever she needed to call on this memory it would always be there for her. She'd never let it go.

"You'll have to take care of Roxie for me," he said, and these would be the last words he'd ever say: "She's yours now. Give her a good home."

"I will," she promised, and she would deliver on that, would make sure the retired police dog never wanted for anything for the rest of her natural life.

He kept his nearly transparent hand on her shoulder for a while, the two looking into each other's eyes, when she saw that he was fading…fading…fading…

Gone…

She stood there, alone now, just her and the call of the birds and the chittering of the squirrels and chipmunks, the breeze moving the humidity around but not doing anything to quell it. She stared curiously at the ruins of Amber Hollow. For a second she thought she could see what it must have looked like centuries ago, when the world was a much simpler place, before electricity and the chaos of the Industrial Age. It hung before her eyes like a mirage, and as quickly as it was there it was gone. She swallowed once, her heart hitching in her chest, trying to contain a sob that couldn't be stopped no matter how hard she tried.

Tears running down her face, she turned away from the village, crossed the barricade, and began the long walk toward Crandon.

The End

Printed in Great Britain
by Amazon